Tranzen

Nigel V Hewitt

Copyright © Nigel V Hewitt 2012. All rights reserved.
ISBN: 978-1-4476-7055-1
nigelh@nigelhewitt.co.uk

Cover image by: Alan Foreman
poisonedal@o2.co.uk

Published by: lulu.com 2012

to Caroline

This is a collection of short and not so short stories written over many years basically because they were there. Most of them started as a silly idea but once the 'silly idea' scene had been written then the rest just demanded to be set down. So here you will find the dragon beating the knight and winning the princess, you will find the person on the ultimate 'bloke trip' where he has power, wealth, status, the works beyond all you can imagine however he never notices and many more like them.
I have to apologise about the continuity lapses in the Tranzen universe. The stories were written over many decades and many of the ideas were only full developed in the later ones. If you find contradictions it is because I do not want to rewrite a story that has become an old friend because several years later I used an improved explanation for some point. Conversely sometimes an off-hand remark in one story spawned a whole new universe.

I hope you get to enjoy them as much as we have.

Nigel V. Hewitt 2012

Contents

Grail 11
Lotti 23
Traitor 47
Devon 65
Jilly of the Fifth 127
Fortunate Tigers 149
Dizzy & Flipper 171
Vestel 243
Zwei 277
The Dragon of Arnoc-fell 341

Grail

Princess Grail held her composure as they tied her hands behind her back. Her mother wept openly. Her father sat on his throne, his head buried in his hands, unable to watch. The rope was not painfully tight but she had never been restrained in this way before. She looked at one of the palace guards who surrounded her and realised his eyes were wet with tears and she nearly broke down herself. She stared at the great crest high above the door till the bonds were tied.
She held her head high as they lead her down from the castle. As they passed through the common people and out through the main gate she turned her head neither to the left nor to the right. Only when they were outside the walls did she look about herself. There before her was the scorched corpse of a horse and beyond it was the suit of armour, still standing, but with all its heraldic motifs burned away and smoke still balefully rising from the visor slots.
She had already forgotten his name. He was selected as the best, the most noble and he came with the best possible references. If he had won the day he was to have been her husband and, since she had no brothers, heir to the kingdom. "Oh well," thought Grail, "I suppose for me it was not much of an alternative. If I am to be meat for the market at least I shall now be served well cooked."

The dragon waited. The palace guard seemed in no hurry to march her onwards but the sight depressed her. Anxious not to let her resolve drop now, lest she should show fear, she stepped forward herself. The dragon was big and waiting. As she walked onwards she felt the weight of the rope dragging behind her. She realised the guards were afraid to come closer. Men. Never brave at the last. She would show them how a princess could die.
She stopped just in front of the huge beast. It towered above her. She looked up and said "Well?" The dragon looked down and seemed to nod slightly. Then he reached out and grabbed her. In a moment she found herself seated in his hand with his thumb across her waist keeping her firmly in place. Worse still he had leaped into the sky. His wings were beating in great gasps. Grail closed her eyes and waited for the end to come.
The end did not come. The gasping gave way to a smooth rush but she was still alive. She ventured to open her eyes. What she saw made her head swim. The great yellow and green body was above her and the wings billowed out on either side. She was facing the legs and tail which streamed behind and a strong wind blew about her head flaying her face with her hair. She looked down and saw the inestimable

distance below her, Far more than from the Aix tower from which she had looked as a child. She closed her eyes again.

Time passed. To Grail who had hardly expected time to ever be bored again in this life this seemed strange. Then, finally, the wind seemed to lessen a bit and the gasping sound returned. She opened her eyes to see the great body turning to become more vertical with the wings spread out above. Then silence. The feet were resting on the ground. The feet were walking.

She craned her head round to see where they were going in time to realise the walls of a great cave entrance were closing around them. She could hardly see. Then she felt herself being placed on the ground. She sat up awkwardly, restrained by her tied hands. Slowly light spread around her.

The dragon was fiddling with a glass ball on the cave roof that became steadily brighter. Grail began to look about and realised that she was not on the ground as she had imagined but on a shelf. She was about thirty feet above the floor of the cave. The shelf was soft as she sat on it being floored with a woven tapestry. It had a low balustrade around it. She watched the dragon.

Satisfied with his light the dragon turned his attention to the cave mouth which he closed with a huge door. He looked back at her. He reached up to another shelf, she could now see that the walls were lined with them, and took a small knife down. He turned towards her. It was a very big knife. Inside she wondered if she should be afraid.

"Let me cut your ropes," said the dragon. "I am afraid the knots are far too small for me to untie." Grail did not move but just sat and stared at him. However the trailing rope hung over the edge of her shelf and so as the dragon pulled gently she had to turn or be dragged nearer the edge.

She never felt the knife but her wrists slipped free and at once she tried to crawl away to the back of the shelf but her hands were numb and she flopped onto her face. She sat up and watched the dragon put his knife away. She watched him wind the rope into a little bundle and place it on a shelf also. Then he sat back on his tail and watched her. Finally Grail could wait no more. "What happens now?" she asked. The dragon looked at her silently. "What are you going to do to me?" she crawled to the balustrade and glared at him. "Do I just wait in the larder till you're hungry?"

The dragon seemed to smile. "Dragons do not eat people," he said. "If you are hungry then call and I will prepare food for you. If you are thirsty look to your right. When you are tired look to your left." With that he got up and lumbered off out of sight. Grail rested her chin on the balustrade and sighed.

Time passed. Grail stood up. The balustrade was low and only came to her knees so she kept well away from the edge. The shelf was long and to her left she found a pile of blankets and linen sheets. There was no bed but since there was nobody to make it perhaps that was for the better. She certainly felt able to make a sandwich of blankets and sheets within which she could sleep.

To the right was a pool fed by a spring. The spring was cold but the pool warm. She trailed her fingers in the water and tasted it. It was slightly salt and luke warm, clearly undrinkable. The spring that bubbled from the rock was cold and fresh but she had to lap at it like a dog. Further still to the right the shelf ended with a notch in the wall. There was a wooden seat in the notch with a hole in it. She sniffed. It might look like a garderobe but it didn't smell like one. A bit more privacy would help but the condemned princess had eaten a hearty breakfast with wine so it was a pressing need.

Time passed. The dragon reappeared. "You will need to eat," he said and placed a bowl on the shelf. The bowl contained bread slowly sinking in a meaty stew. Grail ate it slowly with her fingers then washed her hands in the pool. The dragon returned and fiddled with the globe. "It will be dark soon" he said, "You may wish to prepare yourself to sleep."

The globe started to dim. Grail hurried to unfold the blankets and finally kicked of her shoes and crept into the pile before it became totally dark.

For most of the night she did not rest well but finally, near dawn, she fell into a deep sleep. When she awoke the cavern door stood open. There was the feel of a summer morning. Grail pulled herself from the heap of blankets and groped for her shoes. She clawed at her hair enough to stop it hanging in her face.

The dragon entered the cave. He was carrying a dead rabbit by its hind legs. He hung it from a hook below one of his shelves. He looked at Grail. Again he seemed to smile. "Your dinner for tonight," he announced, and then added as if by way of explanation "You eat meat so I bartered it from a fox. I prefer not to kill creatures myself."

Grail stared at him incredulously. "You won't kill a rabbit? What about poor Sir what-ever-his-name-was?"

The dragon sat back on his tail. "That was regrettable," he said, "I explained to him that my demands on your father were just and honourable but he chose to fight. His death is a pity but he was a hired mercenary. I regret more having to kill the horse."

"Taking me. Was that just?" argued Grail.

The dragon tipped his head to one side. "You were to be part of Sir Endart's reward, so as victor I naturally had to claim you. Was this not explained to you? A nineteen year old bride with a kingdom in her dowry is a fine prize for a forty year old knight but perhaps a poorer one

for a dragon who has seen more centuries than you have summers. My greater reward is that your father is now bound by his oath to be a just king, not a tyrant and your cousin Lethen is to be his advisor and heir. Lethen is a kind man and the people will no longer weep under their bondage."
"What about my bondage?" shouted Grail.
The dragon stood up. "I will get you some bread," he said, "and some other clothes so you may wash yourself. We will talk again later, when you smell better."

Grail ate her bread angrily. She was angry that he had taken her, she was angry that he imprisoned her so easily, she was almost angry because she had not be able to die defiantly. She was also very angry at being told to scrub every part of her body and to give him every stitch of clothing so he could wash it. However she found it very hard to be angry at the sheer beauty of the simple shift dress he had provided for her. It was dazzling white and was smooth and shiny. She did not appreciate the short sleeves nor the fact it would only come to just below her knees but aside from that it was exquisite, fit indeed for a princess.
Grail slipped into the pool and felt the warmth of the water run over her body. The bottom was almost hot to the touch but the water felt tingly all over her. She lay back in the water almost floating and let her worries drift away. When, as a little girl, she had become filthy and been dumped in a tub to be scrubbed with lye she had always viewed it as an experience to be avoided. But this was bliss. Only the pull of the white dress drew her out.
Grail sat by her balustrade as the dragon picked through her clothes. "Quite fetching," he mused, "but such coarse cloth. Perhaps when it is washed it will feel smoother."
Grail said "It was never like this." She ran her hands over the whiteness as it cascaded over her legs. "What is it called?"
The dragon smiled again. "It is silk. It comes from far away. I hoped you would like it. I have more for later. I do not want you to be sad."
"I don't understand you," said Grail, "You bring me here and everybody at home will think I am dead and yet you want to be kind to me. You treat me very well for a prisoner."
The dragon sat back. "Yes. They will all believe you are dead. This frees you from them. You will understand later why this should be so."

Dawn the next day came and again Grail awoke to see the great doors standing open. She waited but her captor did not appear. Finally she became tired of waiting. "Dragon," she called, "Dragon. Where are you?"

He lumbered into sight and asked "What? Little Grail, are you hungry already?"
He placed a basket with bread in it on her shelf and hung another dress over the balustrade. It was a deep blue and had longer sleeves. "For after you bathe," said the dragon.

Grail sat with her legs between the bars of the balustrade leaning her arms on the top. Her feet swung in space over thirty feet above the floor. The dragon was washing the white dress in a small bowl of water that steamed slightly. "If you are bored I could find you a book to read. What type do you prefer?"
Grail tipped her head to one side. "I can't read," she said.
The dragon looked up from his bowl "That is sad. You miss out on so much. I will have to teach you."
Grail smiled at him. "Princesses don't need to read. They have people to read for them," she pointed out.
"Ah," said the dragon, "but you have nobody to read for you. Does that prove you are not a princess?"
Grail pondered. "You know, I don't miss them much," she said.
"Miss who? Your parents or your friends?" The dragon was squeezing the water from the white silk dress by clenching it in his fist.
"Well nobody, that's just it," Grail continued. "I suppose I never really had any friends. The servants were just servants and I only ever really saw my parents for meals. The only person I ever knew well was my governess and I loathed her, simply hated her."
The dragon was silent for a while. He hung the white dress up to dry. Grail waited waving her feet as they hung in space. The dragon turned. "Perhaps we will manage to get on better," he said.
Grail thought for a moment. "Dragon," she said, "how long are you going to keep me prisoner?"
The dragon looked across at her. "Until you do not need to be kept a prisoner any more. Oh. My name is not Dragon. I am Ekta. I have a longer, deeper name but Ekta will suffice."

Next morning as Grail lay in her bath and waited for Ekta to bring today's dress she wondered about her situation. For three days now she had been a prisoner of a dragon. In the weeks leading up to the big fight she had rehearsed several futures in her mind, most of them involved a sudden and rather unwelcome wedding and the others ended abruptly, but none were remotely like her current situation. She lay back and her hair spread out through the water. She realised that she felt comfortable and relaxed. Being a prisoner had real advantages.
A large piece of stick came flying over the balustrade and landed near

the pool. It had a rope attached. Grail sat up like a shot. She crept out of the bath and peeped over the edge. Below her was a smart young man in an expensive cape. "Tie the rope on," he called softly. "I'll climb up and rescue you."

Grail picked up the stick and the rope and peeped over the edge again. "You can't come up," she hissed, "I've got nothing on."

The young man was clearly perplexed by this response. "Well put something on," he called, clearly annoyed, "the dragon might be back any minute."

Grail ran to her bed and pulled a sheet from it. She wrapped it round herself just under her arms. It was too long to be easy to walk in, like a ceremonial gown, but at least it was decent. She looked over the edge again. "I don't think I want to be rescued" she said.

"Look," said the young man again, "you are being rescued and you are being rescued now. Tie that bloody rope on."

"There is no need to swear little man."

"I'm sorry it just slipped o..." the young man froze.

"Oh Ekta," said Grail, "Please don't hurt him. He was just trying to rescue me."

The young man turned slowly. Ekta sat on his tail in the doorway. They all waited.

Finally Ekta spoke. "You are Prince Randel I think. Your father is Mardoc, king of the Denvish Lowlands. He is wise and prudent. It is a pity you have not inherited those traits. Perhaps they will develop with age. Does your father know you are here?"

The prince was looking straight into the dragons eyes. "My father forbade me to come to your mountain for fear that I should meet you," he said.

"More likely for fear that you would fall off my mountain and break all your bones," said Ekta. "You may go. But you must first promise not to speak of anything you have seen here and you must walk out of the door past me. Promise!"

The prince trembled. The dragon held his gaze. "I, I promise," he said, "but do not make me walk past you. I cannot do it."

"And yet you must," mused Ekta.

The prince took two steps forward and froze again. "Go on," called Grail.

"I'm frightened," wailed the prince.

Grail looked down on his head "He told you to go so you can go."

The prince looked up at her and asked "But what if he is lying?"

"Men lie to you," hissed Grail, "He is a dragon."

Ekta sat passively as the young prince moved slowly towards him and watched him squeeze through the gap between his side and the door post. He moved to one side so Grail could see the form of her rescuer

scampering down the slope away from them. He turned and looked at Grail. "You have made the sheet all wet," he said. "Give it to me and I shall dry it. Finish your bath."
Grail sat in the warm water. "Why did he come?" she asked.
"Not on a plan to save you I am afraid," said Ekta. "Denvish is some ten or twelve days journey from here and your father's kingdom is even further in another direction so no news could have travelled between them. He was adventuring as boys are wont to do. They often come here. I hope I judged him right and have frightened him enough to make him cautious and not addled his wits. His father is old and I fear he will be king soon."
Grail was not satisfied with this explanation. "But how did he know I was here? He certainly entered the cave to rescue me?"
Ekta seemed to smile. "Well he sat outside and watched you through the door for an hour. I saw him as soon as I left but I walked on past and when he stopped watching me I watched him."
Grail was horrified "What? As I was having my bath?"
Ekta looked across at her. "Console yourself with the fact that he was quite a long way away."

Grail did not take to reading easily but as the winter came and passed she found that she knew her letters and could pick out simple words without help. With effort she could make the sense of what she read. Ekta was pleased and suggested that they take the book outside and sit there. Grail sat in the crook of his elbow and placed a hand on his shoulder to steady herself and he lifted her from her shelf and carried her through the great door.
Grail sat on a rock and read slowly to Ekta. The sun shone down and the day was warm and no wind blew. When the page was done they just sat and rested in the sun. A fox walked past and inquired if they wanted any rabbits today but Ekta declined. Grail was hardly eating any meat now. She was doing well on the green stuff and dried fruits he had in store.
The day slowly passed and they walked home. Ekta gently lifted Grail back onto her shelf and lit the lamp. They both were tired and slept well.

The summer sun was hot and Ekta slept on the grass while Grail swam in the pool beside the cliff. When she was tired she walked up and sat beside him, leaning on his side. "I think my hair is falling out," she said. Ekta made a noise to indicate he was listening but nothing more. "It used to go right down my back but now it barely reaches my shoulders and it feels awfully thin."
Ekta put a hand on her shoulder. "Don't worry," he said. "Hair always

looks strange to me. It's not like an animal that is hairy or furry all over and it's not like me either. I'm not hairy at all."
Grail rubbed her back against his smooth side. "You're all right," she said.

Autumn curtailed the days out in the sun and Grail began to began to hunt around the cave for things to do. "This place is a mess," she scolded. "You have piles of things you don't even remember. I'm going to tidy it up and throw out the rubbish."
Ekta was very defensive of his rubbish. "I know it all," he argued, "What there is that has no use has memories I cherish."
Grail waved a little hank of string. "What's this then?"
Ekta smiled. "A memento of a princess. Put it back."
The clear out proceeded slowly. Not many things went but at least they became more ordered. One day Grail found a tall box with racks of hanging garments. There were all sizes. She took one of the tiniest and carried it outside to see it better. It was a simple silken dress in the purest white. It was tiny, if she could have squeezed into it it would hardly cover her tummy. However the quality of the workmanship entranced her.
Ekta trundled home up the hill with a net full of apples and looked at it. "Sweet," he said.
"You used to give me dresses like this to wear," said Grail, "Why don't you do it any more?"
"I don't think I have anything in your size," observed Ekta and took his apples inside.

It was a crow that brought the news. Crows do not distinguish between men and other men well but even he knew that men that burn houses and barns are a tale worth telling and a crow likes to be taken seriously. Ekta was pleased to have the report but was troubled by the implications. He determined that he would have to go and see for himself. Grail insisted that she was coming. Insisted.

In the first light of dawn Ekta landed on the hill in the edge of the forest. Grail let go of his neck and slipped down off his back. Ekta pointed out the small wood where the family was hiding. The marauders, finding nobody home, had elected to sleep in the house out of the rain and confined themselves to acts of petty vandalism. The farm, however, was clearly a wreck. Ekta made Grail wait at the edge of the forest while he crept down to the house. There he sat in the yard and waited for the occupants to wake up.
When the cock crowed one of the sentries awoke and saw Ekta. It was like a mummers farce. He looked. He rubbed his eyes. He looked

again. He walked forward and looked again. He swore vigorously and ran into the farm house shouting unintelligibly. Ekta sat in the yard smoking gently. All the windows bristled men and weapons.

Ekta, who had no wish to damage the farmer's home, waited for them to discover the back door. The trap was not to be sprung here but on the meadow below the farm. Perhaps these bandits had heard it said that the place to face a dragon is on open ground as buildings burn excellently but none wished to be the first to venture outside. Finally a party was dispatched, perhaps by threats, to try the way and when the dragon stayed put in the front yard the rest decamped after them. When he was sure they had all left the house Ekta stood up so he could watch them over the roof. The whole band retreated behind the barns and up to the wood above. They skirted the edge of the trees and moved across a patch of open ground to a coppice. Soon they would have to move onto the meadow to effect an escape. Ekta wanted to pin them against the river. It was deep and you cannot swim in armour carrying a weapon. He could hence disarm them and send them on their way. Those that survived the militias that were already gathering against them would be a dire warning to others who might be planning a fortnight's pillage between getting your own harvest in and winter's coming.

Grail watched the band skirting round behind a small hill. They were hidden from Ekta but from her higher vantage point she could still see them. As they approached a clump of bushes a figure broke from cover, running up the hillside towards the woods above. The runner was encumbered by skirts heavy with the damp of spending a night in the rain and was caught in moments. Grail gasped as she saw the flash of a blade but the runner did not fall to the ground but froze. Then the band moved on. The runner was held from behind with the glint of a polished blade at her throat.

The band moved out from behind the hill and into the bend of the river. When Ekta saw them again the trap was ready. He leaped into the air and flew in a great arch to land next to the fleeing brigands. A great sheet of flame turned the runners into the crook of the river. They were driven like sheep to the river's edge. It ran deep with autumn rain and was too deep to ford. Breastplates, helmets and heavy studded jerkins littered the shore. Those that chose to swim with any armour never reached the far side. Only the smallest of arms could be carried. Grail looked for the girl. She could not see her. Why had she not waited on the bank for Ekta to rescue her? Grail suddenly realised that Ekta did not know there was a captive and the captive would fear the dragon as much as did any of the bandits.

Grail ran. She ran like the wind. As she ran she saw the great mop of cloth that was the girl in all her skirts now soaked with water. Grail ran, almost skipping over the ground. She saw the face turn upward and gasp a breath of air before being rolled over by the weight of her clothing. Grail ran past a startled Ekta and plunged into the river. She grabbed the girl and stood up. The water barely came to her waist. She carried the girl ashore.

Ekta made a great pile of weapons and wood in the farmyard and set it alight. The girl seemed shaken but dried herself by the fire. An old bearded face sneaked a glance round the edge of the barn. Ekta sat back on his tail and called "Come Farmer. Come and comfort your girl. She is wet and fearful. I will not harm you."
The farmer's wife came first. Wrapping her daughter about with her own cloak. The farmer, two lads and another girl crept slowly forward. The farmer said nothing. Ekta motioned Grail to climb on his back to leave. As he lifted into the air they heard the wife calling "Thank you dragons, thank you."

Back at home Grail threw her arms round Ekta's neck. "You were wonderful," she cried.
"But you saw the girl," said Ekta, "Alone I would have lost her. I would never have known she existed and she would have surely drowned." Grail smiled. "Team work," she said. They were both exhausted, they snuggled into Ekta's bed and fell asleep in one another's arms.

Winter came and finally turned to spring. Ekta received news that the king of the Denvish Lowlands had passed away and the new king, Randel, had placed a dragon on his crest and the motto 'Wisdom is preferred'. He called himself Randel the Bearded but was rapidly becoming known as Randel the Wise.

The sun was setting. Grail and Ekta sat in the cave door and ate their way through a tray of last year's dried apricots. "Do you know," said Ekta, "That it is now two years to the day since I fought Sir Endart and carried you off."
Grail leaned across and rested her head on Ekta's shoulder. "Not a bad day's work," she said.
"No regrets?" asked Ekta.
"No, none," Grail replied, "Should I have?"
Ekta leaned his head on hers and put his arm around her. "I hope not," he said.

Grail was uncomfortable when she woke up. She said she felt bloated, too many apricots perhaps. She was uncomfortable all day. Ekta did not go out but stayed with her. Finally in the early hours of the next

morning she laid an egg. At Ekta's guidance she placed it in the pool of water on the shelf in front of the door. She rested in Ekta's arms.
Grail watched her egg turn slowly in the warm water. "Will it be all right?" she asked.
"Yes," said Ekta, "and that should be 'he' not 'it'."
Grail was surprised, "How can you tell?" she asked.
"Boys come from eggs," said Ekta. "Didn't anybody ever teach you the facts of life? Don't you know where girl dragons come from?"

Lotti

"Say it again girl," chided Veldor. Lotti recited the word he had so carefully taught her but still the thrush sat in the tree and ignored her. She turned into the room "It doesn't work," she said, "Will you show me again."
Veldor rocked his chair forwards and looked through the window. "Chepith," he said. The thrush cocked its head and flew onto the window sill. "Chepith," said Veldor again holding out his hand. The thrush flew to him and perched on his fingers. "Yes, you know your name don't you," he petted it. "Now fly along home." The bird was gone.
"I am sorry girl," he said. "There's no magic in you at all. Yes, you have a good capacity to learn and, true, magic sticks to you well, but you have not got any personal magic. That's all there is to it. I can't help you."
Lotti, however, was determined not to take no for an answer. "There must be a way. There is nothing else I want to do," she said to the old man, "There must be a way I can get some magic."
Veldor sat back in his chair. "There are only four ways you can obtain magic. I was born with it as many are, some get it through necromancy but that is inevitably black so I will discuss it no further, some are awarded it for a great endeavour and some have it conferred on them by a master after much training."
An hour later, with the address of a master magician carefully memorised and a three day 'safe journey' spell stuck to her, Lotti sauntered down the hill and started on the long walk to Draftfelt. The road had a dubious reputation for bandits so she hoped that Veldor's spells were as good as he promised. He said she was not to stop except at night and she would not be harmed. He insisted that she turn back when she realised how foolish she was being. It rained torrentially. Lotti was soaked to the skin before she had walked a mile and by nightfall was almost ready to give up the whole enterprise. She sat under a tree and told herself she was a fool. She agreed but decided to go on anyway. She said "Chepith" to a bird sheltering with her. It ignored her but it probably was not a thrush. The tree dripped on her all night.
The next day was cold, windy and it still rained. She squelched on through the mud. No carts passed going her way so nobody offered her a lift. That night she slept in the open, curled under her cape, because she was too tired to care and slept well despite everything. In the late afternoon, true to Veldor's word, she arrived unharmed but hardly pleased at the house of the master magician of Draftfelt.

Lotti knocked. A young man answered the door. "Oh. I suppose you are the cause of all this rain," he said. "You had better come in and dry off." Lotti sat by the fire and warmed herself a bit. The young man studiously ignored her and packed dark powder from a big bin into smaller bags. There was a strong herbal smell. "What is it?" asked Lotti expectantly. "Tea," said the man.
Lotti was disappointed but decided that maybe this was just the hired help. "Is the master home?" she ventured.
"I live here alone," said the young man.
Lotti mentally checked the address. She was sure she was at the right place. Perhaps he was testing her. "Then you must be the master magician of Draftfelt," she said.
The young man paused. "Well we are in Draftfelt, yes, and I suppose that I am Kemf the magician, and I do not know of any other magician in the town save a few spell grinders but Draftfelt is hardly a major city so perhaps I am the master and the fool."
Lotti rummaged around in her bag and pulled out Veldor's letter. Naturally, despite the general sogginess of the bag, it was bone dry. Kemf opened the seal and scanned the sheet. He laughed twice as he read but when he put the letter down on the table he looked troubled. Lotti tried to glance, offhandedly, at it but the sheet, to her eyes, was totally blank. "Well," said Kemf, "You have passed poor old Veldor's first test. He quite believed it likely that you would turn home faced with all that rain. Since you are going to stay you had better come upstairs to the workshop and I shall get you a bed and a place for your things."

The house was just two large rooms and a stairway that lead between them. The place Kemf called the workshop was long and low and in the slope of the roof so you could only stand upright in its central section. Lotti was awarded a bed set into the wall with swinging doors to keep out the cold and afford some privacy. There were shelves at both head and foot ends and a single whirl of glass set in the wall to let in some light.
"Keep your personal stuff on the shelves. Keep any special things I shall give you in this box," he told her. The box was strong, iron bound and very heavy. He dragged it over and pushed it into the space under her bed.
As she unpacked her bag he asked her a few questions about her family, but as Lotti had left behind only an exasperated aunt with two daughters there was not much to tell. Her parents had died when she was tiny and she knew their graves, Kemf was quite insistent to know that, and nobody would expect her back. She had wanted to be a witch, a white witch of course, since she was a child and when Veldor turned

her down what choice did she have but to come to a master?
Kemf watched her unpacking. He still seemed ill at ease.
"Oh well girl," he said finally, "I suppose we have to find out what you are really made of." He poured water into a basin and started to wash his hands. "Please you take your clothes off. Cover yourself with those towels, just keep enough covered to be decent please, and lie on the table."
Lotti dropped the socks she was putting on the shelf and froze. "Pardon?" she said.
"Look," said Kemf, "To teach you magic is actually quite dangerous and I would not do it but for Veldor's request. There are things I have to know to make it safer. I am sorry. I know it will upset you but it won't hurt and it will hardly take an hour. Measuring your mind will take much longer and will be much harder for you. So just take your clothes off and lie on the table. I must start by checking your body."

Lotti shivered. Slowly she pulled layers of damp clothing off. She sat self consciously at the edge of the table with one arm hooking a towel across her chest and her other hand clutching the other resting in her lap. The table was long and wide like the kitchen table at home but the surface was finely polished wood and it was inlaid with a pattern of hexagons. Kemf seemed to ignore her and pulled a set of long armed frames up to the table. Finally he said "Lie down then." She clambered up onto the table top and lay down, straight and flat. Her hands wavered in the air, unsure what to do but he caught her wrists and lightly placed her hands, palm down, flat by her sides. Lotti breathed deeply and looked up into the rafters.
Suddenly there was a bright light. He pulled his chair up by her head and said "This won't hurt now but it might be a little uncomfortable" and proceeded to poke something very cold in her ear. The examination progressed slowly. A great magnifying glass passed over most of her body, pausing over every spot and blemish. Lotti was thankful that he spent longer examining her teeth than some other places.

Lotti sat in the kitchen, wrapped in a blanket, and drank her tea. Kemf hauled the tin tub back into the yard. "There," he said as he returned, "Clean and bug free. If you wash all your clothes in the morning then we will have heard the end of those lice. How do you feel?"
Lotti was not sure how she felt. She knew she smelt very funny, soap all over and strange stuff in her hair. If he had not seemed so disinterested in the whole affair she could have wept with embarrassment. "All right I suppose," was all she could say, and then at length she added "Am I all right?"
Kemf sat back in his rocking chair. "You'll do," he said.

In the morning Lotti took on the tasks in the kitchen. She swept and scrubbed as if she was at home. She laid the fire under the great copper in the yard to launder her clothes. As she worked people came to Kemf and sat in the kitchen. They came and spoke softly and he spoke softly to them. Some bought the bags of tea from the shelves, some did not.

They ate at midday and then walked down into the centre of Draftfelt. The market trades people were packing up to go but Kemf managed to buy all the items he wanted. He also carefully introduced Lotti to each of the stall holders.
Finally they came down to the quay side. To Lotti, who had never travelled more than two hours walk from home before, the sea was a glorious sight. The waves lapped on the sands and the fishermen worked at their repairs. The tide was low so most of the little harbour was sand with boats propped up on boards. As Kemf walked past the fishermen Lotti noticed them salute him but shake their heads.
At the far end of the bar an old man in an oiled cape walked up. "I saw one Sir," he said, "But it was only little mind, and it slipped through the net as I reached for it."
Kemf thanked him heartily and introduced Lotti as "my new assistant". The old man pulled off his cap and shook her hand vigorously. He looked at Kemf. "We'll keep looking Sir."
As they walked back up the hill Lotti asked "What are they looking for Master?"
Kemf smiled. Lotti was pleased that he had accepted the title because she did not dare call him Kemf when the rest of the world seemed to call him Sir. He did not answer at once but when they had climbed up through the now empty market he stopped and turned to look back at the bay. "Out in the sea lives a little silver starfish. Sometimes the trawlers or the mussel dredgers find them. Every year, when I bind the fishermen's boats against storms, I ask them to keep any they can find for me but for several years now they have found none. Maybe old Yam saw one but maybe his failing sight tricked him. At least they are still looking."

With some guidance from Kemf Lotti cooked the evening meal. They ate together in silence. Lotti gathered her clothes from the line in the yard and stowed them on her shelves. As night drew in they sat either side of the long table in the workshop. Kemf gave Lotti a book to read. "Read slowly and carefully," he cautioned her. It was stories. She was surprised but read slowly and carefully.
There was no magic in the stories, no adventures either, just ordinary

people doing very ordinary things. Finally the light faded and Lotti went to bed leaving Kemf still apparently reading and making notes.

When Lotti pushed the panel doors of her bed open the workshop was empty. She dressed and ran down stairs. Kemf was talking to a well dressed young woman. "Why will you not help me?" she was asking. Kemf spoke softly. "I have told you what you must do. To go beyond that is not love it is greed. If you choose not to heed my words now it is your choice, but remember them as they are the only true way." The woman gathered her bag and left.
Lotti put the kettle on the range. "What did she want Master?" she asked.
Kemf sighed. "She wanted a love potion. She is totally enraptured with the son of a poor merchant and she cannot see that until she sets aside her pride she will never win his heart. For all her desire she would treat him like dirt."
Lotti was interested. "Could you make a love potion then Master?" she asked.
"Nothing is simpler," sighed Kemf, "But I reserve them to place in the cups of the bride and groom when I am at a wedding for the good ones run deep and can, when misplaced, bring untold sorrow."
Lotti poured tea for them both. As nobody else came to the door she sat down and asked "Do you do magic for many people?"
Kemf smiled. "No. Most people who think they need magic only really need advice. Some only need somebody to talk to. Magic is too strong a remedy for most things."

In the afternoon they walked down through the market again. Kemf made Lotti lead the way. She faithfully traced the same path as the day before. "Good," said Kemf, "I will be able to send you on your own tomorrow. That will leave us some free time to teach you something." Lotti carried the basket of food round by the wharf where the fishermen were and noted that they all looked at them. She also carried it all the way back up the hill, anxious to prove that she was able to do the task. Back at the house they fanned the fire in the range and Lotti prepared the meal. Kemf folded paper to make packets and then ladled tea from his box into them. Lotti asked "Where do you get the tea from?"
"Magic," said Kemf.
"What?" she asked, "You just magic it up?"
Kemf did not look up from his work but said "What is tea? It is taste, it is scent and it is colour. There is nothing there. There are no leaves left from my tea in your cup because it does not exist. You taste the taste, you smell the scent and you see the colour but then it has been drunk these are no more. This is slight magic. It is harmless magic too. It

gives pleasure without hurt. Greater magicians than I have had to make a living from far more dubious labours than making tea."

Lotti sat in the dusk and read her book by candle light. She was reading about a farmer planting potatoes. As he drew each one from his bag he looked at it to see that it was whole and ready to be planted. He pressed a hole with a wooden stake he carried and dropped a potato in. Then he pushed the earth back with his boot. Lotti read in detail about seven long rows of potatoes. When the farmer stood up at the end of the last row his back hurt. Lotti's back hurt as she crept into her bed. She shut the doors and left Kemf to read on into the night.

When Lotti awoke the sun was quite bright in her little glass window. She pushed open the doors and seeing she was alone dressed quickly and hurried down stairs. Kemf was washing a large sore on a man's hand with water. He dusted on a little powder. The man offered payment but Kemf deferred. "Pay me when it is better," he said. The man left.
Shortly there followed a fat old woman towing a girl not much younger than Lotti by the hand. The old woman told a long tale of how she had taken pity on her niece and taken her in after her parents had died "of the diphtheria." How the girl was feckless and slovenly, "just like her father, I cannot see what my sister saw in him". She had beaten her resolutely "for her own good" but she had not improved. If the magician could not help then she would be forced to "Turn the brat out to learn her lesson the hard way."
Kemf sat and listened impassively. Finally the story ended and he reached out and snapped his fingers in front of the fat woman's face. She froze. She was like a statue. Her eyes did not blink nor did she appear to breath. "Now", said Kemf to the girl, "you can tell me your story."
At first the girl was unready to talk but Lotti made her some tea and Kemf slowly prompted her. An awful story unfolded of the girl nursing her parents and her younger brother until they died. She was clearly totally distraught.
Kemf listened as she talked. Lotti wept. Finally Kemf walked round behind the girl and spoke gently into her ear. The girl collapsed backwards from the stool into his arms. Lotti opened the door to the stairs and they carried her upstairs. Kemf lay her on the table and left her asleep.
"Master. What are you going to do?" asked Lotti.
Kemf sighed. "For the girl forgetfulness. Just a little. To soften the pain of bereavement and yet leave her the memories of the happy times before. For the Aunt some kindness and humility. She has the makings

of tuberculosis in her and she will need the girl's support over the years to come." Kemf pulled one of the long arms of his strange frameworks out and rested it on the girl's forehead. A light faintly throbbed in it. He took a bottle down stairs and left Lotti to watch the girl.

That afternoon Lotti made her first visit to the market alone. She had a list but as she approached each stall the trader already had the expected item ready for her. They seemed far more talkative without Kemf there. Before they had been respectful and quiet but now they were almost jolly. She walked on down to the wharf and walked along it. The fishermen positively waved at her and indicated by gesture that they did not, sadly, have anything for her today.
Lotti walked back up through the market. As the barrow traders were clearing away she could see the shops behind. As she walked up the hill she saw a woman she recognised step from the door of one of the shops. It was the woman for whom Kemf had refused to do magic. The shop keeper stepped from the door and spoke with the lady. He was a total contrast to her. She was tall and smart while he was short, fat and dressed in greys and browns but with a bright red fez on his head. She was holding a little paper packet which she placed in her bag. She walked on up the hill. Lotti stepped slowly after her.

The next day climbing in the same place Lotti stopped to inspect the shop. It was dark and had shuttered windows where all the others around it were open to display their wares to any last passing possible customers. There was an engraved plate with the inscription "Gordin, Magician" and much fancy patterning about it. As Lotti turned to move away a hand grabbed her wrist, nearly causing her to drop the shopping basket.
"You are Kemf's girl? Yes?" It was the man she had seen yesterday.
"Y... Yes Sir," she stuttered.
"You're pretty. I didn't think he was interested in girls."
Lotti did not like the implications in that. "I am his apprentice Sir," she said.
"Apprentice?" the man almost laughed, "Is he going to teach you magic? I have a skull that will do more magic in an hour than he will do in a year. He is a magician who is afraid to do magic. Which is a pity because he certainly has a great power. If you want to learn magic I will teach you. I can always use a pretty girl. Good for trade. When you want to learn magic come and see Gordin."

That evening Lotti read about a blackbird building a nest. A black bird does not build a tidy nest and it probably gives less thought to it than went into writing about it but she read it all, twig by twig. When she had closed the doors of her bed she began to wonder about what Gordin had said. Was Kemf really afraid to do magic? She had hardly seen him do any. He made tea, he healed wounds, he had helped the girl and her aunt but had he done any real magic? He always seemed to refuse. Did he really not do magic because he was afraid? If he was afraid would he teach her any real magic?

The next day when Lotti climbed the market street she stayed on the far side of the road from Gordin's shop and looked in the shop windows until she was safely far past it. She was not anxious to renew his acquaintance yet.

When she arrived home Kemf took the shopping basket from her and hustled her out of the house again. They walked up into the hills above Draftfelt. Despite Lotti's questions he refused to say what he wanted them to do. "It is too likely to be a disappointment," was all he would admit. Finally they reached a small piece of level ground in the shelter of a cliff. There they sat down on a low boulder. "This will be as good a place as any," said Kemf. He spread a deep blue cloth across Lotti's lap and on to his own. They sat silently.

After about an hour Lotti was passing the time watching rabbits browsing on the scrubby grass. She was bored but she had had to watch goats for days on end when her aunt's daughters were sick. Suddenly Kemf whispered "Keep still, keep silent but look slowly to your left." Lotti turned her head slowly. There was nothing special in sight but a white horse standing on the scree. The horse stepped nearer and stopped again, inspecting them carefully. As it came closer she saw the horn on its head.

Lotti took a deep breath but remained silent. The unicorn cantered a few yards neared. It came to the very edge of their grassy platform and stopped turning sideways to look at them again. Then it slowly and deliberately paced forwards until it stood right by Lotti. Even more slowly it knelt down and placed its head lightly on her lap. On Kemf's blue cloth. Lotti patted its neck. It turned its head slightly so that the horn ran straight across Kemf's lap also. Slowly Kemf moved his hand to the base of the horn. Then, in a sudden sweep of his arm, he pulled his hand right up the length of the horn.

The unicorn jumped up and backed off a few yards. Kemf placed the knife from his hand into the cloth in his lap. The blue cloth was littered with white flakes. He folded the cloth down its length to trap them and rolled it up.

"Send him away," he told Lotti.

"Oh... But he is so beautiful," she said.

Kemf placed a hand on her arm. He said "Yes and if he flees back to the high hills that are his home he will keep his beauty. Here there are

many that would covet all his horn and his tail and his meat besides. Send him on his way. He will obey you."
Lotti stood up. "Shoo. Go home," she called. The unicorn stared at her. "Go home. You're not safe here," it stepped back and turned to face her. In a graceful flowing action bowed its head so the tip of the horn touched the ground and then it turned and cantered up the slope. Silhouetted against the sky it turned and looked at them again and then was gone.

That evening Lotti read about unicorns. The habits and habitat of unicorns. She discovered that unicorns have a fascination with purity and have an unfailing eye for a virgin. Virgins, well virgins old enough to legitimately not be virgins, exercise a peculiar attraction to them. If you want to capture a unicorn you need a silver chain and a virgin.
The book then began to itemise the uses for unicorn horn. It covered a broad swath of preparations but they were mostly antidotes. Unicorn horn to purify the blood, to remove warts, to provide immunity from the evil eye. While Lotti read Kemf carefully moved over his blue cloth with his big magnifying glass picking every last flake and sliver of horn and placing it in a glass vial.

The next day, when the train of visitors had ceased, Lotti pointedly sat down in the visitor's chair. Kemf recognised the signal. "And now Miss," he started, "What seems to be your problem?"
Lotti grinned. "Well I hardly know how to begin," she said. This was the standard opening line of a woman who came almost every day and it usually prefixed the wildest speculations about her neighbours. They both laughed.
"I came here because I wanted to learn magic," she started. "And I know it takes a long time, and I know I need to get magic because I have none of my own, but I do feel I ought to have done something by now other than the cooking, the cleaning and the shopping."
Kemf smiled at her. "You're feeling discouraged?" he asked.
Lotti rested her chin in her hands and said "Very."
Kemf smiled again. "You are actually doing very well. I know you will be able to do magic, no Grand Master I know, but a good competent spell worker. I want you to learn things properly so you have to understand what the world is really like first then you can understand how to change it to get the result you want. If you don't understand you just go blundering in and you end up spending most of your time sorting out the side effects of your last spell rather than getting on with the next one."
Lotti looked at him disapprovingly, this sounded like he was getting ready to say no to her next request. Kemf continued "You have no

magic of your own yet so you could only do chemistry magic or transitive magic. You need to do a lot of learning before you try chemistry, rules for opening, closing, washing, grinding and mixing - you have to practice for ages on flour and soot before you dare try real active ingredients or you get all muddled up in your own spells. But I could teach you a simple transitive trick, a "call" spell. If I teach you to do it to me then it uses my magic. It might be useful too. You could call me from the workshop, or for that matter anywhere in Draftfelt, without making a sound and you can send simple one word messages. Would you like that?"

Lotti was so expecting to be told she could not have any magic yet she almost neglected to say yes. That evening she practised sending random words from the story books to Kemf who sat at the opposite end of the workshop. At first she found it hard to impress another word on his name and sometimes he laughed so what she had called to him was not what she intended but before she went to bed she could send any word she chose and Kemf got it right every time.

"Now remember," said Kemf. "This is like a letter where the recipient has to pay the postman so it is impolite to send too many unless you have an agreement with that person. Also it takes nothing from you. You only have to set the right state of mind through the incantation and the message inevitably goes through." Lotti was so happy she would have hugged him if she had dared. Now she felt she had really started.

The next day Lotti woke at dawn. She pushed open the shutters of her bed and looked about. Kemf was not in sight. In bare feet and just her night dress she crept down the stairs. Kemf was not in the kitchen. This still left the privy in the yard but the back door was still bolted. The front door however was not.

Lotti was alone. She slipped back up the stairs.

Lotti was not particular what volume she took from the shelf just the shelf she took it from. She wanted a spell, a real spell. She wanted to make something, even something simple. She lay the book on the table and turned through the first pages. There was a list, and against each item the number of the page on which it was to be found. She glanced down the list to take whatever fancy took and selected - love potions. She selected one that seemed safe. It was a powder to be mixed with water to produce an active salve. It acted on one person on contact. If you anointed their fingers they fell in love with the first suitable person they touched, if their eyes and it was the first they saw. It was particularly recommended for anointing the lips. It had no harmful side effects. It was "Secure" in that it did not generate incorrect attachments only bondings between men and women. It was inactive when in powder form. Quickly she drew from the vials of the workshop the ingredients and mixed them in the mortar. She had watched Kemf and felt she knew the trick which was not to touch anything so the spell did not get onto you. She ground the powders together and poured the result into a fold of paper. This she placed amongst her things and then she tidied away the book and all the vials. Then she carefully washed out the mortar rubbing away all marks of her work. She dried her hands feeling satisfied that now she owned her own personal charm to go with the spell she had learned last night.

The morning passed and with afternoon came the trip to the market. Lotti took up the basket and walked down the streets through the stalls. She bought the fruit, the vegetables and a small cut from a ham. She was hardly concentrating when she arrived on the wharf. The fishermen were gathered together in a group and when they saw her they excitedly called her to come. They proudly showed their catch. In the bottom of an old broken bottle was a silver starfish. It was in a few inches of sea water and actually moved as she watched it. Lotti was delighted. "Oh Kemf will be so pleased," she said "He has wanted one for so long."
Lotti took the star fish in its little pool and wedged it carefully in amongst the shopping. She dabbled her fingers in the water to touch it and her hand tingled. Lotti thought "I can feel the magic in it". She started back up the hill.
She was walking along head down watching the little creature in its water and did not really notice where she was until it was too late. "Ah, Kemf's girl again," said Gordin. "Learnt any magic yet?"
Lotti looked at him. She set her mind that she did not like him. He was short, fat and bald, on Veldor this had been good but on Gordin it was very bad.
"Some," she said, "but it is slow and sure."
"What?" demanded Gordin.
"Spells and charms," she said, "Simple stuff." She turned to walk on up the hill but could not resist one final dig. Back over her shoulder she said "Oh and we caught a Unicorn."
Gordin rushed after her and grabbed her hand and demanded "A Unicorn? Where?"
Lotti found it hard to answer for a moment as her hand seemed to shock her whole body. Her head filled with stars and a sudden jangling noise. "Where?" demanded Gordin again.
"On the hill. He came and laid his head on my lap," she told him.
Gordin looked shocked, "You are a virgin? I thought you and Kemf... Pah. Typical of the man. What did you do with this unicorn? Where is it now?"
"Oh Gordin. Don't be cross," said Lotti. "Kemf scraped some of its horn

and then we sent it away."
Gordin almost howled with rage. "You sent it away? It will be a hundred leagues away now. A Unicorn. Here."
Lotti placed her hand on his shoulder. "It isn't that bad. I'm sure we will find another. I'll help you. I will."
Gordin looked suspiciously at her. He seemed uneasy at the gentle hand hung round his neck. "You will?" he asked.
"Yes," said Lotti, "You know I'll do anything for you." She wondered how to cheer the poor man up. "Look," she said, "The fishermen found a sliver starfish for Kemf. Perhaps you had better have it. Please don't be sad. I didn't know you wanted a unicorn too."
Gordin still seemed very doubtful of her intentions but he led her inside his shop. He sat the glass on the counter and stared at the little silver star fish. "What is it for? What is it for?" he asked. Lotti put her shopping basket on the floor and stood next to him. She held his arm at the elbow and rested her head on his shoulder. Gordin was wonderful. He would work out what it was for. She was glad that he seemed happier now.
Gordin moved to a book case and stared at the spines. "No, no, no," he seemed to be ticking them off. He stretched up and lifted a volume marked RT from the top. As he did so his red fez fell off his head and dropped on the floor. As he placed the book on the counter next to the star fish Lotti picked up the hat and carefully placed it back on his head. He glanced sideways at her and pushed it straight with his hand. He poured over the fine text still muttering "What is it for?"
Lotti peered over his shoulder as he leafed through the book. Then he stopped and read a section. He turned forward to another page, he turned back. He leaned back and said a self satisfied "Ah".
"You've found it," said Lotti, "I knew you would. Show me." Gordin ignored her and read down the text. Lotti tried to read over his shoulder but the text was small and she did not know many of the words. She draped her arms round Gordin's neck and said "Come on, tell me."
"Well," said Gordin, "There's a whole section on starfish here. They seem to, in general, have strong therapeutic powers as they can regrow lost limbs. Medicines are always good business. Nothing opens a purse faster than pain or fear." He turned the page. "There are a few formularies for... for... Oh. Toothache. That's a good one, and woman's trouble.
People always pay better when it hurts." He leafed forwards and backwards. "But nothing specific on silver starfish. A moment. I'll try white starfish." Gordin reached down another volume marked WZ and scrabbled through pages. He grunted "Ah, just as I thought," then he read "White, sometimes silver, starfish, er, see starfish. Bother. Ah. And see death star."

Gordin seemed elated as he reached down DE. "This sounds more my line than Kemf's," he said to Lotti who carefully moved the two previous volumes to make way for the third. Gordin thumbed through the pages. "Death, death, er, death star. There's a lot here but it's all astrological and botanical." He turned the page, "Ah. Starfish. Death star. White or silver star. Dead man's hand."

Gordin's eyes seemed to bulge as he read. "No wonder he was so anxious to get it," he exclaimed, "It's a stabiliser."

"Wonderful," said Lotti, catching his mood. She added "What's a stabiliser?"

Gordin carefully moved the starfish, in its seawater into a little glass dish. "Magic is transitory. Magic is illusion. Anything I do will surely undo itself in time. I can heal a broken arm by straightening it and making it seem strong and by the time the magic has worn off the bones are knit back together. Good business is to use a little magic, let nature take its course and then claim all the credit. Just as you should never take gold from a magician. You may bite it, melt it, scrape it and weigh it but in the morning it will be base metal again," he paused.

Lotti waited. Gordin was not getting to the point. How was she to learn if he did not tell her. "A stabiliser?" she asked.

Gordin smiled. "A stabiliser does not make a spell itself but like salt to food it makes it strong and makes it last. With a good stabiliser I can convert a little charm for making a man strong for a day into something that would make you Hercules for a year."

"I thought you said it regrew things," said Lotti, "being a stabiliser is better?"

"Yes," said Gordin "The book says it can regrow limbs. So then I can have an inexhaustible supply."

Lotti smiled, "Like Kemf's tea."

"Well," said Gordin "Let us see the fabulous regrowing of limbs." He lifted the starfish out of its water and placed it on the counter. He rattled around in a draw and produced a knife. He cut a leg off the starfish. He waited. He watched. The starfish did not regrow a new leg. As it lay slowly drying on the counter it started to curl up a bit. Gordin began to look worried again. He placed the two parts back in the water and pulled the RT book open. "It says it here, it can regrow limbs, yes. Maybe I cut too much off." He got the starfish out on the counter again. Gordin tried twice more but the starfish refused to regrow even the smallest part of a limb. In fact it responded in the far more normal way for a creature and it died. Gordin shouted at it but it remained dead. "Poor little thing," said Lotti.

Gordin turned back to his book and muttered "That's a pity. Most of the stuff here needs live starfish. There is a bit on dried starfish, it's good stuff, but hardly exciting. I suppose I shouldn't have cut it up."

"Kemf could help I suppose," said Lotti "Shall I call him?"
Gordin swept a page over. "Sure," he muttered, "Call Kemf, call the ten great wizards, call the arch-angel Gabriel. I'm sure they'd all like to help a poor old necromancer with a stolen starfish."
Lotti patted him on the shoulder. "You didn't steal it," she said "I gave it to you. I'm sure they will all help but I only know how to call Kemf." Lotti set her mind to call Kemf. She wondered what the one word should be. Poor Gordin so needed help she decided to ask for that. "Help" she muttered as she called.
The effect on Gordin was electrifying. He sat up like a shot. "What did you just do?" he cried, "What did you do?"
Lotti looked at him shocked. "I... I called Kemf so he could come and help you" she said.
"You can't call. You have no magic," shouted Gordin.
"Yes. Yes," cried Lotti. "I can call him because he taught me to. It's his magic not mine."
Gordin grabbed Lotti by the shoulders and shook her. "That's all I need right now. A master magician legging it down to my shop as fast as he can run and me with his starfish dead and his girl fawning all over me. He'll eat me alive."
Lotti pushed her hands against his chest to stop him shaking her. "No he won't. I'll stop him."
Gordin let go of her. "You'll stop him? What with?" He paused. He took a deep breath. He suddenly seemed more composed. "Tell me," he said, "exactly now, tell me the calling spell." Lotti took his hand and carefully recited her lesson.

Gordin held her hand and pulled her into the back of the shop. It was dark, gloomy and smelt of damp. He heaved open the lid of a trunk and rummaged around inside. "I had one, I know I had one," he said. He was sweating and wiped his head with a rag. Finally he pulled a piece of black and white cloth from the bottom. "Ah," he cried "I knew it was here." He turned to Lotti. "Quick girl. Put it on."
Lotti looked suspiciously at the thing. It was only as long as her arm. How could it be a garment? Gordin shook it out and as it hung she recognised the pattern in white on the black. It was ribs, a spine and a pelvis. It was a crude representation of a body. But it had no arms or legs. Gordin pushed it into her hands. Down the front it had a row of tiny buttons, each part of the embroidered vertebrae. She took a deep breath. She remembered the first night with Kemf. How he had made her lay naked on the table. Gordin was only asking her to bare her arms and legs.

Lotti tucked herself in as dark a corner as she could find to undress and put on the skeleton garment. As she closed the buttons it hugged tightly around her as it was made of a stretchy cloth. She was a bit perturbed by the fact that nothing went over her shoulders but it relied on the top button being tight to hold it up. Lotti sighed, a few years ago she could not have worn it at all. Also it was hardly discrete as it seemed to emphasise rather than hide the shape of her body. She pulled at the front and got it a bit higher but it still left an awful lot of her showing. She stepped carefully back into the centre of the room, wary of treading barefoot on the deep carving. Gordin was setting a dark wooden box on a plinth facing a great wooden pentagram on the wall. "Is this all right," she asked.

He stopped and looked at her. He seemed to take two deep breaths. "Yes," he said. He picked up a chair and placed it in front of the box. "Come and sit down," he said patting the seat.

Lotti sat down gently, not relishing the cold leather on her unprotected legs. She was facing Gordin's box. Gordin walked over to her and placed a black string thing in her hands. He then opened a drawer and carried a deep red jewel over to her. He carefully fitted it into the strings so it was held. "Hold it carefully," he said, "The gem is old and has many cracks and flaws. We must not break it." He walked round behind her. He took the ends of the strings and together they lifted it together to her neck. He tied it. As he finished he placed his hands on her shoulders. Lotti leaned her head to touch one with her cheek. Gordin paused, he seemed to shiver slightly.

"Now stay silent and do not move," he said softly. He went round behind the box and slowly hinged the lid up. The box had a fine velvet lining and in it rested a small white skull. Gordin stayed behind the box but bent down as if whispering where an ear would have been. The skull seemed to light up and two red beams came from its eye sockets and played for a moment on the jewel at Lotti's throat. As the light died away Gordin closed the box lid.

"Oh he will be here in a moment," Gordin was sweating again. "Come girl," he said. He drew her up to the great pentagon carved on the wall. He dug around in his pockets and produced a piece of cord. "I'm sorry about this but this is how it has to be done" he mumbled. "Please hold your hands up." He carefully tied her wrists together and then tied them to a turned peg that stuck out of one of the upper points of the pentagon about level with Lotti's eyes. "I hope this will do," he mumbled. "I ought to tie you to all the points, spread out, but there just will not be time."

"Don't worry," said Lotti. "I'm sure it will be all right."

"Now when Kemf comes in you say his name, understand? Before we say anything else you say "Kemf" Gordin insisted "That's very important." Lotti nodded.

Gordin backed away and stood behind the skull's box. He almost seemed to melt into the dark curtains. They waited.

Time passed. For a moment there was a breath of cooler air and the sound of the street became louder. Then it was as before. They waited. The curtains beside the pentagon moved. "Kemf" cried Lotti. The jewel at her throat bust into light. Kemf froze.
"We have him," cried Gordin. Lotti looked. Kemf was caught in mid step. He was frozen in an impossible position with his weight transferring to a foot that had not yet touched the ground.
"Well Mr. Kemf. How nice of you to visit my humble premises," Gordin mocked "Having you around lends an air of respectability doesn't it. Even my customers don't respect me but they know I will always help. I fix the ones you refuse - they pay better. It's a pity you can't speak to congratulate me."
"I can speak," said Kemf.
Gordin jumped back to his box. He stood with his hand on the lid looking carefully at Kemf. Then he slowly walked forwards and poked Kemf. Kemf did not move, he still almost hung like a picture of a man walking.
"Yet you can talk," said Gordin.
"Yes," said Kemf.
"You know Kemf, we have never been introduced, we have never really meet but I feel I know you quite well." Gordin pulled his chair into the middle of the floor and sat on it back to front so that he could lean his arms on the back. "I've heard all about the advice you give. I always enjoy finishing the job for you."
He paused for a moment so Lotti interrupted "He does. He gave the woman the love potion."
Kemf asked "Who? Miss. Telleridge? What did you give her?"
Gordin waved his hands. "That's her. Gave her the sulphur and mistletoe one. Good stuff. I used it myself as a young man. No nasty long term effects. Stop the dose and off they go, home to mummy and that's the end of it. Nobody wanted to be my mother-in-law, they were just glad to get their daughters back."
Kemf interrupted him "Gordin you are despicable. You incriminate your soul in everything you say. I also notice you have picked a potion that will mean the customer must keep coming back."
Gordin laughed "Yes Mr. Kemf my astute business sense. But is not your tea just the same? They have to keep coming for more. You don't give them your bottomless barrel do you? Are my customers under any more compulsion than yours?" Kemf did not answer.
"The girl has served her purpose for you," said Kemf, "Release her."
Gordin laughed. "Yes. She has brought you here and she has let me

convert your little message sender into a powerful binding spell. You feel its strength Kemf? It is powerful is it not? It is your own magic that binds you. As you well know a spell that fails comes back on the caster. How shall you break free of that?"

Kemf frowned. "But you don't need the girl now," he said.

Gordin walked up to Lotti. "You think I am keeping her here by force? Do you want to go girl?" he said.

"No," said Lotti. She looked into Gordin's face. "I'll stay with you." She shivered.

Gordin looked at Kemf. "It's not my magic. It's her own choice," he said. Kemf ignored him. He said to Lotti "I never harmed you." Lotti swung round on her bound hands, suddenly cross.

"You used me," she shouted "I was servant and maid to you and all you gave me was books and more books. And you humiliated me. Do you think I enjoyed lying naked on your table that first night while you poured over me? I wanted to learn magic not just be another thing for Master Kemf to study." Lotti's sudden anger fizzled out and she started to cry.

"Wait," said Gordin. "Kemf. You went over her whole body? Does she have..."

"No," said Kemf, "She is totally pure."

Gordin shook his head. It was impossible to tell if he was pleased or annoyed. "Not much use to me then," he mumbled.

"No," said Lotti pulling towards him as far as she could reach. "I'll be all right. I'm sure I don't have to be pure if that's wrong for you..."

Gordin snapped round. His face was red. "Shut up girl," he shouted. "Why can't you think about yourself for a moment and stop worrying about me. Can't you even manage to be frightened? Will you stop trying to make me happy."

Lotti cowered away from him, "I'm sorry," she whimpered, "I don't want to make you angry." Gordin clenched his fists and looked up. Then he took his fez off, threw it on the floor and stamped on it.

A bell chimed with the sound of the shop door opening. "Ah," said Gordin, "A customer. Now don't either of you go away now." He bustled off to the front of the shop and could be heard indistinctly through the thick curtains.

Lotti looked at Kemf. Only his eyes seemed to move. As he spoke his lips barely fluttered. "I know what has happened," he said, "You called me and that was right. I know you are confused but trust me."

Lotti sighed. "I wish you would not fight with Gordin. He has had an awful day. He was so upset when I told him about the unicorn and when the starfish died..."

Kemf interrupted her. "Starfish?" he asked. "Yes," said Lotti, "The fishermen found you a starfish but I had to give it to Gordin to try and cheer him up."

She looked at Kemf for some approval. "Don't be cross, I know it was yours but he was so sad."

Kemf was silent for a moment. "You touched the starfish?" he asked.

Lotti pondered, "I suppose I did. Did you know it's a stabiliser"? Gordin explained it to me."

Gordin walked back in. He looked around and found his fez. "There," he said, "We must not let pleasure interfere with business must we." He pushed the red hat back into some sort of shape. As his hands ran over it it became more and more intact until when he placed it back on his head it appeared totally undamaged.

"Well Kemf," Gordin said, "It is not my choice that you are here but I am sure I can find a way to profit from it. I have followed your career with interest. You live a pretty bizarre life for a magician don't you? You know we do have a reputation to live up to now. I know I've done some odd things in my time but how you can combine Chapel going and magic I do not know." Gordin was wagging his finger at Kemf, almost scolding. "But when you suddenly produced this girl, well, most of Draftfelt was impressed, but the old fishwives would be most disappointed to know she can charm unicorns."

Kemf answered softly. "If they whisper evil against me then may God forgive them for I have done her no evil."

Gordin laughed. "And why did you take her in then? Is she not desirable?"

Kemf seemed to choke. He was almost unable to speak. Finally he said "I took her in on the direct personal request of an old man I care for dearly, but who has perhaps forgotten that I am still a young man." Kemf was perspiring freely.

Gordon smiled, "So she is desirable Mr. Kemf. Even to you?"

Kemf rolled his eyes to look for a moment at Lotti and replied "Yes."

Gordin walked over to Lotti. "You hear this girl? You have awoken the coldest heart in Draftfelt. I salute you. This makes you mightier than either of we magicians here. Am I to be next to succumb to your charms? For certainly, after Kemf, I am the man in this town thought the least likely to fall in love."

Lotti swung on her rope and turned her head away. "You are just being cruel," she said. "Just make him go away. He has not hurt you and he has not hurt me. Please Gordin, don't you hurt him."

Gordin sighed. "But," he said, "There is a fourth person here who should be consulted. I must never forget my partner needs to be asked what he wants." Gordin gently opened the box lid and exposed the skull.

"So," said the skull, "we have caught our prey." Its voice was clear and slight without the sign of breath. It did not seem to come from the skull in the box but appeared to fill the room. "Well done Gordin. We shall be well rid of Kemf."

Kemf spoke. "If you will destroy me there are many others in Draftfelt who will oppose you and your works. It is more the prayers of the chapel folk than the labours of Kemf that keep virtue alive here."

"No Kemf," said the skull, "I do not wish to destroy you. You are far too valuable a prize for that. I have whiled away the long hours shut in this box dreaming of the day I could have someone like you to ride. Gordin has brought me tramps and beggars and I have entered their eyes and walked in them round the town, but they were poor and weak and had so little magic in them that they slipped easily from my grasp. They were like this girl here, but for the traces of gross physical matter she is almost not there. Yet you would be firm. I could hold you to the ends of the earth. Kemf. In your heart you must know that you will never lie in the Chapel yard. The Dark will have you and then you, like me, would seek your immortality in this world."

Kemf could not move but his voice carried contempt. "There is no immortality in this world. From your speech I gather you were a magician when life was in you. Yet even Gordin wears a fire ring to guard against your fate. He would use you but he would never take your place. Neither of us will come to a grave but the fire that comes after death will at least release us from this world. We shall be judged as all men are judged and if we find mercy so be it. Your time will come."

The skull sneered. "Pretty words Kemf. But tonight the power is mine. I shall have your body, Gordin will have your power and you shall go and find what mercy you can. Draftfelt will be ours but that will be an incidental pleasure. You are the star of our night."

Gordin carefully took a large knife from a wall rack. He carried it forwards resting either end on just his finger tips and placed it at the centre of the pentagon carved in the floor. He stepped quickly back behind the skull's box.

"Well," said the skull, "We have the two magicians, we have the knife, we have the victim to act as the intermediary. We shall now transfer the power."

Gordin stuttered "Er, the girl..."

The skull interrupted him "Don't worry Gordin, I will not damage your plaything. I am pleased to see your taste has improved."

The skull began to glow in its case. The red beams slowly grew from its empty eye sockets and played on the knife blade. The light seemed to reflect about the room. Lotti felt it brush over her body like a physical presence, washing over her exposed arms and legs like a gentle velvet cloth. She saw the light play on Kemf still caught in mid-step. A tension

seemed to be growing between them.
The light grew. The floor seemed to be vibrating with power. She shuffled her feet as the carving seemed to cut into her. She swung round a little on the rope at her wrists and looked at Gordin. He stood behind the skull's box, lit by the light in the room. As the vibration intensified he put out his hands to steady the box. The vibration became like a low organ note then with a sound almost like breaking glass it stopped and the darkness fell again.
Gordin bent down beside the box. "It didn't work," he almost shouted, "He is stronger than you. Even bound like this he should be a gift to an apprentice rain maker and still he confounds your power?"
"No," said the skull, "The girl is the problem. Gordin what is this new assistant of yours?"
Gordin stuttered. "She... She is not my assistant. She just came to me. She was Kemf's assistant. She gave me the starfish because she had helped him, not me, with the unicorn."
"A unicorn?" wailed the skull, "Gordin. You have not brought me a virgin on whom a unicorn has laid its head?"
"Er... yes," said Gordin, "But I put her in the death garb, I tied her to the pentagon. What more should I do?"
"Kill her," said the skull, "Kill her now. Her body and blood will serve where she herself will not." Gordin stepped forward and slowly picked up the knife from the centre of the floor. He raised it to Lotti's face.
"No Gordin," she said softly looking into his eyes. "Please don't kill me. Let him kill me but don't kill me yourself." Gordin looked into her eyes. He looked at the knife. He slowly tucked the blade under the amulet's collar. The blade was tight against Lotti's throat.
"Now" said the skull. Gordin's knife arm jerked. The Amulet collar was cut and the jewel fell to the floor and smashed. Another stroke with the knife and Lotti's hands came loose. Kemf finally finished his step into the room.
The skull's eyes burned two red beams at Kemf, but the beams seemed to reflect off him. The beams splayed back over the skull. The velvet and the box began to burn.
The skull screamed "Gordin, you have betrayed me," the two beams flashed out again. Two holes appeared in Gordin's chest before the skull itself began to burn and dissolved to powder before their eyes. Lotti dived to Gordin's side, her eyes filled with tears. His shirt was filling with blood. "Oh Gordin," she cried, "Don't die."
Gordin caught his breath. "I wish I could prevent it, but none can do that now," he said. "Kemf. Kemf. How did you turn aside the skull's power?" Kemf was silent.
"Come on," gasped Gordin, "I tried to save you and the girl. Do I not deserve an answer?"

Kemf looked down at Gordin and said, "Under my tongue I have a sliver of unicorn horn."

Gordin wheezed "Not enough. It is not that powerful."

Kemf hesitated then said. "All the books speak of is dead horn from a dead unicorn. I trusted myself to horn from a live unicorn that still roams free. I knew it would be stronger but it is better than I hoped."

Gordin said nothing more. His body slowly relaxed. Kemf reached down a hand to his face and closed his glazed eyes. Lotti wept. Kemf slowly pulled her away from the body. She sat and looked.

Slowly flames seemed to light inside Gordin's left hand. They spread up his arm and into his body. It was if the flames were burning within a glass man. There was no heat, no sound of the rush of fire. Then in a moment he was gone. The place where he lay was empty, no trace left of his passing.

Kemf took the white shard from his mouth. He turned Lotti's face up and gently squeezed her cheeks so that her mouth opened. He placed the piece of unicorn horn to her lips. "Under your tongue," he said, "But do not swallow it." Again Lotti found her head filled with stars and a sudden jangling noise.

Lotti stood up, her right hand throbbed a bit and her head was slowly clearing. "I loved him," she said slightly shocked.

"I know," said Kemf. "I missed the ingredients as soon as I went to look. You washed the mortar with your fingers perhaps?"

Lotti cupped her mouth in her hands. "I'm sorry," was all she could say.

Kemf swung his cloak about her. "Take the death garb off," he ordered. He buttoned the neck of the cloak and pulled it closed about her.

Lotti's eyes filled with tears again. Under the cloak she fiddled with the buttons. "What about Gordin?" she asked.

Kemf did not look in her eyes. "I cannot tell," he said. He paused. Lotti finished her buttons and bent and slid the thin material down her legs and kicked it away. She looked Kemf in the face. There were tears in his eyes. He said "We know that God is merciful. We know Gordin did not harden his heart when he was called upon to show mercy. Perhaps he in a way loved you too. In truth. For there was no charm on him for it."

Lotti sobbed. "Be careful," said Kemf, "Don't swallow the bit of horn." She lifted the cloak to her face and wiped her eyes "Why not?" she asked.

"I cannot tell but I suspect that you would then remain a pure virgin forever" said Kemf.

"Oh," said Lotti "I don't want that because I'm going to marry you next summer." She fished around with her tongue and pushed the sliver of horn onto her finger. Kemf carefully transferred it to a glass tube.

Lotti hung her head. "I'm sorry," she said, "I didn't mean to say that. It's

not even a plan."
Kemf almost smiled. "That is the problem I had. Did you know that you can only speak the truth with a piece of unicorn horn in your mouth?"

Traitor

"Look! I love you. I want you. You may not think this is a serious relationship but for me it is!"
I wince. I can tell when she is not happy because she shouts at me. I do not need to be a psychologist for that.
"Jo, I'm not trying to hurt you." I try. "I am trying to tell you something you ought to know about me." She is not mollified. Not in the slightest. She puts on a pained voice. "Brian I know you're older than me. I know you're probably lots older than me. I know that people will think I'm mad and that you're a dirty old man but I..."
"Oh Jo" I interrupt, shaking my head and trying to sound hurt, "You don't know and if you will stop getting all heated I will try to explain." I suppress gritting my teeth. This was getting worse by the minute. She has got to be allowed to get mad but this is more than I expected.
She bumps down onto the floor leaving me alone on the sofa behind her. Bozo, Jo's uncle's dog, looked up hopefully, it might be time to go home. Jo is supposed to be walking Bozo. Bozo is getting fat.
I sigh pointedly. "Let me show you something strange" I say to her back. "Come on, touch me on the shoulder." She ignores me to prove that she is cross.
Bozo yawns, gets up and wanders off to the kitchen where he likes to climb into the laundry basket. I wait, knowing she will relent. She turns slowly. I smile. She smiles even more slowly and then reaches both hands towards my shoulders, turning her head slightly to kiss me.
When her fingers touched the body shield she freezes, momentarily shocked and frightened. I wait for her to speak. "I can't reach you!" her voice starts to break up. I cancel the shield, reach out and pull her into my arms.
"And now you can" I say adding as much strong reassurance as I dare. She gasps. "What is it?" Her face was suddenly wet with tears. She is over reacting again. I squeeze her.
"It is the proof of what I am trying to tell you. Proof because nothing on earth can duplicate it. It could not come from earth."
I pull her round beside me to sit on the sofa. I brush her wet hair from her face. I have my arms around her and decide to risk starting from the beginning again. Softly. "Jo, how old are you?"
She looks at me despairingly. "Sixteen" she whimpers.
"How old am I?" I ask.
"Twenty something" she mumbles.
"Try again" I reply as softly as I can.
"Thirty something?" she is crying again but clinging to me, not pushing me away this time.

I try to be very soft but very distinct "In ordinary years, the way you count them, I am six thousand eight hundred and sixty two. I am Varhyn."

Wet eyes looked up at me. She sniffs and asks "What does that mean?"

I snuggle an arm round her so she will watch my face as I explain. "I am part of the team that is trying to help humanity to go from savagery to civilisation in thousands rather than the usual millions of years. What you just felt was the body armour that has kept people from stabbing, shooting or otherwise making holes in me over the years. I normally hide it just on the surface of my skin. I just..."

"You're telling me we have to stop seeing one another?"

"No Jo. No I'm not. Just the opposite. I'm trying to tell you about me because I want to keep you but I won't keep you without being completely honest with you. I am ordered to keep my identity secret but I am excused these orders for family. Family can be trusted. After these last few weeks... Well, I think you are a bit family now."

She tries to smile a bit. She wraps her arms about my neck and touches her forehead to mine. She sniffs. She suddenly smiles broadly and says "I seduced you."

I smile ruefully, "Maybe I seduced you," I offer trying to give her an excuse but knowing it was not really true, "or maybe I didn't resist as hard as I should have. We are not going to argue about that one now. There are lots of things I want to tell you and lots of things I'd love to ask you."

She snuggles up closer. "So I can keep you. Daddy will hate it."

Daddy hates it. When this Brian Wallace person asks to see him he wants to shout at him, give him a piece of his mind and throw him out. I only asked to see him so he could shout at me not Jo. She might be able to pass as older some places but never at home. He has a little girl and I did not qualify as one of her little friends. However I am a senior project psychologist with six thousand years experience of getting humanity to do sensible things despite their personal inclinations and Daddy is a forty year old civil servant. I hit him with as much credibility as he can take. I use my understanding of how the human mind works to present myself as a suitable friend for the daughter and let him lie to himself about my apparent age. We call the tricks we use for this psi and although this is perhaps not an appropriate use of psi it staves off an aggressive confrontation which must be good.

"Jocasta is a head strong girl" he warns me, "I fear she may be leading you on." I smile. I know she is head strong. Wildly so. Daddy introduces me to his wife as I leave. "This is Jocasta's young man". I shake her

hand and go. She says nothing, she just stares at me open mouthed. I suppose I will have to visit her soon.
Jo was out walking Bozo. I wonder what she will think when she gets home. All in all not a bad evening's work I congratulate myself and suppress my reservations.

I sit on the sofa and draw a message to Zey. I must introduce Jo to him one day. I wonder about how he will react.
"Jo this is Zey." I rehearse to myself. That is not his name, it is a title with implications of 'Father' or 'Guru'. He doesn't really like it. I do not know what he is actually calling himself at the moment. I have told somebody about us. I have used a measure of psi on somebody else. That is not quite within the rules, I am sorry, but I did it and it all must be logged. He insists that everything we do is recorded. They will want to know their history and what part we played in it. I think he will like Jo. Anybody would like Jo.
I scratch on the pad. I try to describe Jo in a few brief formulae so Zey could see what she is like. However she seems to look rather ordinary on paper so I give up. I picture her in my mind. My favourite image is walking in the park. Bozo, half Toy Shetland Collie, half powder puff, jumping up at us. She wears the absurd combination of a thick warm jacket and the incredibly short skirt that she seems to like so much. I see Jo kicking fallen leaves, Jo running, Jo climbing, swinging and laughing. Jo being Jo.

Jo skips school the next afternoon, it is games on Wednesday. She turns up at the flat unexpectedly. I am laying on the sofa trying to redraw the diagram of British politics. I hear her key in the door. I pretend not to hear. I expect to be sneaked up on but am surprised when she lands on top of me knocking my papers about.
"What did you do to him?" she wants to know as I try to recover my breath.
"Him? Oh, I, er, I calmed him down a bit and explained a few things." She is elated. "Well he was going to murder you. Poor Bozo was exhausted when I got him back to uncle John's. I was scared to go home. Did you hypnotise him or something?"
I try to untangle myself a bit into a position more suited for having someone sit on my tummy. "I may have used a few tricks to get him to listen but nothing too special."
She leans forward and rests her chin on her hands and I feel the shield cut in to reduce the pressure of her elbows on my chest. Suddenly she says "I'm here without Bozo." True it is unusual but hardly significant. "What, don't they let you take him to school?" I mock. "Good thing too. Your uncle will be mad at you teaching him to come to that silly name".

She tries to justify herself, "Mummy called him Bozo first. Uncle John is her brother."

I smile up at her "That only proves your mum is as nuts as you. Nice one Mendel." We both laugh.

"Well since I'm here..." she says sitting up. She pulls off the hated school tie and kicks off her shoes. As she undoes the top button of her shirt I grab her, pull her down on top of me and kiss her in case she was planning on going further. I have a rough script for our next meeting planned but it is not pillow talk. I reason that a kiss could not possibly be seen as rejection. She soon settles down a bit and is ready to talk again.

"Can I feel that thing again?" she asks.

"What? The body armour? You'll have to get off my chest first."

She pushes herself up and looks down at me. I activate the token outer shield of the multi-level system. I feel somewhat relieved as it pushes her knees out of my ribs as the normal shields are concerned with life and death issues and are oblivious to comfort. She reaches out slowly and slides her fingers over the invisible barrier a few inches above my body. "It seemed so hard to believe" she murmurs. I collapse the shield and her hands land on my face. She laughs.

I sighed contentedly. Jo is nice to cuddle up to. We rest on the sofa and I ask her little questions about her day. The ones that I know she likes to be asked. She gossips about her friends and their friends. She whinges about a teacher. She tells me things she was told in strictest confidence. I go 'oooh' and 'humm' at the right moments but hardly hear her. I stroke her face and enjoy her company.

"Are you going to marry me one day?" she asks.

"I'd like that" I muse, "I'd like that a lot."

She is interested. "When?"

I am wary. "It might be a good idea to finish school first."

"I finish GCSEs in the middle of next term" she suggests.

"Oh, I was thinking of A-levels or more." Not popular.

"That takes years" she whines.

I try to be reconciliatory. "We've got years, they'll be good years."

She sticks an elbow into me. "I'll be an old woman at that rate."

I take a deep breath. She has got to be told soon so I might as well do it now. "Well, no you won't actually." I do not not use psi tricks on Jo but I made the implication of something-to-tell pretty strong. She snuggles down with her nose in my ear. "I can feel a lecture coming on" she says.

I am defensive, "You don't have to know." I offer.

She knows I will anyway. "Go on" she says.

"How's your biology?" I ask as a preamble.

"Lustful and energetic" says the nose in my ear.

"School biology you silly kitten." I scold.
"Straight A's." Predictable, she is smart and quite prepared to tell you.
"Well I am six and a bit thousand years old and still going strong so you can guess that I've got something extra." I pause, she waits. "The trick is a thing we call a 'D-repair cell'. It rebuilds tissues according to the pattern the body was originally made to. We have modified these for use on humans and some of those have been getting into you - rather like a sexually transmitted disease."
She sits up like a shot. "Is that bad?"
I sigh, "It's pretty good. Now shut up and listen." The nose goes slowly back into my ear, a hand sneaks across my chest and under my shirt. She is listening, she was just pretending not to.
"'D-repair cells' that you get will vastly improve your resistance to illness and help you recover from injuries. They will also slow down your ageing. At the moment it is down to about a fifth but if we got married you would stop ageing totally. It does not stop the ultimate internal processes so you do not live any longer than you would if you lived a disease free life but it's a pretty good deal."
"You mean I can stay sixteen for years and years?" she squeaks.
"Well, sort of" I reply. "You get the birthdays but not the wrinkles and such."
"You really are a dirty old man" she is laughing at me. "You are going to keep me sixteen while you go on sexually transmitting your cells into me. And you six thousand and whatever - you should be ashamed of yourself." She doubles up with the giggles. Knees in my side, forehead banging my face. She destroys in a moment all my scripts. She goes home late for tea so she won't be coming round later and Bozo will only get a quick walk. I never finish my diagram.

They come for me at two in the morning. Tranzen military security is ever so good but we never use it. We just have to accept problems and try to repair the damage caused afterwards. However this is the worst bust ever. I get a message from our security people with a request that I co-operate as they have some questions about how I had been discovered. As the Brian Wallace secret identity is clearly now destroyed I might just as well do that and see what we can find out. Suddenly the room is full of armed men and I am tied, gagged and more in moments. I travel down the stairs on a trolley through the wreckage of my front door whilst my flat comes apart behind me. The street is full of police cars, patchy olive brown trucks and an ambulance. It is a long and bumpy ride.

The skies are turning grey as they unload me and wheel me to a low building and into a lift. We go down a long way. Two men are locked in a cell with me. They cut the plastic straps around my wrists and ankles and remove the gag. Then they present me with a bundle of clothes. "Thank you" no response. "Can you tell me..." I stop. They show none of the normal reactions to speech I would expect. They are not just ignoring me, they are not hearing me. I feel cold. If my captors know to use profoundly deaf guards then they already know too much. Finally I am left alone.

We all always have current plans for a bust but lately, for early twenty-first century Europe, they are mostly about showing the shock and disorientation that an innocent bystander would have and using mild psi on the interrogator to make them think that it is all a silly idea. Mild because they will watch their own questioners carefully, or at least they should. I start playing the part, but without much conviction, rubbing my hands together and massaging my wrists as if the circulation had been impeded. I put on the clothes and sit on the narrow bed and look round. One table, one chair, one bed and no window. The only light comes from a bulb behind a glass behind a grill.
A slot in the door snaps open. Eyes look in. It snaps shut. No video surveillance? but video can be tapped into. They know we are high tech. They maybe do not know just how few we are. There is no great team here. Just one starship. I have no-one waiting to rescue me because I do not need rescuing. Well I hope not. I never have had. For the worst case security just dummy up a corpse and do a substitution.
I lie back on the bed and close my eyes. I think of Jo. What bad luck to be just getting involved with that lovely girl and then being grabbed. They must know about Jo. They will probably question her. Daddy will hate it. Zey will not be too pleased either. Since I have nothing better to do I go back to sleep.

It is many hours before my silent warders are back. They take me to a room with a table and two chairs. I sit down. They do not. We wait. I rehearse a whole sheaf of possible interviews. I feel ready to take on a questioner. I can better him. Time is on my side. He will be expected to produce results. I can wait. I can wait years, decades if need be.
Time is our greatest weapon. Zey says "Never plan against a single man no matter how evil. He will always be gone sooner than you expect. Plan against the institutions that give him the power to do evil." Where is this questioner? I want to get started. I am having trouble waiting minutes. Minutes grew to hours. My guards are relieved. I wait.

"Mister Wallace. As you will have realised we know a lot about you and about your organisation. We really did not want to stage the operation last night but as you must understand we felt we had no choice. I would

like to be on friendly terms so please don't let us waste time pretending to know nothing. My name is John and I am here to ask you a few questions. Just to allay our natural fears of... Well, outsiders."
He is big, bluff, balding and about fifty. The speech is well rehearsed and his voice almost completely masks his feelings. I can read him. He does not like me and he is frightened of me. Good. If he is frightened of me they did not know very much. I am not human. I needed in-depth psi training to be able to lie so as to maintain my cover. I could do him no more harm than a kitten. If he does not know that I can use it to my advantage.
I choose to be direct but obscure. "What can you offer me in exchange for information? Can you promise that anything I tell you will be kept secret? Will you release me afterwards?"
"There might be charges laid..."
Use a little psi. Be friendly, almost condescending. "Don't be silly John. Unless you invent some new laws nothing has been done that is illegal."
"Is that your price then? Secrecy?"
"I could tell you some things in return for a guarantee of total confidentiality and my unconditional release." He looks perplexed for a moment then his face clears.
"We could arrange a new identity in return for evidence..."
I laugh gently "Don't be silly John. I'm not a super-grass or a traitor. Go and speak to your superiors and come back with it in writing. Secrecy and release. Then I will tell you the story." I stamp the words with finality. The interview is over. He starts to gather his papers together. I relax. I have won the first round.

I feel better back in my cell. I hope that if they follow through with my proposition I can tell them enough to keep them happy but not enough to start the project rocking. We have told lots of people just what we are about down through the years and it never makes public knowledge. There are lots of good reasons for that which I would be pleased to explain but this is not the place for maths. I wonder what the time is? They dim the light. How thoughtful. I prefer to sleep in the dark. I sleep well. I dream of Jo. We are walking in the park. She is dissecting a flower for me, naming all the parts. Bozo is running around us, he always did like me.
Bang. Whoosh. Through the door. In a dark room. A bright light. Wake up quickly. Get your wits about you. Think.
"Look Wallace the girl told us everything. Not that we didn't know already." I cannot see him against the light. "Do you get some kind of perverted kick out of messing about with school girls? People like you make me sick."

The intro tells me that Jo has not told them a thing. If I sit here and smile at this new questioner long enough they will bring John back in with 'a deal'. I must wake up and think. The sleep fades away and I am clear and lucid. I smile at him. I can win this one too.
"We've got people round here who would just like to sort out nasty little pervs like you. You're in trouble and if you don't start telling us what we want to know you are going to be a very unhappy little man indeed."
I answer just enough to keep him verbal not physical. He does not say anything new after that. He often nearly hits me but if I read him correctly he is not allowed to do that yet. I sense the 'yet' loud and clear. He would like to bang me about. This may be harder to handle. I can fake moderate bruises but it is very easy to lose track and get them in the wrong place. Zey will not be pleased if I start being too inhuman. I am resolved to handle this on my own. I am after all a senior member of the team. I do not need any help with a few questioners.
"...no real woman would want a little shit like you so I suppose..."
Where did they drag this guy up from? His briefing is so bad. The average human male is so out of tune with the women that he claims to love you would think they were a different species. I act normally, I am unaggressive and helpful and I find I have to fight them off. Sadly adult human women are about as mentally messed up as adult men. Maybe that is why I like Jo so much. I could not see that they had been watching me for very long if they do not know that. Maybe they did not recognise it. I wonder how they got onto me?
"Sling the creep back in the cool. I'm up to here with him."
I wonder what the time is? It seems ages since they brought me back. If the light is bright I wonder if it is daytime? Next time somebody talks to me I must try to estimate their circadian cycle. That should give me a guess. If I cannot keep track of the hours I will lose track of the days. Unnumbered time passes.

"Wot you in 'ere for?" This is a farce. They spend thousands busting me with troops and hordes of police and they think I will believe they are short of cells. He is either a snooper to try and get something out of me, a thumper to be agent and fall guy on a beating or just a moron to drive me mad. I fear it may be the third which is the worst option by a long margin.
What is the time? He has just had breakfast. He reckons it is about eight thirty. I wonder if I get breakfast? It cannot still be the day they busted me so it must be Friday. Or is it Saturday? He does not care. "It's all the same in 'ere." How can you not care about what day it is? What are the effects of not caring about the date? I wish I had something to write with - I cannot do maths like that in my head. What are the effects of not knowing the date?

My companion is listless. It is a great relief when he finally announces that he 'knows wot I done'. He is clearly briefed. Injuries sustained in a fight with another prisoner are more acceptable than a beating by interrogators. Good. If they care about that then letting me go is on the agenda. I ask him what I did as I have yet to be told. He does not really know. Just innuendo, something nasty about a little girl. I tell him a little about Jo. He has never known much affection. He has never had a woman he did not pay for. I paint Jo the blithe free spirit. She chose me rather than I chose her. We kept meeting in the park. It was not my choice nor hers. Well, not at first. So we talk.

We leaf through his childhood and subsequent career as a military bully. Never out of trouble but always performing well enough in the field not to be thrown out. We talk about his drinking. We talk about his fights. I keep asking "Why?" and then explain why. Slowly he learns to answer for himself and then to ask the questions.

"God I'm a shit. Where am I gonna be when I'm fifty?" Then they come and drag him away. I think he will make it. I never see him again.

They do like music here. For hours they have played the same stuff but played it far too loud. It is still going when they wake me up for breakfast. It must be wasted on the guards. It must be morning because no kitchen would serve porridge for supper. I think that makes it Sunday.

"Mr. Wallace, I have a proposition to put to you." John finally makes it back. "If you can convince us that you are no threat to the nation and the world you can have your secrecy and release."

I can accept that but I must not let him get away with it that easily. "No John, no. I am a threat to everything your nation and world stands for. I am a threat to those who would grab a man from his bed in the night. I am a threat to those who bully, interrogate, who beat and kill. That is hardly a deal."

He ignores me. Well done John. "I have a document here that states that everything we discuss shall be covered by the Official Secrets Act. Everything will be classified and not revealed even under the thirty year rule. You too are to be bound by the same conditions. Is that clear?"

"Who signed it?" He pushes the paper towards me. I do not recognise the name but the title sounds good. I do politicians not civil servants. I reach out and pick up his note pad and pen. "Tomorrow." I say, "We start tomorrow. For now I am going to write a love letter and you can find me a postman."

Dear Jo,
As you probably know I have been invited away for a few days to assist Mr. Plod with his inquiries. All in all I am not being treated too badly. Do

not worry about me as I can look after myself. Please write so I know you got this letter. Put the time and date on your letter so I can picture you writing it. I think about you a lot and I miss you like crazy. I cannot say much now but I hope to see you soon.
Brian.

I sketch a note to Zey too. Story so far. I am worried about Jo. In fact I am worried about me too but I don't want to admit that yet..

"Are you ready to talk now Mr. Wallace?"
"That rather depends on the questions."
"Who do you represent?"
"The Tranzen."
"And what is your function?"
"I am a mathematician."
"Where does your income come from?"
"I am the recipient of various sums held in trust. It makes a reasonable income. Doubtless you have already traced this."
"We are aware that trusts were set up but the people who put them in place are either rather hazy about you or are no longer with us."
"I hope you are not suggesting..." I trail off to allow him to tell me what he is not suggesting.
"No. We wondered but we are sure that there is nothing amiss. It is just inconvenient that so much of the work was done by old men, often with terminal illnesses."
"Very reputable old men."I could laugh. I told him that I am a Tranzen mathematician and most of the galaxy knows what that implies and he is off talking about money, a concept that is only understood by primitivists and historians.
"Certainly reputable. I am just curious. And how do you live on your reasonable income?"
"I keep a flat. I frequent libraries, restaurants, theatres,..."
"And schools?" He interrupts abruptly. I remember the bright light and the dark room. John will have had the same briefing, he will know as much.
"John." Use psi. Offended. Accused. Forgiving. "John. Surely you are not going to bring in Jocasta. She is a sweet little thing. I am very fond of her but most men are attracted to females younger than themselves. Have you seen her?"
"I have. She looks little more than a child. Until you met her we were wondering about you."
More psi. Tell me what you mean John. "You were wondering that because I did not have a girl friend I might be gay?" His body says yes. His face says that that would have been a great disappointment, but he

says nothing. They know that what I am means I would not be a homosexual. I wonder if they know why? How do they know why? "We wondered for a while," he muses on, "but now we know." I have over done it. He did not mean to tell me that and he knows he did not. He is suddenly worried. Frightened of me. He gathers his papers and leaves. My two silent minders take me back to my cell.

I have blown it somewhere. John is certain that I am something special and I have spent so much time being just plain ordinary. I cannot see the answer. It seems to be associated with Jo. I lie down to rest but I am hesitant to sleep. I know my flat was not bugged. I know Jo would not give me away. I have told no-one else since I became Brian Wallace. Now my interrogator lets his confidence show. I rehearse the arithmetic of that interview. He won, but if I can reason out why he is so confident I can win it back. I cannot. I do not sleep well.

Dear Brian,

I found out what happened from Jenny who lives over the road from you. I cried and cried. Then a police man came and tried to ask me lots of questions about you. I got hysterical and wanted to shout at him but I just cried lots more. Then this morning he came back and gave me your letter and said he would return this evening for a reply.

Why was your letter so short? I miss you to talk too. You always understand. With you gone Bozo is the only friend I can trust. I have him with me all the time now.

Daddy says that he can recommend a good solicitor if that would help. I miss you so much but I promise to try not to worry. Please try to be back as soon as possible.

I love you so much.
Jo.

All they show me is a photocopy and they will not let me keep it. Pity. They must fear that Jo could be passing something else in it. Do they suspect Jo of something? Is she at risk? They have taken John's note pad and pen back too. Time passes. The music continues. The light goes dim. Maybe that means it is time to sleep. Maybe they are getting that other interview room ready. I sleep lightly awaiting the sudden snatch. It never comes. I wake up. More porridge. Am I to live only on breakfasts? Is it Tuesday?

John reads me a long list of items from my flat and asks me where I got them. I could get them all right but I decide to score an average rate, most right, a few wrong, some can't remember. He is keeping to certain ground, wary, after our last meeting. Drawn game.

Back in the cell. The light does not seem to have gone dim for days. Or was it just before the last interview? When was breakfast? Perhaps they only dim it when they want me to sleep. I am not sure if I am tired or just lethargic from lack of exercise. Maybe I am sleepy. I settle down to sleep. When I awake the light is dim. It must be night. The music is playing. I wait for hours till the light becomes bright again. Breakfast never happens.

"Tell me about Tranzen" John is straight to the point at last.
"Why not. You won't believe me and nobody you tell will believe you."
"Try me."
Use psi. Don't let him interrupt. Make him interested so he does not take notes. I lean forward and lower my voice to help the air of confidentiality. I adopt a voice that I know is very hard to record on electronic apparatus. Use psi so that he understands the mumble.
"Once upon a time, a very long time ago there was a world full of people rather like you. They lived and died short brutish lives until they began to realise that this was not such a good idea. Little by little they discovered how to live together and so made the first step towards real civilisation. For thousands of centuries they moved forward. During this time they learned to communicate over, and even to travel across, the vast reaches of interstellar space. They visited their neighbours. They tried to help one another in the quest for civilisation. They had no desire to take one another's worlds, no lust for conquest, no conflict. This was the golden age of the galaxy. A time of peace. These are my people."
"Then first one, then another whole world of beings dropped out of communication. Nothing more was heard from them. Then messages of greeting to 'a great fleet' were heard from a world then nothing more. Ships were sent to inquire and never returned. Then finally special ships were designed to go, to see and to return so fast they could not be harmed. They brought back news of devastated planets and a vast battle fleet devouring and stripping them. Then each world started to make provision for its defence. But the enemy moved inexorably onward. No weapons stopped them because the weapons were designed by people with no wish to harm and wielded by those who had no heart for killing. Maybe they preferred to die rather than become destroyers like their foes."
"The enemy moved slowly, always with all their strength and the worlds almost despaired. They could not halt them without becoming like them. Finally one world made a defence for the galaxy. As the fleet closed in about their home they chose to die in their own way. They had mastered their star and neutralised the radiation pressure that keeps a star inflated. The star collapsed, the outside rushing inwards until it passed beyond the boundaries of normal space. Into a singularity. A singularity so improbable that mass and energy could not exist there.

As the sides of the gravitational well became vertical the minuscule but finite possibility that any particle was outside that mote became greater than that it was inside and the entire star vanished into a momentary blaze of tunnelling photons. A growing sphere of light that destroyed everything in its path."

John is getting restive. Use more narrative action. Do not get so technical.

"The galaxy waited. As if it were holding its breath. Waiting to see if the enemy was really destroyed. They never were seen again. Then came the debate and the decision that every world would contribute to a fleet of our own to protect our worlds against such a foe. A fleet to fight the battle away from the populated planets. A fleet drawn from every people and benefiting from every technology but controlled by none. A fleet trained to destroy an enemy to save the populated worlds. Psychologically able to fight."

"First they set down the rules and called it after the dead world. The vanished people were the Tranzen and so they framed the Tranzen Law to control the Tranzen fleet. They codified the morality they shared. Then slowly, no world building more than one ship at a time, each always far more sophisticated and powerful than the one before, the fleet grew."

"And what do they do, all these crews? Armed and patrolling a galaxy at peace for the two and a half million years since then? They try to watch the worlds that are not civilised yet. Will one breed a new enemy? They try to help. To save all the thousands and thousands of dead ends. They take mathematicians like me and train us as psychologists. We are to measure and to guide. We are to encourage the good and to hinder the evil. We invest our lives in planets like yours. Meanwhile they guard, they are always watching. They protect both the civilised worlds and worlds like your world. If another destroyer comes they will be ready."

I sit back to indicate that I am finished. He has believed me more than I would wish. What I have told him is exactly true. Lies take planning. I can only tell one lie at a time so I only use them when I bound by the law to hide something.

"That is just cheap science fiction. How do you prove it to me?"

"That is just science fiction. I am a normal man. You have nothing to worry about. You are most definitely wasting your time. You may as well let me go and get on with something important."

"All in good time." John is not wearing a watch, what does he know about good time?

It has taken me about an hour since I got back to my cell, or maybe more, it is so hard to tell, but I have made myself a full aural block. I can turn off the music at source. I damp down my ears as if they were hearing a very loud noise. That is a real relief. I sleep better. I dream of Jo. She is dancing by herself. She wears jeans, a loud tee-shirt and has bare feet. She dances alone. I am not present in my dream. I am not there with her. Pity.

Porridge. Silent guards. John.
"We want to talk to your superiors. If you have our interests at heart as you claim we want to negotiate a deal."
Talk him out of it. Use his fear. Suggest the boss is far more dangerous than the minion. "John you can hold me but you could not hold him. I cannot deliver him into your hands like I am. You would have to free me when he arrived. If he comes there would be no deal done, what he thinks fit will be imposed on you. You do not want to see him."
"We must see him. We must have proof of your good intentions. You can go after that. You will have to leave our country. Best if you leave our world."
"I do not want to leave the country. I want to go home. Back to my flat and my friends."
"Back to the girl?"
"Yes, back to Jo."
"You are fond of her?" Strange intonation. Am I missing something here?
"I miss her. I know she will miss me. I don't want to hurt her. I want to see her again very much."
"If you bring the chief here then we will bring her here also."
Round to John. What do I do? What do I say? Even a psychologist is subject to his own psychology. I am at a loss for words. "I can ask him."
"When can he be here?"
"I can ask."
"Tomorrow morning."
"What is tomorrow? What is today? What is the time?" My irritation bubbles to the surface.
"It is just after ten o'clock on Saturday morning."
Saturday? I do not make it anywhere near Saturday. "Give me a pad and a pen."
"Another letter?"
Back in the cell I slowly draw a message. I could use the voice communicator but then I might get asked questions and I don't want to answer any questions. Tomorrow. Please will he come. John wants to see him and I think I need rescuing. I am not in any physical danger but I am emotionally teetering on the brink. I am frightened for me. An ambush is almost inevitable. I check the message carefully. I mark it

with the communications ready symbol. I wait until it is completed. I doodle over the message to hide it.
Will Jo be there? It is about twelve o'clock now. It is Saturday morning. I think I lost. I do not know. Why do I not know? How did they find me? Will Zey come? Will Jo come? The music has stopped. No, I blocked it... No it really has stopped. I miss it, but not because I liked it.

Porridge. Sunday morning. John and the guards. We go up the lift. We walk outside. The sun is bright. I look round. An army camp, maybe, or air force. It is quiet. I look round again. We are standing by a helicopter pad.
"How will he come?"
"I don't know John." I answer but I doubt he will use a physical space craft.
A police car appears driving slowly towards us. I hope. It might be. It is. Jo and Daddy. Jo runs. Jo does not care about the rest of the world now. She just wants to cling to me. Oh Jo I love you. I would do anything for you. Have I done too much? Have I betrayed what I am? Am I a traitor? Oh Jo hold me. I am frightened. We do not speak.
John looks at me. He looks at Jo. "Well?" he says. I do not know what to say. We are still. Daddy and a policeman wait by the car. Jo and I together. John is standing, waiting. "Well?" he says again.
"You wanted to see me?"
John spins round. Jo gasps and presses her cheek into my chest. He is hardly frightening to look at. Only as tall as me, glasses, slightly plump, typical Varhyn to human map, casually dressed, hands buried in jacket pockets. Jo reaches for and squeezes my hand. I hardly feel her.
"It's you" she whispers. I know what she means. Several million years of a stable population and thinking carefully about our children has diminished our gene pool. We think we kept the best bits.
There are armed men all around us. They are running towards us. I expected a trap. I warned him. Jo sees men with guns and is terrified. It is silent.
"You wanted to see me? I am Alharan Anahe," says Zey. "I am the project manager." John looks at me and back at him.
The running men are running. Time passes. They are always coming nearer but never getting here. "What is happening?" asks Jo.
"Do not be afraid," says Zey. We are not afraid. John stares around him. He says "You... you're doing something."
"Yes."
Jo looks up at me. "He's saving us?"
"Yes."
"How?"
"I think space is dilating. I don't know."

He looks at John. "Tell me what your purpose was." No psi, no loading, he just says it.

John looks round. "We've known about you for years. Then we found him. We knew he was an alien. We don't want to be invaded. What if we don't want your so called civilisation? How come it is so right?"

I start to protest. Some things are self evident but Zey stops me. "We cannot know. Plus and minus are arbitrary in the mathematics of psychology. However there is only one choice and the great moral religions of your world would agree with us on which is the desirable direction to aim in."

"But that should be ours to discover for ourselves."

"But at what cost? I understand your fears. We can be no threat but you will not realise that for a while. How did you know he was alien?"

"You are so clever. You are so correct, you are so squeaky clean. Do you realise how many whiter than white people there are in the real world? Precisely none. You stick out like a sore thumb to anybody with the eyes to see. He can't be harmed and he can live on wet saw-dust and he can make his worst enemy his friend. And we had his description."

"Or mine?"

"Does it matter? We searched and we found him. But we had to be sure. We tried everything and got no proof, only a growing conviction that he was all wrong and we were right. So we manoeuvred the girl to him."

"No!" shouts Jo. "No Uncle John!"

"Yes," John turned towards us, and then with desperation in his voice says "Jo. Who introduced you to Wallace?"

"Nobody. We just met in the park."

"No." John is triumphant. "Richmond introduced you. He was trained to. He was our informant. He carried the listening device."

Richmond? I am bewildered. I look down. "Jo? Who is Richmond?"

"Bozo" she stammers.

"You bugged the dog? He used to come and sit in my kitchen?"

"Yes. We were getting nothing. We were desperate. Then by chance we sampled the rest of the tapes. When she was alone, walking with the dog. Talking to the dog."

"I betrayed you," gasps Jo, "I didn't know. I didn't mean too. Oh Brian." Zey laughs. "She confided in the dog? Priceless."

Jo is sobbing on my chest. I stare at John. I am bewildered. "Jo is your niece? You set us together up even though you thought I was dangerous?"

"No. We knew you were not dangerous. What we didn't expect was that you would get sexually involved. As soon as I realised what you had done I insisted that we brought you here. We knew you were small fry.

But we needed to see you in operation. Then we wanted to see the top man."

Zey walks forward shaking his head. "John you are a brave man but you are fighting for an order that is passing away. The days when men sacrifice their children for their tribe have gone. They have gone forever and you will not bring them back. Soon your world will know about the Tranzen, within a decade or less I hope, but now is not that time. I am sorry but I must stop the information spreading for now."

"If you kill me others will take over."

"I could not kill you. I could not even want to kill you. No-one will take over. I promise you we will only do good to your people but you must keep our secret for us. You must close down this operation. Trust me." Psi, commanding. "Trust me."

"Trust you..." repeats John as if shell shocked.

I am awe struck. I never imagined such power. John has been turned around in a moment. I hear the layers in Zey's voice. I realise how saddened he is at touching John's mind. Even if the whole world was at stake he would regret taking that freedom from just one man. Morals are about individuals not planets. It is so hard to balance the future of a world against the rights of a man's soul. We have had to set aside this moral principle. This is the price we paid to become Tranzen, we are submitted to the Tranzen law. Zey is a civilised man. He accurately steers the middle path. He is what we are. He is what we desire for this world. I am proud to work with him.

I too would regret...

I remember Jo's father.

What have I done?

What have I become?

Devon

Sunday morning

Jane leant on the back of his pew and asked "Have you got a few minutes? I'd like to ask you something." She watched him carefully. Alan Poll glanced at his watch, so it was official, and smiled, so he was happy. "Plenty of time," he said, "Fire away."
Jane sat down and rested her chin on her folded arms. Alan half turned towards her. "I hope you don't mind me taking advantage of a friendship but I think you could give me some advice." She paused. Actually she wanted him to do a lot of things but jumping on somebody for a big favour in church just after the morning service was hardly fair so a request for some advice would do to start with. Alan made a sort of 'carry-on' grunt and smiled amiably.
"I've got a problem sister," explained Jane. "She's always been the wild one and now she's vanished."
Alan looked quizzically, "What? Departed and not left a forwarding address? It's legal and more often caused by carelessness rather than anything sinister."
"Uh hu," grimaced Jane shaking her head. "Three weeks before the end of college term and leaving most of her things behind? Mum is worried stiff and the college are writing nasty letters and all that stuff. Worse, her friends think she was mixed up with the Goonies."
Alan sighed. "And you, as the staunch, heroic, Baptist have been delegated to find her?" he asked.
"Not really," said Jane looking up and down the pew. "I just remembered that you once said there was no such thing as a missing person to the Tranzen, they could always find your address."
Alan smiled. "You were talking about running away I seem to remember. I was joking. You were joking. But yes... I suppose we can."
"Soon?" asked Jane trying to presuppose an offer from the context.
He sighed again. "It's no problem. It only uses available information. The computer is in the car. I'll just give you a lift home from church and do it there." He thought for a moment. "All of you," he added smiling deliberately.
Jane wandered round and found Megan and Angela her flat mates chatting. "Got a lift," she said.
"Alan?" asked Angela. Jane smiled and nodded.
"Will he do it?" asked Megan.

They sat in the front room of the flat and Megan plied Alan with tea. He had placed the small satchel with the computer in it on the floor next to the table. He did not seem to be in a hurry. Jane felt nervous about

65

bringing up the subject again but she caught Alan's eye and he lifted the computer out of the bag and placed it on the table.

It was a small lap-top rather similar to Angela's. It switched on as he opened it. "What was your sisters last address?" he asked. Jane read it from her diary. "And can you give me a date when she was there?" Jane counted back and offered a range. "I'll set it for three in the morning on the previous Wednesday," said Alan. "That's a pretty obvious time for somebody to be home."

He hunched forward. "Now," he said, "Let's see." Jane jiggled her chair over to sit next to him. He moved slightly sideways to make more room. Megan moved to his other side and leant on his shoulder to see the little screen. They waited.

Suddenly the screen flickered with words or patterns that vanished almost at once. Perhaps Alan's fingers resting on the keyboard had moved. Then an address appeared.

"Here's it is," said Alan. "Exactly as you thought. She is staying at a big country house with lots of other like minded Goonies as you called them. She is not being held against her will and, as there is no law against stupidity in this country, she stays as long as she likes I suppose."

Jane took a piece of paper and copied the address down. "Tiverton," she mused, "We could be there in four or so hours. I'm sure if only I could get to see her that we'd get it all sorted out."

Alan cocked his head on one side and asked "We?"

Jane bit her lip and said nothing.

Wednesday lunch time

"Thanks for popping in," said Jane. "Are you going to have a sandwich?"

"I've ordered. They said they'd bring it to the table," answered Alan. Jane dabbed at her mouth with a paper serviette. "Sorry I had to start without you but it's the only way to bag a table. I hope I didn't drag you away from something too important. The telephonist in your office was a bit funny about contacting you. I almost got the impression you were in China or something."

Alan's lunch arrived. "Thank you," he said but the sandwich maker had already rushed off to try to stay abreast of the queue. "Don't worry. They contacted me." It was a polite brush off and Jane knew it.

She paused in thought for a moment. "Alan just can't lie," she thought. "Even those little pleasantries like 'you didn't disturb me' or 'I don't mind' can't quite make their way though him." She took a deep breath. "Now I am going to pressure him to do something he will not want to do."

He smiled. "Come straight to the point. You've dragged me back from somewhere, it wasn't China, but I came because you've something important to ask."

Jane smiled back. She looked him in the eyes. He looked back, soft and gentle as always. She dropped her eyes and said "I want you to come to Devon with me. You're the only person I know and trust to do the right thing. I'll go alone if I have to but I just might do something silly and make matters worse."

He nodded thoughtfully. "You might just. And the fact that I'm protected by Tranzen security might just help too. I still remember the news reports about the Goonies and that little incident last year. They may have publicly disowned the lads involved but... Who knows?"

"Also people can't lie to you," Jane continued emphatically. "I've seen that. And if the worst comes to the worst you are much stronger than you look."

Alan raised his hands as if to protect himself. "Hey, you know too much for comfort. I am supposed to maintain some security. I can do all these things and more than you could ever dream of but you may have noticed that my policy is to avoid conflict, not to go looking for a fight."

Jane moved onto the attack. She had rehearsed this all morning. "I want you to come. I need you. If it goes wrong and I'm on my own what will you do then? You know that what I am doing is right. I can't just abandon Jilly just because she's made a few choices I disagree with. I have to go. I have to ask you to come. So will you come with me? Please."

As she spoke Alan rocked back on his chair, almost as if he was being blown back by the force of her words. As she finished he slumped forward again. He took a deep breath. Although he lowered his voice it was strong and he spoke quickly and firmly.

"Look Jane. I am strictly forbidden from doing just this. I am too powerful. I am not allowed to use the tools or abilities that I have just for personal whims. There are rules that are framed to protect me or I'd be off on one crusade after another. It is not my business to combat evil in detail but to work against the causes behind it. There are only a few exceptions to those rules but you don't qualify right now. I wish you did. I am no fan of the Goonies and would quite like to dismantle their little operation, but I can't. Right now you do not qualify."

"What would I have to do to qualify?" asked Jane latching onto the reason.

He shook his head. "I am not allowed to tell you. That would be deliberate evasion of procedure."

"How do I find out then?" She pressed him. Alan swung his head left and right.

He pulled a face like he was in pain. Suddenly his face lightened a bit.

He picked up the satchel and gave it to her. "Ask the computer," he said, "It's not just an ordinary one. It is my personal assistant and does that sort of thing for me. It won't tell you either but it will answer any question and if you can figure it out I'm happy with that."
He smiled awkwardly and turned and left without saying goodbye.

Wednesday evening
Jane put the satchel on the kitchen table and unzipped it. Inside was the quite ordinary looking lap top computer. It was not heavy. Jane looked at it. It had nowhere to plug things in to it like Angela's machine, just a clip at the front which when she pressed it opened it up slowly like an expensive cassette player.
The screen cleared and a box appeared containing the text:
\>> Who is there?
?? _
Jane wondered if this was like the "login:" of the shop computer so she typed "jane" and pressed the enter key.
\>> Jane Naughton ?
?? _
asked the computer
Jane decided to type "yes" but as soon as she had typed the 'y' the screen cleared and displayed
\>> Hello Jane. Alan has authorised me to answer questions on law, regulations and approved practices for you. I may not pass information concerning the Planetary Plan nor may I answer open, speculative questions.
?? _
Jane wondered what an 'open, speculative question' was. She preferred the direct approach. She typed
?? does alan want to help me rescue my sister
\>> He has stated that he does. There is no security reason to force him to lie in this matter.
?? why cant he help
\>> Regulations prohibit unapproved activities for personal reasons except under special circumstances.
?? why
\>> The world is full of worthy causes but the long term goal must not be neglected to fight temporary battles. The team must direct their energies towards the primary objective. Zey has said "Do not fight an evil man, he will be gone sooner than you think. Correct the causes that dispose him to do evil and the structures that permit it."
Jane decided that this was not going in the right direction and wondered if she should try a different subject.
?? what do you know about the goonies

>> Full security cleared analysis runs to over 400,000 words. Please ask a specific question or request a summary.
?? summary
>> The Church of Gnosticism (COG) was founded in 1992 by Gordon Stone. Its tenants of belief, as stated in its early publications, are a combination of New Age holistic teaching and eastern mysticism. The COG does not derive any theological traces from the first century Gnostic heresy nor the Scandinavian cult, it merely adopts its name being Greek for 'knowledge'. The COG has owned James Manor near Tiverton in Devon since 1995 for use as a teaching and retreat centre. The COG has been the centre of a series of scandals involving accusations of using mind control techniques and at least one sexual misconduct incident. The general consensus of Tx observer reports on the COG is that it has degenerated from a quasi religious operation into a mere front for the personal aggrandisement of the Grand Abbott, Gordon Stone. The adherents are expected to contribute either their money or their labours to the enrichment of the COG.

Jane paused and reread the description. 'So the Tranzen know about the COG' she wondered. She typed
?? what should be done about the cog
>> Current assessment is that the COG is undesirable but that it is not harming society in general. The result of its removal would probably not enrich society significantly. It primarily preys on drop outs and failures. It provides food and shelter to many. Although Gordon Stone has been exposed in the press as a sexual deviant these acts are acknowledged to be performed by consent so although socially abhorrent are not legally delinquent.
Jane read this several times then typed
?? will the tranzen help me rescue my sister
>> Alan instructed me to co-operate with you fully. I have authority to make all necessary arrangements as required.
?? alan wants to help me
>> Correct.
?? but he cant
>> Not at the moment.
?? when will he be able to help me
>> If you qualify.
?? how do i qualify
>> Open question
?? who qualifies
>> Parents, wives, children and a mentor may request personal assistance and should be supported. The law permits leave of absence from duties for such requests.

?? i cannot become his parent or his child
\>> Correct
?? what is a mentor
\>> A respected leader, a moral or spiritual guide.
??
Jane thought about the Tranzen and their work. She remembered the name, or perhaps it was a title, of the Tranzen leader that Betron Fahl, the spokesman, always referred to as 'the Boss'.
?? zey
\>> Zey is mentor to many of the team.
?? to alan
\>> Prohibited line of questioning.
Jane wondered what that implied. She looked back up the screen and read the previous answers. This gave her a new idea. It was silly but somehow you can ask a computer a silly question without embarrassment. She typed:
?? could i marry him
\>> Yes but his current work assignments call for him to be available for off planet duties. This calls for body form changing. This will continue for some time. During this period is not considered acceptable for him to enter into any long term formal relationships.
?? what do i do then
\>> Open question
Jane was annoyed. The machine seemed deliberately obstructive at times. "Perhaps I just don't understand yet," she thought. She read back up the screen looking for another branch to follow. She was stumped. "Come on girl," she said to herself. "You're a history graduate with added teaching qualifications. All that learning and logic has got to be worth something more than just equipping you to serve in a book shop." She remembered a tutor pressing the point that you do not assume that words mean what you think they do. There was one pivotal word.
?? define wives as used above
\>> Wives. Plural of Wife. Wife. Female spouse. Non-species dependent definition of spouse. Person or persons in a relationship where young may be procreated and reared. Person or persons in a relationship like or appertaining to that in which young may be procreated or reared. Person or persons with an apparent relationship as above.
The last sentence mystified Jane. Certainly this definition was not the one she carried in her head. This was worth following up.
?? what is an apparent relationship
\>> One that to a reasonable observer exists.
?? a fake

\>\> Faked, acted, simulated. An arranged or temporary marriage is still a valid marriage.
?? so if i called myself mrs poll
\>\> If you acted as and were accepted by him as Mrs. Poll then that would be a wife within the non-species dependent definition.
?? did he know this
\>\> Correct
?? I would qualify
\>\> Correct
?? why didnt he tell me
\>\> His psychological profile would make it almost impossible for him to make such a suggestion. Also to point out such a loop-hole in the regulations would not be considered acceptable behaviour. Remember he must log his reasons for his actions. "I went to Devon to help my wife assist her sister," would be acceptable as your sister has a valid claim on you and hence on her brother in law. Also, frankly, his character is such that he would be seriously embarrassed to make such a suggestion.

Jane paused. She thought about it. Being a wife had several implications and some are more significant from the outside. She was embarrassed too. There was a question hanging and she might as well just ask it as not.

?? would i have to sleep with him
\>\> It would hardly be an apparent relationship if Mr. and Mrs. Poll had separate rooms but the law does not intrude into intimate matters. If to an outsider the relationship is apparent what goes on behind closed doors is private.

Jane had got the idea

?? provided the chambermaid does not find half the bedclothes on the sofa
\>\> Certainly.
?? if we book into a hotel as mr and mrs poll it is ok
\>\> Certainly.
?? he could then help
\>\> He could help you. Your sister does not directly qualify but he may assist you in your endeavours as a wife. He can guide, assist and protect you.
?? how do i contact him
\>\> He is busy. He has to clear a lot of work to be free from Saturday afternoon. Shall I contact a hotel? There are two that offer a computerised booking service which I can access with his American Express card.
?? will he approve
\>\> He estimated it at 85% that you would solve the problem and at

90% that you would then wish to proceed. You have solved the problem but are you both willing and able to live closely as Mrs. Poll for over a week? Your inexperience of him implies that you must pose as newly-weds or you will quickly betray yourself. As a new wife any errors you make will be viewed as amusing not suspicious.
?? a honeymoon
>> Naturally

Jane sat back and wondered about that. Try a little method acting. Imagine walking along with an arm round him. Having eyes for no-one else. Could be worse. It would be a long way from home so nobody would know her so no-one would think badly of her. She looked back up the screen in case there was anything else she needed to consider. Only one item stood out significantly. Being honeymooners would definitely mean appearing to sleep with him. How would Alan take to that? It was go or don't go. She could manage. It was much too important not to manage. Somehow.
?? ok
>> There are two hotels. The more expensive currently has the honeymoon suite vacant for next weekend and next week. I shall book it. Please wait. Done. He is currently busy but I have sent a notification to him.
??

Jane looked at the screen and wondered what she had just accomplished. The thrill of solving the problem passed and the normal doubt and uncertainty that most people use to contemplate the future returned. She realised that she had not asked the most vital question of all. She considered typing "will he be pleased," but decided not to. There are some questions better left unasked. She carefully closed the computer's lid.

Saturday
Jane was packed and ready to go Saturday at two o'clock sharp. Alan picked her up at the flat in a new looking white car. "How did you get the time off?" he asked as he piled her cases and his computer into the boot. "Surely Saturday is the busy day for a book shop?"
Jane smiled and climbed into the passenger side. "I just told them that you were going to help me rescue my sister from the Goonies and that was that. He's got a lot of respect for you has the old man."
"Humph," grunted Alan climbing back into the driving seat. "I trust you did not go into too much detail of how we are doing it. I might want to show my face in that shop again sometime." He put his hand in his jacket pocket and pulled out a little box which he gave to her.
"Oh," she said, "a present?"
"No such luck," he mocked, "It's your disguise. And I need it back

afterwards."

Jane slowly sprung the lid open and inside was a smooth, shiny gold ring. She sat and looked at it as Alan negotiated the city centre. As they began to get onto the open roads she took it out of the case and tried it on. It was neither tight nor slack but when she tried to take it off it was stuck. "Is it special?" she asked.

"Not really. Just if anything happens that means I have to call for support it will identify you as being on our side so to speak. Nothing more. In fact anything more would be profoundly outside the rules I should abide by. With that on the guard would pull you out intact and put you somewhere safe for me to collect later. Mostly I told them to relax, assume I know what I'm doing and don't interfere. Aside from that if you are Mrs. Poll most people would be expecting you to be wearing something like that."

Jane waved her fingers in front of her face. "It's nice. I like it," she said. And then more as an aside, "I could get used to it." Alan seemed to tremble a little, then he smiled and pretended to be concentrating on his driving.

By Bristol most subjects of trivial conversation were exhausted and the boredom was becoming physical. Jane flopped around in the big seats. "Tiverton is a long drive," she thought, "and even if you go the long way which is faster and even if Alan speeds a bit it still takes hours."

"Are you ready for being a married woman?" asked Alan, trying to sound bright.

"Doesn't feel too hard," grumbled Jane. "I'm just a newly-wed wife feeling shattered after a long drive."

"The resource department has promised to set everything up so we appear to be quite normally, if recently, married and they should have arranged several things to precede us including a couple of greetings telegrams. Remembering to be Mrs. Poll should be no harder for you than any newly-wed. We are registered as our home being your address so you should remember that and you got married yesterday morning. OK?"

Jane perked up a bit. There were things she ought to know. "I ought to know what you do for a job too," she asked, "though I don't even know what you really do..."

"I am Alan Poll. Computer engineer. That frightens most people off and anybody who wants to talk shop to a man on his honeymoon is going to get politely told to get lost. My age is two years older than you. We have not got things like joint bank accounts and credit cards sorted out yet so I pay for everything. All you documents still show your maiden name. I have a wodge of cash for you in my briefcase. You work in the book shop etc. just as you do."

Jane rolled her head towards him. "I am a qualified teacher. I do special

needs. I am just between jobs at the moment," she said. "Is that there?"
"Everything is there," he agreed. "Anything else you need?"
Jane felt slightly deflated. He seemed to have thought of everything.
"Er. What are we going to find out about the Goonies?" she asked anxious to get off the subject of their roles as she felt very ambivalent about it all.
"Can you reach my briefcase?" he asked, "It's behind your seat."
Jane struggled to drag the black thing out of the rear seat well and to pull it between the front seats. She placed it on her lap and pressed the catches and it opened. Immediately obvious on top of the internal tray was a blank faced spiral bound volume and a bank's plastic bag containing a block of bank notes.
"Put the money in your purse and take the book," said Alan not watching her as he drove on. Jane pushed the briefcase into the back of the car.
"It's rather a lot," she said.
"It's what? Oh the money. No. Just some folding money for incidental cash. I will get more if you need it. I plan to cover most of the expenses on the old credit card. The book is a full survey on the Goonies. I think we take the weekend to read it and go to work on Monday. People will probably expect us to wander around aimlessly so we can go where we like without suspicion."
Jane did a rough count and realised she was holding two month's salary. "Look," she said, "I can't take all this."
"That's OK," Alan replied breezily, "Keep hold of it for now and give it me back when we come home again. I don't want you to be caught out short for a taxi, a meal or even a bribe if it comes to that. Don't worry. I'm not expecting you to account for it in detail."
The miles rolled on.

The hotel was a modern refurbishment of an old building. A middle aged woman behind the desk, wearing a formal blouse and skirt, welcomed them with a thick, if slightly inappropriate, Scottish accent. A young lad carried their bags, Alan carried his briefcase and computer and Jane was left with two greetings telegrams and rude sea-front style postcard with a cartoon involving a bride, a groom and a small boy asking a question with a double meaning.
The lad placed their bags in the room and pointed out the facilities. Just as Jane expected him to leave the woman from the desk bustled in pushing a trolley with a bottle of champagne in a bucket of ice.
"Complements of the house," she said and bustled the boy out leaving Jane and Alan alone.
"Built into the bill," muttered Alan, "But a nice thought anyhow." He picked up the bottle and read the label. "A reasonable brand I think but

I have no idea what constitutes a good year. Do you like this stuff?"
"Not really," said Jane. "You have it."
Alan sniffed. "All I'd get is water and bubbles. My body shield treats alcohol as a poison and transmutes it for me." He placed the computer on the table and made a squeaky noise. The computer paused and went bip. "That's good," he said.
"What's good?" asked Jane.
"Just a routine security check. We are not bugged, not overlooked and not being spied on by any detectable means. Provided you don't raise your voice quite considerably you cannot be heard outside this room. You can't always count on this but I'll check regularly." He flopped onto the bed and started to clean his glasses.
"It tells you all that from one beep?" asked Jane sitting down beside him so that she would not have to raise her voice.
"Yes. Well. I didn't say it was speaking English did I? It's speaking Phase. Now let's be frank. I'm speaking Phase now but I've got a little implant in the side of my head that translates most modern languages at brain stem level. Phase is just a lot quicker when you want details and much as I like English..."
Jane pulled a face to indicate that she was getting too tired to care. Alan could get annoying when he rambled on and he cared deeply about subjects that put most other people to sleep. "I'm hungry," she said. She had been too nervous to have lunch before starting out.
Alan hauled himself off the bed and scrabbled around on the writing desk. "Here we are," he said, "The Hotel menu. They're open now and ...", he paused, "Not bad for a hotel. I don't think either of us feel like hunting down a picturesque restaurant so let's eat in house tonight."
Jane took the proffered menu card and scanned down it. "Bit pricey," she said.
"Careful," said Alan, "Our ID is a pair of newly-wed yuppies. Don't start going stingy on me or we might have our first matrimonial tiff. This just goes on the bill."
"OK OK let's eat. I'll feel better with something in my tummy." Jane got up and picked up her jacket.
Alan started towards the door. Then he paused and turned back.
"Jane," he said, "There's something I forgot. Come here a moment."
Jane walked up interested. He stood in front of her. "Touch me," he said. "I don't think I have actually ever touched you since we were first introduced and I shook your hand. Now I'm going to hold your hand as we walk down to the restaurant and I'm going to enjoy touching you and generally playing about over dinner. But I need to start gently." He held his hands out, palms up. Jane took his hands and held them. "It's easy," she said.

"It isn't. Well not for me." Alan hung his head. "I know what to do. I want to do it. In fact because I'm rather fond of you I will actually enjoy it but I'm sorry. I'm dreadfully embarrassed. I've never taken a girl to a hotel who is pretending to be my wife before." He paused and sighed. "Gosh, doesn't it sound sordid? Just bear with me."
Jane squeezed his hands again. "I know how you feel," she said, "I'm sorry. I'm letting you carry all the load. You seem so strong and capable and I feel so weak."
"No. It's not like that," he said, "You can't see my emotions because they are hidden. I can act human. I can do everything but I do it deliberately. But it doesn't stop me feeling inside."
Jane put her arms round him and squeezed. "It's all right. We're here to do something good. We have agreed to do it this way. I'm sorry I'm not quite as supportive as I could be. I'm supposed to be your wife and a good wife looks after her husband. You've had a long drive and you need something to eat. After that we can have an early night. That's what they will expect us to do anyway."
She sighed. It was not as hard to support him as it was to see him so competent. "Alan," she thought, "If I was really your wife I'd kiss you long and hard right now." She gave him another squeeze and said, "Come on. Let's eat." They had the restaurant to themselves but Jane played the part because she felt he needed that sort of help.
Replete and sleepy they kicked of their shoes and sat on the bed to talk. Jane was looking at the greetings telegrams. "Why did they bother to put messages in them?" she asked.
Alan lay on his back. He sighed. "Because they are real greetings telegrams. So you have to say something. 'All the best from Mum and Dad' works well for me. I like the post card more. The only thing that worries me is I recognise the signatures from the office and I wonder if Resources reproduced the known signatures from file or merely circulated it to be signed. Since I can't tell, if it's a fake it's a good one."
While Alan was in the bathroom Jane got out the nightie. She had bought it on Friday because she was worried about what to wear in bed. She felt it was very suitable for a new bride while not being too unsuitable for not actually being a bride. She was wondering what Alan would say. She expected him to be good at playing the part fully in public but this was going to be a very private time.
Jane took a deep breath. She had never really had any boyfriends other than friends who were boys. Yes, she had gone out with people and had had a steady date for periods but nothing that even mildly prepared her for this. If they were really married it would be easier. She sat on the king-sized double bed and wondered what to do now.
Alan came out still towelling his face. He was stripped to the waist and had bare feet. "All yours," he said referring, Jane assumed, to the

bathroom. Jane gathered up the nightie and her sponge bag and went into the bathroom and closed the door.

When she was finally done she paused and looked at herself in the mirror. Close up she felt she could almost see through the nightie. It was white and just a bit sheer. Short without being too short. She hesitated before she unlocked the door but decided that it was OK. Ish. Alan was sitting in bed reading the local guide. He was not wearing a top. She went and sat on the bed next to him not daring to get in. "Have you found anything?" she asked.

"The house is in a valley with a cliff path running right past just above it. We can go and spy out the land. I have some equipment to help. It's woodland so I expect we can remain hidden. Look..." he pointed at the map.

Jane leaned forward and looked. "Get into bed," said Alan. "You'll get cold. By the way. Nice choice of night-wear. I was worried you'd bring something either too frumpy for a honeymoon or too brief for my peace of mind. We get breakfast in bed here so appearances are important."

"Thank you," said Jane, trying to hide her relief as she slid into the bed. "I did wonder if I ought to wear anything if I was playing the part to the full. Er. What are you wearing?"

"Pants," said Alan flipping pages in the guide. "I think I know what to do now. I'll check with our security people tomorrow morning but I think I'm done now." He closed the guide and put it on the bedside table. He slid down into the bed and said. "Look. In the morning. When breakfast is coming I'll wake you up and if you could snuggle up to me that would help. Keep up the image so to speak. The tale we have is that the COG is pretty paranoid about security so we could run into their contacts anywhere. Any time we are near any other people you act the newly-wed wife. Understand?"

"Snuggle up how?" asked Jane wondering where image started and ended.

"Try," said Alan and as she slid over to him he wrapped an arm round her. Jane felt an awful lot of her touching an awful lot of him. She put and arm round him and then a leg. "That's right," said Alan. "Not so much sexy as comforting."

Jane was far too aware of 'sexy' to notice 'comforting' but she said "You're not so nervous now are you?"

He smiled in her face and looked into her eyes from just a few inches and said "Well, yes, but I couldn't have done this earlier. Just hold on to me. It gets easier by the minute."

Jane held on. Sexy did begin to dissolve into comforting, then comforting began to dissolve into comfortable and then soon into sleepy.

The phone rang in the security office. The duty guard looked at the clock. He sighed and picked up the phone.
"This is Stone," he heard.
"Yes Master," he replied respectfully although he felt a bit silly, a bit comic book.
"Anything to report?"
"Nothing specific. We are making the usual week-end checks." He wanted to be seen to be dutiful but there was nothing. There was normally nothing.
"Keep me informed."
"Yes Master," he replied again and heard the line hang up. He sighed again.

Sunday
She was dreaming. She was floating in a huge mass of downy feathers. She seemed to be tumbling, weightless, through a bouncy castle of softness. She could feel feathers delicately sweeping over all parts of her body - delicate, exciting but not quite tickling.
She seemed to be swimming through this mass. She was reaching out for Alan. She could not actually see him in the white fluffiness but she knew he was there and somewhere close to her. He was coming closer to her.
Slowly she grasped him and held him. She was holding him and wrapping herself round him as they seemed to float down and settle to a level in the down. He was stroking her cheek. She went to kiss him but he spoke.
 "Wake up. Come on wake up," he said, "Breakfast is almost here."
Jane hardly had to move. She was snuggled right up to him. She was slightly aware that her nightie was a bit rucked up and her tummy seemed to be touching his side. She decided not to enquire further but whispered "I'll pretend to be asleep," and closed her eyes again.
The door knocked. Alan answered and breakfast arrived with the turn of the pass key. As Alan sat up Jane straightened her nightie. She wondered if Alan had noticed. Would he be embarrassed?
Jane picked at her breakfast and Alan finished it off for her. She went to the bathroom to prepare herself for the day. She pulled off the nightie and looked at herself in the mirror. She was a bit perturbed by Alan's almost indifference to her body. He should either be embarrassed or excited. Somehow either would be preferable to being ignored.
She turned before the mirror and told herself that although she was no starlet she was in no bad shape for 24. She never quite vocalised the thought but she felt somehow that he should make a pass at her, he should try to take advantage of being in bed with her. She would resist, of course, and call him to order and he would then apologise. They

would have an understanding then. They would be sleeping in the same bed on her terms. It was not like that though.

She stepped into the shower and forgot about it all in the inevitable struggle for a reasonable temperature that is an unfamiliar shower. Alan was dressed and sitting on the bed with newspaper of some description open before him.

"Do you fancy Independent Methodist?" he asked. "There's no Baptist in town."

"Are you sure you want to go to church?" asked Jane slightly taken aback.

"But I always go to church on Sundays," said Alan, looking slightly perplexed. "And so do you. What's the matter?"

"I don't know," replied Jane. "I suppose I'm just a bit freaked at some levels by pretending to be Mrs. Poll. Somehow it seems just about acceptable with people I don't know but with church people it seems slightly more wrong."

Alan nodded. "I know what you mean," he said looking up at her. "I have it all the time. I don't advertise my non-human nature but am I lying to people by looking human and just letting them assume it? Yes I am, I admit it. Is it wrong? Possibly, even probably. Do you know that it took us all a lot of time and a lot of training to be able to lie enough to maintain just that amount of security? Things like lying don't come easy to a person with the mindset of a grade A civilisation."

He took her hand. "Look. What we are doing here is right and being Mrs. Poll is part of that. I'm not going to say that the ends justifies the means in all circumstances but they need to be considered. We are going to church because that is a right thing to do too. Then we have lunch and then we walk out over the cliffs and see if we can look down on the house and discover anything. Going to church does not interfere with our reason for being here but if our reason for being here interferes with going to church then perhaps we need to ask some more serious questions about it."

Jane felt a bit better. "Think 'secret agent'" continued Alan, "Because that's what you are. If anybody asks your name just say Jane. That's friendly and it's true. Just relax. Everything should be all right."

The church was a turn of the previous century building and was tidy but a bit dilapidated with a strong flavour of new paint on old wood. A tall young man with a beard welcomed them enthusiastically at the door and sent them into the main hall which was filling slowly. Alan chose a pew at the side and they slid sideways in and sat on thick felt on hard wood.

"Rather like home before the refurbishment," whispered Jane. Alan smiled.

A pretty girl came up and gave them a soft bound song book each. "I missed you at the door," she said. "Are you visiting?"

"Just down for the week," said Alan slightly artificially.

"Oh I do hope the weather picks up for you then," the girl replied. "It's been so blowy and wet these last few days. No good for a break at all."

"We're walkers not beach people," laughed Alan, "So it's not too bad. But, thank you, I'd rather it didn't rain too much."

There was a pipe organ clearly visible but right on time a piano started to play and the beard from the door appeared at the front, below the pulpit, and started to sing enthusiastically. The church seemed to be populated with many young people with small children. The morning service was clearly a family affair.

Jane began to feel reasonably at home and when the beard preached a reasonable sermon on 'calling the lost to come home' she took it as a good omen. When they rose to leave the girl was there again, this time with a toddler balanced on her hip.

"I do hope you enjoyed the service," she said.

"Yes thank you," said Jane.

"Good sermon," added Alan.

"Will you be here next week?" the girl asked.

"No," said Alan. "We plan to be going back home on the Saturday."

An older gentleman came up and joined in the conversation. Alan got side-tracked to him and they seemed to Jane to be discussing something to do with the harbour.

Jane was still taking with "Prudence, but everybody calls me Pru," Pru inquired if they went to church normally and said "That's nice," when told where.

After a while, because nobody had asked her why they were there so she had not been called upon to say it was a honeymoon, Jane tried a touch of secret agent and ventured "I do hear you have one of these funny cults based nearby. Does the church do anything about that?"

"What the C O G?" spelt out Pru. "Well, they keep themselves much to themselves. We do know some people who work at the house and live in our road. Nice people. Young. They do the business side of things. Organisation. You know. They're not sort of converts but staff. We get to see quite a bit of them now."

"Oh," said Jane, "You haven't met a Jilly Naughton have you?"

"No," Pru said slowly, drawing out the vowel. "Is she a friend?"

"My sister," said Jane. "She may be with them. I just wondered."

"I could ask," said Pru. "But I don't think they discuss things like who is there."

"Oh no," said Jane lightly. "Don't worry. I just wondered if you might know her that was all." She looked round nervously. "Now where's my husband gone? We must be getting back to the hotel for lunch."

She caught up with Alan by the door and slipped her arm into his and when he turned to her and smiled she said "We must hurry. When you're ready."
Alan was speaking to the man with the beard. "Duty calls," he laughed. "Well, good luck with the hunt for a new minister. If we're ever down this way again we'll see if we can drop in again."

They walked back to the hotel. It was dry but a bit cold. Lunch was billed as a light snack although Alan seemed to have rather a bit. They changed into walking boots and heavy outdoor stuff for the afternoon. Alan stuffed a couple of items in a ruck-sack and they made their way out of the town and westwards along the cliff tops. Slowly the house appeared through the trees.
Alan sat down on a tree stump and produced a bar of chocolate and waved it at Jane. "No thanks," she said, "I'm still full of lunch."
Alan shrugged and broke up the bar through the wrapper then tore it open and started eating slowly. Jane looked quizzically. "You do seem to eat rather a lot," she said. "Is there a reason?"
Alan smiled and ducked. "You see? You're living too close to me and seeing hidden things. Now you know that I have to eat about twice the amount that a normal human does because I handle your food inefficiently as it's not my normal diet. Plus I need supplements on top of that. But you aren't going to tell anybody are you? Just help me hide it. But remember, if you're peckish, I've always got another chocky bar somewhere in my pockets."
Jane looked at him and smiled. She was rather pleased to be taken into his confidence in these things. It would be awful to be living so close to somebody and to feel that they did not trust you. She turned and looked down on the house. "What can we find out by looking from here?" she asked.
"Well I want to move a bit further up," he said, "I want to get the place in the widest possible profile. Then I can go through the place room by room and see what I can see. If I see somebody who looks like Jilly I'll get you to look and confirm it."
Alan lay on the edge of the ridge with his binoculars studying the house. Jane sat below the crest and stared out to sea slightly at a loss for something useful to do. Time dragged on. Alan stayed virtually motionless for about half an hour. It drizzled despondently.
"Come and look," said Alan, "I'll have to hold the glasses for you as they weigh getting on for thirty pounds."
Jane moved up close to Alan and he reached an arm round her so he could hold the binoculars both sides of her face for her. As she put her eyes to the lenses Jane snuggled her shoulders under his arm. "This is almost as much fun as sleeping with you," she whispered.

"Hey," said Alan with a smile in his voice. "Don't say things like that unless you don't mean them. I'm an involuntary telepath and at this range the chemical surge you get from being provocative like that makes me go all wobbly."
Jane shut up and looked. The view was steady and showed a room. It was as if the wall and part of the ceiling had been removed to let them see in. "Is that her?" asked Alan.
It most certainly was. It was Jilly wearing a long translucent skirt, a sparkly bra and something glistening in her hair. "Why the 'Arabian nights' costume?" Jane asked.
"Dunno," mumbled Alan, "It's a strange get up to be wearing just to sit alone in a room at a desk to read a book. Perhaps Stone has moved on from eastern mysticism to a bit of eastern promise." He moved the glasses a trifle and Jane took it as a signal to look round. Alan rolled onto his back and put the glasses on his chest. "I've mapped the house out but I don't see any excuse for a kidnapping. I didn't see Stone either. He must be away."
He looked at Jane. "You must be getting cold," he said. "Let's go find some tea."

Jane sat on the bed and watched Alan working away at the little computer. A picture of the house was turning slowly on the screen and becoming more detailed as he worked. He picked up the binoculars and looked through them in the vague direction of the bed and Jane realised what he was doing.
"Do they record?" she asked. Alan grunted an acknowledgement. Jane asked "Can I see Jilly again?" He looked through them again and worked the controls on the top then he handed them over to her. They were very heavy so Jane rested them on the bed and peered into them. Jane looked at Jilly. Seen through smoky walls. It was just as she remembered it. Jilly always was the pretty one and frankly she could carry off the sparkly bra and chiffon dress look. Remembering the cold wet wood Jane smiled to herself and said "The house must be well heated."
"All double glazed," said Alan. "With just top opening fan lights. Unless you have a big hammer and don't mind shredding yourself on the broken glass the windows might as well have bars. Definitely draft proof and warm though. Must have cost a pretty packet to set up."
"Why the belly dancer look?" asked Jane still perplexed by it.
"And why Jilly?" asked Alan. "Just about everybody else in the place is in jeans and T-shirt order. This isn't something she gets up to in the privacy of her own room and nothing to do with being here is it?"
Jane was mildly shocked. She thought for a minute. "Not as I remember. Jilly was always the one for long skirts or jeans and big

bubbly woollies. I was always the one for the short skirt and the tight top."
Alan chuckled and smiled at her.
Jane pouted at him. "I calmed down a bit at university. I was busy, involved in the CU and stuff. I didn't feel the image was quite right and anyhow the church there was a bit stuffy and I just fitted in."
"So would you or wouldn't you wear Jilly's sequinned bikini?" asked Alan.
"Probably not any more," admitted Jane. "Maybe never."
"So has Jilly just gone the other way?" he asked.
"This is the girl who once called my miniskirt 'soliciting'," remembered Jane. "She's gone a long way if she has."
Alan shrugged and went back to his plan of the house.
Evening drew in and Jane sat in bed in her nightie and waited for him to finish. Finally he looked at his watch and said "Grief. Why didn't you point out the time? Newly-weds should be tucked up in bed ages ago with the lights out." Within minutes he was through the bathroom and back by her side.
Jane lay and looked across the pillows at him. She rather liked the intimacy of last night but lacking an invitation to touch him she felt inhibited.
Alan snuggled down and smiled at her. His face seemed to slowly fall. "Are you all right?" he asked.
Jane pulled the bedclothes round her shoulders. "I'm not sure. It seems different from last night. I'm more self-conscious."
Alan smiled encouragingly. "Try to sleep. Tomorrow I want to check out the local library as I believe they have placed books there and there will be old maps so we need to be fresh." He reached for the light switch hanging over the bed. "OK?"
Jane tried to smile back. "OK," she said. She looked into the darkness where he had just been and felt the bed move as he settled down. Somehow she just knew it was going to be hard to sleep tonight.

The phone rang in the security office. The duty guard folded his paper and picked up the phone
"This is Stone," he heard.
"Yes Master," he replied.
"Anything to report?"
"We have a couple reported in the hotel. The attended the Glover Road Church and the wife inquired about us and specifically after Miss. Naughton. Our contact reported her to be a relative."
"Watch them," commanded Stone. "Report anything further."
"Yes Master," the guard replied.

Monday

Jane was dead to the world when breakfast arrived. The night had been long and it was a hard crawl back to alertness. Breakfast was not on her list of things to do so Alan ate it all.

Jane washed her hair because that usually helped her wake up. She was feeling generally annoyed with the world in general and annoyed with everything in it in particular. Sisters were high on the annoyance scale. She walked back into the room with her head in a towel and stubbed a toe on a shoe she had left in the middle of the floor. She muttered a rude word to herself.

Alan stood up and walked towards her. "You didn't sleep well? he asked.

"No," said Jane with quite reasonable malice.

"Come here. I can fix it. We need you in good condition today or things will go wrong." Jane wondered at this but feeling resigned to the world walked towards him.

He held out his arms and slowly embraced her. The world seemed to go soft. She was sleepy and seemed to melt into him. She sighed and that seemed to carry all the angst of the night away. She was slightly taller than him even though he was wearing shoes and she was not. She ran a hand up his back and ran her fingers through his hair. She was kissing him with wide open-mouthed kisses and then suddenly it was over with a jolt.

She removed her mouth from his and felt a bit silly. "What happened?" she asked.

He was embarrassed now. Red and troubled. "I'm sorry," he said. "I only wanted to pass wakefulness and alertness to you but I went two-way without realising."

Jane did feel wakeful and alert but she had never put her tongue into somebody else's mouth before. "Did you make me kiss you?" she asked.

He was still embarrassed. "Not really," he said letting her go and stepping back. Jane wondered if that was an apology. And what did 'two-way' mean?

She got dressed while he was in the bathroom and they set out for the library. Jane held his hand because that is what they did but she was more careful than before. What Alan found at the library mystified Jane but he seemed to be making notes from old newspapers and books and when the reference section turned up plans of the house, admittedly plans submitted prior to its current modifications, he seemed pleased. Jane was wondering if Alan's renowned ability to side-track onto fields that interested him was beginning to take hold but she chose to say nothing.

They walked back through the town looking for lunch as Alan was always ready to eat and Jane was beginning to regret dismissing breakfast so readily. They found a small café and sat on plastic chairs and had filled rolls with coffee.

"Was there anything good at the library?" asked Jane.

Alan smiled. "Well now I know what changes they made to the house which gives me some clues to what is going on but more importantly I have got enough data to warrant doing more than just pulling Jilly out of here. I think I have a good case to rate the Goonies as a very harmful influence to our work and so if I could find anything that was illegal I could make sure they were closed down. Then 'Bingo', I put the two together and the place is way off planning permission. They have huge cellars built like bomb shelters The place is a fortress. And they have guns too. Lots of guns. I never looked in the crates yesterday but they are there in the recordings. So we can run them out of town any time we want."

"Guns?" said Jane suddenly worried. "This could be dangerous for us and Jilly. Are you suggesting that we just hand the whole matter over to the police?"

Alan pulled a face. "At the moment no, because I think that that could be more dangerous. If this degenerates into a shoot-out then there will be no winners just a lot of casualties. I have no wish to see anybody harmed."

Jane began to get worried. "Look. Is it safe to continue? I don't want to stir up trouble I just want to talk to Jilly and explain. Then I'm sure she will see sense and come home."

Alan paused then said. "You are assuming a lot there. If she is being held against her will they will not just let her out because you ask and if she is there by her own choice why do you expect that you can change her mind quickly? Let me finish investigating and see if we can do something more subtle."

Jane looked at him slightly askew. There was a time for direct action and this might be it. Alan always turned away from direct confrontation. She remembered that he once said 'but why bother?' when she discovered that he had been short changed by a shop keeper. He could be a bit of a wimp at times. Perhaps he had been the wrong person to bring along after all. She kept silent.

On the way back to the hotel Alan stopped into the newsagents and bought a lot of confectionery and two tins of Coca-Cola. This all vanished into the rucksack. He also emptied a whole lots of litter into a road-side bin. Jane sniffed. "You do eat a lot of junk don't you?"

He laughed gently. "I get hassled by our medical people for not eating enough. My Tina is always going on about proper food and roughage. However she approves of chocolate. It contains lots of good stuff and I love it. It has become very popular back home now too."

"You export chocolate?" asked Jane, rather surprised.

"No chance," Alan almost laughed. "There is nothing that is worth transporting over the distances involved between stars. It is always easier to make it where it is wanted. There is no galactic trade and very little travel. The only people who are found out in space are the military because that is where the threat will come from and that is where you want to keep it - well away from the inhabited worlds."

Back at the hotel Alan sat down to compose his morning's researches into a document. Jane made an excuse and left him to it. She went down-stairs into the lobby and moved to one of the telephone booths beside it. She looked up the number for the COG in the directory and dialled it.

"Hello. Karma House."

"Hello. Can I speak to Jilly Naughton please."

"I'm sorry. Jill is not taking calls. Can I help you?"

"I did want to speak to her."

"Who is this please."

"I'm her sister."

"At the moment Jill is in novice training and it is very important that you are able to relax and not worry about the past at that time. I will make a note that you rang and in a few weeks, when she has finished, I will see she is told you called and then she can decide if she wants to call you back. I can't promise anything because that is her decision of course but we do try to encourage students to maintain friendly relationships with their families."

"But I need to talk to her now."

"But she needs time to be quiet and not to be worried by the world. That is what she has chosen. I'm sorry I can't change that. I have recorded your call. I won't forget to see that she knows about it. But I'm sorry, that is all I can do."

The phone went dead and Jane hung it up.

The COG receptionist dialled the 'last caller id' number and carefully wrote down the number. Then she picked a CD from a rack and dropped it into her desk top computer. She typed in the number and wrote down the name of the hotel on the card with her other notes. She dropped it in a wire tray for security to look at.

As the evening drew in Alan suggested a walk down to the harbour and that they could sample the restaurant there. The rain had gone and it was a warm evening. They dressed how Jane thought newly-weds should dress. She began to relax. Back to the method acting. They stood at the harbour bar, leaned on the railings and watched the lights of the other side reflect off the waves.

Alan gently pulled Jane into his arms and snuggled her close to him. "Be a wife," he said. "Somebody is watching us very closely."

Jane did not really care. "Nothing much else to watch," she offered snuggling her arms under his open jacket.

"Maybe," Alan's face was nuzzling her neck. "But one of the people is that girl from the church and she seemed to be pointing us out to the others."

He suddenly held her very still. "Don't move. They just took our photograph."

Jane suddenly felt that that was much more sinister. "Should we go back to the hotel?" she asked.

"No," said Alan. "Play innocent. We didn't notice them. We have nothing to hide. They have the wrong people. Kiss me. That proves we are not thinking that we are being watched."

It was harder but Jane did as he requested. She pretended that she had nothing to hide, that she had forgotten that anybody could see them. Mostly she pretended that this was her husband and kissed him with big wide open mouthed kisses. She touched his tongue with hers. It was not so bad now it was deliberate.

Slowly they began to relax. "They're going," said Alan catching breath. "Just a few moments more."

Jane relaxed and rested her head on his shoulder. "I enjoy being a secret agent," she said.

Alan chuckled. "I don't," he said. "But I quite like being kissed. You do it well. It makes up for the other things. Now. Time to eat."

"Slowly," said Jane. "We don't want to give anybody left watching the idea that you think more about your dinner than your new wife do we?"

Alan was in bed before Jane left the bathroom. She got into bed and looked at him. He smiled and reached for the light switch. "Sleep well," he said in the darkness.

"Alan," she asked, "Do you think we are in danger?"

"Not us," he replied. "I can protect you. But I don't want to start anything off that might put other people at risk. Not just Jilly. There are lots of other people in that house and I don't think that we should going in, action hero style, guns blazing and leave a trail of bodies to rescue just one victim. In their own way they are all victims."

Jane sighed. "I'm a bit frightened. Will you hold me?"

Alan's arms closed round her. "Don't worry," he said. "I'm looking after you. That's why you brought me. Just let me run things and it will all be well. We will succeed and do it safely. We will go home with Jilly."

Jane moved closer to him. The warmth of his body seemed to envelop her with that strange downy feeling again. She seemed to sigh and the fear began to dissolve away. She wrapped her legs round him. It seemed very natural to kiss him again. Big kisses just like they shared on the harbour wall. She had the strangest feeling that he was tense

but his body felt soft and compliant.
"Jane. Stop," He barely whispered it.
Jane stroked his face and unable to see him let her nose touch his.
"Don't you want to kiss me?" she asked.
"I want to kiss you very much but that was not the deal we came here on. Stop and think Jane." He was nervous. It was in his voice.
"It's all right," she said. "I want you to kiss me too. I want to eat you up. I know you're making me do it but I love it."
"No! Stop!" He was not loud but loud for a person who was talking into your face. "Remember. When I said to you on the cliff top that I am an involuntary telepath. I meant just that. I can't control it. I can't stop it. If you were attacking me I could defend myself but while you keep wanting me and desiring me and loving me I'm helpless. Don't you see that? It's not me doing things to you but you doing things to me."
Jane paused, shocked. "You mean it's me that's wanting to do all this?" He nodded. She could not see him but she knew.
Jane rolled her head away from him and did some soul searching. She took a deep breath and admitted several things to herself.
"You're right," she said. "I do want you to hold me and kiss me and I probably even want you to... to do more. I just want it to not be my fault. I'm sorry."
He was soft and gentle in her arms. "That's all right. If you understand it you can control it. We'll manage."
"Alan, am I falling in love with you? I think I might be."
"Um. Well a bit. You're just not used to being intimately living with somebody like this and you're adjusting to it all too well. You're doing the right things for the situation and I'm picking it up and reflecting it back at you. It would make for a wonderful honeymoon but we were not in church Saturday morning we are just pretending, and it would be totally wrong of us to take advantage of each other in this way."
"Alan. If I really pressed you you would let me kiss you and you might even let me go further?"
"Probably."
"How would you feel about that?"
"Elated at the time and then desperately ashamed later."
"OK," she said and took a deep breath. "Look. Can you help me to go to sleep like I did the first night? You held me and I slept well and everything was all right then."
She sensed him smile, but how she did not know? The world went soft, downy and faded away.

The phone rang in the security office. The duty guard folded his paper and picked up the phone.
"This is Stone," he heard.

"Yes Master," he replied.
"Anything to report?"
"The couple reported in the hotel. The woman phoned from the hotel and asked for Miss Naughton. Naturally reception refused. We are running identity checks."
"Amateurs," Stone chuckled. "Check them out. Put a trace on them if it helps. I want to know what they are doing. Is that all?"
"Yes Master," he replied again and the line hung up as abruptly as usual.

Tuesday

Jane woke up alone to the drone of the shower. The usual knock came just as Alan switched off the hot water but she was left to receive breakfast alone. As soon as the lady had left Alan appeared with a towel wrapped round his waist. He sat next to her and devoured his share. He smiled as Jane ate better today.
"What do we do today from a cover point of view today?" he asked.
"I've put in a report on what we've found out so far and the inquisitors have asked that we do not do anything with the COG for twenty four hours while they consider things. I'm hoping that they will OK busting the whole operation up which lets me stomp around officially."
"Will that be safe?" asked Jane remembering guns.
"Oh yes. If we do it we start by stealing all the weapons then go in with huge force and speed. At minimum I should get clearance to remove Jilly without consulting her and I will explain because she will believe me."
"Your funny powers again," sighed Jane and leant back on the bed head. "Look will you explain them to me because I'm only getting quick snatches and you seem to assume I understand."
Alan turned to her and smiled. "OK. But dead secret. OK?"
"Mum's the word," she tried to smile but it didn't come out well.
"I am a telepath. That is I can read your mind. Now this is quite recent to me so I can't quite control it very well yet. I can't help but read emotions but reading thoughts takes concentration, because they are such a small part of what is going on in a brain, and recovering memories is even harder."
He moved closer and dropped his voice conspiratorially. "Along with receiving signals I can also send them so I can:"
<Hello>
Jane jumped. Alan smiled. "I can put thoughts straight into your mind. Now at an emotional level this tends to be a bit automatic at close range which is something I didn't realise before. When you get your head within a foot of mine I tend to receive your emotions and amplify them and echo them back to you."

"Oh," said Jane. "Hence we run away with ourselves. I'm sorry about that."
"Not your fault," said Alan. "But I'm a beginner here myself. I am still just learning to control these abilities. There are worse things happening and distracting me. My whole concept of 'now' is falling apart - but that's another story. Don't feel that I'm rejecting you. I'm not. I just feel we will both be happier to stick to our conventional morality." Jane tried to agree with him but then the funny side hit her. "Alan," she said in her best school marm voice, "I'm not sure I can take a talking too on our conventional morality from you when I am sleeping with you under an assumed name." Then they both laughed and the tension that had been developing ebbed away.
"Back to the question," said Alan when they has calmed down a bit. "What do we do today from a cover point of view today? We can mooch about and be just preoccupied honeymooners and not care a thing about the COG."
"Exercise?" said Jane. "I'm eating too much trying to keep up with your meal rate even if I only nibble. I usually go swimming twice a week and pedal Angela's exercise bike most days."
Alan rolled off the bed and poked at the writing desk. Within two minutes he had found a gym and a swimming pool in the leaflets. Jane looked at the gym leaflet. "It's men on Mondays, Wednesdays and Fridays and women the other days so we can't go together. What's the pool?"
"Public nine till five then private groups in the evening. Let's go swimming."
Jane looked at him. "I didn't bring swimming things," she admitted.
"So we go shopping first," said Alan. "You can buy something really racy to prove that being a married woman doesn't mean you're going dowdy yet. It's in character."
Jane looked at him and smiled and wondered if she should call his bluff.
The bikini was minimalist and racy. Jane normally wore a slinky tight dark blue one piece designed to swim in not be seen in but she chose this bright yellow item for its looks. Alan did not see it till he emerged from the gents changing rooms onto the pool surround.
Jane was still trying to adjust the shoulder straps to permit her to feel confident to dive in. She had, she admitted to herself, gone a bit to skimpy here because it was more elasticised than she thought. She slid into the water, which was to her taste a trifle warm, and postponed diving in.
Alan flopped into the water and generally seemed to bob about rather than tread water. Jane looked at him and then looked up the pool. She set off with a lazy crawl, touch turned at the far end and stroked back

again. Alan was still much where she had left him.

"Do you swim a lot?" she asked.

"Not for a while," he admitted. "It doesn't come very naturally."

"Would you be happier at the shallow end?" Jane offered.

Alan smiled. "No worries. I float. I can't drown. Anyway I can't play this game at the shallow end." He promptly duck dived and reappeared the other side of her about six or seven seconds later.

"You go swim," he said. "Exercise. Remember?"

Jane rolled lazily onto her front and stroked off up the pool again. She tumble turned for effect and came back to discover Alan talking to the life guard.

"... and it's not a good idea without proper supervision," said the girl, pushing her goggles onto her forehead.

"If it troubles you I won't do it again," replied Alan. "But don't worry. I stay well within my limits." He paused. "However," he continued.

"Thanks for worrying about me." The girl hauled herself muscularly out of the water, smiled and then walked off along the pool edge.

"What happened?" asked Jane.

Alan looked crestfallen, like a little boy found out. "Er... I was doing negative buoyancy stuff. Sitting on the bottom when she pitched in above me. So I scooted out of the way and she followed me. So I came up and discovered she thought I needed rescuing. Just a misunderstanding really."

Jane looked at him. "How long were you down?"

"Just a couple of minutes. Nothing a normal person couldn't do. I can go longer but that rather gives the game away if I'm trying to appear average and I'm putting in international competition level free dives. Two minutes is just practised snorkeller stuff. She over reacted."

"Do you always make trouble?" asked Jane slightly exasperated.

"No," he said rather abruptly. "Go swim." He upended in the water and dived out of sight. Jane steadied herself on the side so she could look down into the water. He was sculling across the bottom of the deep end and as she watched he pulled to a halt and pulled up his feet to sit cross legged on the bottom.

"Is he with you?" It was the girl life guard again.

"Yes," said Jane, trying to flash the wedding ring. "Don't worry. He's quite good at it. Snorkeller." As she watched Alan converted his crossed legged squat to a crouch and then jumped towards the surface. He gulped a huge mouthful of air and breast stroked slowly towards them. The life guard walked off.

Finally Jane decided she had had enough and sent Alan off to change. She stood under the shower rinsing the pool out of her hair and wondering what they should do next. Probably eat knowing Alan. Just as she was about to make her way off to the locker area the life guard splashed in through the foot bath and marched past her into the locker room. Jane felt the shower stop and could not justify another push at the button so she pulled the elasticised key from her wrist and looked for her locker.

Jane was perplexed. She went swimming often and she was a creature of exact habit and her things were muddled. Her first thought was that somebody had been at her possessions but a careful check showed nothing missing. She had exactly the right amount of money and her watch and her cross on a chain were present and correct. She wandered into the foyer and found Alan already waiting.

"Do you want to eat?" she asked looking at the sign for the cafeteria.

"Yes," he said, "but not here."

As he walked out of the doors he held her hand but said nothing but when they had gone about a hundred yards he said "My belongings were searched. Just mine alone in the whole male changing area."

"And mine," said Jane suddenly catching on. "Things were not as I left them. I don't think anything was taken."

"No," said Alan "but a small clip was added to my jacket and one to your purse lining. Security want us to go straight back to the hotel and change as the protective devices that I am using make it hard to assess them when they are close to us."

"Could they be bugs?" she asked.

"Not sound. They seem to be tracers as they are emitting radio signals but not complex enough signals to carry more information than 'here I am'. They are rather small. Their suggestion is that we use another jacket and purse if we are going somewhere important and these when we are going somewhere innocent."

"Wow," whispered Jane. "Real secret agent stuff. You are sure we are safe?"

"Absolutely. This is an attack and by law the Tranzen may not lose in a direct conflict. I am arguing to try and slow things down now where as three hours ago I was wondering if I could get some help."

"Will Jilly be safe?" Jane asked.

"I have registered her as someone I want held for me to question," Alan assured her. "Since she is a member of the COG organisation I am worried that if it came to a fight she might be given a gun by her superiors. If Alacia puts troopers in and anybody is fool enough to shoot at a trooper they tend to shoot back automatically. Registration means that in the event of a ground attack she would find herself in a holding cell waiting for me to collect her virtually before anything happened."

"You think it might come to that?" she wondered.

"I don't but for some reason they have enough guns in that place for everybody living and working there to have five each so who knows?

Our surveyors however assure me that only two people show signs of ever having operated a firearm and none recently so it may just be posturing by Stone. Certainly all the guns are crated under lock and key several layers deep. Nobody is going to just pick up a gun without keys, a crowbar and some knowledge of gunsmithing."

Back at the hotel they changed for lunch. Alan's jacket hung in the cupboard and Jane's purse was thrown in her suitcase. "We'll take them with us when we go out to eat tonight," said Alan. "To prove we don't know about the bugs."
Jane was worried. "They know about us then?" He nodded. "They must know we have come about Jilly." He nodded again. She took a deep breath. "Look. I need to tell you that I've perhaps gone a bit far myself." Alan sat on the bed and patted the space next to him. "Sit down and tell me slowly," he said.
Jane sat down close to him and as she started to explain about how she had asked the girl Pru at the church about the COG she realised he had wrapped his arm round her shoulder. It was nice but it seemed inappropriate. "Alan," she asked, "Did I do wrong?"
"Not wrong," he said, struggling with his words, "Perhaps a slight economy of judgement."
Then the crucial question "Are you cross with me?"
"No. But you will be. That's why you need a hug. Pru is good natured but a simpleton and although she believes gossip is a sin she has no concept of a secret or that anybody could pose a threat. She is the sort of person who leaves her back door unbolted because if there is nobody to say 'come-in' when you knock then you can't come in. She probably went straight up the road and asked them. Is there anything more?"
Jane stopped, suddenly embarrassed. Did he already know? How awful. He was all set up to forgive her for making a mess of things. "D... Do you know?" she asked. "Are you reading my mind?"
He looked away and shook his head. "No. I don't do that. You just emoted relief then further apprehension so clearly there just had to be a part two or more."
Jane took a deep breath and told him about the phone call. He laughed. "No worries," he said. "That will have told them nothing more and just convinced them they are dealing with amateurs. Might be for the best. They will not worry about people so clumsy."
Jane was slightly offended. "They couldn't have traced the call," she argued.
"Did you dial 141 to hide your id?" he asked. "If not they could have it on a display as they spoke to you or at least dialled 1471 to get the 'you were last called by' recorded message."

Jane slumped down in his arm and rested her head on his shoulder. "I didn't think of that," she said. "I even use it at home. What a dolt. I'm sorry. I've given everything away. All our secret in pretending to be married all gone to waste."

He gently patted her. "That wasn't why we did it. Don't you remember? You are my temporary wife so I can help you. I can support you, help you and defend you. Because you are my wife the Tranzen will protect you absolutely. Don't worry."

"Apparent wife," cried Jane, her eyes wet. "So an outside observer would think so."

"Oh?" said Alan. "Is that what you wanted? I put temporary wife by common consent on the notification. But only for a week or so though which is why we must be careful. The Varhyn are very precious about marriage and I've always been very careful to observe appearances scrupulously so we don't want to stretch things more than we have to."

Jane's tears dried and she wrapped her arms round him. "I need a cuddle temporary husband," she said. "I need to know you forgive me." They wriggled by consent into the proper line up the bed and clung to one another. Finally Jane sniffed and said "Thank you," he smiled. She took a deep breath and said "Can I kiss you?"

"Certainly," he said.

"You don't mind?"

"I never minded. It just seemed inappropriate to get too involved."

"Am I really your temporary wife?"

"Um... You are recognised as such under Tranzen law."

"So I can kiss you?"

"You don't have to be my wife to kiss me."

"Could we have..." she hesitated and took a deep breath and decided to ask it straight because it worried her. "Could we have made love? Was I that much your wife? You implied you would be unhappy with that. I was pleased but it seemed strange for a man."

"For a Varhyn man it is normal. Don't worry it is nothing to do with your own sexual attractiveness but simply that you are going to stop being my temporary wife soon and go home. Back to Megan and Angela, back to the church and out of my life a bit. I don't think we can ever have the same cool, just friends sort of relationship as before after sharing this but how would you feel, sitting in church knowing we had taken full advantage of this opportunity?"

"Probably not as bad as you think," she said. "But I see what you mean. It would be far worse to go home and say 'goodbye, see you Sunday', after that. A real let down. I'd want to stay married and I'd probably give you trouble trying to get you to agree to it."

"I'm not there yet. It's complex and I need to sort a lot of the changes that are happening in me out first. And there are other people to

consider. Don't go away but don't hold your breath as they say."
"Just promise you won't write me out of a chance without discussing it. That's all I ask," she said.
"We'll talk about it," he said. "I will promise that. But first, in best yuppie speak, let's do lunch."
"OK. But I still am not quite sure, am I your wife, really? Is it like common law?"
"Temporarily. Lunch. Now. Please."
They sat in a restaurant and Jane picked at what was basically a starter while Alan ate a meal. Swimming normally left her ravenous and as she felt she had earned it she normally ate well but today other things were overcrowding her mind and messing with her appetite. She watched Alan eat and listened to his simple small talk and made appropriate replies. She wanted to get him back alone and to ask questions but, although she wanted answers, she was very uncertain as to the questions were.
Finally back in their room Alan said. "I don't know what to do," and sat on the bed. I promised to give the inquisitors the rest of the day but now I feel that the rules have changed. They have made an assault against us and that just seems to alter the state of play a bit."
Jane sat next to him and placed a hand on his arm. "I feel that," she said. "But I don't know what to do either."
He was fidgeting. "We can't do anything about the COG because I promised to let the inquisitors make a ruling but I don't feel able to just wander about," he shook his head. "But I suppose if we don't know about the bugs we would just wander about. We went swimming and had a good time. We had lunch. Now, what do our two happy newly-weds want to do this afternoon. It's wet," he forced a smile like a wild simpleton and looked at her.
Jane sighed. "I don't know," she said. "What do newly-weds do? I suppose if I was really a proper newly-wed and looking out at a wet Tuesday afternoon I'd be asking the same thing. We didn't pick a nice time of year for a honeymoon."
Alan leaned on her. "We must be too much in love," he smiled. "We couldn't wait for nicer weather and we couldn't get a Mediterranean booking so it just had to be Tiverton. We wanted to get married in a hurry."
"Careful," said Jane, trying to lean on him as well. "You're find that you're implying I'm pregnant if you're talking about getting married in a hurry. Gosh. Do you think people could think that?"
He chuckled. "It's a rather tortuous logical link you have to admit. More it's likely we picked a day and perhaps we are not as well off as we like to appear. Perhaps Tiverton was all we could afford. To live well in Tiverton rather than to scrape by on a package to Minorca."

"I've never been to Minorca," said Jane. "I've never really done the holiday thing. My Dad used to drive us all over Europe and we'd stay in B and Bs so I've done capitals and major sites but not much flopping and resting. It would be nice even to go to Tiverton and have nothing to do. Just walk and flop about with somebody special. My holidays these days are just going and spending a week with my parents and, much as I like them, it's always just a bit hassled. Mum always seems so edgy. If we're not doing something she thinks she is failing as a host. I just want to flake out and watch the garden grow."

"Eh?" Alan made a questioning noise. "You never seem to let on to that. This is Jane the organised? Miss fix it? Jane of the notebook and the plans? I shall look forward to taking you to an island one day, where somebody else looks after the food and there is nothing to worry about and see how long you could flop before you had to organise something. Would you make twenty four hours?"

She elbowed him, but gently. "Watch it husband," she growled. "I might be able to organise a better honeymoon. Do it properly."

He lay back on the bed. He laughed. "You could probably organise a better husband too."

Jane sat silently and wondered if she was in love. If so what should she do about it? If so what would he do about it? She was tensed up and wanted to do something physical. Kicking him was not quite justified but kissing him seemed to be ruled out at the moment. Life was so complex.

He was breathing softly behind her. She waited but he did nothing. She finally twisted round and put a hand either side of his chest and looked down on him. "Alan," she started, "I've probably spent more time in these last few days thinking about us, what we are and what we aren't than I have thinking about Jilly. I was ambivalent before we came about it and now I'm totally confused. Do you know what is happening to me?"

His hands appeared on her hips. "Your body is sending you messages. More than I expected. You must realise that sharing a frightening experience together, deliberately choosing to be seen together and, crucially, sleeping together is bound to have profound psychological effects. We are becoming more and more dependent on one another. We have enemies but I trust you. In fact you are the only person here I know I can trust. I can't trust hotel staff, swimming pool staff, not even church people but I can trust you. That is important."

She shook her head. "I think it is sleeping with you that is the biggest problem. I almost think I could cope with an affair more easily than this pretence. I get into bed telling myself it is just a cover story. It is all right really because we're not making love but it isn't. It's wrong because we're not making love. We shouldn't be in bed together if we're not really serious about it. It's not that I want sex. I'm a twenty four year old virgin and I don't believe in sex before marriage, strongly, just somehow I am offended by the whole idea. If Jilly was still at college and we had brought ourselves down here for... for a dirty weekend that would work. It would be wrong, but ordinary wrong, but somehow honest."

His hands rose to her sides and pulled. She took that as permission to lie down across his chest. Her head rested on his shoulder and she felt him breathe deeply before he answered. "Jane. Be careful. If there had been no Jilly problem you would never have spoken to me like that. We would never have got so close as to be discussing this. I liked you, now I am very fond of you. I would never have considered what you just described but now I could be tempted by it. Remember where we are from girl. We met because we are members of the same church. Either of us would be offended if the other suggested a dirty weekend."

"Yes Alan," she said "But you do see don't you?"

She felt a chuckle. "I not only see but I feel it too. I would love to tuck your nightie under your pillow and give in to all those natural desires. It would help us cope with the pressure. But we can survive the rest of the week without it and we will survive going home much better for foregoing it. I'm sorry it's been so hard for you. I did think that you had not thought it through completely when you decided to go through with it."

"I hadn't. I asked the computer if I would have to sleep with you and it said marriage would hardly be apparent if we had single rooms and then when it suggested that we were to be newly-weds I knew that that ruled out separate beds. But I did say yes deferring thinking about it. After that I began to worry. I bought the nightie because I was thinking about being in bed with you. I even wondered if I should go on the pill just in case but when I looked it up you needed to take it for a month before for it to work and I only had days. I didn't know I was going to want you but I rather expected you to want me and I wanted to be prepared in case I felt it might be appropriate. I didn't expect to find you fighting me off."

"You didn't expect a wimp. I'm afraid the Varhyn male is not the stuff that great romantic novels are based on. We tend to react to our wives and you are stirring some very basic reactions in me. I tell you what. We make a deal. After we get back from this trip, successfully I am sure, you give me some time to settle down. Let me get my abilities sorted. Let me get 'now' sorted out. Give me some space for a few months to get all the other complicated threads of my social life together and then we'll see if we can do something about falling in love properly. But remember. Until next weekend we are Mr. and Mrs. Poll. We are on the same team. We are allowed to kiss and to cuddle and to go to bed together. That we have decided not to do everything in bed that we might that is a joint decision because we think we will make one another happier in the long run by it. Now. I want a big hug and a big kiss because that will make me happier now."

That was a deal. Because they had a deal they were free and the afternoon sped by. Finally, sleepily, Jane looked at her watch and said "It's six o'clock," did we doze off?"

"Maybe," said a voice in her ear. "Maybe we should doze off some more because it's still a bit early for dinner."

Jane felt soft and relaxed and she laughed. "So the newly-weds spent the afternoon on the bed," she said. "Then a quick meal followed by an early night. We're finally getting the hang of it. All the walking and swimming was wrong. We had no idea had we?"

Alan chuckled lightly again. She liked that. She did not want to kiss him or anything specific any more, she was just happy to be sprawled out on the bed sort of wrapped round him. Time passed without effort and a suitable dinner time presented itself.

They ate in a Chinese restaurant and came home feeling bloated and tried to find a card game to play but nothing appealed. They went to bed early and carefully remembering the deal snuggled up. Alan watched the clock and at an appropriate time Jane faded away and slept deeply and dreamed happily of things she did not remember next day.

The phone rang in the security office. The duty guard sighed and answered.

"This is Stone," he heard.

"Yes Master," he replied.

"Anything to report?"

"The couple from yesterday. It is indeed the sister and her new husband. She is a shop assistant and he works from a computer firm. Short. Soft. Not a problem."

"So they have come secret agenting? If they want secret agent give it them. You can arrange a fight? Have them beaten up."

"Yes Master," he replied.

Wednesday

Breakfast eaten Alan switched on the computer and almost immediately said "Good." Jane looked up hopefully. He smiled at her. "We have two days and after that the COG organisation will be dismantled. Ideally we can remove Jilly and Norcon will pass the scans of the place to the Police and offer to stop access to the weapons while they raid the place.

If Jilly is not here by then it will keep things simple. It all ends Friday morning."

"OK," said Jane. "What now?"
"A walk along the cliffs with my wonderful wife," he said. "I want details of the alarm system and such. If I am to go in and bring out Jilly I would prefer to do it surreptitiously and let Mr. Plod set off the alarms bulk later."
"Right," said Jane slowly. "So it's gone beyond the 'I get to talk to Jilly' scenario now?"
Alan screwed up his face and said "Well I don't think that was ever on. Firstly because they would not let you in and secondly because they have had long enough to ensure she would not listen. We need something to shock her round a bit and Stone being dragged away in chains and lorry loads of rifles being loaded into police vans should do the trick."

"But everybody stays safe?" asked Jane.
He took a deep breath and nodded. "Unless something changes inside the house I don't see why the status quo should not remain for another few days. Jilly will be reading in her room when suddenly we remove her to a safe distance. She watches in horror as the truth is revealed and, with perhaps a little help to unstitch any brain conditioning they may have used, finally collapses into her sister's arms crying 'how could I have been such a fool'. It's a plan anyway."
Jane began to get her walking clothes together. "So no heroics today?" she said.
He paused. "I don't plan anything but a simple walk and look session. It's a nice day so we could walk a way up the coast and back. To enjoy it. OK?"
It was a nice walk. They had finally got away from the COG miasma that seemed to cover the town for them. The sun shone and they walked three miles out well away from the house and then walked back along the cliffs. Alan was quite quick as he knew what he wanted. He looked and recorded and they walked back down the hill and onto the sea-front and down to the shops to replenish his goodie bag.

Nobody ever gave Karl orders. But he had friends. And sometimes they suggested that he might do something. If he wanted too. But he was not predictable. So they did not ask too often. He had a picture. Tall tart and some shorty bloke. Karl did not like people like that. Somebody wanted them out of town. Out of town was too good for them. They had a posy white car so they would just go somewhere else. Karl would fix them.
He had waited. Waited a long time. They were not helping matters by hiding. He was going to get them. Karl was going to prove something. He was going to prove how hard he was. It was a new idea. They

would have to respect him now. He sniggered to himself on the harbour wall. He was so clever. So brave. So hard.

Alan and Jane were wandering along holding hands and looking in the shops. Alan liked the chandlers but waited patiently while Jane, ever hopeful, sorted through a tacky souvenir shop hoping for something worth buying. "I'm not actually sure what I would do with anything I bought," she complained. "It's not like I can give things to my friends saying I bought this for you on my temporary honeymoon. I'm not sure if I would actually tell people we were here. It could just get too complex to explain."

Alan was getting jittery. He could not say why. "It's a 'now' problem," he tried to explain. "But I don't know if it's a soon 'now' or a distant 'now'. I haven't had a chance to get used to it. To calibrate it so to speak."

Karl walked towards them. Just another person in a relatively deserted street. The weather kept people away and if he was quick and efficient hardly anybody would notice.

Alan looked up as the burly man said "'Scuse me. v'y got a' time?" He tried to look at his watch. He tried to be polite but it would not come. Jane looked at him with troubled eyes and began to raise her own wrist to look at her watch to satisfy the enquirer to make him go away.

Karl grabbed at the knife under his jacket and hunched down to shoulder Alan out of the way. He aimed his shoulder for the middle of the little man's chest and aimed his knife for the woman just below the ribs. He was quick and he was strong and that is what he relied on.

Alan felt Karl's mind become evident as the man pressed near to him. This came as a shock to him as the only mind he had ever sensed other than deliberately was Jane's and that was a total opposite experience. Karl's mind was concentrated on his simple plan. 'Kill the woman first as the man will not scream. He is too middle class. He will freeze. Then kill him. Then leave quickly.' Horror flooded Alan as these ideas entered his brain directly without any of the careful processing he applied to normal information channels like reading or hearing. He accepted Karl's intent as a plausible future. Something rose in his mind about shields and something about mind control but it was overwhelmed by a sense that this was wrong and it should not be and Karl must leave. The new senses welled up in his mind and he pushed Karl away from him. To get him away from Jane. Beyond fast. Beyond this instant. Beyond understanding. And for a moment it was clear, simple, he understood and he did it. Then he realised what he had done.

Karl and the rapidly approaching knife vanished and Jane automatically grabbed Alan. She was panting with the shock of what she had just seen then she realised that Alan was trembling in her arms and not trying to hold her. She pushed him back and looked at his face.

Uncontrolled emotions ran over him. Suddenly she realised that if he was human he would be crying or worse. She held him close in her arms and asked "What happened? What is the matter?"
He clung to her. He was still trembling. He made two attempts to speak and then taking a deep breath said "I didn't mean to do that."
"You saved me," said Jane. "He wanted to hurt me at the least."

Alan struggled to speak again. "No," He managed. "He wanted to kill you and he was so close I felt it and I just reacted against him. I threw him from me. I didn't mean to do it but for a moment I felt his will to kill you and I had to protect you. I was thoughtless. I didn't know I could do that. I must be more careful. I don't want to do that again."
"You saved me," said Jane again. "That was good."
"I could have just touched his mind. Stopped him. Instead I threw him in time. I just had to get him away from you and at that instant it seemed the easiest way, the only way. Time is becoming a problem to me."
Jane pushed him back and looked at his face. "You moved him in time?" she asked incredulously.
"About twenty five minutes into the future. Very roughly."
"So if we stay here he will come back?" she asked becoming nervous.
Alan slumped forward into her embrace again. "No," he gasped. "In twenty five minutes the earth will have moved tens of thousands of miles in its orbit round the sun. And the sun moves too. In twenty five minutes he will reappear into empty space and in seconds he will die. Jane in over six thousand years I have never thoughlessly killed somebody with my hands and now, in an instant, I have killed somebody with my mind. I don't even know who he was."
Jane clung to him. She kept him close. She took him back to the hotel and sat with him. He could do nothing. She held him through dinner and she finally lay in bed and hugged him till they both fell asleep.

The phone rang in the security office. Two guards were waiting. One picked up the handset.
"This is Stone," he heard.
"Yes Master," he replied respectfully
"Anything to report?"
"A strange event. We sent a usually reliable contact after them with clear instructions that we wanted them injured but although they were clearly very shocked by something our contacts at the hotel report they are unhurt. We are unable to find our operative either at home, in custody, or hospitalised. If our contact is at the bottom of the harbour our little man may be more than he appears."
"More likely the girl. I will have to meet them. I shall be with you late tomorrow evening."

"Yes Master," he replied again and heard the line hang up.

Thursday
Jane awoke to breakfast. As the lady left she looked at Alan and asked "Do you feel all right?"
He smiled cheerily. "I have slept. It may be unresolved but it is at least assimilated. Oh and thank you. You did exactly the right thing. A Varhyn boy learns from the cradle that when a woman hugs him like that that everything is all right, don't worry, calm down. I was in a bit of a state and it helped, it helped immensely."
"I didn't understand anything more than that you hurt. To hold you seemed the imperative thing to do. To be a comfort."
He shrugged. "I hurt. Shock. It wasn't a bad thing to do. I regret anybody's death but I suppose I've got used to it. The guard would have shot him without hesitation. If they had showed up and done that I would not have complained. I just surprised myself. Time was once so simple. It just passed. Now, somehow, I don't seem to live at the instant with a clear past and a prospective future but I am all smeared out. Things that happen to me start slowly and continue to happen for a while. Somehow I am learning a whole new idea of time and space and it seems to be so simple at moments but I wonder if this is because I will understand it soon and it is leaking back to me."
Jane patted his hand and said "I understood all the words you just said but I don't think I have an idea of what is really happening to you."
He took her hand and squeezed it gently. He smiled sheepishly. "Neither have I," he mumbled. The smile broadened "But it will not interfere with our job here. I can control it better now and I know it will not give a further problem in the next few days or I would sense it. Silly isn't it?"
She smiled but did not dare reply.
When Alan wandered out of the shower Jane asked him what they were doing. She was sceptical about doing anything after yesterday's incident. Alan sat her down on the bed with a strong feel of something important to say.
"Tonight I want to enter the house and look the place over. I will go in with full Tranzen protection and snoop about. You don't need to worry about me because in that mode I could take a direct nuclear strike so their little pop guns won't trouble me. Hopefully I will find Stone and he will have no choice but to talk honestly. I will work overnight, that's the way we do it and in the morning I will collect Jilly and bring her out. She will come and I will explain. I will arrange that we have an opportunity to talk before the police get involved. It will be up to you to convince her she is going home with us but I will expose the COG and she will believe me. To use my tricks for more than that would be unfair."

"Now I want you to stay safe. We go out this morning and do some sort of honeymooner thing away from the COG. Stay near me so you are safe then this afternoon we come back here, eat early, read the TV film list over dinner and then cuddle off to our room implying a cosy evening in. I sneak off via Tranzen transport and you run the room for two. Lights down and lights out early so anybody watching thinks they know what we are at. I will call your mobile as soon as I have something to report but not that night."

Jane looked at him apprehensively. "A day or so ago," she said "I would have been very sceptical of that. You never seemed to do anything and I thought I was the one really investigating. Now I'm so pleased you are taking it on. I'm sorry but I'm pleased that you're not taking me with you because I'm frightened now. I'm glad we came but I'm so glad that you have come. What do I do now?"

"You can hug me because I'm nervous," he admitted. "Until I get started and the importance of getting it right takes over I am going to feel bad about this. I can do it, I know that, but the waiting is very hard. I don't like doing it this way but only in this way can I move through the place and assure myself of everything and reduce the risk of anybody being hurt. There are so many young people doing all sorts of things there and we want to close it down without any problems. The inquisitors will brief the Police and the Home Office today and promise to provide a totally weapon free entry for tomorrow. But by then we will be gone and Jilly will be gone. Questions might be asked but the Police will know that any records of us are for people acting under Tranzen authority and they know what the official channels are to ask questions about that."

Jane looked at the head on her shoulder and then snuggled her ear against him. She remembered he was close to her and grasped a little of the implications, he would sense her feelings. She tried to feel confident in him and it was not too hard. She hoped he could feel it. "What do we do for Jilly when you get her here?" she asked trying to assuming a success.

He rocked his head. "I don't remember anything in her room to pack so she might need a lot. If all she has is the clothes she stands up in you may need to share your wardrobe out."

Jane sniffed. "I've got enough for two. Well most things. We only have to survive the evening and the drive home. Yes. I have enough," she added it up.

They walked out along the harbour wall that morning. It was wet and a blowy squall slapped the light rain against their faces. The shops were not interesting and Jane could not even interest Alan in the confectioners. She had to admit they were just passing time, more marking time before the evening. The boats in the harbour were doing uninteresting things and even the gulls sat in the rain and looked bored. Finally when they had wandered far enough they just turned round and strolled dissolutely back the way they had come.

Lunch was strange. Jane realised that she had actually eaten more than he had. When she got him back up to their room she sat next to him on the bed. "Are you nervous Alan," she asked, worried that he was getting more and more silent.

He bunched his fists and said "Yes."

She was not used to seeing him like this. "Is there anything I can do?" she tried.

He sucked on his lower lip and said. "Nothing practical. Look. I'm sorry. I'm not used to doing things like this and the waiting really gets to me. I can't do anything else because I'm so on edge so I'm just stuck with sitting here like a coiled spring annoying you till this evening when, stupid of stupid, I shall go very calm, very clear headed and get on with the job. If I am really going to drive you mad you could pop out to the shops or something. I won't mind. I know I am being unreasonable. I'm sorry."

"Could I get you anything?" she offered. "Or should I hug you? That helped before so you said."

He breathed a deep quaking breath. "No. I don't need anything. A hug would be nice but it might be a bad idea. This is one of those points when a man needs a permanent wife or two to generally unload all his troubles on. I need to wind down a few notches. I need distracting as I'm not doing anything useful here, all the plans are made, I am just consuming energy and getting on my own nerves. I'm sorry."

"You don't need to keep apologising. It must be awful. I would not want to go into that place with all those guns and confront Stone to his face. I admire you but I'm glad it's not me. When will you go?"

"Dinner at eight. Leave at nine. Enter the house around ten when it's nice and dark. Hours away."

Jane put her arms round him. He seemed to lean into her. She smiled and reached deep into trying to help. "Look. Shall we take our things off and get into bed? Those are the best hugs."

Alan turned and looked at her somewhat pained. "You do wonderful hugs Jane. But I am not in control like I usually am. Don't complicate my life." His voice was abrupt and a bit fierce.

Jane sat back a bit. She had expected a gentle no, even an apologetic no but this sharp, point blank, refusal startled her. She sat back a bit so he would not have to feel what she was feeling. What was coming out now the pressure was on? Was this a 'real' Alan? One she had not met previously? It was not as if she had offered more than they had already done and enjoyed. Nothing she had suggested was off limits. Outside the deal. She worried. Perhaps it was. That would not have been just a cover hug because they were newly-weds in bed but a hug because they wanted it. He had said she could kiss him? This was only a hug? Well more than a simple hug she admitted.

Jane got up from the bed, she sat at the desk and leafed aimlessly through the pile of brochures. She just needed to pass the time. He was under stress and if she got stressed too it would not help. She was not stressed much.

Jane began to wonder about what Alan really was. She mentally remembered her image in the bath room mirror and asked herself if being a moderately attractive human being was any use. What did he look for? What sort of alien creature was he anyway? He looked human and could be carried away with human affections but what were the things that excited a Varhyn male? Was she doing everything wrong? Then she asked the alternative question about herself. Did she care? "Frankly Jane," she told herself "Are you better out of this? He is a bit weird, nice but weird. It will all end in tears. Monday night. Was it that long ago? Then I virtually offered to make love to him and he turned me down. Men didn't do things like that. So I have heard. Even Christian men I suspect. He really doesn't want me and I ought to admit it rather than keep kidding myself. He has come here and he is helping and that is just what he had promised and here I am trying to write the cover story into my life script. He is not human. Do not ever forget that."

Jane sat at the desk. Alan sat on the bed. The hours passed excruciatingly slowly for both of them but pass they did. Finally they agreed dinner time and Alan managed to demonstrate some of his normal public character and Jane did her part by holding his hand and making light conversation but after the long afternoon she felt mind numbingly dull. Again Alan ate badly and as they climbed the stairs back to their room he seemed to sigh with every step.

Alan was getting ready to go. Jane hovered wondering what to do, to say. He put on his rough walking jeans, a shirt, a woolly and finally his hiking boots and his drab anorak. He emptied out the pockets into a pile on the bedside table and threw the sweet wrappers in the bin.

Jane picked up the ruck-sack and said "Do you want any of this?" pulling out some of the snack food but he shook his head.

"I shall not be human for long once I have left you," he said. "None of it would be appropriate then. I have to do it this way. It is at times like this that I forget how much the Varhyn are like humans and remember how unalike we are."

"You aren't going to show me what you really are?"

"We never let humans see us as Varhyn. We used too once and it was a mistake so we don't do it ever now. Tonight I must be the hunter, the predator, but you must not see that. You would never think of me as human again and I would miss that. It would hurt me more because now I would feel it in your mind."

"I wouldn't think of you differently now," Jane said. "I know you too well to think badly of you whatever shape you were."

He shook his head. "You're wrong but thanks for that. Anyhow I will make my way to the borders of the house before I discard Alan Poll and I will take him up again before I see you again. He may be a disguise but he is a happy one. Please try to forget that I am ever anything else. We will both feel better for that."

He opened the window and looked out. "Now just stay here and leave the computer on so it can watch over you and I will call in the morning. I know we will win here but how and questions like that I can't answer yet. I promise you that on Saturday morning we will put our bags and Jilly in the car and drive home. That I know but that is seeing a four hour drive which is easy. I just wish I could see the moment by moment of the next twelve hours but I am muddying the waters by doing complex things in them."

Jane felt his words wash over her head. She looked at the window and said "We're a long way up."

"Don't worry," he said. He smiled. "Wish me luck."

Jane dithered and tried to smile. He was gone. She did not try to look after him but gently shut the window and sat on the bed and stared at the wall.

Alan looked down on the house and sighed. He fumbled for the mapper control and clicked it to zero. He vanished. He made a quick check by stepping in a muddy puddle. No mark and no ripples. He smiled. He flexed and stretched suddenly feeling long quiescent muscles activating. It was funny to be a Decapod again after all this time. It was years since he had last set his mapper to anything other than one of his range of human identities but he did not have a human zero position. He bounced down the hillside to the wall in the low gravity. He jumped and pulled himself onto the top, about ten feet up. He smiled. He was holding barbed wire and standing on a detector strip but his body shields were taking the cue from the mapper and providing undetectability. He stepped over the wire and dropped down the far side and walked across the lawn towards the wide conservatory.

Jane was fidgety. She was not used to being here alone. She looked at the computer. It sat closed on the table. Was it supposed to be on? "You got me into this," she accused it. She idly clicked the catch open and let the lid slide up. The screen cleared and a box appeared containing the text:
\>\> Who is there?

?? _
She smiled with a sense of familiarity. She typed "jane" and pressed the enter key.
>> Jane Poll?
?? _
asked the computer. Jane looked at it. The computer was in on the deal. It had explained things in the first place. She somehow almost thought of it as intelligent after its protestations as to how Alan could not volunteer the trick of assuming the guise of his wife.
Becoming his wife. Again she remembered the discussion at lunch time two days ago. She was his temporary wife he had said. Not apparent but temporary. Now the computer asked if she was Jane Poll?
She typed y
>> Hello Jane. What service do you require?
?? _
That was not a yes no question so Jane screwed up her face and looked away. It was too early to go to bed and a bit too late to go out. Anyway, she should not be seen alone, the plan for tonight was that they were 'both' spending a night in. What a honeymooner thing to do. She stood up and walked round the room. She could not put her hand to anything. She experimented with the TV remote but she detested TV at the best of times and tonight it seemed banal beyond belief.
She looked at the computer again and it was still waiting for her to choose a service.
?? Am I his wife
she typed and hesitated. Finally she pushed the enter key.
>>You are Mrs. Jane Poll.
You were married six days ago at 10am to Alan Poll by a notary certificate issued by the Central Inquisitors Office four hours earlier under the Abnormal Inter-Species Registration procedures and at a request issued in the authority of the Director of Mathematics. Customary formal declarations by both parties were waved under Alan Poll's recorded statement that both persons were agreed and in common cause on the issue. The certificate is notified to expire after ten days unless notification by both parties or one party speaking for both parties request an adjustment of the term of the certificate.

Mrs. Jane Poll read that several times. She sat up and clasped her hands in her lap and said "He married me," to herself twice in slight shock. She read it again and said "I really am Mrs. Poll." This felt strange. She was so used to playing the role as if acting a part it felt strange to read it like that. Her brows slowly furrowed. "Why didn't he tell me?" she asked herself. Several answers presented themselves. Most of them involved him perceiving her weaknesses. She sighed.

"He was trying to protect me I suppose," she whispered to herself. Then she added it up on her fingers. "We were married on Saturday then, that's six days and we remain married till next Tuesday. Or was it we stop being married on Tuesday? At ten?" Ten days seems so short a time and she had already had just over half and she was only just getting to know him.

She rolled onto the bed that they had shared and asked herself "But if it is temporary does it make any difference?" She pulled a face and thought. "I am alone now. This is how it will be every night next week. And next month. And I won't even be able to talk about it to anybody or they will all think me a silly loose woman. I couldn't even tell Megan and Angela. They just know we are going together. Not that we are posing as newly-weds."

"No," she corrected herself. "That we are newly-weds." She rolled over and dabbed at her eyes with the sheets. "And I am a silly loose woman. I wish I didn't know that he really married me in some sense. He was right not to tell me. It makes not being, well going to not be married to him so much worse." She sat up and bunched her fists. "It's all wrong," she declaimed out loud. "This should have been a honeymoon. A great honeymoon. Walks. Talks. Dinners in nice restaurants. Snuggly nights."

??why didnt he tell me

she typed.

\>\>Speculation impossible

answered the computer which just about matched Jane's view.

??why did he marry me

she simplified the question

\>\>The Varhyn have a strong view of marriage and Alan has many years association with the church and he felt it was impossible to pretend you were his wife. He took advantage of the fact that temporary marriage is recognised by several of the species that are Tranzen so the Inquisitors were able to authorise a cross species temporary license. That you were intent to live with him and call yourself Mrs. Poll would have given you status under old British Common Law so he used that to justify the temporary licence.

Jane read that twice. "Alan," she murmured. "Why are you so mixed up? So you couldn't even go to bed with me without marrying me and even then you turned me down when I wanted to act like your wife. Are you really so inhuman under that disguise that I'm not even a little bit attractive to you? Is there no way I can make you want me for your wife other than to keep your conscience clear? Alan what about my conscience? I am getting into bed with you every night and thinking I'm just acting? Would a temporary wife feel better about that?"

Suddenly she hated the room and the bed and all it did not stand for. She took a deep breath. "I'm going out," she said to herself. "A quick walk." She got her coat and things and she swept up the computer in its bag. "I may need to know more," she thought. Closing the door behind her she stopped and pressed her head against the door frame. "Cash," she groaned. "Don't leave home without it." She grappled for the key, dived back into the room and grabbed her purse from the suitcase and headed for the stairs.

Alan walked round the roof. He looked over the edge and felt the draw of the three story drop. He pushed it away. The lovely feeling that a steep edge gives you was a childish pleasure. The way it seemed to pull you over to fly and to glide and to balance on the updraft. Some humans felt this. For a moment he wondered if the draw of the edge and the desire to fly was leaking through into all those daughters in all those families. Later he told himself. Think about that later and keep your mind on the problem in hand now.
Here was a skylight but below it was only roof space. Ideal. He could rest his body in the roof and allow his mind to move through the building. He needed to keep them close together or he rapidly got very disorientated but here, near the centre of the roof space, he could cover the whole house right down to the storage cellars where the crates of guns were. The skylight was a new fitting in an old hole. He pressed the catches on the inside with his mind and they opened. He pulled the skylight and it did not move. He unwound the two security screws and it finally opened. He slipped inside and carefully closed it behind him.

The phone rang in the security office. The duty guard looked at the clock, it was early. He sighed and picked up the phone as usual.
"This is Stone," he heard.
"Yes Master," he replied respectfully.
"Plan seven for either or both of them," Stone ordered. "I shall be there tonight."
The guard looked at his notes. "Seven," he said, "Yes Master."

Jane sat in the bar and looked out of the window at the harbour. She decided that it was not pretty. Utilitarian maybe but not pretty. She began to wonder if she should be getting back. She would probably regret staying longer and another glass of wine would definitely be an error. She gathered her purse, her coat and the computer. She had carried it all the way here and never opened it. It would not be able to help anyway. She admitted that what she felt was unreasonable. Not a computer's forte. Home. Well back to the hotel. To bed and with some wine inside her to sleep more easily than without. In the morning Alan promised they would have Jilly so it would be all right then. She walked out of the front door and looked up the road to be sure of the obvious route back to the hotel.

It was a moment. Hands on her shoulders and a pad over her face. A deep breath and then choking to breath as a raucous taste hit her throat then it all began to fall apart. And to fall.

Alan curled up in the roof so he would not have to worry about supporting parts of his body while his mind was elsewhere. He checked and he was still more than invisible - he was mapped to nothing. Slowly the point where he perceived his mind to be descended through the building, when he hit the chalky soil he moved up a bit and he, lacking a better word, looked round.

It was a large room with a raised platform at one end and on the platform was a central table. Alan was perplexed to notice that it was made largely of chip-board but had stone cladding glued to it. It probably looked better if you were not sensing the structure below the surface. Next to the table was a large, raised, ornate chair. The main floor of the chamber was empty with a large pentagonal pattern painted on the floor. The walls were equipped with various strange devices. As Alan's mind brushed over them he was reminded somehow of the art of 'putting a question' some four hundred years earlier but he found them strange as there were no hot irons or such. Perhaps restraint devices? But only if one stretched the imagination. Pretend restraint devices perhaps? Did the cult play locking one another up? It seemed hardly likely. Even the strongest chance, a chair with clamps on the arms and a sort of shutter board for the feet would hardly restrain an unfit man for a few minutes. This implied rites and co-operation.

He drifted through the wall into the armoury. It was hardly bristling with weapons. They were packed in boxes with the tops lustily nailed down. Rifles. Clean and still wrapped in the oiled paper that preserved their fresh from the factory sheen and they were all in need of a trained person to spend time on them and put the parts together and bring them to working order. "About two minutes per if practised," though Alan.

However he wanted them gone and the strange ideas in his mind said it was easy.

He reached into a crate and he, again wrong word, grasped one. He tweaked it to move. It slid in the direction it was already going and vanished. He could sense it, about twenty seconds up time moving with the earth and with the flow of time. He picked up a small fragment of torn oil paper and waved it about in the space where the rifle had been and it was certainly gone. Perhaps only he could sense it hanging alone in the future.

He smiled to himself. This was going to be easy. No troopers stomping about loading crates into transport frames with the risk of discovery and somebody walking in on them and trying to stop very heavily armed girls with strict orders and strict time scales with all the embedded risks. He was going to hide the guns and bring them back when it was too late.

It was effortless. No. Moving them was effortless but somehow the act of being able to move them was tiring him. And there were so many. He wondered about moving a box at a time but he did not seem to be able to hold something in his mind in this way that he could not seem to imagine he was holding in his hand. He plodded on through interminable boxes.

Finally at about two in the morning he finished and swept his mind through the entire complex looking for weapons. The nearest thing he found outside of the kitchen was a slightly rusty diver's knife underneath a lot of scuba equipment in a bag on top of a chest-of-draws in the staff quarters. He left it there.

He was exhausted and he now wanted Stone who was still not here. Everybody would be asleep so he could sleep for a few hours. It was not what you would expect the action hero to do but since he had a while free he supposed it would be all right. The mapper gave him perfect protection anyway so he set one of the timers of the armour to wake him in four hours or if anybody entered the roof space or the gun storage rooms and folded his mind to sleep. He would awake at six and sweep for Stone again. He knew he would be there then but he could not get any details.

Jane awoke with a headache and she felt nauseous and disoriented. Someone was stroking her face. 'Alan' she thought not yet remembering her concerns and tried to smile as she opened her eyes.
"You came for me," said Jilly.
Jane tried to jump with surprise but her body would not co-operate.
"Relax," said Jilly. "They carried you in and put you on the bed nearly an hour ago. They said to leave you lying on your side in case you were sick but just to wait till you woke up. They said you'd feel awful and probably relapse to sleep a couple of times. Not to worry."
"What's the time?" Jane asked putting some of the past day together.
Jilly looked at the tiny watch on her wrist. "Just gone five," she said.
"It was about eleven when I left the wine bar. So I've been out for nearly six hours? That was not chloroform or ether. I have a real headache. But look. Are you all right?"
"Well," mused Jilly. "I'm locked in a little cell and you've got the only bed," she sighed. "Depends what you mean by all right."
"Do you want to get out of here? The COG I mean."

"Definitely. Instantly. With attitude."
"You don't want to continue the training whatever that was?"
"The training was learning to close your mind down to forget all your old ideas and just accept Stone's teaching and his ideas. It sounds so plausible at first but it gets harder and harder as you get into it because it really doesn't hold together. When you find a contradiction he just amends it," she sighed. "But for a while I believed it and I didn't mind because I thought I would finally understand one day and he was so interested in me and so wanted to help me that I knew it would all work out for the best in the end."
"Why the funny clothes?" asked Jane.
Jilly looked down at what was at this range evidently a bikini top with sequins glued on. She pulled a face. "He suggested it as something I wore in private and with him to cure me of my fleshly fixation on clothing so I could concentrate on the spirit. I believed him till last night."
"What happened last night?" asked Jane.
"He got back late. He's been away. About three I think. He buzzed me to get up and we were talking and he was teaching me and he got onto the subject of sex. When I said I was a virgin he said that was inhibited and that he would have to help me past that. I realised what he meant and said I was not ready for that yet. He said don't worry, relax it's not such a big thing. He was walking round me as I stood before the altar table and as he went behind me he undid the string on my top and it nearly fell right off but I caught it on my elbows. I screamed 'don't do that to me' and he just told me to calm down but somehow all the frustrations seemed to blow up in me. I just screamed and screamed at him and finally he called for the guards and here I am in a cell."
Jane reached out and squeezed her hand. "Pervert," she whispered.
"I see everything differently now," said Jilly. "The clothes, the talks. Even the times when he left me alone in the chapel and he told me to stand naked before the altar and make my own peace with the spirits. I bet he was really watching. I have been a crass fool. I have been taken for a tart. I've been thinking. There are security cameras most places. I bet he's got me on video. He probably thought I'd just jump into bed with him and thank him for his kindness for helping me. In fact given another couple of weeks I might have done it. What a fool. What a stupid, thinks she's so clever, fool I've been."
"It's finished now," said Jane. "You're coming home with me."
Jilly sighed. "Yes," she said firmly. "I want nice, decent clothes and I want proper night things and I want to be private where I don't think anybody is watching me. All those things you just assume are normal."
"We'll get you out," said Jane, "I have friends who will rescue us."
"Do they know you are here?" asked Jilly. "You were drugged or

something when they brought you in."
"I am sure they can find us," said Jane. "But they might not know to be looking yet. I was supposed to stay in the hotel and pretend Alan was there while he came here and he probably assumes I'm still there."
"Who's Alan?" asked Jilly. "Is he this friend?"
Jane paused and wondered how to answer it. "Someone I trust and someone who will not let us down," she settled for.

Stone gave his coat to the attendant who carried it away. He walked into the basement chapel. Everything was as he requested. He looked in the purse and counted the money. He opened the computer case. Clearly it was battery powered and had a switch based on the cover as it displayed box appeared containing the text:
\>\> Who is there?
?? _
Stone smiled and typed
?? Alan Poll
The computer paused then launched the current version of Windows. An operating system that Stone recognised from most of his office machines. It was too easy. They had not even put a password on it. He routed through some folders that contained a few personal letters, a hotel booking, a form letter that was clearly intended to be a thank you for wedding presents. Nothing about the COG and nothing about Jill Naughton. Almost disappointing. The machine was set up totally to defaults. It must be new and hardly used. Nice model though, fast. He sighed and walked away leaving the computer open on the stone table. It was time to talk to the girl. She should be awake by now. Time for some fun.

"This," said Stone sardonically, "is an electric cattle prod. If you poke a bull with it it quickly jumps away and avoids you. If you poke a person they scream and roll about on the floor and cry. And that's just the men."
The two girls moved back and watched him carefully. He smiled amiably. "Now you, Mrs. Jane Poll, were previously Miss. Jane Naughton I believe. A sister I think? We ran a few checks because at first I thought you were fakes but no. We have real newly-weds happening to turn up on our doorstep. Dear me. At this time of night you should be tucked up in bed with that new husband of yours not wandering the streets and sitting alone in down market wine bars. Not a tiff I hope? So early? So sad."
Jane felt Jilly squeeze her hand. "What is she thinking?" she wondered. She took a deep breath. "He'll be looking for me," she said trying to sound at least a bit menacing.

Stone sighed. "Well he ought to guess where you are, so as soon as he's ready he'll be right along. He does not seem to be quite as inept as you are but I expect we will have to bring him here too. You did not seem to be finding us."

"I trust Alan," said Jane.

Stone smiled. "How touching. Now. Why don't you both relax and we can finish this business in the morning. If we find him wandering about looking for you we'll bring him in. Sleep well."

As the door closed Jilly said. "He's always been a bit strange but he's never been like that before. What have I got you into now? And what was that about Mrs. Poll? What have you done while you have not had me to keep an eye on you?"

"Don't ask," said Jane wondering if there were hidden microphones. "I'll tell you about him later. He's super. You'll like him."

Jilly snuggled down a bit. "I can tell you like him. Wow. Mrs. Poll? What has been going on while I've been here? I didn't get to be a bridesmaid. I thought we had a mutual understanding?"

"They don't pass on your messages and mail," said Jane.

"You wrote?" said Jilly.

"So did everybody. And tried to phone. They took messages. We wondered if you were ignoring us. Mum was worried to death."

"Stone said it was sad that you didn't care enough but he was not surprised as lots of churchy people cut you dead if you go off the party line. He encouraged me to write and told me to leave any mail with the front desk who would stamp it and post it. He even warned me that they sent things second class unless I specifically asked for first. The lying wotsit."

"Too late now," said Jane. "We all know the truth now and Alan will come when he knows I'm gone. He would never let me down. Gosh. I'm still so drowsy I think I am going back to sleep. I can't seem to help it."

"This poor husband of yours is going to have to be pretty magic to rescue us now," said Jilly. "Sleep it off. You were drugged and we may need you very clear thinking in the morning. There is nothing you can do now but thank you for being here. I'm sorry I wasn't there to be a bridesmaid."

Jane was too dizzy to protest and the world went away again. Jilly sighed and moved so she could comfortably sit on the floor next to the bed and waited for the morning.

Friday

The guards placed Jane in a chair and Jilly up against a wall and left. Jane was shocked. She had barely woken up even with the surprise of it before it had happened and was over. Jane pulled her hands but they

were held by metal clasps about her wrists. Something was restraining her feet but she was not sure what. She looked at Jilly. The poor girl was still in her crepe skirt and bikini costume and was now spread out, held by her hands, standing against a wall opposite her. "Crucified," thought Jane then dismissed it as over dramatic.
The guards were gone and the lights were getting dimmer. Jane worried they were going to be plunged into darkness again but then the music started. A deep chord swelled and sounds rose drawing to a fanfare as the lights at the altar brightened and Stone entered.
"Cheap vaudeville," thought Jane, almost offended at the idea that somebody could be impressed by that, or even think the somebody else could be impressed.
Jilly however knew the formula "Hail Master," she cried loudly and fervently.

Alan woke and moved his body in the confined space. He checked. The guns and ammunition were still gone. He could just make one move and they would all click back into place in time for the search later today but nobody would be at risk then. He smiled to himself. Now to find Stone. He set certain parameters in his mind and swept the building. There was a flash of familiarity in the chapel deep under the central hall and then the sense of satisfaction as he found Stone's mind.
"This man is evil," he told himself. "I have seen the consequences of his actions." Finally he assured himself "He does not deserve mental privacy and I may save many from his abuse," and so Alan dived into his brain.

Stone walked over towards Jilly who visibly cowered. "You see my sweet," he said. "You see what happens to those that refuse my honours?" Jilly looked at him pleadingly.
"You won't hurt her," she said.
"I might," said Stone. "If it amuses me."
"I'm sorry," said Jilly. "I was wrong. Just don't hurt her."
"Bit late to bargain," said Stone. "More the time to serve and be rewarded."
"I'll do anything," said Jilly her voice faltering. "I will be very attentive."
"Even the thing you ... declined... before?"
"Yes," said Jilly her breathing getting a fraction laboured. "I was frightened before. I didn't expect it. I must have been inattentive in my studies."
"And that virginity that was so important to you?"
"Just a flesh thing. To be subordinated to the spirit."
"You have remembered your lesson well. And then you would hope for

a reward?"
"If I find grace in your sight Master."
Stone smiled. "You want this sister?"
"Have her sent home Master. Her time may come but she is not of us yet."
"You have learned your lesson. But what if she speaks of us and our secrets?"
"I shall be with you Master. She will not speak and if she spoke why should she be believed if I were to deny it? She would feel my life was hostage to your favour."
"Yes. Yes," said Stone. "Fear is good. Fear teaches you obedience. But fear still allows for hate. You might fear me and obey me but still hate me. You have one more hurdle to cross."
"Yes Master. I am willing. What must I do?"
"Despair," he laughed softly. "Once you have despair and hope is gone then you serve and obey without question. You have gone beyond love and hate then. You submit to every whim without question."
"I am ready Master."
Stone watched her, now standing directly behind Jane.
"But my dear," said Stone. "You might better understand my place and role in the universe and your place and role in the universe if you were first to watch me kill this sister of yours. It is all a matter of who is in control and who is called to serve." He carefully reached round and showed Jane the knife. She gasped.
Suddenly the computer went 'bip' paused and went 'bip' again.

Alan moved slowly through Stone's mind. It is impossible to describe it to a non-telepath but imagine a tunnel sloping gently downwards. Information, think of it as lights, was sweeping forward, downward past him. He was drifting slowly from raw senses to interpretation and understanding. He saw streams of thought moving through nodes and becoming refined. Lines, edges and colours become patterns, groups of patterns become objects, objects pick up connotations and implications and become personal responses.
Hearing swept past him. There was a rhythmic pulsing to the sound. Stone was hearing something going bip, bip, bip. Pretty monotonic and he was ignoring it. Alan let it rush on past.
Alan touched the stream of sight. He saw. He did not just see as Stone was seeing or what Stone was seeing but he saw it as Stone saw it. He saw Jilly. Stones eyesight was poor but he knew Jilly was held to the ring in the wall by a handcuff so he saw it. Alan saw it.
Stone was standing behind a chair and a glance down revealed another head of long blonde hair. Stone looked at the table. There was a lap top computer sitting open on it. Stone did not recognise it. Alan

tried to reach back to more primitive sight but Stone looked away. Alan thought "That could well be my computer. But I left it with Jane."
Alan slowly moved in on what he was searching for. Here was the area of Stones mind that vetted his thinking. Perhaps it would be called a conscience. Streams of information was flowing into it. It was a mass of activity. At its core neurones were throbbing at nearly their full rate but nearer the downstream side the activity was lessened and only a fitful flow streamed on.
"Alive and well but inhibited," thought Alan. Sure enough a big ganglion of inhibitor links were trained into the output fields. The conscience had slowly boosted its activity to try and compensate for its lack of effectiveness but it was all strangled at the end. Alan caressed the inhibitors. It would be so easy to just prune them down a bit. Stone's conscience was so big and strong it would not take much to make it heard. This was not a person who lives a life that is bland and their conscience is rarely stirred and becomes dull, this was a lusty sinner who has fought to have his way despite knowing better.
Alan watched the cells fire and the neurones carry the pulses away. A cell fired and then relaxed while the chemicals it produced washed away. Every now and again he sensed a cell somewhere around him die, thousands die every second in a normal brain, the bi-products of their own operation kills them and as a last gasp they lock on and kill themselves. The mind is very intolerant. A cell works perfectly or dies and so the system fails safe. When it is gone it is gone forever but its neighbours carry on the work.
Alan mused sadly. It was pretty much as he had expected it. There was no excuse here for a psychological make over. Stone might be a thoroughly unpleasant piece of work but he was reasonably sane. Sane for a class G worlder. Perhaps he ought to stop looking at the mechanics of Stone's mind and start to hunt for something in his thoughts. But that was not within the intentions of the rules. He had already bent things a bit to be here. He hesitated.

Jane's mind was in torment. Everything was happening too fast. Why didn't the computer stop bleeping.

Alan touched hearing senses. There was that bleeping noise still. It was vaguely familiar. No, not familiar to Stone, familiar to him. He grabbed for raw hearing and heard the computer talking phase.
[Alharan. Stone has Jane. He is threatening to kill her.] It paused.
[Alharan. Stone has....]
Alan did not wait to hear it in full again. He reached for the conscience. The inhibitors flared. Locked full on. For a moment Stone had no conscience, no limits. He flushed with power. He was incarnate evil.

Alan hung on to the cells as a man might a mad dog. The node began to fade. Burning out. Poisoned by the stream of chemicals they released. Alan held them on. Forcing them to stream. Stone threw back his head and laughed. He was free of restraint. He tightened his grip on the knife.

The cells finally died. The whole inhibitor node was a burnt, destroyed clump. The inhibition was gone and there was nothing left to replace it as the brain cannot grow new neurones. Stone choked. He was looking with terror into his own mind. At the desires and intentions. What he remembered thinking was now more than any worst dream.

Alan's world was becoming chaotic. "I've done it now," he thought. "I have created a saint." Stuff the rules. He pulled back out of Stone's mind and as he wanted to be with Jane, now, he let the new abilities run over him. Space and time were not a problem. He grabbed his own body from the attic floor and then dragged it across the distance to the room below him simultaneously screwing the mapper control back to familiar old Alan Poll.

Suddenly he stood in front of Jane. Stone looked at him. "Better put the knife down," said Alan firmly but not daring use any mind control tricks knowing that Stone would be almost traumatised already. Stone looked at him open mouthed. "It is best that you go and sit down for a while," Alan continued. Stone seemed to accept this and staggered up to the altar end of the room, dumped the knife on the table and collapsed in the big chair.

Alan's tucked his fingers under the wrist clamps. He pulled hard enough to hurt and the armour's shields cut in and protected him by tearing the screws out of the wood. Jane stood up shakily and put her hands on his shoulders and leant on him. She could neither talk nor cry nor even think clearly. She just breathed in big gasps. As she slowly subsided she could hear Stone sobbing.

Alan lead her over to Jilly. He opened the clamps that held her to the wall and the sisters embraced. Jane looked over Jilly's shoulder at Alan and smiled at him. Both girls were trembling but she knew it was time to smile.

"Oh thank you. Thank you," said Jilly. "I didn't know that he was like that, I really didn't know. Thank you for coming for me Dotty. Thank you for not giving up. Oh Dotty it's over now isn't it?"

Jane held her tight and said "Yes," but glared at Alan over Jilly's shoulder.

"Dotty?" he mouthed. Was he shocked or amused?

"Don't ask," she whispered.

They walked through the dawn towards the tall wooden gates and as they arrived there was a slight crack and two large people in green brown dress pushed them open. Alan directed the girls to one side as people rushed past them. As the sudden crowd subsided they walked out of the grounds into the lane outside. He stopped before two uniformed and capped senior looking policemen and two more of the green brown people. Jane looked at them "Tranzen," she thought "Sort of coloured space suits."

"We are all right. The gun crates are still unopened and," he paused pulling a face for a moment, "ready to collect." He looked at one of the green browns and asked "Can you have Tokimed examine my two assistants?"

Jane was surprised to have another green brown person step up to her and gently take her hand and pull her sleeve up. She was losing track of how many of them there were here. They were exactly the wrong colour to see against the trees and bushes here and they seemed to have everything covered leaving them faceless. An instrument was pressed into the fleshy part of her forearm and suddenly she felt a prick. She looked at Jilly who was receiving the same attention while Alan and the others looked on approvingly.

They walked back from the gates and seemed to pass an endless crowd of cars and minivans with Jilly slightly shivering in the cool morning air. Then they came upon the hulking mass of the space craft. It could not be mistaken. It was a bulky solid smoothly curved mass and dark amid the panelled and striped police vehicles. It sat on four framework legs folded down from its body and it had a large door swung upwards from its side with a ramp running down to the ground. Two police women stood near it talking and ignoring the green brown sentry.

Alan walked up the ramp and was greeted by more green browns and some people who looked just the same but were in white, now clearly space suits or something. He turned and beckoned the girls to follow him.

"What now?" asked Jane.

"Breakfast," said Alan gesturing towards a brightly lit table sat incongruously in the middle of the dark wide open deck. "Then some statements to the police since we seem to have time and some charges to raise and then we phone for a taxi and go back to the hotel." Jane flumped in a chair and looked at a table set with a white cloth and with a conventional breakfast, top hotel style, set on it. She looked at Jilly wearing very little still and now sitting opposite her. She looked at Alan who was reaching out to pour tea for everyone. She looked again around and saw the spacecraft deck and out through the wide open door the trees and road and a police van and two police women and she stopped dead.

"Alan," she asked. "We have nearly been murdered and you are going to have breakfast?"

"Yes," he said firmly. "You don't cope with the wildly abnormal by having some more wildly abnormal to follow. Have some normality. Tea, fruit, cereal, toast. We will face the police and stuff later." Jane found a cup of tea in her hand. It was normal.

"You're doing something to me again aren't you," she said.

"Well I'm trying a bit," he smiled. "But you're not co-operating and Jilly is. Please. It will help."

Looking at him Jane began to find breakfast more interesting and the outside world moved off to a respectable distance. She looked at Jilly who was poking at a glass bowl with grapefruit segments in it. Their eyes met and Jane almost automatically passed her a breakfast bowl and smiled. Then they forgot about the outside world and ate breakfast. Ate a hearty breakfast and slowly began to chatter inconsequentially. Buttering toast Jilly said "You know you still haven't properly introduced me to your husband here."

Jane blushed slightly. Alan said "Alan Poll. At your service. However don't get too set on the title of husband. It's a complex arrangement and not like things humans do but it allowed us to get support from my people here. We stop being officially married on Tuesday which will be rather a disappointment for us both."

Jilly looked at Jane and shook her head. "I'm not going to ask questions about that," she said "as I can instantly see I would not understand. But am I right though? It was something you did for me? To rescue me?"

Jane tried to smile knowingly but it came out more as an idiotic grin and she nodded. "It's just a special, one off, temporary thing."

Jilly cocked her head on one side. "But if you love him so much why does it have to be 'temporary'" she asked.

Jane fumbled for words. "It's a long story," was all she managed.

Alan was buttering toast but he pointed out "At the moment I couldn't undertake any long term commitments of that type. My duties make it impossible. This may change but it isn't that way now. Anyway. It is far more complex than you can imagine. Remember. We are different species. Love is not enough. Love is only the start. Now remember too. You must not tell anybody about us. I am supposed to be a big secret."

"Ah yes," said Jilly. "I remember reading about that. You are not the man who does the press and interviews so you are secret. I used to follow all that stuff avidly but I rather lost interest when I got into the COG. What happens now?"

Alan seemed to chuckle. "Well it would be nice to make some sort of statements to the police so they know what you saw and what you went through but I expect that Stone is explaining that already."

"He'd lie about anything," hissed Jilly emoting such malevolence that

Alan took a deep breath and blinked.
He chuckled again. "Oh I think he may have given that up by now," he said.
"I'll do statements," said Jilly. "I owe him that. I feel good and ready."
Jane was puzzled. "I feel good and ready too," she said. "I've been drugged and such and kept falling asleep and had a totally bad time yet I feel quite good and quite bright. How come?"
Alan gestured with his hands to indicate he had no idea then added "But it could just be that the Tokimed operator dosed you with something to buck you back up. You probably had a lot of rubbish left in your system from that stuff they knocked you out with last night. Make the most of it." He chuckled slightly and continued. "Me trying to wake you up Monday had a few adverse side effects."
Jane looked at him remembering the side effects. "I shouldn't have gone out."
Alan rocked his head. "Well going out wasn't the problem... but you took your purse. With the bug in it."
Jane felt she should gasp and be horrified but somehow she could not. She just shrugged and said "Huh. Idiot. I could have saved myself a lot of trouble."
Alan smiled. "But then you arrived when Jilly needed you. Look I'm sorry about the drugging. I had rather overdone the 'keep her alive but otherwise do not interfere in any way' orders I had given on looking after you. The guard were very edgy about letting you be grabbed like that but believed they were doing what I wanted. It worked out very well so they still think I'm really smart rather than knowing the truth that I was just dumb lucky."
"I was so pleased to see you," admitted Jilly. "It may seem a rotten thing to say but having you there without having to talk to you for quite a while was good. It made me stop and think deeply for the first time in months. I was so sure you were there to rescue me and you had been caught trying. Once I had that sorted out I knew which side I was on and what I wanted to do." She paused and smiled. "Then you should have woken up and it would be a wonderful reconciliation. But unfortunately you didn't wake up, not for ages more. By then I was mad and I was really getting very uncharitable about Stone because of what he had done to you rather than what he had done to me."
"Probably more healthy," muttered Alan. "You are more motivated when it is you that you care about but you never feel so good about it in the long run."
"Today," said Jane. "I could feel good about anything. That is your doing isn't it Alan?"
He chuckled. "I already told you. Normality. I will make it as normal as possible. Look on it as first aid."

Jane looked round and smiled. She recognised that they were perhaps eating breakfast in a strange place and none of them, especially Jilly, were quite dressed right but they were together at last. All that remained were the formalities, the paperwork and stuff so the police knew what Stone had done. Somehow even that was pushed away into that nebulous time known as 'later today' by the sheer breakfastiness of the moment. She helped herself to some more tea.

It was nearly five o'clock that evening when they had finished. Alan leant on the hotel reception desk, got another room for the night and signed Jilly in. Jilly admitted she had given up most of her clothes weeks ago and virtually had survived in what she was wearing now for ages. Jane divided her wardrobe with her as, when they arrived at the hotel, she was wearing Alan's anorak over next to nothing. Jane even parted with the nightie. Jilly joyfully jumped into jeans and a thick denim shirty thing and real, oh luxury, real underwear. They ate in the hotel restaurant and jostled Jilly off to bed as she was visibly fading by nine. Alan rolled out of the bathroom, kicked off his shoes and slowly undressed. He flopped on his back in the bed. Jane looked at him lying there with his eyes shut breathing slowly and wondered what constituted reasonable and unreasonable modesty. She reminded herself that she was his wife at least for the time being so she quickly took off her things and tucked herself into bed beside him facing him.
"It's done," sighed Jane holding the bedclothes over her shoulder. "All finished. This is what I hoped for when I dragged you down from the Deli."
"From Tokyo," murmured Alan rolling over to face her.
"To the Deli. Sorry I'm all confused. What?" Jane was perplexed.
"You said I might have been in China. Now Delhi. It was just Tokyo. Not important."
"You... What... They got you back from Tokyo?"
"It was gone midnight there and so I had a few hours free. I went straight back so I didn't miss much. I had to finish all I was doing there last week so I could be free this week. I knew we'd be finished by tonight so I can pick things up tomorrow evening if I'm to be free Sunday."
"Alan?" she asked. She waited for the slight sound, or was it a movement, that indicated she had his attention. "Will you explain about temporary marriage to Jilly. I can't because I hardly understand it myself. She thinks we're married because Stone told her and she knows I'm in here with you now but what when we take her home to the flat and put her in the camp bed in my room and you say goodbye and leave. She's got to be told before that. I don't think what you said over breakfast sank in. She knows it's different but I think she thinks we're

just secretly married or something."

Alan laughed. "Don't worry," he said. "I will tell her everything in the car again as we drive home. I expect she will think very highly of you for doing so much to come and save her that she will keep our secret."

"It is a secret isn't it?" said Jane.

"It's funny sort of secret. If anybody looked us up now on any of the many government computer systems they would have found we were newly-weds but after we get back that will all vanish again. But nobody you know would even know how to do that. As far as people back home know we went away, we got Jilly and we came back. The COG had a run in with the Police and it's all in the papers. The Tranzen helped. I will have all the bills. You had a nice room that looked over the harbour. I was close by. That's enough. Your close friends, who might delve closer out of concern, know that I am Tranzen so if you say you have to keep some details confidential they will understand. Relax. The only people who find out will be those you tell."

Jane looked at him. There was another thing. "About last night," she started. "Well. Yesterday afternoon."

"I got mad at you," he said apologetically.

"No you didn't," she said. "I was trying to help and I suggested something and you said no rather strongly. Well I wanted to say that I've figured it out now and I'm sorry. I didn't realise."

"I'm sorry too. I didn't need to bite your head off but the whole idea would have been too much the Varhyn fix. That is just what a wife would do for her husband. The idea was so attractive to me that I almost panicked. We had made it through that problem already. Understand that the Varhyn are not like humans, we mate for life so to speak. That is in our blood so that would be how a woman reminds her man that she completely supports him and only him forever. I wanted you and your a sign of your approval so much I had to be so careful."

"I got it wrong," said Jane. "I thought you didn't want me. I thought that now he is under pressure it is coming out. That hurt. When I think about it now you did that because you love me, or at least you like me a lot."

He sighed. "Maybe it was. Maybe I do."

Jane wriggled a little closer to him. "It's all finished then. Just tonight and we go home. Then the weekend and Monday and then I stop being Mrs. Poll and revert to poor little Miss. Jane Naughton. I've spent rather a lot of your money I'm afraid. You couldn't afford me full time."

"Hum," Alan grunted and seemed to think about it for a bit. He pulled out the arm Jane was encroaching on and swung it over her head. She bent her neck up so he could wrap it round her. She felt it all down her back. "Are you sure I'd want you?" He asked, but the chuckle was there.

"I'm sure we'd be compatible," mused Jane. "We do the same sort of

things. We have a similar sort of outlook on life."
"Yeah. Adventurous holidays. Acting. Getting knifed and of course I make it a habit to take pretty girls to hotels and saying they are my wife. If you think you are seeing me as I really am this week you are sadly deluded." He rolled onto his back and stared at the ceiling. "I like my life boring thank you."
Jane was silent. She thought carefully. "He's embarrassed again," she realised. "He can do so much and yet he can't seem to cope with me." She realised the most humane thing to do was to change the subject. "Alan," she asked "Are you musical? Music is so important to me."
She felt him jiggle the bed as he laughed. He realised what she was doing and liked it. He decided to play the game and reached back thousands of years of memory but only a few decades of real time. "It's not really in my ID. However I did play guitar professionally once. In the summer when I was I was seventeen I did eight Thursday nights in the back room of a pub with some school friends.
The landlord paid us a fiver a time and after expenses my share was a bit less than fifteen bob a night. We claimed we played Chicago Blues but it was mostly home transcriptions of old John Mayall Albums. On the strength of that I thought I was Eric Clapton but I when I got back from my first term at university the drummer had sold his kit to buy a car and that rather put an end to it. Later I leant my guitar to a friend and never bothered to claim it back. Nothing remotely serious. My mother hoped guitar lessons would make me into Julian Bream but I wanted to be Bill Wyman. Does that count?"
"You clot," she said and poked him. Hard.
"So I'm a clot. At least I'm a happy clot." He lurched away from her finger.
"Alan?"
"Um?"
"Thank you."
He laughed gently. "I won't say it has all been fun but I think it needed doing. Being with you has been fun though. I like you a lot."
"Alan?"
"Um?"
"Alan. I like you a lot too. When Jilly offered to give herself to Stone to try to get him to release me I wondered for a moment if I would do that for her. I wasn't sure. But I did know I would do it for you. And more."
"Clot," he said. "Of all the people in the world I am the one that does not need you to protect me from the likes of Stone. Stone needed protecting from me. I rather worked him over more than even he deserved."
Then he kissed her. He put his hand on her cheek to hold her head softly and rolled towards her and as their bodies touched he kissed her

on the lips. Gently, not excitingly but long and tender. Jane liked that. "He kissed me," she said to herself. "Not I kissed him." She sighed and snuggled up in his arm and waited to go to sleep in the warmth. She had waited a long time for that and nothing was going to ruin it now.

Jilly of the Fifth

The train pulled in and, as the breeze cleared the steam away, she took a moment to consider it. She had read all the books as she came up from through the school. The one school girl heroine that really appealed to her, always getting into the direst of scrapes, always in the most terrible of dilemmas, always faced by the most complicated of problems and yet she always came through. Now, by the coincidence of name and time, she, Jill Jenkins was now 'Jilly of the fifth'.
Everything unfolded around her as usual. The trunks went on the van, it had been a horse and cart five years ago when she started, but that was during the war. The little ones were marshalled into a crocodile to walk up to the school while Miss. Savage ignored the older ones who could be expected to know the way and the penalties for being late. Jilly looked for some class mates and found the new fifth formers gathered together and postponed starting to walk up through the village and out towards St. Agnes School for Girls set in the woods facing out over the lake.
Jilly looked at them. Amanda had a suitcase. Amanda always had a suitcase so she would have to carry it when the rest of them remembered to put everything in their trunks. Mary had had her ears pierced and she had very tame sleepers in. She had a letter but it wasn't going to go down well. Jewellery never did. Katharine's older sister had eloped and got married. Full scandalous details were promised for later. Elisabeth...
"Jenkins!"
Everybody stopped and looked at Miss. Savage. What had Jilly done?
"Jenkins. This is Felicity Ward. She's new. She will be in your dorm. Take her up to the house."
Sighs of relief all round. Felicity was gathered up and the girls hurried off towards the school before they were noticed again.
Felicity was a short girl with glasses and, as expected for a new girl, every stitch she wore was new. They inquired politely after her family and discovered she lived with her grandfather and although she had been educated at home he had felt a good school would help her finish. She had a brother but no parents. She had lost her father in the war, he had been a Captain in Flanders, and her mother more recently. They didn't enquire closer. She was a bit anxious but was rather looking forward to school but it was the first time she had been away from the family home except holidays. Slowly the conversation turned and they were telling her about the school, the good and the bad, and they arrived and gathered in the refectory for the news on dorms.
Old Savage was right. Felicity was in Jilly's dorm. As a bonus they were

in one of the little ones up in the roof which was one of the perks of being in the fifth. It might not be as warm as those in the main part of the block but they were snug and had a reputation for being where things happened. The five girls inspected it, they approved it although the view wasn't special as the window opened onto the roof and you couldn't see down much so they sat on their beds wondering how long their trunks would take to get to the top floor.

Dinner would be at six and they hadn't anything else to do but just talk until then and Helen had been travelling since dawn so they tried filling Felicity in on the teachers and staff, all their fads and foibles. She looked a bit worried at times but took assurance that things were overall pretty good. She asked particularly about getting and sending mail and explained that her brother was also starting school and they had promised to write regularly.

When that ran out of steam they pressed Katherine for the salacious details of her sister's elopement but it turned out she didn't have much. There were stories of how awful housekeeping for two in a one room bed-sit in Brighton was while they worked up the residency period but no details of what schoolgirls really care about. The conspiracy of silence on what losing your virginity was all about continued. It was either the best thing ever or the worst thing ever but nobody who knows ever tells.

Helen proposed a pact. The first one to do it spills the beans. No holds barred. Every last gory detail. The good and the bad. They clasped hands and promised, not because they cared quite as much as they said but because they were bored and hungry and it passed the time. Then they speculated as to who it would be first. Mary had form because she had danced at a ball. She had had a card. Jilly had only ever danced with her brother. He looked the part as a Second Lieutenant in the Household Cavalry but brothers definitely don't count. The joke ran until the bell sounded and dinner finally released them down to the refectory.

Classrooms were announced over dinner, no surprises, and timetables were posted. A quick rush back up stairs, clambering over the pile of trunks now in the middle of the room, recovered notebooks and the copies were made. The teachers named produced some squeals of delight and some groans but the general consensus was that, aside from Thursday starting with double maths, it wasn't too bad. Time to unpack.

As the first week back unfolded Jilly found it rather fun to see everything as new through Felicity's eyes. Fortunately she was bright and, if anything, ahead of the others so she was spared the terrors of after-hours remedial class. They were lucky to be five friends as they had all known of dorms where angst and spite were the rule. If anything Helen could be a bit abrupt and Gwen failed to stick up for herself and then snapped when she thought she'd been pushed too far but they both meant well. You had to catch them on a bad day for things to go wrong. Felicity was coming out as the bright one, Elisabeth as the gossip while Jilly? Jilly didn't know what she was. She somehow had Jilly of the fifth stuck in her head and yet the fifth was just turning into the fourth with a few more privileges and a bit more responsibility. Reassuring but just a tiny bit disappointing.

Suddenly Felicity was fetched from class. She was packed and was gone. Miss. Mitchell, their form teacher, revealed that her Grandfather had died. She would attend the funeral, the family proceedings and return shortly. Keep her in your prayers. Jilly thought of the kind old man that was her Grandfather. Poor Felicity.

The bed was empty for a week and then Felicity reappeared. Everybody was sympathetic but a bit unsure what to say. Felicity understood. It was expected. He had been ill for some time. That is why they had gone away to school she thought, perhaps, he wanted to die in private. He was like that. He hated hurting people. He was a bit shy. Her brother had been a great comfort and had sorted a lot of things out. Everything was held in trust for them for when they were twenty one. It was sad but Grandfather had been ill for so long. It was hard to see it as the best for him but it was inevitable. We must move forward. Then she'd sniff and apologise for making a fuss. She wasn't coping well but she was coping.

Then it happened again. Felicity was called from class and wasn't there at lunch and only appeared again at dinner time in the evening. Everybody was dreading it being another family member. She said nothing through the meal and in the dorm composed herself and looked at her friends.

"My brother has been kidnapped," she announced and looked at them as if uncertain how they would take it.

They were horrified and bursting with sympathy. Jilly sat with one arm round her while the others tried to think of things to say that wouldn't sound too crass. Jilly was realising that what might make a good 'Jilly of the fifth' story was, in real life, a heart tearing tragedy for a poor girl who had already lost her caring, protecting grandparent and now somebody she clearly viewed as her best friend in the world had gone too.

Felicity tried a brave face. "Harry will cope better than I," she said. "He would tell me to buck up so I'll try. He's probably having a real adventure now. I'm sure it will all come out all right in the end."

Everybody agreed hopefully.

Next morning there were two policemen walking round outside the school. When Felicity was 'excused' games and told to stay within the main school buildings everybody knew she was being protected.

Jilly had the shopping lists for the other girls. They were trying to prepare something special for Felicity who wasn't eating well. Just a couple of treats to produce after lights out, plus the usual luxuries everybody needed from the chemists to replace standard school issue. Jilly was pleased to be out doing something. It was terribly frustrating just sitting about in school waiting for news of Felicity's brother. It wasn't as if there was anything she could do. In real life, not school girl adventure books, things happened far away and you weren't involved. It was probably for the best as she didn't have a clue how you should deal with armed kidnappers.

The stuff from the chemist was discreetly in the bottom of the shopping basket under an old tablecloth and now she could turn to the more entertaining side of the expedition. She had a rough list but what she bought was going to depend on what the baker had on display today. Preferences had been expressed but she had to pick.

She joined the queue which, happily, wasn't long. There was just the baker serving and his lad was sweeping up so she tried to eye up the shelves over the shoulders of the two people in front of her. The woman paid and Jilly was promoted to next but one and she was immediately struck by the accent of the man ahead of her.

"...well pork pies then," he said. "Three of them. And would you be having any bread rolls?" Jilly though he was buying for a picnic but he had money but no bag to carry stuff in. He ended up with four or five paper bags balanced in his arms.

The shopping basket was loaded when she left. She had all the important goodies and a couple of known second favourites. Jilly of the Fifth was still nagging her about the man with the Irish accent. It just wasn't picnic weather. Certainly it was dry but it was getting chilly and there were lots of places that would serve you hot food in the warm nearby. It just seemed incongruous. A clue?

Suddenly there he was again. Arms loaded with bags again as he came out of the grocers. "Even more bags," she thought before her alter ego pointed out that these were all grey paper and the baker had used white. She paused and looked back up the road and watched him out of the corner of her eye. The answer to where the baker's bags had gone became immediately obvious. He walked up to a motorcar and opened the door and loaded his purchases inside.

The direction was spot on. She was in school uniform and the route back to school lead straight past the car. She set off at a determined

pace in case they were about to drive off hoping to get a look.
The man she had watched got into the driver's seat and piled his shopping onto the seat next to him. There were two people in the back. A tall one and a short one. No, a slumped one. Three pork pies explained. Now if the slumped one looked a bit brotherly to Felicity... But no. The slumped one was sort of what they call medium build with short dark hair and that was about all she could see. The real world could be frustrating at times. She was past the car when it pulled away and pulling over to the other side of the road came past her and drove gently off into the distance.

Jilly rehearsed her facts and admitted there weren't any. Three people in a car buying food. Frankly far more likely to be innocent than kidnappers. Certainly not enough to run for the police and probably not enough to be taken seriously by anybody. If it was a story she would know Harry, or recognise him from a photograph but a dim view of somebody with short dark hair wasn't enough. It wasn't even Felicity's colour. Even if she had a word with one of the policemen at the school it was going to go down as an over-active imagination. She'd doubt it if one of the others told her the tale.
As she was starting the final trudge up the hill Jilly saw the car again. She quickly pulled out the shopping list and scribbled down the registration plate number on it as her heroine had been telling her off for missing that before. It was parked in the lane that ran round the meadow by the river. Jilly of the Fifth pointed out that the river ran through a wood and you can get closer to see things from a wood.
Jilly accepted that she was being an idiot but detoured down the lane promising herself it was just an opportunity to take the long way round to the school so she could enjoy the walk. When a break in the fence presented itself she made a further detour into the wood but failed to come up with a convincing excuse for that one.
She crept through the wood trying to be as silent as possible and was fortunately listening and heard voices ahead of her. She paused, slightly unsure of how to interpret what she heard.
"... and yer'd be wiping yer own ass if you hadn't pulled that silly stunt back at the farm but if you wanta be tied up that's what you get. Now. Let's have you back to the car and we'll 'ave some dinner."
"Tied up" was ominous she thought but the rest of it didn't make much sense. However if somebody was tied up she ought to find out enough to know what to tell the policemen back at the school. She wondered about sneaking up closer.
"White blouse," Jilly of the fifth reminded her. Yes, the chase across the moor. Jilly had covered herself with a dark blanket so she wouldn't be seen. Jilly had a table cloth in the bottom of the basket to cover things

and it was dark blue. Jilly smiled to herself. She thought things like that were always a bit far fetched when they happened in stories but, by chance, she had just the thing for the plot to move on.

Even draped in the cloth she was hesitant to get near to them but she now had them as both the same height, just a bit taller than she was, and one was obviously stumbling a bit while the other was trying to encourage him along. They reached the road and got back into the car and were soon engaged in doing something and talking although the sounds the reached Jilly were too muffled to follow.

The idea of them eating pork pies made Jilly's tummy cry out with the unfairness of it all so she delved into the shopping basket and pulled out a cream puff, decided she was having half her share of the feast early, and ate it.

Time passed slowly and it got darker and darker. The moonlight enabled Jilly to see the car but not the occupants. The car had a little light that they turned on at times but it didn't actually reveal much of what was going on inside.

Jilly ate a second cream puff and decided that missing dinner wasn't really too bad. However they would have noticed by now. Miss Hickman, if she was lucky, or Old Savage if she wasn't would have her in the office to explain. If this was a wild goose chase she was in trouble and even if it wasn't things were not going to be too good.

Finally all three people stepped out of the car. Jilly almost sighed with relief as if they had finished their supper and had driven off it would have left her with a serious anti-climax. They were walking towards her so she backed into a bush and ducked down as low as she could under her tablecloth.

They walked right past her. Ten feet away. Still she couldn't get a clear view of anybody as the moonlight might be bright but you just couldn't see the detail of anything. Jilly pulled the table cloth round her and snuggled into the bush. She was finally going to get at least a glimpse of the captive.

Dark trousers, black shoes, a white shirt open at the neck but with a collar. She tried to make it a description. Probably short hair... She ran out at that. He was stooped so she wasn't quite sure how tall he was and his hair looked dark except when it didn't.

Jilly tried to watch carefully which wasn't easy as the moonlight was bright for moonlight but still pretty dim when it came to seeing details. The captive was either tied or hand-cuffed as his hands always stayed together in front him and he was a bit wobbly. He was clutched from both sides and walked down to the water. He did not seem to be obviously cooperating but they were bigger than him so it probably did not make much difference.

"Just get in the boat sleepy head," said the tall man. "You can sleep it off alone tonight as we're going into town for a meal and a beer or three. We've earn't it. We'll be back for you after drinkin' up time and bring you a pie."

Jilly stayed with the table cloth shadowing her face and blouse. She watched them pole the boat across and unload their captive. The island had a shed and lots of wire netting cages, she couldn't see anything she understood and there didn't seem to be anything in the cages.

They fussed about in the shed and when they finally came out they looked round but seemed to look straight past her. One up to Jilly of the fifth. Then they polled the boat back, they didn't seem to have oars, and dragged it back up the bank onto the flat ground and walked back to the car.

She waited while they looked round again and got back into the car. It started and they drove off. Jilly listened to it go all the way up the road towards the village before she dared unwrap herself.

Right. It seemed quite straight forward. All she had to do was get in the boat and rescue the captive from the island. She walked up to the boat. It was rather big but the pole they pushed it about with was still in it. The key thing to remember was to tie the boat up when you landed. She remembered the story where Jilly had to rescue the two girls who forgot that one and were marooned. This should be relatively simple.

Jilly pushed at the boat and it didn't move. She heaved, shoved, levered, spoke to it tenderly and ended up threatening it but it was obstinately far to heavy for her. She sat on the corner and looked round and wondered what to do next.

"So he is in the shed on the island?" she thought. "And he is now alone. What am I to do?"

Well what would Jilly of the Fifth do more to the point? Swim over and rescue him of course. It happened in the sixth book. Well it was similar. But Jilly in the book just happened to have her swimming costume with her and a towel and all Jilly had was a table cloth. "Well" she thought. "The cloth will have to stand in for the towel, be it a bit small, and... and I don't really need a costume in the dark."

This was daring stuff but she wrapped her clothes in the cloth and carefully memorised where they were and stepped into the stream.

It was colder than she expected. And slimier. She gritted her teeth and breast stroked towards the island. It wasn't wide but climbing out barefoot onto the bank next to the little wooden jetty wasn't much fun. She made her way to the hut and examined the door.

It looked simple. There was a bar dropped in frames to stop the door opening. Clearly the hut was to contain things not a habitation as the bar could not be lifted from the inside. This was good as this implied

that no accomplice she had not seen was left. Jilly sighted up the run back to the river as she guessed a pursuer would not follow her into the water. She lifted the bar and pushed the door. It creaked ominously.
"Grief," mumbled a voice. "A Nymph. I'm hallucinating."
"Harry Ward?" she asked wondering if it being him wasn't too far fetched an idea.
"Er... That's me," said the voice.
"I'm one of Felicity's school chums," Jilly assured him. "I heard them put you here. I came to see if I could get you free."
"Wow thanks!" said Harry. "No. Not a nymph. I'm sorry. I'm not thinking very clearly. They've been giving me stuff to make me stay asleep. In the moonlight it looked like you didn't have anything on."
"I don't," confessed Jilly. "You're on an island. I had to swim."
"Oh grief. Gosh thanks. I'll try not to look. Well... I'm tied to a chair. Well I think that's what it is. I'd really appreciate being untied because I desperately need a... er... to urinate. It's getting pretty pressing."
It took a while but they were good knots. Whoever tied them knew what he was doing so they came undone easily when you got the moonlight on them. Harry stepped outside hurriedly and did what he needed to. He returned and stood sideways deliberately not looking into the shed.
"I guess I've got to swim to escape," he said. "Any ideas on how to get my clothes ashore dry?"
"Er... no," admitted Jilly. "That's why I left mine on the other side."
Harry pulled at the door and suddenly he was holding in. "Drop on hinges. That's handy."
"Can we use it as a boat?"
"Far too small. But it should float some clothes and have them arrive dry. I trust, my pretty nymph, that you will not be offended by my naked body."
"I won't look," she said.
"I'm afraid we have to give that up now," he sighed. "We must watch over one another. Swimming in the dark is hardly safe. However we need to escape the island. May I apologise in advance for any embarrassment I cause you but also may I thank you from the bottom of my heart for having the courage and strength of character to come to rescue me like this."

Jilly swallowed. Courage? Strength of character? This wasn't her. What would Jilly of the fifth do?
"Thank you," said Jilly of the fifth. "We must get away quickly. Don't worry about me." Jilly was quite relieved to let her take over.
Harry floated the door, put an old box on it upside down and progressively piled his clothes onto that. Jilly was pleased that the moonlight afforded a bit of decency but was glad she had permission to

watch in a concerned, caring way.
"Do we just go straight across?" he asked.
"Yes," she replied. "My things are wrapped in an old table cloth. It will be easier to find them once we're ashore."
"Right ho. Let's be going. Try not to splash or the water will go over the door and soak my stuff." He was across the stream in no time and lifted the whole door onto the grass. He turned back and as Jilly stood extended his hand to pull her ashore. "A Nereid," he said with an obvious smile. "A beautiful water spirit who saves the poor adventurer in distress."
Jilly looked up and down the bank and saw an anomalous lump. She hobbled off over the twiggy ground to fetch her clothes and the shopping basket then she and Harry took turns with the table cloth to dry themselves and then they got dressed.
"A gym-slip?" Harry asked when he thought it proper to look at her again. "You are in your school uniform?"
"Er... yes," was all she could think to say.
"As am I," he sighed. "I was abducted. I assume you heard? They've been moving me around but this was the first time they just abandoned me all tied up."
"Handy," she said. "What do we do now?"
"Police Station. I really doubt we will have trouble with a return visit from my abductors sitting in a Police Station. Plus I can get them to ring home and sort me out some money so I can run to some clean clothes and a bath. After the last few days... well being in the river, for all that it smelt a bit funny, has probably made me more hygienic rather than less."
"Follow the river to the road then left," Jilly of the fifth took charge. "Babercome Croft has a Police House but it's two miles."
"A bit under an hour then. We'll be there after closing time so we'd better get away from here. Derry has a gun and I don't know about the other man."

It was a long walk and Jilly was already tired, uncomfortable and cold but the prospect of a gunman whose victim she had stolen behind them made her hurry. The Police House had the requisite blue lamp so it was easy to find and Harry knocked solidly. Constable Harris was quick to recognise the face from the newspapers and, once he had spoken to his superiors was happy for them to place a reverse charges call to the Ward home.
"Emmet? This is Harry. Yes. I'm at the Police Station in Babercome. No Hampshire. Look can you get Mr. Peters for me. Right. Thank you. Peters? It's... Yes. Babercome. Look I'm destitute. I have only the clothes I stand up in. I've swum a river with my rescuer to escape. I

need some beans. Can you sort it out? The Police Station... No. Police House I'm told. Babercome in Hampshire. Work magic for me. Great." Mrs. Harris plied them with tea but within half an hour a car pulled up outside and a suited man arrived on the doorstep.
"You have a Master Henry Ward here?" he asked. Constable Harris showed him in. "I am the manager of the Westminster Bank in Staplefield," he explained. "I have been requested to bring you one hundred pounds and assist you your grace."
"Thank you Sir," said Harry. "I am desperately sorry to drag you out in the middle of the night but I have just been rescued."
"No problem. No problem," the bank Manager assured him. "I had read about it all in the papers but I had not realised you were a customer until I received a call from your local Branch Manager. I have my car. May I take you anywhere?"
"A hotel where we can get a bath," Harry asked hopefully, "A night's sleep and getting my clothes laundered would be a godsend."
It was a short drive and a hotelier opened to them. The Bank manager explained things and a room was readied with a gas water heater over the bath. As he left them in the room promising to return for the clothes basket in ten minutes the porter said "Good night Mr. Ward. Miss Ward," and closed the door.
"He thinks I'm Felicity," said Jilly. She sighed. "But I think I'm staying. No chance to get back into school now. Anyhow it's miles. After you with the bath."
"We have gowns and night things," Harry said looking at the pile. "And we have three beds and a sort of folding screen so sharing isn't really a problem."
"I really don't want to be left alone," admitted Jilly. "I'm not traumatised like people sometimes are in books but I'm still pretty nervy. I know I waited for them to leave but I was very scared."
"Well I ought to go in the bath," wondered Harry. "But you've seen me in the buff before so I guess if you want to sit in I've no reason to complain."
"I won't look," offered Jilly. "Just don't leave me alone."
"Would you want a bath too?" he asked hesitantly.
"I was in the same river," she sighed. "And you've seen me dressed as a nymph. I'm not going to make a fuss just don't tell anybody or my reputation is trashed."
"Jilly," said Harry. "If your reputation is in my hands you will be valiant, blameless and pure. I may well owe you my life so you definitely deserve my respectful discretion."
"Well hurry up and get in the bath," she said. "Then we can both be valiant, blameless, clean and get some sleep."

A Police Inspector came to the hotel and took careful statements. He revealed that a search was on for the men and the car. He assured them that the men must have fled the county as they had not been detected. Jilly tried to feel reassured but gunman won over policeman. Still it was time for both of them to get back to school. Two stops up the line for her but quite a trip with changes for Harry.

Harry paid the bill and tipped generously. They had directions to the railway station but the time of the next train was a long way off so they set off at a slow walk looking aimlessly in the shops.

"Would you mind Felicity knowing we 'shared'?" asked Jilly wondering how much she should tell when she got back.

Harry pulled a face. "Felicity I trust but be careful how far it goes. The Police have contacted the school so you shouldn't get too much stick for being out-of-bounds overnight and you have that wonderful injunction from the Inspector this morning not to tell anyone, and he repeated anyone, anything. All in all you rescued me and everything is solved. Good show."

"Would you tell anybody?" Jilly asked. "We shared a bed so some people might think we... we did things."

"Well we didn't so that's that. We swam a river naked so there really wasn't anything new to see, we were far too tired for that sort of stuff and, anyway, the hotel provided night things. Look Jilly you're a spiffing girl. You're as resourceful as any story book heroine and, having met some of Felicity's dumb friends, I was beginning to think they were all totally made up. I really would love to get to know you better and I will write as soon as I get back to school. You will always be the beautiful Nereid who rescued me."

Jilly blushed a little. "I would prefer it if you didn't always remember me as naked."

Harry smiled. "This is a girl with the courage to set even things like clothes aside. That takes more strength of character than most will ever have. Look, you may well have saved my life. We do not know what the plot was yet. The last act where they are caught, arrested, tried and the whole plot is exposed is yet to be played. Remembering you naked in the moonlight as my rescuer will always be both precious and chaste to me."

"No lustful thoughts?" she asked bashfully.

"No... Well not at the time," he admitted. "I confess that when I woke before you this morning and just lay there looking at you... Jilly you are not just resourceful and brave. You are very pretty too."

She grinned at him playfully. "So that was really a yes? I don't mind."

"Well a bit," he laughed. "I want to keep our relationship proper because I want to stay in touch. As I say I'd like to get to know you better. Maybe something will come of it."

"A romance?" she asked.
He dithered slightly. "Well... You're the first girl that has made the idea seem attractive but I admit I haven't got a clue what's involved. Books are always so stilted. I don't believe two people who are planning to build their lives together talk like that. When you see real people in love they might be a bit absent minded about the rest of the world but they aren't doing a Jane Austin. Frankly I suspect that they share everything."
"You wouldn't elope?" She knew it wasn't a fair question but he was sweet when he was embarrassed.
Harry shrugged. "I'm now the titular head of the family. I'm not sure I can elope because that implies I'm going against the family will. Of course naughty goings on is a bit of a tradition, although not lately. My ancestors were not always very nice people. The third Duke was reputed..."
"One of your ancestors was a Duke?" Jilly interrupted quite amazed.
Harry stared at her open mouthed. "Did... Didn't you know? Surely Felicity told you. I am a Duke. Since my grandfather's death I am now the seventeenth Duke of Hallowfield. That's probably what all this mess is about. We own shipping, farming, lots of land in the city and the abduction must have been something to do with that. They either want a ransom, which would be a problem as it's all in the hands of the family solicitors until I make twenty one, or they want to influence something. However nobody said a word to me so I suspect you rescued me from the hired help not the plotters. Jilly. You're looking at me as if I'm mad."
"I... I... " She stammered. The tables were turned on her. Now it was she that was embarrassed. "I've never met a Duke before."
Harry executed a courtly bow. "Well you've now rescued one and he will be eternally grateful. If there is anything I can do for you just ask."
Jilly looked round not sure what to say. She was still clutching the shopping basket so she remembered she had eaten a lot of the cakes and she ought to replace them. It seemed like a simple way to defuse the embarrassment but, really, Felicity should have warned them.
"It's just a silly thing, " she started. "But yesterday I was in the village to buy cream cakes and things for the other girls and... Well while I was waiting for things to happen in the wood I missed dinner so I ate them."
"So we buy some more?" Harry was obviously delighted at having something to do. "What we really need is a pastry chef but I guess that's a bit much for a village so a baker?"
Jilly looked round and said "I can't see one but if we walk on a..."
At this moment she was grabbed from behind and pulled backwards. Out of the corner of her eye she caught Harry ducking, twisting and rolling onto the pavement and then turning to face them. A look of

recognition turned to horror and he ducked behind a pillar box. There was a loud bang followed by a high pitched squeak and then somebody poked her in the ear with something both hard and warm.
"If you don't give up I shoot the girl," said a voice beside her. "Then we both come after you so we'll catch you you be sure. Do yer want her dead or alive?"
Harry stepped out and put his hands up like they do in movies. "OK," he said let her go and I'll go with you."
"No," he said. "She's the one who keeps things simple. You be good and nobody gets hurt." He dragged Jilly over to the car and opened the door. "Now you both get in the car and we drop you both somewhere safe for the night and then, I promise, we sort everything out tomorrow."
"You won't hurt her?" asked Harry walking slowly towards them.
"I will hurt her if you don't get in the car next to her right now," he said waving the gun. "People heard the shot so they'll have the 'Tans coming. If I have to make a break for it leaving you both dead in the road will slow them down but I don't want that and you don't want that. In the car. Now."
Jilly ducked her head to sit into the car but she was pushed by the shoulder then a hand on her bottom threw her to the far side of the car. Harry sat in after her and their captors got into the car and they drove away. Jilly looked round and people were watching. "They will tell the police," she thought, "and when we don't arrive for the train they'll be sure it was us." She glanced back at Harry sitting next to her. "I wonder if they took the car number..." she thought. "If it's the same car the police have the number I gave them."

They drove on and Harry slowly sat back in his seat. "Well," he said slowly. "Are you finally going to tell me what this is all about?"
Their captor made a pure movie gesture of pushing the brim of his hat up with the end of his pistol barrel. "You don't need to know," he said. "It's politics."
"You're Anarchists?" asked Harry. "Or Fenians?"
"We are professionals," he was told. "It's not for you to know who our employers are. Just remember that I won't hurt either you or your pretty girl unless I get orders to do it or unless you make it necessary. Be good and you're as safe as possible.
"OK," said Harry. "And if you get orders to shoot me you just dump her so she has a long walk home so you can get away?"
"Let's hope it doesn't come to that," he said. "Pat and I should be getting our new orders tonight as clearly we are not going to pick up your sister as there will now be coppers beyond your wildest dreams at the school after our little shooting incident back in town."
"Right," said Harry sounding surprisingly cheerful. "Felicity's safe, you'll

139

probably let Jilly go because if you're not getting paid to shoot her you don't shoot people for free. I'm waiting on orders so it's not worth trying to negotiate now. Just remember that I do have access to a lot of money so don't just shoot me without giving me a chance to make a counter offer."

Their captor chuckled. "I'm not telling you more in case orders are to release you. I'd like to keep that nice and simple."

It was getting gloomy when they arrived somewhere and stopped. They were unloaded, shown the gun and told to shut up while their hands were bound behind them. Then they were bundled into a stocky stone built hut with a flat roof.

"Right," said Derry. "We're going to leave you here. Pat tied your hands and as he's a sailor boy he's done it well. The roof is solid and the floor more so, the door is iron as this used to be the blasting powder shed for a quarry. You won't be getting out of this one. We will be making a telephone call and we get orders for you. The way things are going I suspect it will be to dump you and come home."

"And if it isn't? asked Harry.

"Well nothing personal," said Derry. "I don't like shooting kids but it might not come to that. In the big scheme of things it saves you growing old and all the pains and tribulation that come from that. Also I'm good so it won't hurt. You won't even hear the bang. Now I'm sorry to be leaving you tied up like this but we'll have our orders in the morning and we'll be back. If it's to let you go we'll walk you out onto the hills, untie you and point you on the way back to town and set you off. It will take you a couple of hours so Pat and I get well clear. The weather looks to be good so it won't be too rough on ya'."

He smiled amiably, as if he were suggesting an outing, and he was gone. They stared blankly at the door and heard him fasten a catch and then the car crunched off up the track. They were alone.

Jilly sniffed. "I think I'm going to cry," she said. "I'm sorry."

Harry walked up to her and said "Come on. Sit down on the bench. Let yourself calm down. If you need to cry it's well justified."

She tried to snuggle up to him but it was very hard with your hands tied. She got her head on his shoulder and sobbed gently. It seemed to help so she asked "You could have got away if I hadn't been there."

She felt him shrug. "I did the right thing. I'm happy with that. I wanted to be with you until train time. Buying cakes would have been fun."

Jilly sniffed. "Thank you. I wanted to be with you too. I've lost all the shopping now and the basket. What do we do now?"

"I'd like to get a look at the knots he tied. He clearly threaded it very carefully but I don't see why what he can tie I can't untie. I'll just have to look, turn and work by feel. It could take ages but it's got to be worth a try."

Jilly sniffed but he seemed hopeful. "What do I do?" she asked.
Harry rocked his head. "I'm not sure. Perhaps start sitting astride the bench with your back to me so I can see the knots."
It took a long time but finally Jilly pulled a hand free. "You did it!" she exclaimed because any success must be a cause for some hope. Harry smiled at her and she desperately wanted an extravagant gesture so suddenly she put her hands round his head and kissed him open mouthed.
"Wow," he said when she stopped and smiled.
"I... I'm not sure what came over me..." she apologised.
"I'm not complaining," he smiled. "Would you like to try undoing my hands now?"
"Oh gosh," said Jilly. "Yes. Of course. I'm sorry. I was distracted."
He sat with his back to her and she poked at the knot. It didn't seem too complex and she wiggled the loose end back through one loop. "You know Jilly." he said conversationally. "I am becoming mighty fond of you."
"I'm glad," she replied moving another loop. "Lustful thoughts again I hope."
He chuckled. "Not much use for them here but get you to myself in a nice warm room with no chance of an interruption and I could be quite the cad. Every girl's mother's nightmare."
"That's a promise so I'll look forward to it," she muttered pulling at a stiff bit. "But we might be being shot in the morning so tonight could be your last chance."
"I'd rather put my efforts into avoiding that fate but please be assured that I wouldn't consider such appalling behaviour and a torrid affair with just anybody. You have become somebody very special to me."
"Of course," she continued, "If you were to propose first, and if it so happened that I accepted, it would merely be a bit premature rather than totally licentious."
He chuckled again. "Believe me girl. Even if I married you first it would still be very licentious. I respect you because of your character and courage but if you kiss me like that again I will take it as an acceptance and see you in church."
"So is that a proposal then?" she said struggling with a rope end.
"We will need to wait a while," he answered. "I'm only seventeen."
"And I'm sixteen," she insisted. "We could get married at once. It's legal."
"No," he laughed. "Finish school then I have dibs."
"But what if Derry comes back and shoots us?" she complained. "Now I've found a husband I don't want to die a virgin."
He sighed. "Neither do I girl but concentrate on the knots."
The knots finally came undone, she took longer than Harry and actually

levered one bit free with her teeth. Now they were both free they started to explore. It was getting dark and what moonlight there was came through a barred window. The shed, sadly, yielded no forcible exits, the door resisted Harry's shoulder and the flat roof was no better. Sitting on Harry's shoulders Jilly thrust her hands into all the gaps round the roof edge but it yielded a lot of rubble, a Victorian sixpence and a wooden handled spike that might have been a chisel or a screwdriver once. Harry thought it was a rope workers tool but why it might be stuck in a roof he didn't know.
"We're not getting out until they get back," said Harry so we'd better get smart."
"Could we jump them and stab them with the spike thing?" asked Jilly not quite sure if that would work in a Jilly of the fifth book as violence never quite happened.
Harry sniffed. "Well maybe if I sharpen it up by grinding it against the floor flagstones" he said. "But jumping them might not be smart. We need to look like we're still tied up then when they feel safe then we jump them."
Jilly of the Fifth solved this in Book 4, the Welsh Adventure. "We retie the rope into loops," explained Jilly. "Then we put our hands in from opposite ends so it twists into a figure of eight. Then we still look tied up until we want to get free."
Harry was impressed. "That's a top idea Jilly. Did you just think it up?" he asked.
"I... er... I read it somewhere," she admitted.
"I'm still impressed," he said. "Felicity is a dear but I doubt she'd come up with something like that. Look, you try and rig that while I try to put a point on this tool. If I tuck it up my sleeve together with your trick we might just steal a march on them. We'd better hurry as it's going dark."
It was hours into the night when the scrape-scrap noise stopped and Jilly said into the darkness "Harry?"
"I'm finished," he said. "I have an arrow head point on it and it's got a nasty sharp edge on it. It's not a dagger but you could do somebody a lot of damage with it."
"Can you come and sit with me?" she asked.
Harry mumbled something but she heard him moving about. She felt the bench move and a hand landed on her hip and backed off. She reached out and felt him as he sat down next to her.
Jilly snuggled up against Harry's chest. "Hold me" she said.
"Nervous?" he asked as his arms closed round her.
"Obviously," she sighed. "I don't want to say something silly like 'I'm too young to die' but I would feel I'd been cheated of so many big experiences."
"Travel, study, people," suggested Harry.

"Even just the simple things," she said wondering if she should mention the one big thing again that was playing on her mind. He was being a bit dim.

"We don't really have a plan but we have a chance," he squeezed her. "We'll try and get you your simple things."

"Harry," she started slowly, "I did mean what I said earlier. About our relationship. If you want to... To take it further... Well I'd like that."

"Well if you're sure..." he said. "Look... OK..."

Morning came and with it a fresh sense of urgency. They were ready for hours or so it seemed. Finally they heard a car crunch over the rough lane and stop outside.

The door snapped open and Derry carefully looked round waving the gun. He looked relieved. He saw the two captives sprawled on the bench looking groggily up at him. "Good news," he said. "We're going for a walk. Get yourselves up."

"Are you going to untie us?" asked Harry worried that that might give things away.

"All in good time," he was told.

They walked slowly back up the lane away from the hut with Jilly in front. Harry seemed to be keeping up a meaningless stream of banter and Derry was making the very minimum of replies. Derry steered them off the lane and onto a foot path leading up by a dry stone wall and then down into a dip.

There before them was a pile of earth and a roughly rectangular hole. "This is as far as we go," said Derry.

Harry turned and faced back at him. Jilly turned too and looked back. Harry stepped up to Derry. "Oh well. It's a disappointment but perhaps it's best that you didn't for warn us. It would have been a terrifying drag up the track."

Jilly looked at his back as the ropes slipped away and the spike slowly slipped down out of his sleeve.

"I'm sorry I can't find much sympathy for your cause," continued Harry, "but I can see that in your own way you are a patriot so there's some honour there."

He stepped forward another pace. The spike was now in his hand. "Will you send a note, one day, so we can be found and taken home? For family..."

"That might not be possible unless things work out," said Derry.

Harry sighed as if resigned and suddenly snapped round. In a moment he was holding Derry's revolver hand in both his hands. Jilly gaped. Where was the spike? Then she saw the handle was in the left side of Derry's chest. Derry had a look of horror on his face but nothing moved. He slowly crumpled.

As Derry let go Harry switched the revolver to his other hand and said something that sounded like "Sorry," and fired twice at Pat holding the weapon out in front of him in two hands.

In contrast to Derry's slow fall Pat was hurled back by the impact of the shots. He turned as he fell and lay on his face, his back a mass of blood.

Harry let the gun swing down in front of him still gripped in both hands. He was frozen.

Jilly looked at him unable to know what to say. Suddenly she realised that she should act and twisted her hands and pulled them out of the ropes. Gently she stepped up to Harry and took his arm. "Are they dead?" she asked.

"I killed them," he replied tonelessly.

"They had dug our grave," said Jilly.

"That makes it right? Killing them?" Harry began to sound desperate.

Jilly of the Fifth spoke for Jilly. It was a quote. She remembered it because she thought the grammatical error was not quite Jilly. "You did the right thing. You had no choice. I know you could not stand by."

Harry drew a deep breath. "Yes," he said as if trying to convince himself. "I couldn't wait for them to shoot you. So... So what do we do now?"

Jilly pondered for a moment. "The Police again? We need the police. Can you drive?"

Harry turned and looked her in the face. "Enough," he replied. "Not legally of course but after killing two people in ten seconds that hardly seems a problem any more. I suppose the keys are in Pat's pocket."

This time it was a Police Station not just a police house and as soon as they identified themselves senior people were called and a party was dispatched to try to find the shed and the two bodies based on Harry's rather uncertain description. Finally Harry asked to phone home again. "Emmet? It's Harry again... Well as right as can be expected... Yes. She's here too... I... Hello? Oh Peters... Yes. Chobham Police Station. Wiltshire. Look. I haven't got any money again... You will? Right then. We'll stay here and wait. I appreciate that... Yes."

He handed the receiver back to the Sergeant who was watching over them. "He's coming. He's bringing a couple of the estate workers who used to be in the regiment. He doesn't want anything else to happen. It's a long way so they'll be a few hours."

It was one of the larger cars and once they left the police station it became evident both the workmen and Mr. Peters were carrying guns. "If you would like one..." Mr. Peters asked but Harry deferred. It was evening before they arrived at Hallowfield and Jilly looked at it open mouthed.

"I will show you around tomorrow," said Harry. "We do not leave until we have the all clear from the police. We must telegram your family too. But first, after our discussion last night there's something I need to give you. It's a bit of an heirloom so be careful with it."

Miss. Savage took Jilly inside and sat her in the office. "This must have been a traumatic episode," she ventured.
Jilly nodded. She sighed. "I'll give you traumatic," she thought. She drew a breath and reached in her mind for her prepared text. All the trip here in the Hallowfield car she had worked on it. "Yes," sigh again. "Once you have looked at a grave somebody has dug for you I don't think you are ever quite the same again."
"And Lord Ward?" Miss Savage enquired "He is recovering?"
Jilly tried what she thought was a pleading look "We were both very shocked but he is returning to his school today. He is a total hero and a perfect gentleman. However he had to kill two people to save us. He is not of nature a violent man and it is playing badly on his mind."
"You... You were not interfered with?" Savage asked.
"Oh no," Jilly assured her. "I have swum rivers in the dark, untied knots with my teeth, even searched the pockets of a dead man for his car keys but thankfully nobody made any... er... any unwanted advances."
"That's a blessing then," Miss Savage felt she was on ground she could cope with. "You and Lord Ward have become friends?"
Jilly smiled inside. Remember this Savage. She nodded and went for the kill. "It might be just a huge mutual crush but we have promised to keep in touch, to write regularly, and my family and I are invited to Hallowfield for Christmas so we shall see what comes of it. As I said, a hero and a perfect gentleman."
"There you are Savage," she thought. "I've dropped you the biggest hint that I can that I might, just might, be romantically attached to a full Duke. I know I can never view Harry like that but I know you care desperately about nobility. You have a head full of protocol."

She arrived in the refectory in time for dinner and was virtually mobbed by her classmates. "Details later, I'm hungry," bought some time.
Finally they were back in their little dorm.
"You are going to tell us everything that happened even if it takes all night," insisted Elisabeth. It only took half an hour.
"So the big question," asked Helen. "Did you do it? You rather skipped that bit in the story. We got clothes off to swim, sharing a bath, we got in bed, we got locked up and going to die but we never quite got told if you got kissed let alone if you did the deed."
"I promise not to be upset," said Felicity. "I know Harry's super."
"No," grumbled Jilly. "He doesn't know when to drop the chivalry bit."

"Did you actually ask him?" Gwen wanted to know.
"Well I hinted," said Jilly. "Very strongly. You can't just outright say it can you?"
"Maybe you didn't hint enough," suggested Elizabeth.
Jilly was feeling cheated. "I kissed him," she revealed. "And as I said he's seen me naked and I've seen him too, I've been in bed with him. What's more he's told me I was very pretty which I know isn't quite true so I thought for sure he was trying to soften me up. Then, when we were locked up together and it all looked hopeless, I told him I didn't want to die a virgin and waited expectantly and all he did was propose."
"He proposed?" squeaked Helen.
"What did you say?" demanded Elisabeth.
Jilly looked at them and smiled. She opened her collar and reached behind her neck. She undid the clasp and pulled the chain up. "It has to stay a secret while we're still at school..." she said but the girls were staring at the ring.

Gillian Anne Ward née Jenkins. Duchess of Hallowfield. 1904-1992

Fortunate Tigers

The king settled himself on the throne. This was, admittedly, just the largest chair his staff could find in the country house they were now occupying. He looked around himself. He was surrounded by enough of his court to make matters official. He checked the official recorder was ready. He smiled at Tigers. He took a deep breath. "Bring in the prisoner," he said quietly. The Samurai nodded gravely.

The prisoner was a sorry sight. His feet were shackled so tightly that he could only shuffle in tiny steps, his hands were bound tightly behind his back and his robe was muddy and torn. He smiled amiably however. "Hello Dikki," he said to the king.

"Well Alharan the Priest," smiled the king lounging back on his throne, "We finally meet again and, at last, on my terms. You have been a pain to me these many years. I shall almost miss our meetings."

"Oh?" said the prisoner languidly, "Eh... You're going away?"

The king laughed. "Alharan you have been captured trying to infiltrate this castle. I am told you surrendered quite easily. So much for the great warrior priest. Now I am going to cut off your head."

"Try too," corrected the prisoner off handedly.

"Don't play with words. Your tongue is more trouble than your sword and I shall not listen to you today nor give in to your pleas for mercy." The king was annoyed but would not show it. "Today we shall end this business for good. I shall have your head displayed on the battlements as a warning to your followers."

"You've said that sort of thing before," said the prisoner languidly, "Nothing much ever came of it."

"You always had some hold over me before. I needed you to help me in something and you helped at a price that always made things come out other than I intended for all you prowess. Today..." he looked round, "Today I am master of this realm. I need no rescue and none of my family need rescuing. Today I shall deliver myself from you. I have learned well not to listen to you."

The prisoner chuckled. "Perhaps I was lucky but something always did come up didn't it? It got towards the end of that period that I hardly worried about the dangers of running into your men, which was good because I didn't want to hurt any of them, but I admit I did sometimes feel concerned about what escapade you would drag me into next."

The king sat back and folded his arms. "Relax old friend. Today I will burden you with no great task, there is no one to save and no awful problem or mystery to unravel. I have learned my lessons well and I am done with school."

"I think I'm still learning," replied the prisoner. "I assume you're flying

the banner of royal justice if you're doing the condemning today?"
"Of course," snapped the king looking at the quartermaster.
"Sir," the poor man replied. "You expressly instructed that your presence be kept secret. The flags are ready but we were awaiting your precise wishes on this matter."
The king sighed and picked up his fan and inspected it. "Yes," he said "See to it." The quartermaster left at a run hoping he had a banner of royal justice in the flag box. The king waited, probably aware of this and once he heard the feet rushing up the stairs he raised his eyes so everybody could continue.
"That's better," said the prisoner. "Things should be done properly shouldn't they?"
"It's not a problem now," said the king. "When you are out of the way we will mop up this peasant revolt in days. I know better than to show my hand too openly when you are involved."
"Yes," replied the prisoner. "That's why I had to find where you were. Hence my visit. Thank you for running up the flag. It sends the message for me. I told them to watch for it."
The king rolled his eyes. "You don't seem to realise what is happening. This is not like the previous times when I needed you. Today I am going to take great pleasure in watching your head cut off by my executioners who stand right now behind you. It might not remove the stupid smirk from your face, I think that is permanent by now, but it will, at least, stop you endless banalities."
"You flatter yourself Dikki. Stop behaving like the spoiled brat," the prisoner smiled a bit more. He had the manner of a man enjoying a conversation, over a drink, with old friends.
Before the king could reply a tall slim girl behind the throne burst forward. "You shall not speak to my father like that," she almost screamed. "He is the king and you are a... a mere commoner."
"Ah. This must be the daughter that I have heard about," the prisoner looked delighted, "Inherited the family arrogance I see."
"Correct Alharan," said the King. "This is Fortunate Tigers my daughter. She is pretty?"
"Pretty? Yes, certainly. But many would say that a sharp tongue like that needs taming. You have neglected your parental duties perhaps? Not an enviable task I think for some poor future son in law," the prisoner diverted.
"Yes," mused the king. "But where do I find her a husband? If I wed her to one of my junior lords that would only ferment division in the kingdom. What sort of husband do you want my dear?"
"I shall rejoice greatly in whom-so-ever my father the king chooses for me." Fortunate Tigers bowed deeply smiling.
The King shook his head. "I need somebody who does not aspire to my

throne," he suddenly laughed. "There is only one person who that fits that. Tigers! How would you like to be a widow?"

Fortunate Tigers hesitated then bowed again. The king looked past her and said "By my father's that's taken the smile of your face Alharan. What's the matter? Don't you like her? You always had an eye for a pretty girl."

The prisoner hesitated. "The offer of marriage to a royal princess is a weighty matter in the codes of chivalry," he said slowly.

"So you can't refuse without good reason?" The king laughed out loud. "We could have a wedding before the execution. She will make such a pretty widow. Marry my daughter Alharan and then I will cut off your head."

"Try too," he said again but the voice was weaker. He was decidedly hesitant this time.

Dikki smiled to himself. Here was the solution to many problems. Tigers could inherit his kingdom as a dowager queen but not as an unmarried princess. He felt satisfied with that. As a warrior he had often faced the prospect of furthering his own cause by his death and leaving his hard won kingdom to some adventurer seemed a waste. As the widow of a great, virtually mythical, lord such as Alharan the Priest, Tigers would out-rank almost any husband she cared to take to continue the succession. A good day had just become even better. He smiled again, well satisfied with his own cleverness.

A War Lord was dispatched to find a priest and the necessary gowns and trinkets for a wedding. A table and chairs were set and the king sat opposite his prisoner. Alharan's hands and feet were unbound and wine was set between them.

"I think we can simplify the whole matter of wedding gifts," said the king pouring a mug of wine and pushing it towards Alharan. "Weddings are too complicated. I'll give you a gift, call it the Dowry, and you give me a gift, the Bride Price. Then we have the wedding and finally we have a banquet to celebrate. Of course you won't be eating with us because you'll be on the roof as I promised earlier but that aside: What gift do you want from me?"

Alharan still looked troubled. "This is tiresome Dikki. Stop this game and try and cut off my head if you must. I have better things to do that play your silly tricks."

"Now, now," the king scolded. "Fortunate Tigers is getting dressed for her nuptials. We must not disappoint the poor girl. Choose your gift."

"Something along the lines of tax reductions and the disbanding of the standing army?" Alharan thought.

The king thought. "Well if I disband a lot of the army I won't need so much tax so that seems reasonable. It's getting to the planting season soon so a lot of them are murmuring that they want to go home anyway. Probably better that you don't ask for a thing as all you property will shortly go to your widow and Fortunate Tigers has too much clutter already. Now. What are you going to give me? Something magical I hope."

Alharan sighed. His fingers closed on his hand and a ring that nobody seemed to have noticed slid off his finger. "I have used this as a focus to marshal the forces I use to protect myself. It is a simple trick and I can now do it with my mind so the ring is redundant. It displaces me a fraction of an instant into the future and then diverts the things that come to me into the future to me. It keeps me safe because if something too powerful or too intrusive enters its field the time zone tears and the thing is not passed through. It may protect you from some assassins and that will keep the nation from civil war so I feel more than you will benefit from it."

"Words, words, words," sneered the king. "A magician's magic dies with him. So you're giving me a ring. I shall wear it as a memento of you. We had some good times together." He sat back and poured himself some more wine. "Do you remember the Dragon of Lin Por? Your insight that that old thief clan master Ju was not the dragon's servant but its master was the clue and when you recognised the dragon in the evening over the castle was a giant paper kite we had won."

Alharan paused then said "It was actually a hot air balloon but, although we used the fiction that you had slain the dragon to get the locals to assist us in rooting out Ju and his henchmen, I notice you have not seen the need to correct this."

"Too many witnesses saw me fire the arrow with your silver tip and then the dragon burst into flames and fell upon the castle. Who am I to disillusion them? It was a pretty sight though," he laughed.

"And the matter of Dance Ko?" asked Alharan.

The king looked down at his wine and his eyes saddened. "Yes," he said. "It is now two years since she died. She was my queen and all the others are just concubines. Fortunate Tigers is her daughter and so is my heir. I never loved anyone like her. There will not be another queen."

He looked up. "Alharan. She warned me against you. That I could always trust the words you say but never, never assume that you mean something when you do not specifically say it."

Alharan made a 'huh' noise and waited.

The king looked round but there was no sign of a priest or a bride so he continued. "Now. Tell me truly. What do you think of my daughter?"

Alharan drew a breath and radiated annoyance. "She deserves better treatment than you are giving her today. She is being good and obedient whilst you are being petulant and unfair to her. Why not let her make her own choice in this matter? Dance Ko chose you when you were penniless and foolish and waited five long years for you to finish the matter of the succession. That made a good strong relationship not this foolishness. What is the poor girl thinking now? And what will she think in years to come? You never fail to amaze me Dikki. You can always top the previously most stupid thing you have done."

The king laughed. "You will not rile me Alharan. This is a happy day for me. Should a father not rejoice on his daughter's wedding day? Especially if he is spared the rigours of a dowry. You know I like you. I even trust you, it is just that you always seem to oppose me, it's quite simple. With you around I will never get to rest because you will always want to improve me and get me to change things. Relax. I can see you are not really bothered about dying, you never have been. It's better this way. We have one last joke together, well I have told them to set you a place at dinner so that's the last joke, and then it's over."

Alharan snorted. "I've never had to worry about dying because I'm not planning on doing it yet and I certainly am not planning on doing it now. But this isn't a joke. Are you really going to ask your daughter, Dance Ko's daughter, to go through with a wedding and then watch her husband's execution? Don't you expect that she will have set a lot of hopes for the day of her wedding? A lot of fears too? How can you be so monstrously unkind?"

Dikki put his cup down. "What am I supposed to do then? Groom a young general as an heir and then present him to her to legitimise the succession? Please, I have more respect for my daughter than that. This way I give her the freedom to select a second husband without affecting her status. She will be a dowager queen when I, er, move from the palace to the royal mausoleum. Once established she can pick any pretty boy she fancies as a consort. I have not fought to regain my father's kingdom just to pass it on to some fool. Fortunate Tigers will be my heir and I do believe she will actually do quite well."

"Dikki. I've always liked you and I've always put up with your idiosyncrasies but this one has to be the stupidest yet. We've played the 'but next time I will kill you Alharan' game for too many years for you to seriously expect to get away with it now." The priest seemed cross in a mild manner. "Don't drag this poor girl into your games and complicate her life with a husband who, be he living or dead, gives her a very strange status. She is a royal princess and that is hard enough to bear. Let the poor kid at least have some semblance of a courtship and a choice. Dance Ko chose you and waited for you for many years while you followed through with your destiny as the rightful heir. She made, I sometimes feel, a poor choice but she was allowed to make it and to stick by it. Why should Fortunate Tigers be married off just to suit your delusions of dynastic pride. Remember. You only have to count back six generations and it was your family who were the bandits."

"Don't worry old friend," the king laughed. "It won't be for long and by supper time she will be quite over it. She's not what you'd call a very gentle soul so I doubt if she will worry over long. You saw how she reacted to you when you insulted me. Her heart is on the right side and she will appreciate what I, what we, are doing for her today. I'm sure she will wear the appropriate mourning garments for the appropriate time, she's quite good on protocol." He paused. "And don't you worry. You will not have to put up with it at all. You will miss the whole show. I know how you hate that sort of thing." He looked round again and finally saw what he wanted. "Look. The priest is here. Tigers must be ready so we must go. Now. You will not misbehave and upset the priest or Tigers will you?"

"I know how to maintain dignity and religious reverence. A royal wedding is a very auspicious event even if the Father of the bride is determined to undermine it."

The wedding was simple and performed with relative dexterity and skill by a priest found in a cell and suddenly called upon to serve the king. He was more concerned when he discovered who the bride-groom was than the bride. He very carefully laboured the free consent declarations and waited over long in case there was a denial but in the end he pronounced the conjugal blessing and presented the newly married couple to the King as senior witness.

Dikki put his hand out sideways and the requisite gold coins landed in it. He gratefully paid his offering and then instructed that the priest be taken to the door and sent off the premises. The old priest bobbed and bobbed in thanks, then turned, bowed deeply from the waist to the man he had just married and then ran.

"And now my son in law. What now?" the king asked.

Alharan bowed. "Most illustrious and regal father in law. Perhaps I might take ten minutes to talk with my wife before you move on to further matters. It would be hardly be proper to miss the opportunity to introduce myself."

The king waved. "If you assure me you will not attempt to escape you may sit at that far table and the musicians will play for us hence you will have total privacy to talk. I shall be generous: you may have one quarter of an hour."

"The king is generous. I had no intention of leaving," Alharan bowed.

Fortunate Tigers sat demurely. Alharan sat opposite her. He waited till the music started. "You are beautiful," he said, "And you have conducted yourself admirably whilst your father has not been overly kind to you this day."

She took a deep breath. "He means well. I think he actually likes you but feels you are a challenge to him. He hates things like that."
Alharan chuckled slightly. "He always has and probably always will. That's why he needs people like me to remind him that he is just a man like every other or he will start to make a god of himself. He who is the creator of all things does not willingly tolerate that from men."
"Are you not worried?" she asked. "You talk about the gods as if you had a long life to contemplate."
"I have taken a long life contemplating. I have chosen to serve the one god, or perhaps he has chosen me. I have a duty to this whole world and if I am called to serve here then so I shall. I do not believe I am called to die here today so I do not worry about it."
"I don't think he is going to change his mind now," said Fortunate Tigers. "He would lose face and that is not what he thinks being a king is all about. If you want to save your head you need to escape now."
"What?" Alharan looked genuinely shocked. "Run away and abandon my newly wed wife? Even a peasant has more honour."
"You would willingly die to satisfy an honour debt?"
"Certainly. But as I have said I do not plan to die here today. I have other things to do."
"I fear that that is not what my father plans."
"Certainly. However he has agreed to disband his major army, he has agreed to reduce the stupid levels of tax that caused the stoning of tax collectors in the first place. These are not things he had planned to do when he got up this morning but he will keep his promises because that is what he does. He will not need reminding to issue the orders and to check that they have been obeyed. That is a bigger change than any of the officials here expected. Since that is what I have been trying to get him to do for the last six months today must rate as a success. I am sure that deep inside he knows that I have always acted honourably towards him and his family and that if he did cut off my head it would be a most impolite act towards an old comrade in arms."
"He often spoke of you and I knew he felt you were impolite yourself in that you always oppose him in matters of policy and yet in matters of the defence of the kingdom or of the people you were always a close ally."
"We represent the two different sources of authority in the land. The secular and the spiritual. Without just kings and the enforcement of laws no man nor woman is safe and that is the first freedom. But without somebody to teach righteousness and to rebuke sin what benefit is freedom from fear? You are born, you work long years and then you die. What benefit is there for a peasant in his years of toil or what benefit to a princess in her years of enforced idleness if they come to the same end? Without a spiritual guide to point them in the

direction of righteousness their lives become pointless. I cannot teach without stability for it is hard to call a man or woman to consider their soul if they fear for their life but can a man say that a full belly is all there is to hope for?"

"When my mother died I saw my father at prayer," said Tigers softly. "He did not know I saw him but I know he wrestled and finally made peace with his soul. He has never been the same since. He is less careless and he worries more when he sits in judgement. So much so that today he is almost out of character. Perhaps he finds you as a man does an old friend and remembers the days of his youth. He lives for a moment as the youth he once was."

"You see much for one so young," he nodded.

"In the palace the food is assured but most other things are at risk day by day. I know that three times men have tried to kill my father and each time, although he was saved, people that I knew died. A peasant knows that a bad harvest may cost him his life but a princess will get no warning. I have read and I have studied. My father says I am old with books but I fear at times that I know so little."

"You have read the 'Book of Dragons'?"

"A bit. It is hard because it makes you think about yourself rather than just teaching you."

"That is what we intended. That it teaches you about yourself. That we could not write because we could not know all our readers."

"You wrote this? But it is anonymous."

"When you finish it re-read the dedication. You will then understand what it says. If you have read the first part then you will have considered the problem of conscience?"

"That even the wicked man agrees what is wrong? That there may be no honour amongst thieves but when betrayed they feel aggrieved and think of vengeance?"

"Yes, and that a king and a princess are no less bound to do what is right than is a priest?"

"I always feel we have more scope for good or evil."

"Not really. Good and evil are practised in your daily living or they are not practised at all. Yes, you can have more consequences with your actions but not even the poorest slave is able to say my poverty makes me righteous nor that my master's wealth makes him evil."

"Evil is a matter of the intentions then?"

"Motives. It is sad to see a person do the wrong thing for the right motives but they are the simplest person to correct. When you see an evil person doing good out of malice then you expect the turn to come shortly. What I hoped you had learned from that book is to feed and care for your conscience. Your father will try to make you adopt his view of the kingship and if you are to be the queen after him you need to distinguish clearly between what is right for you and what is right for the kingdom."

"You are trying to improve me now?"

"You are my wife. Should not a dutiful husband take pains to see his wife best equipped for the life she is to lead? Has your father done less?"

"You are my husband. I have not really got used to this idea yet. Oh dear. I will not get time to grasp it fully before it is over. I will try to remember what you say so I can be dutiful to your memory. Perhaps knowing that I shall read your book careful will be more comforting to you than knowing that I shall do the formal mourning."

"Mourning is only to comfort the bereaved. The dead have more pressing things to do I am sure. They are entering into a whole new experience of being. We can hardly guess as to what it is like. Certainly the folk tales of heaven are just pictures as we tell tales of foreign lands to children. The real thing will be far beyond our imagination."

"But I shall mourn. Because you deserve it. You have been a great companion to my father in the times of his greatest need. He speaks often of you with honour."

"I shall take that as a sincere promise but it is not my intention that you be called upon to do it. As I have said your father is an old friend and we share many ideals. I am pleased to find them now in you for when you first introduced yourself I had sad visions of a petulant brat."

Tigers chuckled. "And now that petulant brat is your devoted wife. Your only wife?"

"I have no other wife. I have not even considered the prospect for several decades. I am somewhat taken aback by the course of events. I am usually well able to predict what is to happen but I had not considered this as even a possibility and even if I had I would not have calculated it as probable. Dikki, as ever, always manages to amaze me. It will take me a day or two to come to some clear plans. You must forgive me if I seem a trifle distant at moments but I must think things through."

"Perhaps it is your turn to read 'The Light of Sunset'," Tigers offered. "Unless you wrote that too."

A grin passed over the priest's face. "No," he said. "I visited Silumi long after he completed that work but I was entertained by his fellow monks and he just sat silently and smiled at us all. He had an air of peace to him. The book was just another expression of that. It's hard to explain."

"You are old," said Tigers. "I don't doubt you because my father said you were about in his father's days and you never changed. Do you know the writer of every book in the library?"

Alharan shook his head. "The imperial library is considered vast as it consists of several hundred volumes and yet in my travels across this world I have read many thousand. You must never forget the labour that goes into a book. Not just the time to compose the thoughts into words but the time taken to transcribe the first copy and then the long hours of the copyist to make further volumes. Any book is a thing of huge cost and I strive to read and record every one that I come across. If a thought is worth the cost of writing then it is worth the cost of reading even if I may disagree with it."

"Are there many thousand books?" she was genuinely surprised. "Is there wealth enough to buy them?"

"There are libraries and personal collections. I have always made it my business to both search out the books that are written and to direct those that have the ability to either take down their thought or those of their masters and present them clearly. Others I get to chronicle the events. Your father, I believe, has made a full court record of his father's betrayal and his own flight then his struggle to rebuild the kingdom. I have dropped in occasionally and read large parts of this. It is good."

"I read some of it too and I also heard him dictating. When I realised who you were I was cross with you because I always felt that you were unfair to him. I could see how he rather liked you and you always cheated him of the final victory."

"I never did. Perhaps I stopped him making a fool of himself in some silly or spectacular gesture but when did we ever fail to win? He sometimes could not tell the victim from the villain. The average foot soldier was not asked what side he wanted to fight on, he doesn't want to fight, he only kills because the alternative is to be killed. You should not kill the troops and spare the chief who expects to shed everybody's blood but his own."

Fortunate Tigers took a deep breath and composed herself. This was getting too metaphysical for her. She picked a previous remark and turned the conversation to surer ground. "You said I was beautiful. They say you never lie."

"Why should I lie? There was no requirement for me to make any remark but it is true and I judged that you would be reassured by it."

"What would you do if you escaped the executioner?"

"Well," Alharan pondered. "I have a problem in that I have lived for many years as a monk in the On monastery. Although I have not taken their vows they currently honour me, somewhat against my advice, as the Abbot. I could hardly return to a celibate community and bring my wife. It would probably be frowned upon. Perhaps I would have to press my worthy father-in-law to allow me the use of one of his many houses."

"We could go to Deep Min Sha. I have many happy memories of it as a child. It was our summer home." Her eyes softened with her voice.

"Did you find the secret bower at the end of the stone garden?" He asked playfully.

Fortunate Tigers almost jumped. "Where you duck down? How do you know about it?" she asked.

"I laid out the designs for that house and its gardens. Come on, it is my crest over the main door so it's pretty obvious. It is nice to plan little surprises into places. They add to the delight. There must be order and certainty but there must be fun too. Did you find the little room through the tapestry wall in the main hall?"

She leaned towards him and asked "What? The jade dragon tapestry?"

"You press the dragon's nose and the door opens. It's just a tiny room intended only for children to play in. I thought it would be obvious as if you count the windows on the north side there are thirteen but you can only find twelve in the house. I had to put the window in or the gap would have given it away at once."

"I never knew that. A secret room. I would have loved that. If I ever have children I shall be sure to take them back there and let them play in a secret room." Her face suddenly fell. "But perhaps I may never have children."

"Well you have a husband now and that is a start." Alharan answered gently.

Fortunate Tigers sniffed. "When they first brought you in I would have laughed to see them cut off your head but now it is going to upset me. How much longer have we got? I want to remember you because you're really quite nice and it always seems sad if somebody dies and everybody forgets them. When my nurse died I was ever so sad and on the anniversary I wanted to make a gift at the shrine but everyone said I was silly and to forget her."

"Comita Didan?"

Tears started in Fortunate Tigers' eyes. "Yes. How did you know that?"

"She was your mother's nurse too. We brought her up from Tarapi when your father and I destroyed the pirate strong hold on the cliffs. You father was hurt, quite badly, and we had to care for him for three weeks. He was the most intolerable patient ever. He would have been better in half the time if he could just understand what the words 'rest' and 'relax' meant."

Tigers sighed. "Tell me... Tell me about my mother. Everybody talks about my father but I am sure there is so much I could learn from her. She never spoke of those times."

Alharan sat back and looked at the ceiling. "Where to start?" he ruminated.

"Your mother was the eldest daughter of a local chieftain and was not particularly well educated but her nurse, Comita, taught her the stories and parables so she had a well developed moral code. To keep the story to the point as we haven't much time at the age of ten she was promised to son of a local warlord, your father, and she took the arranged marriage very seriously and started to discover everything she could about him and his family."

"I won't go into the details of your father's place in the local rules of inheritance because you must have read up on it already but when his father was assassinated I lifted him from the palace and placed him with a family, a retired knight so it was not quite as simple a home as Dikki makes out, and they brought him up, trained and educated him. He was about fourteen then and your mother was thirteen."
"I made sure he was tutored with books as well as arms and he is more accomplished than he cares to admit. He is quite a musician and worse poets are well remembered. I suspect that he thinks these are unmanly graces and practices them alone or only with those he trusts."
"I knew about your mother so I went to the Castle Dance shortly after I had place him in safety and explained. I had not realised at that point how involved she was in the idea of him. As they had never met I assumed she would be rather indifferent."
"You father was an angry young man and studied war and weapons hard. I dropped in occasionally and sparred with him to quench his ego but it was quite obvious he was good but needed guidance. I decided to let him run out as a Samurai knight and do a bit of seeing that other people have been wronged too. This also meant he could practice his fighting on bandits and murderers before facing properly trained fighters."
"It was about this point that your mother's family decided that she would be better wed than waiting so they found another prospective groom and she just up and ran away when she heard. Be careful, your pedigree on impulsive behaviour is strong. Thankfully Comita had people contact me and I found her before she discovered the truth about the world being an evil place for a young girl alone and I made her promise never to tell her origins without my permission. Then I had to get back to sorting Dikki out so she came along."
"So there was I with a hot headed young knightlet with a head full of honour and idealism trying to prove he could right very wrong in the world and a sixteen year old girl who thought him an idiot but he was her idiot. Well the long and the short of it is that we stomped round the country righting a proportion of wrongs and slowly pushing some idea of what could and what could not be accomplished into their heads. Looking back on it I'd say it was fun but it certainly didn't seem like it at the time."
Tigers interrupted "Is the story of the blindfold fight true?"
"That I had Dikki blindfold me to fight the champion of Titoran? Of

course it is. The trick was that they had beams of light to flash in the face of the challenger at key moments so they would be distracted while the champion knew the signals and could see when his opponent's face lit up. The blindfold simply meant that I was spared the distraction and fought with my other senses. It had the added benefit of making the whole trick the thing of myth. How do you distract a man who cannot see? It gives us an edge in people's minds and they forget that we are three adventurers in a court of a hundred fighting men. I have a trick where I cut arrows out of the air which is great if you concentrate on me and forget to shoot at my friends. Nine tenths of a battle is getting inside your enemy's head, once you have done that cutting it off is a mere formality."

"The story you won't hear told is when I had Ko and Dikki dress up as a minstrel and a tumbler and infiltrate a stockade fort. I wouldn't let Dikki take a weapon in case he started something and he had to find the captive we were there to rescue and lower both her and Ko down the walls then fire the place and run for it. I made him shave his beard, which wasn't very much at the time, and dressed him as a woman. He was, apparently, propositioned by a very drunk Sergeant. Ko thought it the funniest thing ever and Dikki has refused to ever talk about it again."

"Anyhow. Back to your mother. I like to think she was horrified to see this was her betrothed but, although she knew who he was, she obeyed me and never told him. In fact I'm not sure she ever told him that she was his childhood arraigned bride. Anyway for the next six years they argued, threw temper tantrums, fell in love and threw worse temper tantrums. If there was a problem they fought side by side and when there wasn't one they invented one and fought each other. All in all it looked like a good relationship because once it became clear that Dikki was generating the kind of local support to retake and to hold his father throne I knew they would never have a quiet life."

"But that's awful," said Tigers visible offended. "I always thought she was so supportive."

"And how would you support somebody like your father?" Alharan was smiling. "You cheer him on heartily when he is right and kick him hard when he is wrong."

"Oh," Tigers put her hands in her lap smiling. "Maybe I only saw one bit."

Alharan shrugged "She would not kick him publicly, she had more sense than that. However I got on the wrong end of her tongue on more than one occasion and you know when you've been kicked."

"To be frank I trusted them both. They were a good team and, for all the bickering, they needed and supported one another. Dikki is smarter than he thinks and needs somebody to agree with him. Too often he had been with me and my gifts gave me insight I could not explain so I could be right when to his eyes I couldn't know yet. It makes him cautious which curbed his hothead nature. Caution is good in a king but sometimes he needed Ko to tell him to act now."

"So..." said Tigers leaning forward. "Is this what you plan for me?"

He put his elbows on the table and chuckled. "If you need kicking or telling to act I hope you will listen to my words. I think your father is aware that his age is catching up with him and you will soon succeed. The kingdom is ten times more stable now than in the days of his father and, probably, ten times as big although the borders were pretty nebulous in those days so it's hard to be definite. I would have not planned to marry you to act as your guide but it has now happened and we can make a good thing of it. Perhaps your father has done exactly the right thing for the kingdom even though he will deny it strenuously."

"I am," admitted Tigers. "A bit scared at the prospect of inheriting. My father has been going to select me a husband for several years now and I am now seventeen by which age royal princesses are safely betrothed if not already married. I feel I need a strong husband to stand by me or all my training, studies and my father's guidance will all come to nothing."

He looked at her puzzled. "But you have a husband. You have Alharan the priest. Who, in the House of Kia Murama See, is going to forget who I am and what I can do in the defence of a cause I judge to be right? I like the way my reputation goes before me as it keeps me from having to fight. Even when I climbed in the back window here I was pretty sure that I would be recognised and nobody would do anything rash and get hurt. I don't want to hurt anybody in this kingdom. I spent enough time trying to get it back into Dikki's hands. That's why I carried a staff not a sword. I know the way to bang a man on the head so he wakes up in an hour with a headache but is none the worse for it. I've done it to your father twice and I'm sure that tale isn't in his annuls either."

"I have strong views on morality," he continued. "And the conduct of husbands is an issue I think is not taken seriously enough locally. Some men treat their slaves better than their wives and, although I have knocked a man on the head to remind him that a slave is a person and deserves the respect due to any person, a wife should be honoured. Consider it a work in progress."

They were leaning closer and closer to maintain the confidentiality of their words and finally their foreheads touched. For a moment Tigers drew back and then after a moments consideration she gently touched him again. Alharan moved his hands towards her, palms up and she took them. "You would be a fine husband," she sighed. "You would be kind and never beat me unless I deserved it or unless you were very

drunk."
"I do not drink intoxicants if I can help it and when I must they have little effect on me. I have only beaten a woman four times in my whole long life and only then because they had chosen to fight as a man and it was a preferred course to killing them. I hope I am a fine husband. Do not write me off yet. We have had the ten minutes I asked for but we still have the extra five your father granted us."
She squeezed his hands. "If we had another ten minutes I would probably fall in love with you as Mia did Suki in the story. However that would hardly be becoming of a royal princess. We marry to make great alliances not for personal notions."
"Oh?" he asked. "Now am I not a great alliance? You have drawn Alharan the Priest into the royal house of Kia Murama See. You are the heir and you shall bear the future heir. Am I to have that great honour that my daughter shall be queen after you?"
"A son would be a better move," laughed Fortunate Tigers. "Alas we have so little time. How strange to be a virgin and a widow. Has this ever happened before?"
Alharan sighed. "I have heard tales but never met one except for a young girl given to an old king to nurse him and wed to him to counter any scandal. She was sadly misused by her step-sons when her husband died. Her status as one of the King's widows meant that she could not remarry anyone but a royal and they were all her step-sons. She did not lead a happy life."
"Do you think I will be happy?" asked Fortunate Tigers.
Their eyes locked. "I will do everything in my power to ensure it," he said. "I take promises very seriously and in marriage I have promised very much."
Fortunate Tigers glanced around and leaned forward. "You look at me as my father did when I was little. It was the way he looked at my mother. Surely you cannot feel anything for me? My father is playing with you and will kill you."
Alharan smiled. "I have just made promises before the priest and the people and so have you. If the accidents of fate give me five minutes or five decades to live with you am I absolved from those promises by your fathers actions? Anyway. He is an old friend and for all his bluster and banter I wish him no harm. After all. Should a man not respect his father in law?"
"If you're hoping I'll try to persuade him to stop you don't know him that well," she pointed out.
"Certainly not. He'd just get cross and shout a lot. He's like that. Put a knife to his throat and demand that he renounce his kingdom and he would smile and say that it is better to die a king than to live as a coward but tell him he can't have a beer just when he wants one and

you'd think he had bees in his hair."
She laughed. "So you do know him then. I'm almost sorry I'm not going to get time to get to know you better."
"Well tell me about my wife. I was first introduced to a girl who shouted at me because I was insulting her father. Now I discover she is dutiful and concerned to do the right thing. I admit I like the later rather than the former but I begin to see now how they are the same person."
Tigers focused on infinity for a moment and then looked at him sternly.
"I was born at Pep Lee and stayed there, I am told, until I was five. You don't realise you are different when you are little but my mother insisted that I always had friends of my age to play with and to be schooled in their company. What I did notice though was that my father had Comita take me into a large room where he either sat quietly and smiled at people or he shouted at them. It was very boring and none of my friends had to do it. I thought it most unfair."
"I don't remember my mother ever being very well but she did her part in running the various Palaces that we lived at. There was a sort of fiction that I didn't know about the concubines but my mother selected them and they were always very pretty, very sweet and very very dumb. My father was quite happy with that. My role model was to be like a concubine but smart because that is what I thought a good wife would be. I knew I was going to be a wife not a hand maiden as by the time I was old enough to know the difference I knew what a princess was too. I did rather think there would be a son to be king because that is how it is supposed to happen but it didn't."
"Your mother controlled what Concubines went in to your father?"
"It's a matter of timing. I have the rules noted down. It was my father's choice too. I think some of the girls were disappointed. I have a retired concubine running the system now. She's smart enough to keep the notes and do the timing but not smart enough to be tempted astray."
"He trusts you? That is a good sign. Dikki always was a good judge of character. In fact I remember him telling me that if we ever met somebody just like him to distrust them at once and kill them as soon as possible."
"If you had killed him then you would not be in this place now."
"You are right but he would not have sired a beautiful daughter for me to marry. Please continue. I like what I'm hearing."
"You are kind... and I see that it is more than the usual politeness I get from the Palace staff and the courtiers."
Alharan just smiled.
"Well growing up... I learnt to read. I learnt the major local languages. I have read about foreign countries although I have only ever travelled with my father and then not to really foreign places just about our kingdom. I have read religion and metaphysics. I've read some magic

but it doesn't really make much sense. Most of it is statements from evil men who were caught and made lengthy statements to try and save their necks from the executioner. A real magician just wouldn't be caught."

Alharan chuckled and she stopped looking flustered. "I'm sorry," she gasped. "I didn't mean it like that. You're obviously not an evil magician and you chose to be captured. You said that and I respect it even if I don't understand it."

"What do you remember of your mother. She was an old friend and I was sad when I heard she died."

Tigers paused. "Well it's hard to describe her. When she was here she was always here. Having her was normal. You don't realise how special somebody was until you don't have them any more."

"Any favourite memories?"

"Holidays mainly. Those times when she had my father to herself and he stopped being king with all the problems and tasks that brings. Playing on the floor with my father, she was never well enough for that, and snuggling up between them when I was tiny. Feeling them close and together. I felt safe there. Like nowhere I have ever been since. It might be that I just didn't understand things at that age but it always comes to my mind as a happy time."

"You're not happy now?"

"I am happy I suppose but I confess I'm not confident. I trust my father to make the best possible arrangements for me but my future must contain his... his death and then I will be so alone. Alone with responsibilities. Alone with all these people needing me to be right when I know so little."

She sniffed. "Remember I'm not like my father. He has lived the life of a king but also of a poor man, also a merchant, also a farmer and also even a bandit. He knows what people are like, what they need, what is justice to them. I read the laws and do not understand what is behind them. There are laws prohibiting stuff that only wild beasts would do and laws to make restitution in families that have torn themselves apart. How am I, a simple princess who's world comes out of books to rule them?"

"There are worse ways to start than books. They do enable you to cover a great deal of ground is a short space of time. Keep reading. You will find the stories and parables of your childhood also tell your heart what is right and what is wrong."

"Well I have studied. I have watched. I have tried to understand. I think the biggest watershed in our lives was the deaths of first Comita and then my mother. One year robbed me of my childhood nurse and teacher and then of the only person I felt could protect me. I know my father worries about my safety but he is making a mistake in trailing me round behind him with his army. I'm sure I could be adequately guarded at home and this idea complicates his plans and his life enormously. I am sure the army would be in fields under canvas rather than gathered round this old house if he were not trying to offer me some semblance of a home."

"It was convenient from my point of view. Rather than fighting skirmishes and having people get hurt we just needed to remove bridges and flood fields. He slows himself down so much."

"He sets great store by having supplies coming in. He said he never fought his best unless he was a little hungry but very hungry didn't work."

"He pays his men on time?"

"Half in hand and half on account for when they leave to go home. As most of them have either fought for him before or have friends who have they seem to trust him on that."

"I'm impressed. He did listen to some of the things I told him. We will make a psychologist of him yet."

"A what?"

"Somebody who understands people's minds."

"That is him isn't it? Normally he can take an enemy at the first battle because they never expect him and then they do the wrong thing because he has plans for them. He has found these last few weeks most frustrating because every time he laid a trap you weren't there. You understand men's minds too I perceive."

"It is my speciality. That and making people better themselves. Dikki is one of my favourite pupils because he has never realised he is a pupil." She smiled. "He would hate that. I would love to learn war under a master but he would worry about how people saw him. He feels he should know not be asking for directions."

"I wasn't offering war, just bettering yourself. It's the harder one of the two."

"Back to your Book of Dragons?"

"In part. Now you are my wife so you obviously get the personalised treatment."

"That's wonderful. I'll look forward..." Suddenly Tiger's smile collapsed and she dropped her face on her hands. "I'm sorry. I've done it again. That was a most inconsiderate thing for me to say considering you present predicament. I do apologise my most gentle and wonderful husband."

They suddenly noticed that the musicians had stopped playing. They looked up and felt the eyes of everyone on them.

They stood and Fortunate Tigers walked round to Alharan's side and took his hand. "Don't say anything to me now or I shall burst into tears," she hissed. "Just hold my hand as long as you can."

"Sir," said the executioner, somewhat confused for a protocol at being called to execute the King's new son in law especially when everybody was being so friendly. "Your hands should be bound behind you."
"Shall I just clasp them like this?" asked the victim linking his hands behind his back. "It might save time and trouble."
"Er. Thank you Sir. I'm sure that will do. Would you please kneel?" He was anxious to move on.
The executioner was a master of his craft. He checked the prisoner was in position then felt the back of his neck for the position of the vertebrae. He placed two hands on the sword, he rolled it slowly back over his head and looked at the king. On the nod the blade snapped over and down and came to rest in the little hardwood block he had placed on the stone floor to protect the edge of the blade.
"Missed," said Alharan. "Do you want to try again or give up now?"
"Again," shouted the king. The second attempt was no better.
The prisoner sat back on his heels and looked at the king.
"An explanation?" asked Dikki slowly.
"I have already told you," Alharan's smile was back.
"Perhaps I missed it," so was Dikki's impatience.
"You are wearing the ring I gave you?"
The king held up his hand.
"Then take a cloak pin," said Alharan. "And try to pierce your finger so it draws blood."
The king held out his hand and said "Su Shi." The Samurai Lord standing next to him removed the clasp from his shoulder and passed it to the king who pressed it against his forefinger.
"By my ancestors," he whispered. "I felt a moments pain and then it glided through. Look it is sticking out the other side and I don't feel more than a touch. And it slides sideways and the skin closes behind it without a mark. Would this ring save my neck from the executioner's sword also?"
"Yes," said Alharan. He smiled and added, "Is that a direct enough answer for you to save you insisting to try it and scaring the poor man to death?"
"Your 'yes' is sufficient. I don't think I need to test it," said the king pushing an ornate dagger through the palm of his hand. "This ring truly is a gift worthy of a king's daughter."
"Yes. I could have done with it on several occasions when we were together before but it's a new trick. Anyway. The throne was yours by right of birth and then by right of conquest when you displaced those that killed your father," said Alharan. "It should be a peaceful realm and with less army you would have less suspicious neighbours and with less taxes you would have fewer stoned tax collectors. You really need

to plan to live a peaceful old age Dikki. You are not the young blood you once were."

"You're trying to improve me again," Dikki sat back laughing. "I would have thought that you, the old pragmatist, would have given that one up years ago. The trouble is that you're right. We all get old, even you, and we have to make plans for the days that come after us." He sat forward. "And you seem to have reworked my original scheme for Tigers to inherit simply so now I have to admit gracefully that you have outsmarted me again or do I decide that I have finally outsmarted you in that, because of your tenacious honour code, you are now my lawful son in law and, would you believe it, my lawful subject."

"Don't expect to push that one too far," said the priest firmly.

"Oh no," said Dikki stroking his beard. "But it has got to be worth something or you wouldn't have wilted quite so much when I suggested it. I suppose I could use you as a negotiator with Vern up the coast. Yes. He'd have to listen to you and as my son in law you could agree a deal without needing to run back and forth. You'd preserve my honour because that's what you care about and frankly I don't care what deal you do because I'm sick to death of the whole business. There's one. I wonder what else I can use you for?"

"I don't mind doing a few runs like that but I would not expect to take over your whole diplomatic efforts. Be serious. Anyhow. I thought a newly married man was supposed to get a holiday?"

"Sorry Alharan. Duty calls. It's an onerous life running a kingdom and power carries responsibility. Well I wonder who told me that? Couldn't be somebody near here at the moment could it? My memory is getting poor. I must be getting old. I'm afraid I will have to use my son in law to carry some of the load. There are too many people in the kingdom who would suffer if it all goes wrong. Oh well. That's life."

"If I am going to have to put up with you then do I still get the deal we agreed?"

"By my father's yes. If Alharan the Priest is running the diplomatic side I probably barely need a bodyguard let alone an army. When did we ever fail together? Even the bandits will pay their taxes and think it's a better deal than the chance we will come looking for them. I like it. This will be fun. This will be the best of old times and you won't give me much trouble because you must respect me."

"We can perhaps come to some sort of an understanding. Be serious though."

"Come on Alharan. We have a banquet set. We shall eat together and try to resolve our remaining differences over food and good wine." The King stood grasped Alharan's shoulder and pushed him towards the great hall.

"Excuse me?" said a voice behind them. They stopped and looked

round.
"What about me?" asked Fortunate Tigers, her hands on her hips.
The two men turned and looked back at her and then at one another. They smiled then they stepped back and stood beside her. Each linked her arm, her father on the left and her husband on the right.
"To the wedding feast," said Dikki starting forward with an arm stretched out in an extravagant gesture.

Dizzy & Flipper

"I don't really see why you are worrying about these Americans," pointed out Alacia. "It was the British team that stood the best chance of recognising us before time."

Alharan pulled a face that implied 'Yes but'. He waited till he knew he had the whole group waiting for him. "Yes but," he said "The British were largely running their search for aliens on Earth on intuition and guesswork and, because they did not know how to quantify these methods, they never would supply proof positive to their thinking so their political masters did not keep authorising the funds. These Americans however, who are following the lost cause of trying to detect us with technology, where we can eat them alive, just happen to have two of the best intuitive people I have ever seen. They believe in the technology. Yes. Moreover they believe in their technology and they will keep going and they could just get to the right answer despite the fact what they think they are doing is actually impossible."

Betron laughed. "All the facts may be there but provided we keep providing them with false leads they will keep up the UFO search. Take that incident last year when they tried to cover up the crash of the anti-missile balloon platform. We have now destroyed most of the records of the launch so with time it will look more and more suspicious. It is wonderful what you can manage by just adding a little 'Confidential: shred this duplicate copy when out of date' sticker to a file. Maybe one day we should actually fake a real UFO sighting as they seem to be so very effective."

Alharan offered a forced smile. "I don't think that will ever be necessary as the imagined ones are far more fanciful than anything we could dare. I trust we are keeping good documentation as I would hate to be accused of tampering with the historical record on this matter at the end of the project. Remember that, regardless of the inconvenience, researching the existence of alien life visiting Earth is a valid scientific goal. Nothing gets shredded at our behest we have not copied. That aside, who is going to suggest a solution to the problem of Lernski and Henderson? Alacia wants to shoot them or at least stop them abruptly and Betron wants to recruit them, either way will work I suppose but I would prefer to deflect them gently but in a way that ensures they stay very deflected." He looked round hopefully.

Betron grimaced. "We successfully infiltrated the British team and that was very effective. Shall we just do that again?"

A general air of discomfort moved around the meeting. Betron moved to defend his position. "I know that none of us were happy about reaching the key team workers through their children but it was an

insightful plan and brilliant in execution. It also used mere weeks of staff time rather than the months we anticipated it would take and it very effectively ended a problem that was causing serious difficulties." Alacia looked at the documents before her. "Two daughters this time," She noted. "But who is going to do it? Are you offering to try Betron? You are unattached. Do you fancy being a little girl for a few weeks?" Betron sat back and waved his hands. "No. Not me. Beyond me. This is state of the art stuff especially with our strict rules of engagement for children. Only one touch is light enough."
Alharan sighed as everybody looked at him. "Using the same parameters," he asked, "what is the minimum change we need? How little could I get away with?"
"Two girls..." said Betron poking at the computer pad in front of him. "Would you go as a girl?"
"I doubt I could manage that," muttered Alharan. "My CD2 rating would bottom out and I would be next to useless. Try me as an interesting friend."
"You'd have to be more involved than that, they're mid teens. I'll use your AW profile as that seemed acceptable most places. It's a good match. Magic. Wow. Hey. Look at this," Betron was sat back looking at the computer pad. Alacia stood up and looked over his shoulder. She smiled. The others took her lead and gathered round. They were impressed.
"Oh dear," said Alharan as he looked. "Why do I always get the excitable ones?"
"Oh come on, it's a 95 percent hit for four weeks work and they are very nice girls," said Alacia reading the symbol codes for personality. "I can see that and I'm just an amateur at this stuff. You just think that any woman that matrixes with you with a positive delta-two is a man eater. Just relax, be nice to them and they'll eat out of your hand. When do you ever fail to make a good impression? Will you do it?"
Alharan sat down. "Oh all right. I'll do it but it's hard. I don't want to mess anybody about emotionally and I don't want to get all jangled up again. Remember I'm Varhyn, I hurt as easily as they do. I am, so to speak, an easily eaten man. Come on then. Let's do the sums. Can we convert a 95 percent on the estimator into a concrete set of actions or is it just Betron's fictional multipliers again?"
By the end of the meeting they had a plan and, as the group broke up to go and put the first phases into operation, Alacia stopped Alharan at the door.
"Is this really ethical?" she asked. "Children again?"
"You were pushing it so how come you ask now?" he replied slowly. She waited and said nothing.
"I think so," He added and paused. "Well it is more ethical than the

alternatives. I prefer misdirection to out and out misinformation but children always complicate matters. Perhaps you had better put some mechanisms in place to ensure that, whatever happens, neither the girls nor their parents are harmed. Oh. And ride along with me when we get to the critical bit. It helps to have somebody to talk too who does not have to get clearance for things. If you are talking to me and we are jointly issuing orders then nobody, math team or military, says 'but'. However, do not tell the rest of the team we're doing it that way. I want them to stay cautious."

"He looks good I admit," said Bill Henderson as he browsed back down the resume. "There is just something nagging me about him. What do you think?"
Ben Lernski shook his head and said "Well I did wonder if he was a bit too good to be true but when we first approached him he turned us down flat. It wasn't a matter of money just the principle of the thing. He would not leave his current position. I actually took that as done until I heard that they were closing his project and realised he was soon to be out of a job. I just got back in quickly with a provisional offer but he is still not taken with the idea of moving away from his larger family, he has a wife and a sixteen year old boy. Moving from the British Midlands to Montana, away from uncles, aunts and grandparents and such was not what he had planned."
"Oh come on," said Bill. "Pomona is a major town not some truck stop in the hills. We have a school, a hospital, cinema, restaurants. He doesn't have to live on the base. We can get him a nice house, probably bigger than he's used to. What does he really want? Offer him a six month deal to try it out. If he's used to living on British academic pay you can bully him with lots of money. If he's facing being out of work then we'll get him. That's what he has a wife for."
Somehow that seemed to settled it. Roger Woden was to join the project.

A car pulled up outside and Desiree shouted "Dad. They're here."
Ben opened the front door and walked out. "Doctor Woden? Hi. I'm Ben Lernski. I'm glad you found us OK."
Roger Woden matched his picture on the files. He looked a bit flustered. His wife got out of the car on the nearest rear door and a boy ran round from the other side.
"I am pleased to meet you Professor Lernski," he said. "May I present my wife Betty and my son Alan."
Ben was glad to find Eloise and Desiree coming up behind him so he could introduce them also. Roger was very formal. Hands were shaken all round.

"Coffee or tea?" asked Eloise, "You must be frazzled in all this heat."
"No," said Roger. "The hire car has air refrigeration. I suppose that must be normal here."
"I'd love a coffee," said Betty who was far more socially aware than her husband and that allowed them to be ushered up to the house. Ben walked Roger up to the house behind the two wives. He was pleased he had decided not to meet first on the base. Roger could just have found that too much.

The High School principle was explaining the examination systems to Mrs. Woden and was somewhat relieved to discover that the mother of his new pupil was herself an ex-teacher and was quickly able to spot the strengths and weaknesses she expected her son to show on the new syllabuses. The boy would do well so he relaxed and buzzed for another coffee, they laughed about spelling. All that was left was to introduce the new pupil to grade eleven.
Desiree Lernski had already primed the class gossip mill. Alan did not let her down. She was talking with Philippa Henderson at lunch time.
"Dishy," said Philippa "And he talks so cute."
"Careful Flipper," said Desiree languidly sucking soda on a straw, "I saw him first".
"Since when does that mean anything?" replied Flipper patronisingly. "Anyhow Dizzy, you've never had a real steady before, what makes you think now is the time to start now?" They laughed as girls do.

Roger Woden's first day at work was primarily briefings. Personnel wanted to grind through a long list of employment information which was ten times as hard for them as he was a foreign national working on a defence site. This was worse for the personnel people because they knew that they were not being told what he was to be working on, just that it was important. Finally he ended up in Ben Lernski's office just before lunch time.
"Well Roger. We're glad to have you aboard," beamed Ben. "I think you will find that your reputation has preceded you."
"That's most kind of you," the Englishman replied, looking rather sheepish.
Ben trundled on in best meeting mode. "Now Roger. I would like you to meet our Project Technical Director. This is Bill Henderson." He was pleased to see Roger smile.
The two men stood to shake hands and Roger said. "Now there is a reputation that does go before you Dr. Henderson. Am I to suppose that your presence here has been the reason that you have not published anything recently? I doubted that your work would just stop as suddenly as it had appeared to."

Bill smiled. "We have made progress. Here we can concentrate on our work without the distractions of academic life. I don't have to get published to keep my grants up and we don't have to do students." All three men laughed the quiet laugh of old university men admitting the dark secrets.

"What progress have you made?" asked Roger sitting back down and leaning forward.

Ben slouched back in his chair. "We were rather hoping to ask you that question ourselves first," he said. "We have a big pile of stuff for you to review later so you can get up to speed on our results to date."

"We worked for five years and suspected more and more but proved nothing," said Roger. "I once thought there was an extra-terrestrial presence here on earth and that our history is full of their actions and we could easily prove it. Now I believe it more and more but fear we will never prove it. Certainly all the tabloid UFO sightings and abduction reports are just noise. We have lots of data that is consistent but unproved but they do not do that sort of thing. If there is anything it is very precise and very controlled so we had better hope it is reasonably sympathetic."

"So you do still believe it could be proved?" asked Ben.

Roger took a deep breath and said "Yes I suppose so. I certainly did once with vigour but for how much longer I don't wish to speculate. I find myself knowing an awful lot about people that may or may not exist. But you and I know that belief fatigue is a problem in our business. The lack of hard evidence gets to us all in the end."

"How would you react if I said we had proof?" asked Ben.

Roger paused then said "I would be slightly sceptical. They are too smart to leave real proof. Proof, in our business, runs through your fingers like water. The best you get is people who won't tell you things but are not smart enough not to let some things slip. People who might have met the aliens but will try to shield them. You can't break them down because they know they must not tell and they care about not telling with religious fervour. So you reassure them that they are not telling you anything and then drop them hints and let them explain. That's where the patterns come from and the patterns are too consistent and often too complex to have been made up."

Ben had picked a pencil of his desk and was twisting it in his fingers. He said "We've come up against that too. I've often felt that our best data comes from people who are too nice to realise we are cheating on them. However later we will play you the tapes of an interview with an old woman who was dying and loosing track of who was there. She was confiding in someone who she knew when she was young and her story is very consistent with what we already know."

Roger waited to see if he would elaborate then screwed his face up

and replied "Dangerous. Someone telling you what you want to hear is hardly evidence. You have done credibility studies on it?"
"Yes," said Ben confidently. "We used your system and got over sixty percentage points over her whole interview and nearly eighty points on references to Tran-sen, Var-rin and a person called Say."
"Trans-zen and Zey with a soft European zed not an American zee," said Roger slowly. "We are clearly seeing the same things. Zey is the leader who everyone hero worships but who never seems to do anything. Then there is Denn as well who is the one who actually does things but is not approved of because of it. We do not understand if they are similarly ranked or even if they rank in the same hierarchy." He paused again. "Have you investigated angels?"
Ben sat forward and glanced at Bill. "We heard you were working in that area but nobody could explain why."
Roger screwed his face up. "No reason really. I hoped you might have come to it from a different direction. It was just that one of our sources who was good on other areas said as an aside that angels are wrong. They don't have enough wings. I had a strong hunch that that was very significant."
"With many wings and eyes all around?" asked Bill. "You have to admit that the biblical cherubim is hardly a baby boy with pigeon wings stuck between his shoulders and a chubby pink bottom."
"No," said Roger. "Neither is it a white, Italian, renascence, long haired, effeminate male with eagles wings on the back of his cassock. Yet it was once a term clear enough to describe an image but one that changed over the years, faded I think. It was just one line of many. Have you any reason to suspect that they might not be friendly?"
"They could be very dangerous," Ben said firmly. "We'll show you the reports on the 'man without sin' later. Suffice to say they can do mind control beyond that that a science fiction author would invent. Admittedly I have yet to find an instance where their intervention has not been at least partly justified."
Roger sighed again. "Perhaps that is why my project closed. Our funds were cut off when we felt we were getting near to something. Conversely does that mean I may have brought you to their attention?"
Bill shrugged. "We are more public that you ever were. They'd know about us but can they do anything about us? That's the question. They don't do much if they can help it that's for sure. Perhaps there are very few of them or perhaps they are not as strong as we suspect or perhaps our distributed data systems and fully matrixed management is a problem to them. It sure is a bind to us so I'd like to think it carried some sort of an advantage."
"Or perhaps we have all found out already and they have just mind controlled us to forget and to reject that solution if we get near to it

again" said Roger gloomily.

"That's a risk we have to take," replied Bill firmly. "But my assessment is that they never mind control their friends and that they never use mind control where we wouldn't rate somebody as needing locking up or shooting or worse. They might deflect us but not go for the mental jugular so to speak."

"So you think we're safe?" asked Roger.

"I hope I do," said Bill. "That's as much as I can say."

The school was small and so was the class and things slowly fell into place. Alan, generally, was approved of, he thought about things before he did them which helped.

Mr. Fitch the sports master scored Alan a big zero for motivation. He was not competitive. Not at all. He was stronger than he looked and quick. He scrubbed out the word 'graceful' on his notes because it did not seem appropriate for a boy but it stuck in his mind. Woden would not make any teams unless they decided to do competitive trampolining. Mr. Fitch wrote 'high board diver?' and moved on.

Most of the classes were no problem. Alan was new to some of the less traditional elements of the course and most teachers were quite happy because he took up new ideas with delight but when he scratched his head and told Mrs. Simes in maths that a definition of a set that allowed a set to be or not to be a member of itself was 'less than useful because it was bound to end in tears' authority ruled and he had to submit to mathematics as it is taught here.

Roger was pleased to find the books he had suggested would be useful to have had preceded him and were sitting in a box on his new desk. He looked suspiciously at the bulky computer terminal but assumed he could ignore it into submission. He opened the new hard bound notebook and wrote the date at the top of the first page and stared at the wall for a few moments. Then he wrote the headings:
- Language
- Morality
- Mind control
- Polygamy
- Daughters

He paused and looked at the list for several minutes then added
- Angels.

He looked at the list and refused to add the last item in his mind. It seemed that it was that that had precipitated the close of the Warwick project. Once they started looking at the genetic predisposition towards polygamy the roof fell in, the money stopped and friends became foes. He sighed. Good friends, he remembered, had become cold and given up and the project was losing key people to other fields even before their Whitehall bosses pulled the plug. He refused to write it down but promised himself he would remember it. It was, because of the reaction, the clearest clue to date and paid them back for the three months it had taken to get the questionnaire past the ethics committee. He smiled. It would be nice not to do trauma victims though. It was sometimes, well occasionally, a good data feed but most of them were just poor ordinary people who had had to go through very extraordinary experiences. Even the few that might have met an alien were so scarred by the events they did not have any knowledge you could actually assess as meaningful. It had bought the Warwick team into the alien search and it had officially paid the salaries but it was a lost cause.

Dizzy and Flipper sat in the refectory and ate lunch. "Who do you think he'll invite to the form party?" asked Dizzy.
"Don't wait too long," said Flipper off handedly. "It's less than three weeks now and most people who don't have a steady are already getting firmed up. Everybody views it as the run up to the prom at the end of the year. Who have you already turned down?"
Dizzy wrinkled her nose up at the implication but said "Well Tim asked if I might be interested and I said I'd think about it but not to wait for me. Nothing else."
"What if I said Alan had asked me to go with him? What would you do then?" Flipper kept eating.
"Oh I don't know," said Dizzy lazily. "Probably a toss up between locking myself in my bedroom for three weeks to cry or there again I could just scratch your eyes out now rather than waiting till later to do it. Would you say yes?"
"Given the offer," said Flipper languidly. "Do you think he knows he's supposed to ask somebody?"
Dizzy sat up and looked at her. "Surely they have form parties in England?"
"Not all schools here have them so who knows? I suppose we could just invite him. He might not realise that's back to front."
"You or me?" asked Dizzy, her voice more relaxed than her eyes.
Flipper looked at her. "Both," she said. "Then he decides. That's fair isn't it?"
"This could be the end of a beautiful friendship," cautioned Dizzy.
"If he's already invited Rachael we'll both need shoulders to cry on."
"Don't even think that," said Dizzy firmly.

Roger read the report and made some notes. It was good stuff with all the usual missing bits. Somebody had been in trouble and somebody had rescued them. Somebody had failed to use all their unarmed combat skills and weapons and had ended up suddenly very dead and somebody had been mind controlled which made it an alien story not just another human anguish report.

The mind control was interesting. He was a bad man by his record but he had now willingly confessed his crimes but now he was gentle and considerate. Apologetic even. A thoroughly reformed character.

Roger re-read the text and the attached notes. Being evil had clearly dropped out of his life. It was a bad memory.

Roger called up his 'private mind' theory again. Rather than the 'private eye' who was psychologically weak but physically ruthless when riled the 'private mind' was physically weak but could be psychologically violent when cornered. Someone had kicked the evil out of this man as precisely as any terrorist knee-capping an informer. Was it a precise, careful operation for his own good or a violent outburst? Roger wondered. This was as ever the real question under all their studies: could these people be trusted?

"Run that by me again?" said Alan. "I am supposed to invite someone? I've heard that. But if I invite Dizzy then Flipper never talks to us again. And if I invite Flipper then Dizzy runs off and joins a monastery in Tibet. OK? And if I even think of inviting somebody else you both tear me limb from limb and bury the pieces at a crossroads at midnight with a stake through the heart. Simple. I always get such good deals. I think I'll stay home that night and hide under the bed."

"You can't not go," said Dizzy, shocked.

"Seems like the safest option so far," said Alan. "I probably wouldn't enjoy a noisy party anyway. I could take a weekend off and go camping. I'm told the countryside is really wonderful around here and that autumn is the time to see it."

"It's the social highlight of the term. It's the official party not just some friend's thing. We all dress up and there is even a real band," Flipper was beginning to worry that he might mean it. "Everybody goes and most everybody has a date."

He did. "That's not me is it?" he laughed. "I don't do official. Well, not very well. I can't dance to save my life and if you want a status date then surely as the two prettiest girls in the class you can play the field."

"Complements," gushed Flipper, "Will get you everywhere but unless you want to watch a kicking, screaming, swearing, hair tearing bitch fight while we decide for you you'd better make up your mind soon."

"I don't do kinky and I don't do violent," said Alan coldly. "I might do some camping before the weather turns cold."

"Do camping this weekend," said Dizzy in mild frustration. "The party is not till the weekend after that so you don't have to make up your mind yet."

"Dizzy's got a tent. Let's all do camping. We used it in the summer last year and it's beautiful here in the fall," Flipper flowed along. "We could take the bus up to Pike's Forge Saturday morning and walk back down the valley and get the bus home at Little Creek. Back for Sunday tea. Dizzy and I did it in July and it's cool scenery and mostly downhill after the first bit and there won't be any midges at this time of year."
"And we don't discuss the party again till we get back?" Asked Alan and, without waiting for an answer, said "Deal."

"It's only really a tent for two," said Dizzy after Alan had left for his next class. "And are we all going to sleep together? He said he didn't do kinky."
"Camping at this time of year you take off your boots and your anorak and clamber into a sleeping bag in the rest of your gear and, anyway, there's going to be two of us. You don't get to do anything with him we can't both share."
Dizzy pulled a face to indicate that she thought that that was gratuitously crude and asked "What would your Mum say?"
"You are going camping with me," said Flipper very quietly. "She'll say 'do be careful dear and both wrap up warm and I hope you have a lovely time'. If you even hint we're taking Alan with us you'll get us both grounded till after we're on prescription HRT."

Roger sat down with Bill and said "Do you mind me asking the most fundamental question?"
"What's that?" said Bill.
"Well," started Roger awkwardly. "It's the question that nobody ever managed to answer at Warwick... What is our actual objective in all this research? What do the people who are paying us want? Yes, I know that we want to know if there really are aliens on earth but you and I do not have real doubts about that except in the depths of a bad night, but are we trying to invent an alien detector or are we trying to make contact either officially or unofficially? Alan asked me this ages ago and it has been bugging me ever since."
Waaall," drawled Bill. "I suppose the project was set up because of several internal military security documents that seemed to show the mind control trick had been used on security agents investigating in strange places. No, I can't go into details here but they turned out to be typical mind control victims. You know. The really nasty type. The sort of person who makes a good security geek because they don't care about anybody and working for the government gives them an excuse to get away with things. Overall the powers that run such things wanted to know who was defending themselves so well and should they be

worried about it. I suppose the 'who' question is still our objective."
"But what sort of 'who' question is it? Do they just want the phone number or do they hope we can produce a magic box that you point at somebody and it says that they are/they aren't an alien or do they just want the definitive history of aliens on earth? I am personally fascinated by the work but what do I aim for so I have something to present to you and say 'I have accomplished something this month so keep the salary coming'?"
Bill stopped and thought a while. "Our main budget contributors are military and I can't tell you more than that. But we know that they run on fear of the other side so I always reasoned that we are the first probe to try and sense, to measure, the other side."
"So all the picture of the aliens we are building up goes into a sort of threat assessment," Roger rubbed his chin as he thought. "Threat assessment is two way. On the capabilities side our aliens are dangerous but on the intentions side? I have rather developed the feeling over the years that they are no threat. In fact they are a rather beneficial influence but I suppose that might only apply while their self interests happen to coincide with ours."
Bill sat forward on his desk. "That may be the key issue. If as a result of our work we did come up with the right phone number, so to speak, then it would be up to other people than us to do a deal to ensure our safety, certainly as a nation and, I would hope, as a whole world."
Roger looked him in the eyes. "So perhaps there might be a danger of them doing a deal with whoever finds them first?"
"You've read the reports. The secret ones that we trust. You know they have very smart tricks they can pull. They can definitely get into and out of locked rooms. They can survive poisons and radiation. They can do tricks in your mind. We have hints of very sophisticated and powerful weapons. If any nation is going to have a share in that I'd prefer it to be mine. I don't claim we're the best or even good but we have a history of backing away from conflict and preferring to use power to blackmail rather than to flatten."
Roger nodded quietly. "I can live with that. But what am I trying to do? Find that magic phone number?"
"That would help," said Bill. "Failing that write the history and put a zero to ten reliability number on each chapter."

Alan was climbing steadily but he still said "Hey. Slow down a bit."
"What's the matter?" asked Dizzy.
"Well I'm getting hot," he said. "This snow suit thing is intended for later in the year I think."
"You'll be glad of it when we hit the top of the ridge," said Flipper. "It's going to be windy."

"I hope so. I feel like I'm wrapped up completely and then with the anorak pulled over my head I can't unzip it and get some air in."
"They are the kit to have," said Flipper. "It's just handy you're my Dad's size."
"It was good of him to lend it," said Alan. "You must thank him for me if I forget." The two girls looked at one another behind his back and choose not to reply.
"In the holidays," continued Alan regardlessly "We could do this in the week as it's nice to be at home weekends as Dad is there then. During the week he works late here just like he did at home."
"Bug eyed monsters don't do sociable hours in the week," said Dizzy. "But they never work weekends."
"Do you believe in the aliens Alan?" asked Flipper.
He did not reply at once, then said. "Why not. There must be other planets with life in the universe. It only stands to reason that humanity is not alone. Now abductions and stuff, however, that's just junk, just people looking for publicity."
"But do you think they're here?" asked Dizzy.
"Dad thinks so," said Alan cautiously. "He's studied it for years. That's good enough for me. I suppose I've never thought about his evidence because I've not seen what he's seen."
"Did you see ET in England?" asked Dizzy.
"Oh no. We're such a cultural backwater we don't have cinemas yet. We're just trying for 'fire' and if that works out in next century we'll try for 'wheels'," He paused and took a deep breath. "Of course I've seen it. It's daytime TV now. I reckon it's worse than Close Encounters as that's just being weird for the sake of being weird. ET is just weird and slushy. I prefer films where they spell out the plot, or at least where you can work back to the plot at the end."
"What would they be like?" wondered Flipper who loved ET but had to admit to slushy.
"Lots of different planets would mean lots of different shapes and sizes," suggested Alan puffing slightly as he caught them up. "We might not even recognise some as beings."
"A super intelligent shade of the colour blue?" asked Dizzy.
"Douglas Adams," said Alan recognising the quote.
"Well done," said Dizzy. "Or could they just have two heads and three arms?"
"You name it. Does your father talk about these things?" asked Alan.
"Sometimes," said Dizzy. "But I glaze over till he stops."
"My Dad won't tell me anything," said Flipper. "He's into secrets. He doesn't think we notice that when he goes to walk Scrappy the dog he times it to run into your father Dizzy. Whenever he goes they seem to meet, talk for a few minutes and walk on. Then he gets home and sits

in his den for a while."

"Maybe they're plotting to take over the world," said Dizzy preferring to nudge the conversation away from parents.

"Maybe they're the aliens," exclaimed Flipper. "I can see it all now. The Base is the secret head quarters of the alien invaders. That's why it's an airfield with no aeroplanes. And one day our Dads will unzip their human suits and step out as aliens, catch the next UFO to Washington and take over the government."

"That makes us at least part alien," laughed Dizzy.

"They only tell you where the zip is at the last moment," suggested Flipper.

"Why does everyone think they're a threat?" asked Alan.

"Would they bother to come if there wasn't something in it for them?" pointed out Flipper. "It's a long way from anywhere."

"Maybe they can't go back," suggested Dizzy. "Perhaps their space ship is broken."

"Interesting," said Alan slowing down. "So what we're dealing with is a poor bunch of Robinson Crusoes, striving to scratch out a living in the backwoods. Hoping against hope that they will be rescued before the essential supplies run out. Surely they wouldn't hide. They would do a deal?"

"Perhaps they've done a deal with the Russians. That's why this project is so hush-hush," offered Flipper. "We're fighting the 'Red Menace from Mars'."

"Not Mars," said Dizzy.

"How come so?" asked Alan. "We would be the obvious next port of call?"

"They're strong. Dad says that is more gravity," pointed out Dizzy.

"My Dad thinks they fly so wouldn't that suit less gravity?" responded Alan.

"Boring," said Flipper. "Don't talk aliens when I'm hungry. Who's got the bag with the candy bars in it? I feel a chocolate attack coming on."

"You have," said Dizzy. "Hold still and I'll dig it out," she added starting to pull at Flipper's rucksack. She pulled things out. "Here Alan. Hold this," she said and as he took the three bars from her she resealed the ties and flaps.

They trudged on up the path eating slowly. Flipper said "We'll be at the top soon. From then it's all downhill and once we get down to the trees we can stop and put the tent up and start to make dinner."

"I could look forward to dinner," said Alan. "I'm carrying it and I don't know what it is."

"Never you mind," smiled Dizzy. "We both have excellent grades in home management so you are going to enjoy it."

"I shall look forward to that," said Alan. "What then? You unzip your human suits and abduct me?"

"No," said Flipper. "You must be one too. That's why they brought you all here. Just before the final invasion."

Alan laughed. "That's why my Dad's talking about getting a dog. I trust there are a lot more alien kids. We can have a big party to celebrate total world domination."

"No," said Flipper. "Just us three. No others for billions of light years."

"Ah," Alan laughed again. "So that's why it's so vital to you I have to choose one of you for the party. You never told me it was as serious as the continuing of a whole species."

Dizzy pushed at him and said "You haven't heard the polygamy thing?"

Alan and Flipper looked at her. Pleased to have their attention she continued. "Alien women are big and tough and in charge while alien men are soft and marry lots of women."

"So alien women know how to share?" said Alan. "You two can't be aliens then."

"No," said Dizzy stumbling on the track as she lost concentration on walking. "They marry lots of human women."

"Where does that leave the alien women?" asked Alan, sounding perplexed.

"I don't know," grumbled Dizzy. "That is just what Dad says."

"Where does this leave things like Roswell?" asked Flipper.

"They're fakes," said Dizzy.

"But who faked it then?" asked Flipper.

"The aliens," said Alan brightly. "They want us to believe in the wrong sort of alien."

"Pah," said Dizzy crossly and stomped on ahead.

"What's your theory of aliens Alan?" asked Flipper moving alongside him. "Don't kid us that you haven't thought about it."

Alan looked up at her and was silent for a moment. "Dad may have told me more than he was supposed to so if I tell you you don't tell. Right?"

"We're all in this together. We're all project families," said Dizzy back over her shoulder to prove she was still listening.

"Well the aliens have been here forever. Dad's got stuff on early Egypt and Mesopotamia and stuff that he refers to and he thinks they were already here long before that. Also he has this jump theory of civilisation that was developed by his department that says that new ideas happened and then spread fast across the whole world as if you only had to hear the idea to accept it. And finally there is the idea that they can get into people's brains and make them change. Like a ruthless conqueror who suddenly becomes an efficient administrator and stays home to raise grandchildren. I put all this together and think that they are refugees from a lost civilisation who have landed on Earth and they quite like it and they quite like us and provided we don't cause

them problems they generally look after us so we keep a comfortable world running and they can live amongst us as a hidden, super rich elite."
"So we're not aliens then," said Flipper. "As I'm not super rich."
"Why would they be rich?" asked Dizzy. "They would only want what they want and human riches would only make problems."
"Dunno," replied Alan. "Given the choice I'd be super rich. Whatever I wanted would probably be much easier to arrange then. Money may not buy happiness but, as they say, you can buy a much better class of misery."
"Money is just a means to an end. If they were really smart they'd go straight to it and cut out the middle men," said Flipper.
"Perhaps they have already taken over the governments," offered Dizzy. "They control things so that we look after them. And the base is a place for aliens who like mountains to live in and your Dad, Alan, he wanted to move, so here he is."
"He didn't want to move but I'm quite happy to be here," replied Alan. "In that case maybe we are aliens because I have to admit I live a happy life in amongst people I like and I get to do fun things."
"Except that you have to go to a party next weekend," said Flipper with emphasised sympathy.
"But I have the choice of two of the nicest girls to take," countered Alan. "If I could take you both I'd be in clover. A pretty neat weekend as you say. Admit it. I've got a better deal than Michael who has asked everybody and probably couldn't even get Martha to consider him if she suspected the custodian hadn't got to work that evening."
"There are a lot of boys who would think that taking two girls camping in one small tent was a pretty neat weekend," simpered Dizzy.
"I think it's pretty neat but I'm not fool enough to start expecting too much. The night I slept with Dizzy and Flipper will be a great story but I don't expect to do much more than talk and sleep. I've seen how thick these sleeping bags are. Between two of them even a close cuddle would be something your mother wouldn't turn a hair at. Of course if I get to sleep in the middle that would be a real bonus if I was to boast about it."
"Who would you boast too?" asked Flipper. "Do you kiss and tell?"
"Oh naturally I deny everything. So we shared a tent but that's camping. It's not as if they're cute, good looking or sexy is it? This is just old Dizzy and Flipper. Great folks to have along on a camping trip. Hey! Great countryside you have here. I saw mountains, trees, and, er, things like that."
The two girls laughed. It was nice to feel that he accepted the situation and also nice to feel that he appreciated them. Dizzy took his left hand and walked alongside him and Flipper, seeing this moved to Alan's right

side and offered a hand and was pleased that he took it. They walked silently as a threesome up to the top of the ridge.

Roger and Betty walked from their car up Bill's drive and were drawn into the warmth of the house. Bill waited until a polite interval had elapsed and then invited Ben and Roger out to 'the den' to leave their women folk to talk.
The den was a basement full of the detritus of a hobbyist engineer. The benches were hidden under a litter of part made or even unmade items and tools and the walls were hung with the trophies of successful endeavours. They sat and drank bottled beer of a innocuous strength and talked about nothing and took a long time over it. Bill knew dinner was casseroling gently above them and the best policy was to wait till they were called and the afternoon passed as lazily and as gently as you could wish for.

The wind blew. "Wow. Windy," said Alan. "I see what you mean. You could tie a rope round my middle and use me for a kite. It stings your face but you stay warm as toast in the suit."
"We only exist to serve," quoted Flipper. "But you have the rope and we're getting a bit late so if we could continue down rather than fly you now. We've got to cross this gully first to get into the shelter of the forest and as I remember it it's a bit of a scramble."
"In a red snow suit the Rangers would report a UFO flying by and that'd annoy the aliens back at the base," said Dizzy. "You keep forgetting that we are supposed to maintain some sort of security. Come on. Another mile and it's supper time."
"Hey," laughed Alan. "I'll drink to that."
Slowly they descended over the rock and scree towards the trees. They looked down on the stream. Flipper sniffed at it. "Well it is about ten times as big as it ever was in the summer so maybe we just have to look for a narrower bit. The rule is search upstream."
They trudged along the bank but it did not seem to improve. "With every little rill that joins it the main stream is less until you can cross," pointed out Flipper.
"I haven't seen anything join it yet," pointed out Dizzy "And it just seems steeper and faster."
"But narrower," pointed out Alan hopefully.
The tree bridging the stream looked almost artificial. Flipper inspected it and said that "Man made unless the local beavers have started investing in chain saws. Look at the cut end."
"So it's a bridge," said Alan. "So we cross. Right?"
"Right," said Flipper.
Dizzy said nothing. The bridge was nearly five miles long and at least

ten miles above a raging torrent. It was a disaster movie waiting to be filmed. She looked at the others. They were serious about crossing it. If they could do it then she could. She wasn't going to fade out. But she wasn't going to go first.
Alan walked slowly across keeping his arms spread out. "It's a bit slippery in places," he said. "But if you mind the mossy bits it's OK." Flipper looked across at him. She stood on the end for a while and thought about it a bit. "I'll crawl across," She said. "I feel better if I've got things to hold on to." She got three feet and stopped, took a deep breath and continued. It was long and slow. Dizzy wondered if it was possible to give up and turn back, perhaps Flipper did too but she never told anybody if she did. As she finally crept off the far end Alan reached out to help her up and she stepped straight into his arms and held him tight. "Scary," she breathed feeling Alan's arms wrap round her.
"You're OK," stated Alan patting her back. "Take your time. Calm down. Then we must get Dizzy across."
Suddenly Flipper was embarrassed and let him go. They looked back at Dizzy. She was looking down into the stream. "It's OK if you crawl," said Flipper. "Don't look down. Watch your hands."
"I'm OK. Don't worry about me," lied Dizzy and started out. It all went well on will power and deliberately ignoring the drop until she was nearly half way across. Alan watched her stop and hunch down.
"What's the matter?" he called.
"Scared shitless," shouted Dizzy panting.
"Relax and wait till it passes," offered Flipper. "You're most of the way," she added generously.
Dizzy took a deep breath and moved forward six inches and stopped again. "Just wait," she gasped. "I'll be OK."
"Shall I come out and help you?" asked Alan stepping onto the end near to him.
"No," wailed Dizzy. "It might not take the weight of two of us."
"It's new wood," said Alan. "It'd take twenty people. Just take a deep breath and go another step. You'll be OK."
Dizzy flopped down and slipped. Suddenly she was no longer in a crawling position but flat on her tummy with a leg scrabbling on either side.
"Hold tight and relax," Alan contradicted himself and started to climb back onto the trunk. "Don't worry I'm coming."
"Hang on in there," shouted Flipper trying to be encouraging but at a loss for something specific to say.
Alan dumped his rucksack on the ground and stepped cautiously onto the tree towards her. "Just wait," he counselled. "Take it easy."
Dizzy in desperation saw him as saviour and forgot all ideas of physics

in her desire to hold something or someone she had confidence in. As soon as he was something that could loosely be described as near she lunged towards him and slipped sideways. For a moment she seemed to be caught on a branch and then she was not. "Oh bother," said Alan as Dizzy hit the water.

Flipper ran down stream and Alan, almost unable to move, watched her scrabbling down the scree towards the narrow bit below the pool beneath the trunk. He watched Dizzy cast towards the bank and suddenly she was on a rock near Flipper. She was holding Flipper's hand as she stood in the water. She was on the shore and the two girls were weeping deliriously in one another's arms.

Alan looked down at them, slowly shook his head in disbelief and then quietly activated his communication unit. [Thank you Alacia.]

[She is on the right side now. She will not notice that we helped.]

[You are probably right but with that rucksack full of camping stove she should have sunk like a stone.]

[You need to get her dried out quickly or we will need to do something more. I assume this impacts your plans to recruit them today?]

[I never intended to recruit them as such. Just to plant ideas that leak back home. Our big fireside after supper chat which was to be the key ingredient of this weekend is probably still on. We shall just have to see what we can manage to recover.]

Alan shrugged and slowly turned on the spot by shuffling his feet and walked back across the tree bridge.

"I don't like the look of that sky," said Bill. "The forecast was fine but that looks like it's going to pitch it down."

"That will ruin the girl's weekend," said Ben.

"Oh?" said Roger, interested.

"Our two crazy daughters have taken it into their heads to bus over the other side of the mountain ridge and walk back over the top, camping overnight," explained Bill. "They took all the cold weather and wet weather gear so I guess they'll be OK but I did not expect rain or I would have objected."

"Oh," said Roger. "That's a coincidence. Alan was invited to go camping this weekend by some school friends. Do you suppose it's a party?"

Bill pulled a face. "If it was a party Philippa would not go. She's contrary that girl."

Ben said softly. "But would she and Diz take Alan along and neglect to tell us?"

Bill crunched his face up. "Well. Maybe. Together they'd do most anything that was sufficiently dumb." He looked at Roger. "Would Alan go if they asked him?"

Roger paused. Slowly he said "They have all become good friends

these last few weeks. Look. If you were sixteen and two very pretty girls asked you to go on a trip like that, would you go?"
All three men looked at one another and all said "Yes."
"Damn," said Bill. "Now we need an up-to-date weather forecast before we know whether to get mad or get worried."

Dizzy dripped under the tree while Flipper and Alan erected the tent. "I think my oversuit is actually holding the water in," she moaned pulling at her ankles. They got the tent stable and Flipper stuffed her in with her back-pack while Alan bashed the remaining pegs in.
"Every last stitch," insisted Flipper, untangling Dizzy's sleeping bag from the camping stove. Thankful the supposedly waterproof rucksack seemed to have worked a lot better than she remembered that they ever had before.
"But it's freezing in here," complained Dizzy unlacing her boots.
"Once you're out of the wet things towel yourself off and then, when you are really dry, get into the sleeping bag and towel your hair. I'll pass you in some dry clothes and you can get dressed inside the bag but we need to get you bone dry first or you will just get the new things wet and then you really will freeze and there's no fixing it." She looked at Dizzy struggling out of the sodden clothing "And let me see your toes before you get into the sleeping bag" she insisted remembering her first aid.
Alan looked at the pile of clothes that Flipper handed him. "Yes," he said, looking at Dizzy's underwear like it was going to bite him. "I'll feed it onto the rope so it can't blow away and tie it between two trees. It will dry quickly in this wind."
Flipper looked at the sky. "Not if it rains," she said and dived back into the tent.
Flipper rooted through both their sets of spare clothing and passed the warmest and woolliest items to Dizzy and the sleeping bag contorted itself as she got dressed inside. Soon she began to looked a bit warmer.
"Sorry," muttered Dizzy. "I panicked. Heights do that to me."
"I nearly did too," confided Flipper. "I just kept looking at Alan. I promised myself a big hug. It got a bit obsessive but I made it."
"Good thinking," smiled Dizzy. "You got your hug. I was just thinking about me slipping off and getting a soaking so guess what I got."
"Well I'll cook the supper and tell Alan he's got to cuddle you to keep you warm," offered Flipper "Then, once we've eaten, we can all snuggle up together and get some sleep."
"Alan in the middle?" asked Dizzy.
"Yeah," said Flipper. "He's not used to the cold so it's our duty to keep him from harm."

"He came back to get me didn't he?" Dizzy mused. "Do you suppose he's not bothered about heights?"

"He took it very slowly. I suspect he's a bit nervous but perhaps he just controls himself better than we do."

"He's not just showing off is he?" Dizzy looked at her sideways.

"Anyone else I'd say maybe, but Alan?" Flipper paused, "I don't think so. If he was showing off he'd fool about. When he does something smart he always seems to have to laugh at himself as if to excuse it. I think he was just genuinely concerned and got on and did what he hoped would help."

"Is that because he's with us or because he's English?"

"I don't think it's English. On the TV they're like us but talk funny. Better. I think it's just him. He's at ease with himself and it rather makes me feel at ease with him. Don't you feel it?"

"Sort of. Do you think he wants to be a boy friend rather than just a friend? He's never tried anything. Not even a hug." Dizzy almost looked worried.

"We've both hugged him before now and we both held his hands on the way up. He's sweet but I think he's shy."

"But we have to start everything. Could it be that he's always got both of us around and he's too nice to tell one of us to please get lost for a bit?"

"Well I've looked and looked and he's definitely not interested in any other girls in the class. Even when I found him talking with Rachael as soon as he sees me he just beams that great big smile of his at me," Flipper grinned. "He always seems so pleased to see us but, no, I'd love to say he prefers me but I can't prove it."

"He didn't want to take either of us to the party," worried Dizzy.

"Or did he not want to not take one of us? He can't say yes to one because that would mean he had to say no to the other?"

"Oh Flipper. If he just offered me some kind of affection. So I could be sure it was me. I think I'd fall totally and madly in love with him at once."

"You and me both sister," sighed Flipper. "Still. We should know by next weekend. And win or lose, no hard feelings, we're always friends."

"Yeah," said Dizzy reaching out and grabbing Flipper's arm. "But the loser's allowed to cry a bit." They smiled at one another. It was not much of a deal but at least it was a deal.

Alan flapped at the tent door. "Are you decent yet?" he asked querulously.

"Grief," said Flipper. "We've left him out in the cold. Come in" she shouted.

Alan pulled up the zip and pushed a bundle at them. "The small things are all dry," he said, "But I'd better bring in the rest of the stuff though they're still a bit wet as it looks like it is beginning to snow."

The girls looked at him and he did indeed have snow on his jacket. "Oh wonderful!" said Flipper.

Three sets of parents looked at one another. "We don't want to make a fuss if the weather stays good," said Bill, "Not to people like Park Rangers anyway."
"I'll give them fuss when they get back," said Eloise.
"Don't worry," said Becky Henderson. "It will be all right. You are safe if you are not stupid and they are not stupid and they have done the training."
"I wasn't thinking about the weather," said Eloise.
"Relax," said Ben. "Remember when you went with Jimmy and me up to Turner's farm and we stayed there? Nothing happened."
Eloise did not seem comforted by that. "We were at college then so it was different. These are just children. They shouldn't do it without asking."
Ben put her arms round her and pointed out. "No. What I mean is that a party of three tends not to be like that. Anyway. Flipper's taller than you so what was that about children? They didn't ask because they knew we'd say no. Just like we didn't. We were three days and I didn't even get a kiss. These kids are just out overnight in a tent that promises no privacy. Alan is in no danger I assure you."
Somehow they all laughed and that defused the tension slightly. It was good to be able to feel good about something. Ben said "Look. If they are going over to Pike's Forge and back down the trail to Little Creek then they go past the Ranger station and the rule for hill walkers is that you check in. We can ring."
"Yeah," said Ben. "And get their latest weather report too."

Flipper set up the stove in the open end of the tent. Thankfully although the wind was strengthening it had not changed direction and that end was still downwind. She was trying to revise the menu. It was supposed to be lots of fun things but she was beginning to think in terms of what she could bung in together, heat up and call nutrition. This was not going to be an idle evening under the stars as the snow was now going past horizontally and it was getting dark early.
"The snow suit's dry," said Alan. "Shouldn't you put it back on?"
"Yes," said Flipper. "After the soaking you need every bit of warmth. Then we all get into our sleeping bags in our snow suits and snuggle up."
"It will be warmer but I'll have to take my jeans and stuff off again first," said Dizzy.
"I'll sit here and face the door then," said Alan. "Or I'll go outside if you want but I don't want to disturb Flipper."

"That's OK," said Dizzy. "I may need you to hold the torch for me as I'm wearing two of Flipper's cardigans and I know I buttoned them up wrong so I may never get out of it by feel alone. I'm decent underneath."

"Oh," said Alan. "I'm disappointed. I thought you wanted me to help remove Flipper's cardigan."

"I hear that," laughed Flipper. "Do you want to eat this dinner? If you are doing something naughty back there remember that I'm here to see that I get my fair share."

"Don't worry," said Dizzy. "You just get on with the cooking. Alan's just going to help me take all my clothes off."

"Oh goodie," muttered Alan.

"Alan," said Flipper. "I somehow can't see you lecherously smoothing Dizzy's nubile young body into her mum's cast off snow suit. You don't seem the type."

"Well I can dream can't I?" he was laughing.

"Hold the torch straight," said Dizzy, having trouble with buttons. Alan turned round to look where he was pointing just at the crucial moment when it all came undone. "Oh," he said and turned away again.

"It's a bra Alan," said Dizzy crossly pulling her arms out of the cardigan. "You make such a fuss." Flipper turned to see what was going on and caught the pot with her sleeve.

Dizzy sat in her snow suit and put her boots back on while she watched them clean up. "It's a good thing it spilt inside the tent," said Alan. "Plastic ground sheets rule. We can always wash off what we don't eat when we get home. If it had been outside I'd have thought twice about eating it once we'd scraped it up."

"You don't have to eat it," said Flipper, slowly calming down.

"On the contrary," said Alan licking his fingers. "I'm ravenous and it tastes far too good to miss. If you can do this in the woods, in the snow and wind on a portable stove I've clearly fallen in with the right two girls."

"It's cooked," said Flipper sadly. "But perhaps I should put it back on the heat to warm it up again and hope that kills any germs."

"Don't worry," said Dizzy. "I'm ready to eat anything. Do me a bowl full and I'll sort it out as I go. Where's the bread?"

They zipped the door up and lounged about eating the meaty, savoury goo with squashed French stick. "All in all," said Alan. "It's not worked out too badly. Not quite as we planned but not too badly."

"Well done Alan," muttered Flipper. "Total disaster and he says 'not too bad'. About the only thing that could happen to make it worse is that we really are abducted by aliens. How would we explain that when we get home?"

"Especially if they are the wrong sort of aliens," said Alan.
They ate on and Flipper was thankful that she had prepared too much as they had probably lost over thirty percent. She sighed and thanked her luck that it was good and filling and warm and left them feeling contented.
She looked at Dizzy who was not as pink as she should be but she was in control for a girl who had been swimming at a bad time of year. She wondered if it would make a joke so she offered. "Next time we come up here we must bring our bathing things."
"Oh?" said Alan, "I thought we did? It's just that Dizzy forgot to change."
"The lure of high diving," said Dizzy wiping a bit of bread round the bottom of the big mug she was eating from. "I never had the chance before because I never made it to that high board. Couldn't pass up an opportunity like that could I?"
"You are so brave," treacled Flipper admiringly. "But if you had left Alan the ruck-sack your spare clothes would be drier."
"Well," said Dizzy, leaning back and smiling, "I did think about taking off my things and passing them to him but I forgot to put my swimmers on under my snow suit so I'd have embarrassed everybody so I just thought, what the heck, and went for it."
"I wouldn't be embarrassed," said Flipper. "We've known one another to long and Alan's just a friend. He's very understanding. I'm sure he'd have carried your clothes back for you and he'd be a gentleman and not look, would you Alan?"
"Oh certainly. I would never look if either of you were splashing around naked in a pool. I'd just sit on the bank and watch for fish and see the birds fly by and relax. Well. I might need to watch a bit. To see you were safe. I would feel so bad if there was an accident. In fact my conscience would probably force me to keep a careful watch at all times. You're very vulnerable with nothing on you know, you could easily come to harm."
Flipper laughed. "Oh Alan. You're so sweet. Always diligently putting our interests before your own. And you would help us get dry too?"
"Towel you down? Why certainly. You must not get cold or you might get a chill. I would never forgive myself if I neglected you. It would be unforgivable."
"Oh what a pity," said Dizzy. "Flipper made me undress completely and dry myself carefully before she would give me any clothes to put back on. I did it all myself and I didn't need to. We left you out in the snow. How inconsiderate."
"Don't worry," laughed Alan. "Next time just ask. You know. A quick shout of 'Alan I'm stark naked and I want somebody to rub me all over' and I'll be straight there. I promise."
"I'll tell you what," said Flipper conspiratorially "You can unroll the

sleeping bags and then you can help me take off my anorak because its next to impossible to do it in confined space with a snow suit underneath. And then, if you're really good, for a real treat, Dizzy and I will help you take off yours."

"Oh," said Alan. "I am honoured. I am not worthy. Pass me the rucksacks that I may serve." He fussed about and they bickered good humouredly about who's sleeping-bag was whose and then they came to arranging them.

"Alan in the middle," said Dizzy.

"Well you're the coldest," said Alan.

"Don't argue," said Dizzy. "It seems to be going quiet."

"Snow," said Alan permitting himself to be diverted. "It deadens the sound but it's not too bad as actually it's an insulator."

Further hilarity was occasioned as they took off the anoraks and bundled them into the sleeping bags so they would not be frozen in the morning. Flipper carefully reminded them that gloves and boots needed to be in the bag too or they would regret it when they woke up. They scavenged round the ruck-sacks for some final treat and found two chocolate bars and after a complex debate came up with a way of dividing them exactly three ways as everybody insisted that they would not accept an atom more than a fair share.

"Now we get a severe weather warning," complained Bill. "No sooner do we get confirmation that they checked in at the Ranger cabin at the start of the trail than the Rangers tell us that it's a change of plan on the weather and suddenly it's going to be wind and snow big time."

"Thank goodness they checked in by name," said Ben. "At least we know for sure what's going on. They have snow suits and waterproofs and food and both girls have done mountain skills courses. Provided they don't get too distracted they should be alright. Hell. Kids. Who'd have them?"

"They're probably sitting round a fire full of good food and thinking about turning in for the night," said Bill.

Ben sniggered. "They have Dizzy's tent so it will be cosy but with the two of them Alan's going to be disappointed if he hoped for a snuggle."

Roger smiled. "He's never been the type to try but he gets lots of offers."

Bill was still looking out the window but said. "Well Flipper's been wandering about like a lost soul for a couple of weeks so she's probably in love again. Gee. Wasn't it hell being young? They're probably both besotted with poor Alan and fighting over him."

Ben cut in "...but they could never negotiate a deal. You couldn't ask for a more diligent chaperone for Flipper than Dizzy and vice versa."

"So all we worry about is snow?" said Bill. "That's probably quite

enough for tonight. If it does snow hard do we ask the base to help?"
"You mean ask the General?" asked Ben. "Make his day that would."
"Into the car," said Bill. "Let's get onto the base while we think about it."

"Time to get into the sleeping bags," said Flipper. "I'm starting to get chilly and in them we're OK to way below freezing."
"I only just put my boots back on," complained Dizzy.
"Sleep in your boots," said Alan. "We won't tell your mother and provided you haven't stepped in the dinner they were washed and clean."
"What's that noise," asked Dizzy. They all froze and listened. There was a distinct huff huff noise by the tent door.
"Aliens?" said Flipper with an air of 'I don't care, let me go to bed'.
Something pushed the tent and it leaned about them. Flipper grabbed crossly at the zip and pulled it up and two bright eyes caught Alan's torch light and teeth.
Flipper screamed. It was no fake but right from her roots as a being. The bear snarled in response but as it moved there was a snap and a blue flash like an electric spark and it jumped backwards. Flipper's torch followed it as it stood waving its head looking at them.
"Bear," said Flipper, unable to manage more than a single word and still unsure whether she was going to scream again.
"It's the food," said Alan grabbing for something to hold. "It wants the spilt meaty stuff. The torch must have frightened it off."
"It will be back," said Dizzy. "Never get between a bear and its food. We must get away till it has finished. We must get out of the tent. It smells of meat. Don't tread in it."
Alan pushed Flipper out of the door and Dizzy followed them grabbing Flipper's hand. The bear was circling round the tent. "Run towards the rocks," shouted Alan pointing towards the stone outcrop that sheltered the tent and turned towards the bear.
[Threat assessment] he demanded of his armour.
[Male Grizzly Bear. 220 Kilos. Single specimen within area. Shield effective.]
He took a deep breath and wondered what to do. He drew himself together and looked at his hands. He was holding tightly to a tin of Coca-Cola. He smiled at himself. So much for the big strong man. I'm armed with a can of soda. [Suggest weapon.] he asked the armour querulously.
[We will take care of this Sir] said a trooper as she took him by the shoulders and pulled him gently back. [Commander Denn suggests that you should go and assist the young ladies.]
Alan looked as the outlines of the battle armour of the soldiers eclipsed the bear. Five of them were gathering round it but they did not seem to

have any weapons he recognised in their hands. He took a deep breath and ran towards the rocks. That was their problem and they knew what to do more than he did.[Alacia. I have never been more pleased to see troopers on earth.]

[I may quote you on that. Be serious. This is not a Vestel. It is only a little scavenger on a low gravity planet. You could rip it apart with your bare hands.]

[Be serious yourself. I have never ripped apart anything more threatening than an unwanted invitation. Where are the girls?]

Alacia must have switched something because suddenly his mapper switched to infra-red vision and he immediately saw the two of them huddled in their snow suits in a gully near the top of the pile. He jumped up to them and crouched down saying "It's staying at the tent."

"What did you do?" asked Flipper, her voice harsh with fear.

He wondered how to answer and still feeling the can in his hand said "Er. I threw some tins at it but it was more interested in eating our food so I think it will stay distracted. Hey it was big. I know you promised an exciting weekend but I never thought you could deliver real bears."

"A bear," said Dizzy dissolutely. "I thought the local park rangers were still collecting money to buy a stuffed bear from Canada so people would know what used to live about here."

"We get all the luck," said Flipper disconsolately.

"I hope you weren't planning on lending the tent out next weekend," said Alan wrapping his arms round them. "It looks a bit second hand now."

"Stuff the tent," said Dizzy. "If we get out of this alive I will never venture into these mountains again. Look we need the tent or we freeze. We haven't even got our anoraks. We're in real trouble now."

"Don't worry Dr. Lernski," the General exuded confidence. "The well being of the whole team is important to us. We have their route so we just send a party with Jeeps to go over it from both ends. Lots of my men here have families so there will be no complaints and we have some of the best mountain people in the state. We often help out the Park Rangers. We'll get them down unhurt. Don't worry."

Back in Bill's office they looked at one another.

Bill shook his head. "Now comes the awful part," he said. "We just gotta wait and hope they didn't do anything stupid."

"They wouldn't," said Roger.

"Have you met my daughter?" asked Ben.

"I have," said Roger then paused.

"Damn," said Bill. "If they had some sort of radio. We could have called and discovered they were OK. I don't care what they're up to. I just want to know they've got the tent up and they're out of the cold. We can't even use the helicopters in this wind so it's just sweat it out till somebody calls."

"We need a UFO," said Ben.

"There's never one when you need one," grumbled Roger. "Then three come along all at once."

"They do tend to help people," said Ben. "And hell we need some help now. Listen to that wind."

"If I had a phone number," said Bill, "0800-ALIEN" I'd call it."

"0800-TRANZEN," said Ben. "Get them right."

"They'd want a deal," said Bill. "Hands off us and you can have the children back."

"No," said Roger morosely. "They never do deals. They just do what they think is right. If they stopped or waited we'd have not a clue. But they say 'But that is wrong' and fix it and then try to cover up afterwards. It's like they are just wandering around doing things we cannot comprehend and suddenly somebody does something that really offends them and they fix it and then they say 'Oh bother, time to do some security'. One of our people at Warwick reckoned they were watching us and were almost automatically protecting us. We had a fire and the alarms went off even though they were supposed to be down for repairs. Just one of those things said security but it just worked out that nobody was hurt."

"So if the kids walk down the hill tomorrow and say 'snow? what snow?' we give up because they have got us wired already," murmured Bill. He sighed. "Look. I don't normally drink but I've got about half a bottle of Jack Daniel's in the cabinet for visitors. Split three ways it will help pass the evening without being enough to be irresponsible. Dawn is a long way away yet. In cases like this they find them at dawn and then it is either too late or it isn't."

Roger looked at him. "I don't normally but don't count me out yet. It could be a long night yet."

"Come on Bill," said Ben, stretching himself out on the big leather arm chairs in the meeting room end of the office. "That's needlessly morbid. They know what to do and they've got the right gear. It snows so you pitch camp and wait it out. They know they checked in with the park rangers so they know we know they're up there so all they have to do is wait on the trail and they get found. If two gals and a guy can't keep warm in a small tent then teenagers have changed since I was one. Pour the whiskey. Later we will need it inside so we'd better put it there now."

"OK OK so I'm a worried old Papa," said Bill rattling glasses out of the cabinet. "But it seems only yesterday that those two were tinies playing together on the hearthrug. They were such darlings."

"You didn't say that when they took the garden hose into the lounge to

water the house plants as I remember," said Ben taking a glass.
"And left it on the sofa," grumbled Bill. "Roger. Never have daughters. Alan can't have been like that."
"No," laughed Roger. "Boys are wonderful. We all were boys so we know that for a fact. Alan never did anything like that. In fact I can't remember anything he did to upset me at most ages."
"Typical academic father," laughed Bill. "Just about remembers he has a wife because the dinners on the table must come from somewhere and wonders if the plastic ducks in the bath means that he has children." He raised his glass. "To a happy outcome gentlemen."
Roger looked perplexed. Bill laughed. "Come on then I didn't mean it."
Roger sat back and took another sip at his drink. "Don't worry," he said, "For a moment I didn't seem to remember any of Alan's childhood but it's obviously just tiredness. Darn it I'm the trauma expert. I'm just getting a taste of my own back. Perhaps I should fill out one of those wretched Kerr-Wilson forms."
"K W? Were they useless or what?" Ben reached the bottle round the others. "If the candidate was calm and relaxed and reading poems it was a zero and if they were covered in blood, much of it their own, had most of their clothes ripped off and smelt of urine, much of it their own, they scored ten. Interpolate linearly to get trauma coefficient. Fifty questions to decide that was unmitigated crap."
"If we're doing trauma shouldn't we get insights into our problems?" said Bill.
"I think the Jack Daniel's is an antidote to insight," said Roger. "So we'd better be insightful soon before it hits our blood too hard."
"In Tennessee they'd say it was the other way round but I have some questions that bug me so I'm game," said Bill. "It will pass the time and the night will be long. Do you want to play?"
Roger shrugged and Ben said "I'm game."
"Right," said Bill, "First question. Why do the stories say there are more alien women than men and yet all the people we hear about are men?"
"Easy," said Roger, "Human society is based around men so they just appear as men. If you have ten limbs and wings you have to wear a big disguise to be any sort of human so pick your sex to suit the job in hand. My turn with a question?"
Ben grinned. "Sure."
"If the men keep marrying human women what genetic effects would we see?" said Roger.
"Some inherited characteristic?" wondered Bill.
"Is there an alienness gene?" tried Ben.
"Hang on," Bill tried again. "They are always affluent and successful so even if they did not pass on any genetic material then we would see an increase in the sort of women they are attracted too."

Roger wondered "If they are reversed to us then we would expect that to show."
"What?" said Ben. "Reversed hunter-gatherer?"
"I suppose so." replied Roger. "I was thinking it would be more subtle but think it out."
"Female hunters and male gatherers?" offered Bill.
Ben scratched his jaw. "I thought there were few men?"
"You only need a few men for the species." replied Roger.
"A stud farm?" contemplated Bill. "That's not the image of the men we have?"
"If the women are strong are the men smart?" tried Ben.
"Surely that's taken are read?" laughed Bill.
"No," followed Ben. "I mean where do they invest their growth? Human women invest in their immune system so they may not be as strong but they survive better for the sake of their children so these men invest in brains?"
Roger thought it through "So smart men and strong women have alien forbears?"
"Well," Ben was disappointed. "Something more specific I was hoping."
Bill considered it "OK. So how many people would have aliens in their ancestors?"
"Sounds easy statistics if only we knew how many there were and how long they'd been here," said Ben. "Is it on file somewhere?"
"Try 100 and 6000 years," suggested Roger.
"Where did you get those figures Roger?" Bill asked.
"Blind guess but when I asked the same question at Warwick all of us who had been working on the project for several years jumped for around about those sort of numbers," Roger replied.
Ben turned on the computer terminal and started to log on. Bill banged his glass down on the table and said. "You don't need the computer Ben. With those figures the answer is simple. Everybody has alien ancestors."
"No," said Ben, "But I see what you are getting at. Let's say most of the world's population could have some trace of alien in their ancestry. Would it be equal in all population groups?"
"If your normal mate has lots of wings and you've changed your affections to humans why should you care what colour they are?" considered Roger.
Ben was unsure "We don't see them in African mythology?"
"Mythology has always got its supermen." Bill assured them. "Do we look for bird-men? Anyway all African mythology is word of mouth not written so it has been recently filtered. In cultures like that you need to look at their old art to figure out what they used to believe."
Nobody wanted to follow that so once the silence lengthened Ben said

"My question then?" and received general shrugs of agreement.
Ben looked up at the ceiling and tipped a little more whiskey into his mouth. "What do you make of the reference in the Carlsberg report where the contact said 'they smell bad' and compared with Mrs. Rodes who said 'but they don't smell'. Two of our best sources contradicted one another on points they were certain on."
Bill wrinkled his nose. "I rather missed that as I don't smell much. Are you suggesting we could detect them with trained sniffer dogs?"
"No," said Roger. "I had a report that said that they didn't care about smell so perhaps they do smell bad if left to themselves but when they are under observation they take precautions and do not smell at all?"
"It's strange that people mention things like that," said Bill. "It is rather taboo to discuss personal scent these days. Come to think of it I can't believe that Mrs. Rodes would say that. She was far to proper. Therefore it must be more significant."
Ben put his chin on his folded arms and looked across the desk at them. "Then why would she say they don't smell? I would expect none of her friends did. She was a bit too much of the Cape Cod set."
Roger wondered. "Perhaps they just never smelt. Even when you would expect it?"
"I never expect it," said Bill "But I'm just defective. When do you expect people to smell?"
"Not normally," said Roger. "Even after playing rugger you're hot and sticky but you'd have to leave it before it smells. Tramps smell."
"You have a normal sense of smell Roger?" asked Bill.
"Well yes," he replied.
"Well neither of us have," pointed out Bill.
"It's quite a common sensory deprivation. Alan has very little. He doesn't realise that his mother is baking till be walks into the kitchen and sees cakes while I have been dying of hunger, well... greed maybe, for ages."
"So neither us nor your son would be able to detect an alien by scent and we still do not know what they smell like if they smell at all."
"They smell badly or they do not smell?" rehearsed Ben. "Again I have that nagging doubt that we're missing something obvious here. Is there any way to resolve these two?"
"They fail to smell good?" offered Bill.
"Pheromones?" asked Roger.
"You mean they fail to smell correctly?" developed Ben. "They have a missing smell. But that is a pretty obscure thing to notice and a weird one to comment on. Perhaps it is something that we just take as so normal we don't notice it and when you meet somebody that doesn't smell like that it stands out a mile."
"Maybe we should get somebody in to smell all our specimens in case

there is a clue in them. I'll make a note to phone central in the morning. Monday I mean. Those stupid kids. What are we doing in the office in the dead of night?"

"Drinking and arguing about work because thinking about them is worse," said Ben. "I'd be a lot happier to know they were all snuggled up together making teenage mistakes than thinking that they might be out in the cold and snow."

[Alharan. The current prognosis is that as humans in your current situation you should all be dead well before morning. We need to do something more.]
[How is the tent?]
[Sorry. We were not sure what to do and we waited while the bear tore up much of the stuff as we were more worried about stopping it following you. It was frightened of the troopers I think. The tent is ripped up and useless now and the sleeping bags are already soaked. Do you want us to fake up a replacement and get it erected? We would need about twenty minutes to remanufacture it. Less if you will take approximate or if we steal a similar one from a shop or somewhere.]
[<Diseree> will be beyond recovery without treatment by then after her soaking earlier. <Philippa> is not much better. I need to do something now. It needs be believable even if far fetched. Can you get me a big plastic bag? Say eight foot by four? Like my new mattress came in. Wind and waterproof with no holes but tatty looking, like garbage found in a forest. Quickly.]
[Manufacturing now. It will buy you a few hours. There will be a trooper with it near you in forty seconds. Just get out of sight of the girls and she will find you.]

Alan got up and peered into the gloom and driving snow. "Hold this," he said pushing something into Flipper's hand and taking the torch, "I think I see something."

Flipper pulled at him. "Don't go," she said, "You'll get lost," but he was gone.

"What's he doing?" asked Dizzy.

"Dunno. He doesn't know that the first rule of survival is to stay together," said Flipper wondering what she was holding but Alan was back waving the torch excitedly.

"It's a plastic sack," he said, "It's huge. It might keep the wind and snow off a bit. We can get under it, or even better inside it." It was huge, nearly as big as the tent and transparent with writing on it. He laid it in the hollow with the open end down wind. Dizzy wiggled in feet first, then Flipper.

"Is it OK?" asked Alan.

"Yes," said Flipper pushing Dizzy over to one side away from her.

"Squeeze in."
The two girls tried to move away from Alan's boots as he squeezed between them then let the rounded gully flop them back together.
"Snuggle up," said Alan folding the open end up so a bit of air would get in. "Conserve heat," he added. He clicked out the torch again.
"Gosh it's good to be out of that wind," he finished.
"I'm so cold it hurts," whimpered Flipper into the darkness. "And the wet is getting into my suit."
"I don't feel so cold any more," mumbled Dizzy.
"Don't go to sleep," insisted Flipper. "We just have to survive till the storm blows itself out then they can come and find us."
[Alharan. <Desiree>'s core temperature is still dropping.]
[I thought so. I'm going to turn my body mapper off.]
[Off? You can't do that. We never show our Varhyn forms to humans.]
[It's pitch dark and they are both wearing snow suits and gloves. What they need is an 140 kilo Varhyn male generating three times as much heat as any human and who comes with a built in feather quilt. I have the torch so I control what they see and my hands are very human and so is my face.]
[They will recognise that something is different if they touch your body.]
[They are both wearing snow suits and gloves and, anyway, they are getting past recognising anything already. When the day comes they will assume they dreamt it. The alternative is I hit them with an anaesthetic from my medikit and you put in a Tokimed team to sort them out. How we explain that I just don't know because if you fall asleep in the snow you generally do not wake up. These are the worst people in the world to do that too. We are going to make matters worse.]
[You will do the explanations I am sure. I already have a Tokimed team ready and on the ground near to you. That is how we are monitoring the girls.]
[It's handy to be able to do invisible.]
[Invisible is not worth a light in driving snow but they are as near as we dare get them without being seen. Do you think you can manage things?]
[If this does not work you will have to take over. Oh. If that bear comes back can you do something about it?]
[We will monitor the girl's core temperatures. If they reach the lower limits it is Tokimed and you can start thinking about the excuses. Do not worry about the bear. It is gone. When it had finished licking up your dinner it tried to follow you but I have troopers in the woods all around you so all you have to worry about now is the cold. I told them to arrest it and move it twenty miles away. I was not sure if it was rare or valuable or accounted for so I did not want to shoot it needlessly and

leave another problem for a security clean up.]
[Right. I am glad you have things in hand. Setting the mapper to off.]
"Alan. What's happening?" Dizzy asked.
"Stay close and let me put my arms round you. Stop fidgeting Flipper."
Flipper did not want to be told. "Some thing's tickling my face and something smells funny."
Alan was not reassuring "Don't ask what the sack might have had in it. We might not want to know that ladies."
But Flipper was reassured "Provide its not bear I don't care what I can smell."
"Your voice sounds funny," muttered Dizzy. "And I want to go to sleep. That's bad isn't it?"
"Very bad," said Alan's funny voice. "Talk about something exciting so you stay awake. Generate some heat."
"Argue," said Flipper. "Alan. Who are you taking to the form party?"
He chuckled mischievously. "What if I asked Rachael? Do you think she'd say yes?"
Flipper knew "She'd say 'In yer dreams Buster'. She's dated Andrew as of Friday lunchtime."
"Aww sucks Flipper. Aside from being strong, tall and handsome what has Andrew got the I haven't?" laughed Alan.
"Well Rachael for a start," she replied, "If he plays his cards right. Be serious. He's the academic king, he's captain of the football team and he's totally smitten with the girl. Aside from his being deliriously gorgeous I can't see what on earth she sees in him."
A little voice on Alan's other side asked "Alan. If you want to take Rachael to the party why are you tucked up in bed with Flipper and me?"
"Dizzy I'd give anything to be tucked up in bed with you and Flipper right now," he responded.
Her voice was very quiet. "It feels like we're tucked up in a big quilt. Is that a promise? If we ever get out of all this snow will you do it?"
"Wild," said Alan encouragingly, "You'll have to get Flipper to agree if you want to do a threesome."
"So you do do kinky after all," Dizzy almost laughed. "Shall we make him promise Flipper?"
Flipper wanted Dizzy to continue. "Why not? A girl needs something to look forward too. Sign me up. I'm game."
Alan was more hesitant "Can we think about it later? This might not be the time to plan things like that."
Dizzy poked him. "But you just said you'd 'give anything'."
"It's a figure of speech Dizzy," Alan excused himself. "I want you both to be safe, warm and comfortable. That's probably the most important thing to me at the moment."

Dizzy was not accepting excuses "And I want to be warm and comfortable with you."

"And Flipper makes three? Is she still included?" Alan insisted in complicating the issue.

"Oh yes," cut in Flipper, "Better than a silly noisy party. Look Alan. This is the time to plan things like that. We're either going to die or we're not so I'm not going to waste time worrying about my homework. If it isn't important tonight then forget it, tonight you are very important to us and sex is always important to everyone. That's just human."

"I realise that but don't worry, if we're careful we will make it through," Alan almost sounded worried. "You don't have to plan the rest of your life instantly tonight. You'll have plenty of time to get your sex life together. If you want to include me in your plans I'll be very flattered." Flipper was enjoying the game. "That's not so enthusiastic. You're not changing your mind are you Alan? Dizzy will be ever so disappointed." Dizzy tried to sound hurt "Promise Alan," she pouted. "Please. Flipper. Make him promise."

"Alan you ought to promise," scolded Flipper. "Dizzy is just a poor girl who is offering herself, well offering both of us actually, to you in a moment of crisis. It is hardly gentlemanly to ignore such an offer and positively insulting to turn it down. Anyway don't you think it would be fun?"

"More fun than I can cope with at the moment," he laughed.

"Promise then," said Flipper pragmatically.

"Now. Alan. Please," pressured Dizzy.

[Well done. Less than two minutes and the temperatures are rising. Not to mention hormone levels. Keep them going like this and we have made it.]

[Thank you for reminding me that I have an audience Alacia.]

[Currently the highest access channel on ship-net. Everybody's ready to help.]

"Help. I'm trapped between the two most beautiful girls in the world and they are trying to seduce me," he tried.

"If you don't promise I will go to sleep," threatened Dizzy.

"I don't find that very seductive Dizzy," he explained. "You'll have to come up with something more sexy than that."

"If you even think of going to sleep I'll pinch you," said Flipper finding that a bit too close to things that were worrying her.

"Stay out of this Flipper. He hasn't promised yet," Dizzy actually complained.

"I'm not promising anything," said Alan wondering if anybody could tell the facts from the game, "I demand to be properly seduced somewhere warm when I've got time to enjoy it and to participate enthusiastically."

"You just said you wanted to go to bed with me," whimpered Dizzy.
"Dizzy? I'm not sure I did," he said, but gently not wanting to hurt her.
"Why not? What's wrong with me?" she bit back.
He laughed, suddenly reassured that she was playing the game. "Aside from being cantankerous and twisting my words nothing is wrong with you. I'm sure you'd be wonderful in bed as you've both got the figure for it. You'll have to excuse me tonight. My libido is suppressed by the cold and with two of you here I'm a bit confused. Half an hour in a hot tub and I'd find you both too sexy for words but right now stay in your snow suits, you'd find me a bit disappointing."
"Alan? A question. Seriously for a moment," Dizzy was suddenly gentle again with just a taste of worry in her voice.
Alan could not resist. "Sure Dizzy."
"Do you find me sexy? Not just nice, not just a friend. Don't kid about. Tell me the real truth," she asked.
He took a deep breath. "OK. The serious, truthful answer is yes."
"Explain," she asked.
Another deep breath. "Serious and truthful but no comebacks if you don't like the why?"
Dizzy was taking no prisoners "Tell me. No promises."
Dizzy felt him swallow before he answered. His voice was soft but clear. She was almost worried she had gone too far. "I like skinny rather than fat. I like rounded but not top heavy. I like strong personalities rather than weak. I like long hair but don't mind the colour. I like smooth skin. Pretty helps, spots don't. It's that simple. I'm hardly demanding am I?"
"That's both of us," said Flipper buoyantly. "Am I sexy too?"
"Both of you are very sexy," Alan laughed feeling the tension that had welled up in a moment dissipate just as fast. "So is Rachael but I hear she's taken. Do you see why you're giving me trouble? You're both sexy, really sexy to me and on top of that I like you two both masses as people but then you want me to choose between you."
"So that's why you want to go to bed with both of us," chuckled Dizzy, "I can see it all now."
"If that's how you want to read it," Alan offered. "Can I take both of you to the party?"
"We take turns to dance?" said Dizzy.
"Then we take turns to slide outside for a smooch," added Flipper.
"I thought it might be that sort of a party. You see my problem?" asked Alan.
"Yeah. To get in all the smooching for two you'll have no time to dance," reasoned Flipper.
"He said he can't dance Flipper," Dizzy reminded her. "So it's OK."
Flipper made a hmm noise to indicate she was considering it. "If he can

smooch well enough then we forgive him. Right?"
Alan started to object but suddenly he had somebody leaning on his chest. "I might not... Hey! My ear. I muuummmmm..."
Flipper waited and listened until she heard her friend flop back down and say. "Not bad when you relax and open your mouth. Your try Flipper."
"I..." managed Alan.
"Shut up and pucker up," insisted Flipper fumbling for his cheeks with gloved hands and lurching up onto his chest as he lay on his back. He seemed bigger than she expected but that must be the snow suit. She did not just kiss him she tried everything she had ever imagined just in case it was the last time.
Finally she relaxed and laid her head on his chest. She breathed deeply. "Wow Alan," she said softly. "Where did you learn to kiss like that?"
She felt him bounce as he chuckled under her. "Did I do something special?" he asked. "I thought that's what people normally did?"
Flipper lay still, not wanting to move. "On a sample of three boy friends that is : No, No, and I don't know, I never let him try," she said.
Dizzy was pushing at her to move over. "What was special Flipper?" she insisted. "You had longer than me. Alan what did you do?"
Alan was apologetic. "I'm sorry Dizzy. You rather caught me out. I didn't really get going till Flipper started." He felt the two girls pushing on top of him. Flipper gave way graciously.
"Then kiss me again," demanded Dizzy. "Like you did her."
Alan almost sighed but restrained himself. "OK. But you have to be more relaxed this time."
Dizzy was affronted "You were the one... Oh come here."
Flipper was still leaning up against Alan and felt him rocked by Dizzy's assault. She smiled to herself. She's not cold now she thought. That meant she was a legitimate target. "Stop grunting Dizzy," she said. "You sound like a hog."
Dizzy stopped for breath. She too had put everything into it this time and had got everything back. She was quite amazed. "It was never like that. Ever."
Alan's arms squeezed them both up to him "So you girls do approve of something I do?" he said. "Or are you a bit less critical now than you would be at other times?"
Dizzy was still breathless. "Yeah," she gasped. "But why were you hiding talents like this. We could have been enjoying that ever since you came?"
Alan excused himself. "I didn't know that's what you wanted. Don't Americans know how to ask for things if they want them?"
Flipper huffed, unsure if she was annoyed at him. "Be serious. Kiss me

like I've never been kissed before is not one of those polite introductions we learn at kindergarten."

"Alan," asked Dizzy is a very deep, seductive voice. "Are you a virgin? Because if you do sex like you kiss I could need to revise a lot of those things I learned in Sunday School."

Alan squeezed them again. "Well Dizzy I've never been asked that one before. Not tonight though, so stay warm and don't go to sleep on us." She smiled to herself "I'm not going to go to sleep now. I'm hardly cold any more."

"Well keep your snow suit on girl," reminded Flipper. "Oh and when did you ever go to Sunday School?"

"Before we came to the project. When I was little."

"And they taught you about things like that? We just got wimpy stories. I think most of my Sunday school teachers only had the vaguest ideas about any sin not available to people under the age of five and not involving temper tantrums or candy bars. What did they tell you?"

"Not to be bad, but with no definition. And there was stuff about respecting yourself and things like that. I'm sure they wouldn't approve of sleeping with your steady and such but, at a guess, most of them never had the opportunity."

"Hey..." said Alan but Dizzy interrupted him.

"Don't you start," she said. "I don't approve of things like that either but if I wanted to I could so not doing it counts."

"Damn right," said Flipper. "Smooch and cuddle all you want but if you even think about going to sleep I will pinch bits of you you didn't even know you had. You fall asleep in the snow and you're history. I want to hear some heavy breathing over there. Right?"

Alan laughed. "Gosh," he said. "The practical application of lust to mountain survival. And I thought that that sort of after-school class would be boring. How wrong can I be? Did you have to practice much?"

"Just common sense," laughed Flipper. "If you're short of sleeping bags and you pair them up boy-girl they're bound to stay warmer. Why do you think we brought you on this hike? Just a sensible precaution that's all. You can't be too careful in the mountains."

He chuckled gently. "That's a relief," he said. "I was a bit worried that you might have a dubious hidden agenda."

"Be serious," said Dizzy. "We're not subtle. Our only agenda item was to get you miles from anyone else, alone in a tent with just us. Nothing hidden about that. If it wasn't for little things like falling in rivers, a blizzard and a bear we'd have got along fine. Cramps your style do things like that."

There was a pause then Flipper asked gently "Dizzy. But do you think we would have got to kiss him without all that?"

Dizzy drew and exhaled a deep breath noisily. "Well, I think we could

have come to some arrangement." she said.
"But I wouldn't have realised I didn't mind sharing him until I feared we might be all going to die and that you needed him as much as I did," Flipper replied.
"Turns seem quite sensible," replied Dizzy. "But I see what you mean. If you'd tried to kiss him on the way up I'd have called foul straight away."
"When you held his hand I did too," responded Flipper with a touch of edge developing in her voice.
"Nice wasn't it?" interjected Alan before they could explore it further. "There can't be many lads get to walk hand in hand with their two best girls. I liked it." Somehow it seemed churlish to argue more.
As the silence began to lengthen Flipper, anxious to keep everybody talking, asked "What do you think they are doing at home?"
"My folks are going over to yours. Remember," grunted Dizzy.
"And mine," added Alan.
"What?" said Dizzy sitting up a bit. "You didn't tell us that?"
"It didn't seem... What's the matter?" he replied.
"So we were rumbled before we started," said Dizzy flopping down again. "They probably knew we were all here together before the snow started."
"Is that a problem?" asked Alan. "You are chaperoning one another."
"Mothers don't think like that Alan," pointed out Flipper. "We were actually hoping for a bit of secrecy here. That is why we asked you not to mention who you were going with."
"It will be alright," he said. "I'm sure we can explain."
"To my dad I might explain," said Flipper, "To my mum? Taking a boy camping? It might be screaming, it might be tears, but it won't be listening."
"No," said Alan. "She won't. She might be cross but..."
"You don't know my mum," interrupted Flipper. "When she's cross."
"Wrong," said Alan. "I do enough. You just wind her up that's all. Mothers are a resource and they are there to help but if you won't let them help they don't know what to do and get all stressed out. One cry of 'Mum. Help. What do I do now?' and she'll come over all mother hen and since she has been sixteen and seventeen and more and had to manage it you'll be surprised what she found out."
"Heresy," muttered Dizzy. "No teenager believes that. How late would they let you stay out?"
They felt him shrug. "Never had any problems. If what I wanted to do was seriously late, like early hours, I'd ask if it was reasonable, and safe, I'd usually get told I wasn't to walk home at that time of night and get given cab fare. If you go in confrontational you get confrontation. Go with a problem and you get solutions."
"It never seems that simple," said Dizzy. "Mum. I've got this boy I'm

madly in love with but he's not interested in me."
"She'd probably say 'You poor thing. I've been there,'" offered Alan. "Have you ever tried this?"
Dizzy thought about it for a while. "But would she tell me how to get him?" she asked.
"She might ask if he was worth the effort but she might have done it and be able to advise," Alan replied. "She might advise dumping him and she might be right."
"Mum he's English," offered Dizzy. "And although he kisses well he doesn't seem to volunteer much."
"Careful," he laughed. "She's probably approve of that. Mums tend to think you should start slowly and work up gradually."
"Good," laughed Dizzy throwing an arm round him. "So you think my mum would approve of you. So it's all right to snuggle up to you."
"She'd probably approve more if she was sure Flipper was right here with us and that I have my arms round her just as much."
"My mum wouldn't approve of what I'm thinking about you," said Flipper.
"You're allowed to think," said Dizzy. "They can't take that away from you."
"If they approve of what you do that is the main thing," offered Alan. "If you approve of what you do that is even more. Having both of you to snuggle up to is wonderful and takes the edge off being cold and wet and as long as we are trapped in these suits by the snow I can do anything I want and so can you."
"Anything Alan?" asked Flipper.
"If you can think of anything your mother can disapprove of that can be done in a snow suit go ahead," he said confidently.
"I could kiss you extravagantly and crawl all over you," tried Flipper.
"She probably thinks you do that already," said Dizzy. "Weasel words Alan. What about a promise that we can do anything we like when we get down off the damn mountain?"
"Well," he replied. "I could be open to offers. Negotiation. We'll worry about that in the morning, after breakfast."
Flipper audibly flopped. "Shit," she breathed. "I'd give a lot to know we are going to make it to breakfast. If the wind and the snow don't get us we might not have seen the last of the bear. If this is life we'd better make the most of it."
"I'm cold but I'm not getting colder," insisted Alan. "And I don't think either of you are getting worse now. Just don't go to sleep on me that's all."
Dizzy poked him. "I'm not going to sleep," she said. "I was as I said but being here is... well novel. I've never slept with a boy before."
Alan growled. "The one thing you are not going to do tonight is sleep

with me Dizzy. If you stop answering for a moment I might just tickle you."

Dizzy curled up at the thought. "Don't even think about it," she giggled. "I will fight. I will kick. I will scratch. You will regret it."

"But you will wake up," said Alan. "Cheap at the price. The entertainment value alone could be worth the lost blood."

"By the time dawn comes round," cautioned Flipper. "We may need to resort to more direct measures than that to stay warm and awake. At the moment I feel almost warm but I wonder if I'm kidding myself. I can still wiggle my toes and feel them though and I've been worse than that just walking home from school."

"I want to do something naughty," said Dizzy deliberately changing the subject. "If we're going to get zapped for taking Alan camping I've done nothing yet to be worth the punishment. What do I do Flipper?"

"Put your tongue in his mouth," she replied.

"Flipper. Why should I... Oh yes. Alan I think you ought to kiss me again so I stay warm," Propping herself up on one elbow beside him and reaching over to touch his face with her gloved hand.

"You feel warm to me. Are you sure?" queried Alan.

"I'll be the judge of that," she was insistent.

"But what if Flipper is cold?" he asked.

"I'm frozen," said Flipper supporting him.

Dizzy tut tutted. "Your turn is next Henderson. Patience is a virtue. Remember your Sunday School lessons."

"That's right Dizzy. Share. Take turns," Flipper wanted her rights.

"Just a moment," interrupted Alan sounding slightly worried. "Are you two fighting over me?"

"Flipper and I are just planning the next key event in your life," he was told.

"And what might that be?" he asked.

"A surprise," counselled Dizzy.

"Oh goody. I like surprises," he said.

"This one will blow your mind boy," offered Flipper.

"I think you are over excited girls," he cautioned.

"Nah. This is relaxed girls. When we get back, in the warm, then we'll show you over excited girls," Flipper pointed out.

Another squeeze. They liked that. "I'll look forward to that. For now just stay snuggled up so we don't lose any more heat," He rocked his head one way. "Flipper? What is that you're pushing into me?"

"My nose. I'm keeping your ear warm," she said.

"No. Not that. The cold thing on my neck," he pointed out.

She paused as if having to think back. "It's the thing you gave me to hold."

He relaxed "The what? Oh that. It's just a can of coke. I don't know why

I rescued it from the tent but I ended up with it. Something to eat might have been better."

"No Alan," said Flipper. "You can live for much longer without food than drink but we will not have problems lasting till morning regardless. Come to think of it give it to Dizzy. It might help her stay awake."

"I'm awake," said Dizzy. "But there again if you're offering."

"Can you drink lying down?" asked Alan.

Dizzy did not see a problem. "I'll try. Do we do shares?"

Alan seemed to jolt slightly. "I'm OK but if you girls want to have it I don't think we'll bother to take it home with us."

"Is it a bit shaken up?" asked Flipper anxiously.

"Flipper," cautioned Alan. "I was holding it and looking at a bear so be careful it will probably explode and this entire sack will be full of foam. No. You've been holding it for ages or so I guess it's flat again now."

Dizzy and Alan listened as Flipper shuffled about and finally heard the chuck, phut, creek noise of a ring pull. There was more shuffling and a very unlady-like slurping noise.

"It is coke," said Flipper. "I rather hoped it would have been some of the Doctor Pepper I bought. Who's next?"

"Shall I pass it over to Dizzy?" asked Alan.

"Yeah. Reach over," said Flipper.

"Coming across. Where are you Dizzy?" asked Alan.

She was not ready. "Not yet," she said lurching about. "I need to face outwards. I can't drink lying on my back. I'd just tip it all over my face."

Alan held the tin above him till she seemed settled then slowly lowered it towards her. "OK here you are," he said letting his arm drape across her so she could find the hand with her gloved fingers.

She had her gloves off however so she could feel the tin. "Thanks," she said, then "Gosh Alan your hand is so cold. Where are your gloves?"

"Lost them," he suggested as they would be returned when he mapped back to Alan Woden. "It's the hand from the other side. You're wrapped in my left arm."

"Well give it to Flipper. She'll warm it up," she replied.

Alan was unsure about that. "You drink the coke. I'll look after my hands. No! Flipper? Stop it "

Flipper was pulling at his shoulder and arm. "If she's got a hand I get a hand. You should have mitten strings like we have if you're going to lose your gloves. Pah. Little boys."

Alan was trying to keep his arm from inspection. "You keep your hands in your gloves. I'm OK. Well stop... It doesn't bend that... Flipper!"

Everything went still with a zip noise. "It will be warm now," Flipper assured them.

"Yes. Thank you," said Alan a touch tetchily.

"What did you do Flipper?" asked Dizzy cautiously.

You could hear the smirk. "Unzipped my snow suit, tucked it in a bit and zipped it back up. It was a bit of a shock but it's getting warmer as we speak."
Dizzy enquired "Where's your other hand Alan?"
Alan saw this coming and tried to defend himself. "You're lying on it. It's quite happy. Don't worry. Ouch. Dizzy. Lie still. We have hours to wait till morning yet. Alright. Alright. You win."
"You don't mind do you Alan?" Dizzy felt she ought to ask.
He hesitated long enough to imply he was dubious but said "Well not really. But if I'd tried to put my hand there I trust you would have been offended."
Flipper cut in "Maybe. Don't count on it."
Dizzy sniggered. "Be serious Flipper. We're good girls. We wouldn't stand for that."
"Well. Not without an invitation," she was told.
Alan tried to sound grumpy but failed. "Who was invited? This is bullying. You are taking advantage of me. Look can I ask a question?"
"Shoot," said Flipper.
Alan paused and Dizzy burped. There was a pause again while everybody giggled.
"Up till this weekend neither of you has done more than talk to me and now here we are getting quite intimately acquainted. What brings this on?" has asked. "Is it something aphrodisiac about camping or is it bears? I think I need to know this because it will make a great deal of difference to how I plan the rest of my life. Do I have to have a bear to be a hit with girls or can I get away with just a tent?"
The left side of him said "We really fancied you didn't we Flipper."
Then the right side said "We were waiting for you to do something."
"Boys always start things," finished Dizzy.
Alan sounded perplexed. "But how are they to know when they should? It would surely be wrong to 'start something' unless you are sure the girl approves of you?"
Flipper laughed. "Ha? You're kidding? When your heart is breaking it is never, absolutely never, the right boy that wants to console you."
"Alan. Were you waiting for us to give you some sort of sign?" asked Dizzy.
"Well. One of you perhaps. Something," he mumbled.
Dizzy asked the crucial question. "Which one?"
Alan fudged. "Oh grief. Look. I didn't mind. I like you both. I hoped one of you might just like me like that too."
"No preference?" asked Dizzy not sure if she was relieved or disappointed.
Alan sounded worried. "Well. Not really. A clear sign would help. When Rachael asked me if I had made a date for the form party I said no and

she warned me not to leave it too long or I might miss out and I asked how you knew if somebody wants to be asked and she said they'll just raise the matter casually in conversation and I said but what if the..."

"Bitch!" screamed Dizzy explosively.

Alan paused, shocked while he gathered his thoughts. "No," he restarted, "I'm sure she didn't..."

"Bitch! Bitch! Bitch! I'll strangle her," Dizzy was not interested in excuses.

Alan sounded worried. "No Dizzy. She couldn't... Flipper? What's the matter."

Flipper was convulsed with laughter beyond control. She struggled for breath and finally said "Alan I'm sure she didn't. It was merely coincidence that she accepted Andrew's date just after I told her we were all going camping this weekend. I'm sure it was all innocent and lovely. She looked so black on Friday you wouldn't believe it and I never guessed. Grief I never guessed."

Alan began to sound panicky. "No. Surely you don't think she wanted... Oh no. This is too awful. She must be so offended."

Dizzy needed to clear something up. "Alan. Would you have taken her?"

"No. I wanted one of you," he was suddenly breathing hard. "I thought she was just being friendly, helpful and explaining things. But I should have... Oh I don't know... How do you say no to somebody like that? Kindly?"

Flipper was convulsed again. "And I told her we were going camping in Dizzy's little tent. I said no for you. Slammed the door. Dizzy what do you think?"

Dizzy was upset. "I'm not happy. You can laugh but she tried to pinch Alan. Everybody knew we had first call. What if he'd been too embarrassed to say no? Flipper! It's not funny."

Flipper could not help it. "Oh it is. It is. She tried to pinch him and she got slapped right back. And she's at home now thinking we're up to grief knows what and she isn't getting any."

"No," said Alan. "I agree that it's not funny. She's a friend. A nice person and it's mean to talk about her like that. You are probably making far too much out of an innocent conversation. I didn't know you were telling anybody at school. I think that is a bit silly as they may well read too much into it. It's not like we are doing anything improper."

Dizzy asked very softly "Alan. Do you know where your hand is?"

Alan paused. He replied softly too. "Don't tell me Dizzy. The way you ask that I suspect I might not want to officially know."

Dizzy was pleased with the effect. "It's just on my tummy. But that's not the important thing. We are lying in a plastic bag in the snow. We've been attacked by a bear. I'm still not convinced we are even going to live but it is very important to me that you are here with me. Now, I will share you with Flipper. She is here. She has been through all this. But Rachael offends me. She is tucked up at home in bed. She hasn't crossed any tree bridges. She hasn't fallen in any rivers. She isn't struggling to stay warm. She's probably never even seen a bear. She can stay out of it. If I want to do something improper I damn well will. I have earned it."

Alan went soft and reassuring. "Dizzy. Relax. I'm not interested in her. I will be polite and friendly because I always am. You don't have to worry. Anyway. She hasn't got my hand on her tummy." He paused. "Dizzy?" he asked. "You're not ticklish are you? Because I was stroking you before but I didn't know it was your tummy and now I'm frightened to move."

"Daft Galoot," she said. "It was nice."

He wanted further reassurance "And you aren't really struggling to stay warm are you? You feel quite OK."

She took pity on him "Not now. Everything seems to be moving and working but I was cold before. Badly cold. I was frightened. I seemed to be losing contact with my toes but they're great now."

Alan rolled his head the other way "And you Flipper? OK?"

She wriggled in a snuggley way. "I was cold but I've got a nice warm arm to hold on to. Alan you are just the central heating system a girl needs. I'm sorry I laughed. It was funny though. It might be innocent but Rachael is not the type to be pushy or say anything like that. She'd just hope and show she was willing and waiting so she must have been on edge. But she's a nice girl. Really. Not like those Lernski and Henderson brats."

"Should I avoid them then?" he sounded worried.

"Too late," Flipper insisted.

"Damn aliens. I've been abducted then?" tried Alan.

Flipper followed through "As good as. This sack is just a dummy. You're actually locked on a flying saucer and being used as a sex slave."

Alan was losing touch again "I don't remember anything like that in Dad's files. Are you sure they do things like that?"

Flipper was in control. "You're our first victim so we'll see how it goes."

He tried reference back to a previous conversation. "Do I have to marry lots of you?"

"Just two," she came straight back.

Alan was genuinely surprised. "You would be happy with that?"

"Deliriously," said Flipper giving his arm a cuddle again.

Alan seemed to go silent, pensive, but somehow it was his turn. Finally he said "Flipper?"

"Um?" she just made a go ahead noise.

"Do you have much of a sense of smell?" he asked lightly.

"Not really," answered Flipper, grouping for the usual excuses. "It's my sinuses they say but I think it's Dad's grotty genes. I should to have chosen my parents more carefully. Don't worry. Dizzy's got it worse than me so you can't avoid it. Why do you ask?"
"Butterfly mind. I must be dozing off. Dizzy? You awake?" he diverted.
"I'm more awake than you are. I could stay on subject. Don't worry about me," came the response.
[Well?]
[We are trying. It is not going to be easy to get blood samples in your current position but the Tokimed crew will try to get close enough and we have distance equipment to send them. I will get back to you when we've processed them. It is obviously a possibility but why did you not think of it? You are the psychologist.]
[Too uncommon and both of them too?]
[You said top intuitive people. Is that not super-gene stuff?]
[Yes and sometimes. Get me some results. Do we now understand the two fathers all of a sudden?]
[Well Betron is suddenly working like mad so he thinks it is significant. Just wait. We will call you. If you guys did not get involved with human females there would be no super-gene to worry about.]
[Oh good. It is my fault then. I am sorry. I apologise for all the trouble I am causing you.]
[Well watch out for the other problem.]
[You mean what?]
[If they are descended from you they fall in love with you every time.]
[Not true. So my descendants show, on average, more discernment and a laudable choice in partners but it is not inevitable.]
[A girl who on the pretence of warming your hand tucks it under her shirt and into her knickers is not being sisterly.]
[That from the girl who, to re-enforce my bodyguard, joined my harem. Which one?]
[Both of them. The harem would have been fun if you had not already over complicated it. <Philippa> is in mid sentence. Sorry. I am talking too long.]
"Why did you guess I don't smell much Alan?"
Alan grabbed to get his mind round the sentence. "Er. Sorry. I was idly thinking about bears that smell our dinner and didn't somebody say this sack smelt funny? No reason. Just going gaga that's all."
Dizzy conveniently diverted the conversation. "Don't worry Flipper. You don't smell much because you shower regularly."
"Shut up Dizzy," bit Flipper. "No Alan you jumped without hesitation from one subject to another. You are perverse sometimes. Was it important or is it that you wanted to change the subject? What were we talking about before?"

"You said that you wanted us both to marry him," Dizzy remembered. "I can think of some parents who might ask you to reconsider."
"That was it," Flipper put her mind back into thread. "Don't be funny Alan but seriously. We don't do polygamy in the west but some places still do. What do you feel about it because we discussed it once in class and I was surprised to find it didn't seem too wrong but most of the girls were vehemently against it and most of the boys said they didn't see how you could love two people fairly."
She felt him sigh. "Flipper I suspect it's more down to the culture you grow up in. If you saw your father love several wives and our friends fathers do the same it would probably work for you. But we're westerners and we've never seen it so we'd be bound to get it wrong. Don't worry about it."
A gloved fist banged him on the chest. "No. I'm not talking about us," Flipper growled. "You're as bad as Dizzy. It's the whole idea I'm interested in."
Alan sounded floppy and thoughtful. "Well there is man born for each woman so for humans it would be greedy. Anyhow Dizzy went spotty at the prospect of Rachael taking me to the party so what makes you think you could share a man and retain any cool?"
"Hey," Dizzy interrupted. "I was worried she was trying to steal you away. If she'd come and negotiated with us we could maybe do a deal. A couple of dances maybe."
"And a smooch?" asked Alan fearing the worst.
"A quick one could work," Dizzy confirmed it. "I just don't want to be sidelined just because she gets better grades than us. I'm sharing you with Flipper aren't I? Look. Just because you've got her and Flipper and me after you don't think that you're some kind of super-stud. You play by our rules or you play alone. We like you 'cos you're nice but if that changes we change."
Flipper wriggled, squeezing his arm and said "Not sure we could spare a smooch though."
"Hey," Alan was sounding worried again. "Stop talking about me like that. I'll wish I hadn't kissed you if you just treat me like a commodity."
Flipper was pragmatic. "Be serious Alan. You enjoyed it too."
Alan tried to defend himself. "That's not the point. I'm a me, not a kissing service."
Dizzy supported Flipper. "He's an alien Flipper. What other boy would talk like that?"
Flipper was getting into a game of Alan baiting in the nicest way. "If he doesn't like kissing why does he do it so well?"
"Maybe he was abducted and they taught him," offered Dizzy.
"So why did they send him back?" asked Flipper.
"The thrill is teaching it," said Dizzy. "Alan. Stop making noises. Are you

really embarrassed by us?"
He sounded defensive but denied it. "Well. Not really Dizzy. I just don't want to overstep the mark and upset you. I happen to be very fond of you both and anyway, tonight I think we are keeping warm because we are perhaps a bit more intimately acquainted than we planned."
Flipper squeezed his arm again and said "I don't think there is anything you could do tonight that would upset me."
"Can I quote you on that?" asked Alan cheerfully.
"Must you always be so light?" she could not be cross with him but she could pretend. "We have talked a lot about sex tonight because it's important to a girl. I don't think we're going to die now, unless the bear comes back, but I did rather expect it earlier. And it just annoyed me that that was one life experience I was going to miss."
"We have a boy here Flipper. Go for it," suggested Dizzy.
Flipper was annoyed at Dizzy, that was reasonable. "Be serious girl. Outside these snow suits it is probably below freezing. The bag keeps the wind and snow off but it is cold as cold in here."
"Now girls," suggested Alan. "Much as I get all hot and excited when I think of you I don't get that hot and excited. Another night perhaps."
Flipper wanted to explain. "I know that Alan but I want to believe I could do it. Not in a sort of dirty or loose way but with love. I was joking earlier when I was trying to get you to promise to go to bed with us but underneath I really wanted it. I just needed to play the jokey game to allow me to say it."
They felt him sigh before he spoke. "Wanting seems alright Flipper but doing is out of our reach tonight and when we get home I think we might have more sense. But tonight is special I agree. I feel that tonight we grew up. We go back to the same parents and the same class in school but childhood is over. We have faced the world, we have faced death and seen beyond it. There is no way to know what happens in the rest of our lives but this is a significant night, no argument."
They lay in silence until he said. "Keep talking. We stay awake remember."
"I'm not cold now," said Dizzy. "I was just listening to the wind and feeling you stroke me. Somehow in the dark the world seems distant and sensation seems so major and immediate. We are going to be all right. I know it. But it can never be like this again and that's rather sad. Tonight, perhaps for the only time in our lives, we are totally free."
"Some things you can't do," offered Flipper.
"Only the impossible Flipper," she responded. "Would you hold his arm like this if some things weren't impossible. Would you dare?"
"Perhaps not," wondered Flipper. "Perhaps in a silly way I do feel safe. I can talk like jail bait but there is nothing I can do. I think we're going to live so I don't have to worry about things I've never done. But one thing.

One very important thing. Alan. Dizzy and I have both admitted we would have sex with you, here and now, if it were possible. What about you? Would you do it?"
There was a sigh. Long and deep. "I hoped you weren't going to ask. I hoped I could pretend that I was a good, a virtuous lad. Not taken to lusting after these naughty girls. I keep finding I'm asking myself what would have happened if the evening had run as we planned? A warm autumn night with three of us in one small tent. What could have been?"
"Nuttin," said Dizzy. "You don't think I'd let you make it with Flipper and leave me to watch? Flipper? Would you have popped out for a walk while we both bundled into one sleeping bag?"
"No chance," said Flipper. "And Alan. You wouldn't have considered it. You're awfully nice and we did fancy you masses but what would you have done if we offered sex? Seriously now."
"I... I... I'd have died of embarrassment," Alan sounded genuinely worried but tried to save face by finishing "But only because there is two of you here of course."
"Stop it," said Flipper. "You're being evasive again. Imagine there is just you and me. I'm naked and you are nearly so. I'm saying I love you. I say please. I'm snuggled up against you. I'm kissing you and touching you in oh so many ways. I say don't be cruel I need you. I say you must. I say Alan, now, please."
"Wow Flipper," gasped Dizzy. "That makes me go all wobbly and I've known you for forever."
"Oh shut up Dizzy. This is important," she insisted.
Alan's voice was low and sure. "It makes me go funny too and I've only known you both a few weeks. How much is just the time and place I don't know. Tonight Flipper, actually either of you, you could tell me to come to you and I would. Tomorrow we'd say dumb thing to do but tonight you could probably get me to do anything. Now stop. I'll admit it that I'm lying between the two girls I desire most. I have a hand on Dizzy's tummy, I think, and another on Flipper's hip. Thirty something hours and we'll be back in school. I've got to see you. I have to talk to you. Heck I have to breath. Do you think you are making that easy? Sure I want you, you are both very pretty. Admit it. Presented with either of you warm and naked I'd be unable to resist. You could make me do anything and enjoy anything. You win. You both win. Tonight I can't do anything. Is that good? Yes. Do I like it? No girls I don't. So go easy on me. Just because I try to be the nice guy doesn't mean I don't feel the same strong chemical things. What you feel I feel. Perhaps more so. So don't make it hurt. Please. It's not fair."
Silence lengthened. Flipper listened and heard Dizzy's breathing jerk. She realised she was sobbing quietly. She took a deep breath and said

"Alan. We're sorry. We didn't think," She felt the arm seem to squeeze her. She heard some sort of mumbled words from the other side. They rested and waited and time passed.
[Alharan?]
[Yes?]
[Sorry to intrude.]
[Go ahead]
[I think they are clear. <Philippa> is 62% and <Desiree> is 66%. They carry more super-gene than your immediate descendants. I think you have already worked that out though.]
[The whole enterprise was a waste of time then. Hence they brushed off all my implication. They were just not thinking in that way. From the fathers?]
[We cannot get a fix on the fathers as they are in the base but for over sixty something it has to be strong on both parents.]
[What now?]
[Betron has fixed it. He has delta'ed them. Well not yet but he is sure what to do next.]
[Typical. That easy. I face down a bear in a blizzard and he just plans a phone call. Job done. Go home. I just need to extricate myself.]
"I'm hot," said Flipper. "and it feels clammy. Are we getting enough air?"
"If I can borrow my arms I'll open the bag end up a bit. It would be pretty silly to escape the cold and then suffocate."
[Environmental report please.]
[We are putting in oxygen and we are taking out water vapour and such. You are beginning to overheat them. The suggestion is that you remap. It was a good bit of tactical thinking at the time but the sky has cleared and sun starts to comes up in about twenty minutes so it had better end now or you really will have complications.]
[Are we going to be rescued?]
[Two jeeps are coming up the trail. Less than forty five minutes. We will warn you so you can get out and wave to them.]
Flipper complained "Alan! Mind your elbow in my face."
"Sorry Flipper," he apologised. "Just trying to get some more air in here without too much snow."
At least Dizzy appreciated it. "That's a bit better. The clammy feeling has gone. It's great to be warm again."
Alan hopefully tried "Can I keep my hands now? It's been fun but..."
But Dizzy had other things on her mind "Prob-lemo." she said. "I need the lady's room."
"You'll have to wait Dizzy," said Flipper flatly.
This would not do. "I have waited. It wasn't so bad when I was so cold but now I'm bursting. Alan was rather pressing on my bladder."
"You said it was your tummy?" Alan defended himself.

Dizzy was slightly worried. "Low tummy. Can I get outside if I'm quick?"
Flipper knew that would not work. "You can't go outside. The wind is still howling with blown snow. You'd freeze bits of your anatomy off that you might need one day."
"I'll go in my pants if I wait much longer," cautioned Dizzy.
Alan tried to divert into a solution. "Flipper where did we put the coke can? If I cut the top off with the knife she could go in that and we could empty it outside the sack."
Dizzy was not hopeful "I've got more than a coke can to come."
Alan sounded annoyed. "Have several goes then. Be reasonable, we're trying to help."
Dizzy was urgent. "OK. OK. But hurry."
"Hold on," started Alan lurching about and pulling everybody into a heap as he moved around in the confined sack. "I've lost the knife. No. here it is. Hum. There. I've bent the cut edges down inside so it's got no sharp bits. You can squeeze the top and make it narrower if that helps."
Dizzy sounded panicky. "Well stop talking about it and pass it over. Men. All talk."
"Here you are," he said. "Do you want the torch so you can see what you're doing?"
"Flipper can hold it. You look away," she insisted.
"I thought you were trying to seduce me and get me into bed a few minutes ago," he tried to sound surprised.
"Grief Alan," hissed Dizzy. "If you think the sight of me trying to pee in a coke can without wetting my snow suit could be erotic you've lead a very sheltered life."
Flipper was more concerned with practicalities. "Careful Dizzy. It's nearly full."
"Well quick! Empty it. I'm not finished. It's hard to stop," said Dizzy finding she needed to do something she was not used to.
Alan reached over "Give it to me Flipper. Don't spill it."
"Come on. Come on," pressed Dizzy.
"Keep your hair on. Here you are." said Flipper.
"Oh that's better. Empty it again. I'm nearly done," Dizzy sounded more relaxed.
"Gently Alan," said Flipper passing it over again.
"Some things were never so difficult before," said Dizzy finally finishing.
Flipper tried to sound jolly. "What are friends for? Zip yourself back up."
"I'm even hot now. Alan. We don't need the tin now," said Dizzy relaxing again.
"I just thought that while we were doing it I could use it," he said apprehensively.
"Shall I hold the torch for you?" offered Flipper trying to sound serious but failing.

"That's OK Flipper. I can do it by feel. I'm a boy remember," he reassured her.

After more lurching and some poking around at the sack mouth he announced "Are we done with the tin now? If I put it outside it will blow away. Flipper?"

She hesitated and finally said "Well if we're all doing it... Hold on while I unzip."

Dizzy pointed the torch while Alan looked vaguely at the red lines beginning to show through the trees. "Grief Alan. Boys are so lucky. This is no way to pee in a crisis," said Flipper emotively.

"It's full. Pass it over," muttered Alan.

"Alan? Are you watching?" asked Flipper, less concerned than she expected.

"Listening. I prefer my images of you to stay beautiful and ladylike," he replied.

"Welcome to the real world Buster," she snarled. "Think yourself lucky we're not having periods or you'd really get a slice of ladylike. Have you got any more tissues?"

He winced but managed to reply "Here. What do we do now?"

"Cuddle up, stay warm and wait. The sky is already getting light," said Dizzy wobbling about and grabbing undefined bits of people. They slowly reordered themselves into three side by side bodies with arms wrapped round the outside of others.

"Is it still snowing?" asked Flipper wondering if the hand she held in her glove was Alan or Dizzy.

Alan moved about a bit. "I don't think so," he said. "But it's blowing about a bit still but not falling any more."

"We've made it then," she said, satisfied. "If it's dawn and we're alive and still warm and dry we've made it."

"Alan. You won't forget your promise will you?" asked Dizzy gently.

He paused. "I thought that was still under debate."

"No you promised. Flipper heard it," she insisted.

Flipper took a deep breath and decided to have one last dig at Alan. "Of course you did. You insisted we were to seduce you properly somewhere warm. That's a contract if ever I heard one. Dizzy and I will have to try to oblige just as soon as possible after we get back despite our personal concerns about your morals. I think you said you'd give anything to be in bed with both of us and we agreed in a moment of weakness but it would be dishonourable to back out now."

"Are you sure?" asked Alan. "I seem to remember something like that but somehow it seems different the way you put it."

"Trust us Alan. Would we lie to you?" said Flipper reassuringly.

"What's the definition of jail-bait in this state?" he asked.

"Under sixteen," she replied. "Don't worry. We're old enough to make informed choices. How old are you?"

He seemed to pause. "I seem to remember a sixteenth birthday party, although this night seems to have gone on for years so I might be more."

"No worries then Alan. You can consent if we bother to ask you," she said smugly.

"What if I don't consent?" he wondered.

"Easy. We don't ask you," she pointed out. "Be serious. Nobody is going to believe a boy who says two girls bundled him into bed and made him do it."

Alan digressed, sounding slightly worried. "Dizzy? Don't be silent. You worry me."

"I'm alright Alan," said Dizzy. "I was just thinking that they'll probably have a search party out and they'll find us and we go home and we won't see one another for days."

"And our parents discover we took Alan with us," added Flipper.

"Without Alan we'd be bear food," excused Dizzy.

"Bear poops by now," muttered Flipper not quite sure how Alan would react.

"We're going to get grounded till we're thirty," continued Dizzy.

"I didn't need the allowance anyway," batted Flipper.

Dizzy tired of the ping pong and asked. "Alan. What will your folks do?"

"My Dad will go 'hum' and 'err' and finally say 'that was an error of judgement young man' and my Mum will say 'Oh Alan. How could you?'. Then they'll say 'but we're so glad you're safe'," he said.

"Even when they know you went with two girls?" asked one side of him.

"Yes Dizzy," he replied.

"They know you don't they? They know you wouldn't do anything wrong," she offered.

"Smaltz. I can make mistakes with the best of them and stupidity? You should see me at it," Then he softened. "But no. I wouldn't do anything deliberately harmful, or at least I hope I wouldn't and I trust them to know that. They taught me it."

"Would you go to bed with me if I pressured you then?" asked Flipper.

"You asked me that earlier. I think that would be a mistake," he said.

"I think it would be a mistake too but that's not what I asked," Flipper wanted reassurance. "If I tried, if I really gave you a hard time with tears and kisses could I get you into bed with me? It was yes then. What is it now?"

"Well probably. I'm awfully fond of you. Both of you. But please. I'd feel rotten about it afterwards. It would be wrong and we all know that. I want good things for you," he sounded worried.

"Alan?" she asked.

"Yes Flipper?"

"Does it feel strange having us both cuddled up to you with our arms wrapped round you at once?"

"No. It feels nice. I was a bit unsure when you were both trying to kiss me though. I don't think I was quite prepared for that," he reassured her.

"Alan. I think I love you."

"It might just be the stress of the moment Flipper. Don't make plans yet. You might feel different when we're back home," his voice stayed gentle.

"No Alan she loves you forever and ever just like I do," cut in Dizzy urgently "We did before tonight but we never knew it. We didn't want to compete because we've been best friends since we were tiny. But now we both have you. We'll work it out. And you love us both too don't you."

He sounded worried again. "In a way Dizzy I suppose I do. Grief knows how we will cope with this when we get back home but I suppose I really do."

Dizzy took that happily "That's nice. Flipper and I can share you. It will be all right really."

"Are we aliens then?" diverted Alan. "You said they married lots of women."

Flipper wanted to play the game. "You can be an alien and we can both marry you then."

"And then our Dads can study you," threw in Dizzy.

"I think you can make plans like that later," muttered Alan.

"I'm not really planning. I'm just dreaming happy dreams while I'm awake because you won't let me go to sleep. Shall we marry him Flipper?"

"At the moment I'm not planning on ever letting him go. But what about the honeymoon? He says he doesn't do kinky."

"He'll do what he's told. We'll have a vote and if it's two to one he's got to agree. Its only democratic."

"We'll see," counselled Alan.

"I've never been in love before," announced Dizzy.

Flipper harrumphed and added "Can I name a few names you might remember Dizzy?"

"They were just school girl crushes."

"That's what I said at the time."

"So you were right? I didn't know then. Let me finish. I've never been in love before and I don't really know what to do. Should I leap in and be all physical like they do in films or do I just talk to you or what? What would you like?"

"Unless you want to get suddenly very cold hold the physical."

Alan cut in "Thank you Flipper. But she's right. Tonight just talk to me.

Don't get too wound up about me as we are all too young to go mad. Maybe tomorrow this will just be another teenage crush but if you know don't tell me that tonight because I'm rather enjoying it. I think films go physical so soon because it is easier to show it, and anyhow, some of the audience will pay to get some physical on screen. Physical is fun but it is only part of the deal."

"Boys don't talk like that Alan," pointed out Flipper.

"Some boys don't think. Others are taught that talking about feelings is weak and they have to hurt inside because it would be unacceptable to hurt outside."

"Why not you then?" she followed up.

"Don't know. I just see it and say 'that looks bad, I'm not doing that'. It seems obvious that you avoid the things that hurt and hurt other people but some boys just recover from one fling and they head straight back, the same way, and bound for the same disaster."

"And girls," said Flipper emphatically.

"Carol," said Dizzy.

"Who?" asked Alan

"Miss Easy in the year above us," said Flipper.

"I don't know," said Dizzy. "I don't think she actually slept with anybody. I don't think any of them actually lasted that long."

"You're kidding," Flipper laughed. "I don't think I ever saw her at a dance or a party without a new pair of hands up her jumper. She wouldn't have taken long."

"But probably not a very satisfying experience?" asked Alan. "Using the only way she knows to start a relationship and discovering that it oh so rapidly goes the same way as before. There are times I think the only way to start a happy relationship is by post. So you get to express yourself with the sexual pressure off. So you can get to know somebody and get to like them first. Then you have a basis to fall in love and make a success of it."

"Alan. If more boys talked like you more girls would trust them and they'd get a lot more of the physical," suggested Flipper.

"You were offering me that before," he replied. "Don't try and come Miss Sensitive at me. I already know you are Randy Flipper. The girl who puts a boy's hand in her knickers to keep one of them warm."

"I did too but you didn't notice," Dizzy pointed out.

Flipper chuckled. "Dizzy? I'm ashamed of you! I thought you were better than me."

"Hush Flipper," Dizzy scolded. "We can compare notes later. We mustn't embarrass Alan."

"Just a sec," said Ben. "There's the phone." In a moment he was back at his desk. "Ben Lernski," he answered. The others watched his face for a sign but he shook his head at them, made a few notes on his pad, pulled a face and said "OK" and "Thanks" quite a few times then hung up.

"Heck," he said. "How do you think they knew I was in the office. Its nearly dawn and our Client Supervisor at the Pentagon calls?"

"Don't you get 'Ring me' messages on the answer phone?" asked Bill.

"I do."

"Yes," muttered Ben. "Anybody interested in some UFO sightings? Details coming on the facsimile machine shortly."

"More noise," sulked Roger.

"I thought the Air Force had a department who look after things that fly," said Bill. "We do the behavioural, historical stuff. We don't do lights in the sky."

"This is supposed to be good and desperately secret," said Ben. "We can look at it Monday morning and see if it rings any bells. The nearest thing to a UFO on our books is a Jay and the words were 'they sent a Jay for him because they are invisible' so you're going to get a lot of sightings of that one."

"I hadn't heard that," grumbled Roger. "Was that in my brief?"

"Probably," said Ben. "But also probably beyond the boredom point. We put the good stuff at the start."

"I don't do UFOs," said Roger. "A Jay sounds Var-rin. It flies, it carries people and things, humans can't see it. Makes our job easy do things like that."

"Yes," laughed Ben. "You know I'd really like it to be nice simple detective work. Like a TV show. Clues, thinking, and finally a show down."

"Hump," Bill was not impressed. "If you are planning a shootout at the end please excuse me if I take reports from China. These are not the people I want to get into a fire fight with. I did the last part of the war with a photo reconnaissance unit and I've seen things you would not want to imagine. If the Var-rin have anything like the fire-power we imagine that would look like a tea party."

"But wouldn't it be nice to know we would be away from the situation where the good guys won't tell and the bad guys can't tell?" replied Ben. "I do feel we are on the wrong side at times. Lumps of evidence in a lab would be a nice change."

Roger was not mollified. "A lump of evidence like that would just prove you were on the right track and that they wanted to distract you. We had that with our polygamy studies. As soon as we started on that route all our historical studies people discovered new leads, the ethics people wasted time and money on rewriting our innocuous questionnaire when they passed the Deviant Sexual Practices stuff from the guys next door as read. Finally they pulled our grants for no

progress when for the first time we were making some."
"Henderik says the polygamy stuff is just data skew because it is biased to the eastern cultures where it was practised. We did a bit but dropped it," noted Ben. "Do you think it offended your paymasters?"
"They were financing a department at Clapham who were researching sexual seduction for intelligence gathering purposes so who knows. We just found that in families that we suspected to have recent alien ancestry we found rather abnormal views on marriage. Women who would die rather than find their husband having an affair admitted that if he married the woman, somehow, doing things properly so to speak, they wouldn't really mind. They did not see this as having double standards. It was as if... Well I don't know. Some of them were quite surprised themselves when we pointed out the implications of their answers but were happy to agree that they found the idea of polygamy not just acceptable but rather attractive. Outside this group these views were so rare as to be trivial and normally they showed other deviant tendencies. If you eliminated the wackos the match was even more remarkable. I really thought we had something measurable for once."
"Well I for one would not like to do a study like that." said Ben. "I can't see us sending researchers to Mrs. Rhodes children and asking how would you feel if your husband married another woman. Well. Not if I wanted them to be accepted back again later. That one's too way out for me. I would like nice lumps in the lab. Real hard evidence."
"True, true," murmured Roger. "I don't want to go through that again. I wasn't going to mention it but it's probably the Jack Daniels talking."
"Forget it then," said Bill. "Hey," he turned to the window. "The sun's coming up."

"The sky seems to be getting lighter," said Alan. "So at least the clouds are staying away."
"Excuses time soon," said Dizzy. "What are we going to tell them?"
"Exact truth," replied Alan. "Firstly it does not give you conscience trouble later and secondly it's easier to remember."
"Yes but what do we emphasis?" Dizzy wanted to know.
"Hey! Mum! I'm alive!" offered Flipper.
"Yeah," said Dizzy. "But once they've got over us actually getting back they will want to know why we went."
"Based on our discussions over night," muttered Alan. "You both fancied the same boy but neither of you were going to let the other have first chance. So you both went along to see it was all decent and stuff."
"They'll think we were planning more than that," said Dizzy. "These are parents you must remember."
"Well if challenged you say reflectively 'maybe I was hoping a bit but

with Flipper there I suppose I knew it wasn't going to happen'," Alan suggested. "Be honest about your feelings. Admit mistakes. They respect that. They really do."

"Do I admit that I spent half the night fantasising I was wrapped up with you in an enormous feather quilt?" asked Dizzy.

"Only if they ask you directly," said Flipper. "Be honest by all means but don't jump off any cliffs."

"If they're listening sympathetically it's not that bad. How would you expect them to react if you asked 'Mum. I keep dreaming about him. Am I in love?' They are not going to jump down your throat," Alan advised. "Just pick your moment. If you are getting told off a bit don't come back with something provocative. Just take it and look sad. Say you're sorry, you were silly, and you'll get a cuddle. They won't be pleased, we have to live with that, but they will be very relieved so we must play to that."

"I suppose you're right," said Dizzy. "Where did you learn all this stuff. You don't strike me as the type to be experienced in talking yourself out of trouble?"

"Just watching people get it wrong," he said. "There are times I think I am the only person in the world with eyes and ears because I see, I think, I act, simple."

"Did you plan on us taking you camping when you suggested that you should go then?" asked Dizzy.

"It may have been in my mind but hardly as a formed idea," he said. "I admit that when Flipper offered I did say yes rather quickly in case you changed your minds and I tried to make it definitely you both inviting me."

"What if one of us had changed our mind?" asked Flipper. "Would you have gone with just the other?"

He laughed. "Be serious," he said. "If one had decided not to go the other would never ever have gone. One out all out as they say."

"I'd do it now," mused Dizzy.

"Now is now," pointed out Alan. "If next Saturday morning you were due to meet me at the bus-stop and Flipper called, can't make it, you'd call me and say sorry, we can't go, Flipper can't come."

"Stop it," said Dizzy and poked him. "Right now counts. I won't tell my Dad what I wanted to do to you but I might ask my Mum what it's like to be in love. It's all rather confused at the moment. Already it's not the same as it was in the dead of night and I don't know why."

"Perhaps we're not just going to die," suggested Alan. "When the pressure comes off you can afford to be a bit more selective about prospective mates."

Flipper too poked him, and harder. "We are quite satisfied with our choice. It's just that we might not be pressing ahead with the action

plan quite so fast."
He laughed. "I can live with that. Maybe when we are home we'll be right back to Friday night and have to begin again."
"No," said Flipper. "We can never go back to Friday. Even if we discover we are not in love we can never be the same again after tonight. You can't hold on to somebody and say inside 'if I'm going to die at least I'm going to die with you' and ever look at them the same way again. At risk of sounding morbid, I can't think of any two other people I'd rather die with."
Alan seemed to chuckle slightly. "I know what you mean," he said. "It sounds silly if you just listen to the words but if you hear the thoughts behind it is something very precious that we have shared together. By rights we should have died but we got lucky and made it through. This opens up a whole thing to us that we could have missed out on called the future. I think we both agree."
"Hum," said Dizzy. "I'll be sad to find out I'm not in love because being in love is why I survived. I was cold and somehow I became warm. Just holding your arm in my snow-suit seemed to add just that bit extra so that I got warmer hour by hour when I had been getting colder. You really didn't mind where I put it did you? I am sorry."
He chuckled again. "I was flattered," he said. "I couldn't complain. I had Flipper's knicker elastic pressing on the back of my other hand."
"I'm not going to apologise," said Flipper. "I needed that arm. Not to keep warm but to keep my confidence up. It was as intimate as I dared. Well as intimate as I thought you'd let me dare."
"Don't worry," he said. "Last night I said I thought you could do anything to me and you probably could. But we now have the dawn and nothing to regret except the loss of the tent and the problem with explaining ourselves. You probably stopped at a good point."
"You wouldn't have minded?" she asked
"I wouldn't have said I minded," he corrected.
"I didn't dare," said Dizzy "And I was cross with myself. Give me your hand to hold now."
"You promise you'll keep the snow suit zipped up?"
"Promise. What are you doing without gloves?"
"I just pull my arms up my sleeves and make fists. They're not too cold and I can feel all the fingers."
"Me too. Me too," said Flipper playfully.
"Promise too?" he asked hopefully.
"No. But not yet. But no promise. I do what I want with that hand."
"Alan," said Dizzy sounding perplexed. "You've got a watch on."
"I always have a watch on" he replied lightly. "Except in the shower."
"I don't remember a watch," she murmured.
"I am so disappointed," he whined. "I thought I was so remarkable and

she doesn't remember the plainest details. So much for my reputation as a sex god."

"And your hand feels smoother," she added.

"I was cold," he pointed out. "I may have warmed you a bit but you both unfroze my fingers. Don't worry."

"It's sad," said Dizzy. "It's almost over now," she propped herself up. "I can see you. I can read the writing on the sack. We get to go home soon which is good but you're right. It will never be like this again."

"No," said Flipper. "The next time we get to snuggle up with Alan we will be warm."

"But we won't be afraid," complained Dizzy. "So we will have to be good."

"Hush a moment," said Alan. In the distance they heard the sound of a Jeep.

"Drat," said Dizzy. "I was going to get you to kiss me again first."

"Then hurry," hissed Flipper "Or I'll miss my turn."

Bill looked at the others. "The weather wasn't their fault. The forecast was for it to be good and others were caught out too. Someone is still missing over at Windy Valley. Missing and now presumed dead."

Ben nodded. "And the bear. That's scary. You never expect things like that. Apparently the Rangers took one look at the tent and went straight back to the van for rifles. They haven't found it yet but they reckon it's big."

Roger looked over the top of his glasses and said "But they did deceive us. We were not understanding this as a mixed party."

Eloise sucked her lips and said "Desiree said she was sorry. But they felt they could chaperone each other."

"Alan accepts it was an error of judgement," replied Betty. "If he had gone with one girl I would have been horrified. Two somehow seems less suspect. He says he doesn't want to go camping again."

"Alan did very well," said Ben. "Frankly if he were my son I'd give him hell for going with the girls but be very proud of the way he handled it all."

"Well they're all in bed sleeping it off," said Ben. "And amazingly none the worse for it. I suppose it will go down in their lives as one of the key coming of age events and I suspect that nothing we do or say will actually be remembered. They have faced death and managed to come back against the odds. What sanction or punishment is going to compare with that?"

"Should we stop them seeing one another for a period?" asked Eloise.

Roger shook his head. "No. They need to share the experience. We actually need to encourage them to talk about it. Remember that inside

they are not only saying 'I could have died' but also 'I could have watched you die'. They don't need a hard time or it will come back and haunt them."
Betty nodded. "Blame only attaches to the going together and I suspect that that was more innocent than they would like to admit. They knew they couldn't actually get up to anything but they were playing at it. Posturing. The rest is bad luck followed by a huge amount of determination and courage."
Bill said "That sack was a gift from God. The tent and sleeping bags were apparently ripped to shreds. The bear went through it looking for anything to eat. The wildlife rangers say that sacks like that are uncommon but are the kind of litter that is destroying our countryside but just thank God it blew past when it did. It's almost a pity the rescuers abandoned it. That would be the memento to keep."
Eloise was worried. "Do you think they might be traumatised Mr. Woden? I know you have studied this sort of thing."
Roger shrugged. "I hope not. I think we need to play it low key. Don't give them the 'you could have died' stuff just be pretty normal. Settle for 'I was so worried'. I tell you what. If the girls are up to it bring them round for supper this evening. At seven. We'll leave them in the kitchen with a phone-out pizza menu and some cash and we'll watch TV in the front room and just wander in occasionally for a coffee. That will let them talk it out in a familiar environment. Safe. Unwind. Debrief. That sort of thing. It's the best way to do it."

[So I was wasting my time Alacia?]
[No. Admittedly Betron fixed the problem but without the knowledge that they were carrying so much super-gene your plan would have collapsed.]
[My plan had collapsed long before we discovered that.]
[Yes but because you were there we fixed it. That is what counts.]
[So it just waits for me to extract myself and come back?]
[Looking down your logs that is going to be painful.]
[I can make it easy for them. Remember that now I know they carry super-gene I can be manipulative but nice. Slow them down so to speak.]
[Alharan. I was not talking about them.]
[Look. I will do it. Is that acceptable?]
[No. You have a responsibility to look after the emotional health of all the team members. Since when are you not a team member?]
[...]
[Alharan?]
[Point taken. But how do I allow for the fact that I know what I am

doing? Psychology does not work that way.]
[Integrals. Do the sums, follow the results, don't think. And just relax with them. Please. All of you deserve it because you have been through so much in so little time.]
[I will try but I cannot promise results.]

"How do you think Roger will take it?" asked Bill.
"Difficult to say," pondered Ben. "After the weekend he was saying he'd give anything to go back somewhere where the worst weather is steady rain. Perhaps we let him break it to us that he's not staying after his trial period and we don't fight too hard."
"Conversely," tried Bill. "Could we be wrong. We always said this stuff was not relevant before. Do we just change tack like that?"
"Intuition," said Ben. "You know this time it's right and so do I. Read the report again. Yes, there is so much missing but that's just because they're a bunch of airmen who are not trained in what to look for. We can fix that and then we will get serious data back. Real data too. Just like we've always wanted. Mind you," he paused. "It's going to be hard work and a long haul."
Bill looked at him hard. "I recognise that and I'm willing to try for it. But back to Roger. You don't think we can persuade him to change tack and follow the new UFO leads?"
"He felt it was wrong before," Ben dithered. "It seems that we have a new lease of life here on data we previously thought was rubbish."
"But it seems so obvious now. Surely he will understand?" said Bill.
Ben sat back and looked at him hard. "You don't really think that do you?"
"Well no," Bill shook his head uncomfortably. "It does seem a pity to bring him all this way because we like his knowledge of Tran-sen then tell him we've realised it was all wrong or at least not so significant."
Ben opened his hands and shrugged. "So we pay him a big terminal bonus and give him a magic reference with D.O.D and your name on it. He's made. He's done the years. He should get a chair. Who do we nudge? You know England."

"You don't mind do you?" asked Betty.
"I said I was thinking the same way," said Roger. "When you said it I was relieved that you agreed."
"It would be fairer on Alan too," she added.
"He's English and he'd just work better in England. He's probably dying to see his aunt again."
"Oh," said Betty. "Yes. He used to stay with his aunt so I could work. It's strange. Sometimes he seems almost a stranger and sometimes not. Still. He's turned out a real credit to us, despite getting into this incident

he's actually come out a bit of a hero. Oh I'm tired and confused. How will your bosses react?"

Roger sighed and said hopefully "I'll try to do a deal with L and H tomorrow."

"L and H?" she queried.

"Sorry," he laughed. "I just have to be so careful not to call them Bill and Ben in public in case I laugh and have to explain it. I don't expect they'd be amused. Americans don't find that sort of thing funny."

"E-dop Ipple Weed," said Betty and kissed him. "Be careful now."

"Not grounded," said Flipper. "Well not yet. I don't think it's sunk in with them quite."

"My Mum said that provided I told them where I was going and who I was going with they wouldn't raise a fuss about anything," said Dizzy. "She said 'It is too dangerous to have secrets'. I said 'I've got this orgy planned next weekend' and Mum said 'Doesn't that clash with the form party? Or is that the form party?' and we laughed. She's not so bad."

Alan sat there with his hands in his lap. Silent.

Dizzy looked at him and asked. "What's the matter Alan? Surely your parents did not give you a hard time? They've invited us over."

"That's just it," said Alan. "I'm sure Dad's worried about us. We're going to get post traumatic shock or something."

"Are you?" asked Flipper. "I don't think I am. I'm just pleased to be warm again although if I ever see another tent it will be too soon."

"Another bear you mean," pointed out Dizzy. "If I am ever attacked by another bear I will get nine types of post traumatic shock and then some. Otherwise I think I'm OK."

"Oh," said Alan forcing a smile. "I'll stop worrying then. If we've got no psychological hang-ups waiting to jump out and bite us we can get down to the business of picking a pizza or three. Do we do splits? Dizzy can phone it in."

"You hate making phone calls," sniffed Dizzy, "I don't see why." He gestured with his hands, I don't know, she smiled. "If you were a girl you'd be used to the phone by now. What else are evenings for?"

Do they have bear?" asked Flipper peering at the leaflet. "Revenge is said to be sweet."

"If you want sweet order some ice-cream," said Alan. "I've had enough bear for this weekend."

"Don't you want to go again next week?" asked Flipper. "I hear they are only forecasting a bit of light snow and hardly any wind so it should be quite nice up there."

"No," said Alan. "There's some rotten party I'm expected to go to. Got to meet my responsibilities and all."

"It'll be noisy," laughed Dizzy. "You don't do noisy."

"I do do ham and pineapple," he said trying to read over Flipper's shoulder.

"You're not adventurous enough," complained Dizzy. "What about the special super-spicy?"

"Should we get some coke?" asked Flipper.

"There are tins in the fridge," remarked Alan. "I didn't want to mention it."

"Do you remember that coke can?" gasped Dizzy.

Flipper laughed. "Could I ever forget?"

Dizzy put her head on Flipper's shoulder and said "Now that was traumatic. I don't know how we did it. I'm not sure it's anatomically possible. Especially not in a plastic bag."

The two girls were laughing but Alan merely smiled. Flipper glanced at him to excuse herself and continued "The knickers were the problem. I don't think I'll ever wear knickers in a snow suit again just in case."

"I'm not sure I ever want to wear a snow suit again," laughed Dizzy.

"That will be draughty if we go hiking again and you're buck naked," warned Flipper.

Dizzy scowled at her. "It had better be summer or I'm not coming. Alan will bring the plastic bag just in case."

"Hey. Who says I'm ever going camping with you two again?" he sounded worried. "Your track record lacks that certain something. We first agree which one of you is bringing the bear gun? Anyway, were you planning another hike?"

"We'll fit it in some time I'm sure," said Flipper. "We do that later. We've got to seduce you somewhere warm first."

"Oh yes. We promised didn't we," laughed Dizzy.

"Don't worry about that girls," he smiled. "I'm too smashed this weekend."

"Some other time?" Dizzy looked at him earnestly. "Get your diary out."

He moved back slightly. "You don't really mean it," he smiled.

Dizzy leant on his shoulder and said "I suppose I don't. Last night I did though. Last night I would have done anything for you. I was imagining taking off all my clothes and wrapping myself round you. But somehow tonight it's gone."

"That's good because if Mum came in for a coffee now and found you like that she'd be a bit upset," he murmured.

"We're back in the real world now," said Flipper. "We've lost the magic. Even the love that was so intense then seems more restrained. More reasonable now. You may have to wait to be seduced. Till we feel more in control."

"I'm quite happy with that. I felt it too. Last night our strength was that we would do anything for one another. It was fun to talk like that. To be a bit naughty and a bit sexy. I think it helped us keep warm and stay awake. But we were safe from that then because of everything else. Now we're warm and dry and bear free we cannot take the risks."

"It's strange," said Flipper. "Last night if we could have crept from that sack into my bedroom I would have happily pulled off the snow suit and crawled into bed with you both. Somehow I almost remember it. When we were snuggled up in the dark and I was lying on your shoulder when I had your arm in my snow suit and one of my arms was wrapped round you and the other one was sort of draped across your chest. I pulled off my glove and sort of wiggled my fingers down through the snow suit and touched your warm skin inside."

"I imagined something like that too," said Dizzy. "Stupid really. I suppose we were psychologically undressing you because you had other things on under the snow suit and anyway it wasn't unzipped but I'm sure remember the tips of my fingers touching your skin. But not my hands. Perhaps I was nearer going to sleep than I thought I was. You seemed to be wrapped around us in the dark. It was warm and enclosed. And your arm? Where did the snow suit go? I had arm not sleeve down across my tummy. That's when I realised you were an alien."

"Oh Dizzy. You say the sweetest things. The snow suit was a bit rucked up I think. Well above my wrist but not all that high. When you grabbed my arm you weren't gentle all that."

"I suppose so. I just remember it differently. I suppose we imagined a lot," mused Dizzy. "And we have to trust you because you're just so awful at telling lies."

"I should practice more I suppose," he responded. "Any lies you need telling?"

"Tell us how you're going to stay with us and marry us both," tried Dizzy.

"Oh," he said. "I thought you had laws in this country prohibiting things like that? Wasn't the Civil War about that as well as slavery?"

"I think it still exists," Flipper tried to remember. "It's just that the law doesn't recognise it or something. We did it in history years ago."

"That's not history," said Alan. "History is 1066 and that sort of stuff. That's just recent politics."

"It's history here," insisted Flipper. "We didn't do the stone age in the USA."

Alan did not pull a face by bypassing the translator but paused till he felt a bit happier but by then Flipper had moved on. "Then you explain how everything went right once we got away from the bear," she said. Alan laughed at her and asked "That was right. We nearly froze to death and more. I'd hate to be on a trip you said went wrong. This was aliens poking about and interfering right from the start of the day."

"It started very well," suggested Dizzy.

"No," laughed Alan. "It was going awry before we left home. The weather forecast was definitely a bit alien. No Flipper checked that. She must be the alien then. Dizzy have you noticed anything strange about her? Antenna? Counted the heads?"

"No. We've been together since we were little," growled Dizzy. "We know you get good luck and bad luck but last night all the big things that we couldn't control went wrong and you expected us to believe that we were lucky, lucky, lucky in all the details."

"I was surprised. I admit," he said rocking his head to look at her, "Pleased."

"No Alan. She's right," Flipper cut in. "She fell the best part of thirty feet into a pool full of rocks and swam to the side. She didn't hit a thing, her snow suit was sodden yet she swam."

"Dizzy is a strong swimmer and she was frightened. That gives you strength," he pointed out but without much determination. "Anyway a sodden snow suit is only heavy out of the water. I bet it even floats."

"And you drove the bear off," continued Flipper not interested in the science of it. "Bears don't go away but when you said it had gone we believed you and it had. And that sack. I don't know what to say about that. Be serious now. Brilliant. Magic. You created a new tent out of nothing. We were so impressed."

"Well gee gosh I'm an alien and I never noticed," he was laughing. "I'm so glad you pointed it out to me as I had missed it. I must remember to abduct you at the next opportunity. Look if this is what is important to you I'll be an alien. I would prefer it if you didn't point all this out to your fathers but if this is important to you I'll be an alien."

"No Alan. That's not the important thing," Flipper insisted. "Last night you said you loved us. That's what is important. That's what we really care about. You're a bad liar and you didn't have to say that so it is true isn't it? Even if you go away and we never see you again you did love us, last night you loved us, really?"

Alan looked down at his hands. He took a deep breath. "Last night," he said, "Last night I loved you and today I love you. Perhaps I will go away. Perhaps we will never see one another again but that will always be true. Then and now I love you. I didn't want to love you. I especially didn't want to love both of you because that's confusing. But loving you is more than liking you. It is more than finding you sexy. Loving you is something that I will never lose."

He sat up. "But now," he continued firmly. "If you love me you won't ask any more questions. I've had enough questions, I've had enough bears, I've definitely had enough snow and I'm hungry. I want a pizza and you've talked about anything but pizza so, finally, choose a pizza. OK?"

They looked at him. They all smiled an agreement. Flipper picked up the menu and the pen and idly ticked the seafood special, wrote ALAN next to the Hawaiian and pushed it over to Dizzy. As Dizzy read down the list suddenly she looked up and smiled and asked "So Alan. Now that your plan to get us both grounded has failed who are you going to take to the party?"

He dropped his head on his hands then looked up and said "What if I see if Rachael can be persuaded to dump Andrew and then try to arrange for you both to share Matthew?"

Flipper laughed and jumped up and grabbing the back of his neck with both hands tried to bang his head on the table. Dizzy smiled approvingly and dialled the Pizza shop.

Sequel

"Are we wasting our time with a silly theory?" asked Dizzy Hamilton looking at her friend.

"Silly theory I can accept. Thirty year old romance that got nowhere? It's that too. Want to get to the bottom of it? Must do. We are going to have to ring," said Flipper Standish.

Dizzy pulled at her hair distractedly. "We're mothers with grown up families. Do we really think we should be hunting for a boy we knew when we were sixteen? Is it healthy?"

Flipper was adamant. "We'll go mad if we never know. Alan was here and we knew him. Now we discover he never existed. We lived in the project from when we were thirteen till we went to college and now we know it was on track right up until the Wodens arrived and went then it was sidetracked and the one Woden we really knew never existed."

"It could just be an error," cautioned Dizzy. "Magazines are like that. Just because Professor Woden's obituary says he had no children does not mean that Alan did not really exist. Even then you are making a big jump to say because of that he really was an alien."

"I know. I know," Flipper rolled her head. "But we ring and ask. The Tranzen have an inquiries switchboard that they say is just for this purpose. We've dithered for two days. The worst they can say is, sorry not us, and we then either believe them or we don't."

"No," said Dizzy. "The worst is they say they'll look into it and get back to us and we sit and wait. We don't hang on as it's transatlantic. Expensive."

"My bill. I've discussed it with Garry," Flipper reassured her. "He says that if I've got to know he is happy. It was a long time ago. He's not worried I will suddenly run off with someone. He knows I think he's a gem."

"Oh bother. I suppose you're right," groaned Dizzy. "We need to know. Those few weeks changed our lives. Will they be open? It's a lot of time

zones away?"
"Where's the number again? If they don't answer they don't answer. Shall I do it? Go on. Pick up the other handset," Flipper ordered. "You've got to listen."
She dialled the number for the Tranzen building in England. She waited while the line made the usual noises and then a ringing tone but in two bits.
"Good evening. Tranzen Norcon inquiry line. How may we help you?"
"Er. Hello," started Flipper. "We want to find out if a person we once met was Tranzen."
"Can you give me the name please?" asked the operator smoothly.
"He was called Alan Woden," said Flipper.
"And what is your name?"
"I am Phillippa Standish but I was Phillippa Henderson then. Flipper."
"I detect a second phone in operation. Any information I give needs to be considered confidential. Who else is listening?"
Dizzy was surprised. "Desiree Hamilton" she said. "née Lernski."
"Dizzy," said the operator immediately. Both women gasped. "You will respect our confidentiality?" they were asked.
They both more or less mumbled "Yes," rather than said it.
"Alan Woden was a senior team member. His brief was to divert the Project your fathers were working on because they were too good and were becoming a problem. He is available. If you wish to speak to him I can call him but he may need a few minutes to prepare himself. These sudden re-introductions are very hard for the team and I need to respect that. However his logs for that period indicate that he was happy to be contacted again by either of you."
Flipper looked at Dizzy and was almost unable to speak. She covered the phone and said "Do we want to talk to him?" Dizzy nodded but said nothing. The line was silent as the operator waited for them. Finally Flipper managed to say "Yes please."
The operator's voice was still smooth and gentle. "I anticipated that. I already have him on the line. Connecting you."
"Flipper? Dizzy? Is that really you?" the voice sounded sort of familiar.
"Alan?" managed Flipper.
"That's Flipper. It's so good to hear from you again. The exchange said Dizzy was there too."
"Yes. Me," stumbled Dizzy. "Alan Woden?"
"Alharan" he said. "Alan is near enough and I use it but I'm afraid the Woden bit was a sham."
"We... He died. Your... Professor Woden," said Flipper.
"Yes," the voice sounded regretful. "I went to the funeral. Even the few months I lived with them made me very fond of Betty and Roger. They were good people and we had to mess them about a bit. I always

regretted that."
"And us?" tried Dizzy.
"Oh gosh yes," he said. "I never planned to fall in love with you. That really did mess my job up. I am supposed to maintain some sort of security and it is almost impossible for a Varhyn, even with training, to lie to somebody they love and you kept calling me an alien so, in the end, I just had to agree and pretend I was joining in the joke."
"So the camping trip?" stumbled Dizzy.
"The disaster? I didn't check the weather with our people and they trusted me to know what I was doing. They helped. It was a squad of Tranzen troopers that dragged the bear away. We had a medical team waiting in the snow all night to help if it went wrong and they made, and delivered, the sack for us."
Flipper offered "So you saved us?"
"I got you into the mess so I had to get you out," he blamed himself. "I had to recognise it as my fault so what else could I do? I was falling in love and I thought about what I was supposed to do clearly enough but let the rest of the world pass me by. I don't think straight. Nobody does then, neither human or Varhyn. I wasn't alone. If you had started to get badly cold you really would have been, well, abducted, warmed up, and delivered back in time for our rescuers."
The two girls went silent. Finally Dizzy said. "Did you love us both? or which?"
"Oh dear," he said. "It's the give away. The Varhyn as a species do polygamy. We have very few males so normally we all marry lots of women. Hence I rather fell in love with both of you at once. I tried to help you fall out of love with me before I left and I hope you were down to 'good friends' when we said goodbye but I felt awful. I hope it didn't leak out."
Flipper was sitting down, more relaxed now. "We went home and cried together but it was just sad. You never wrote, except the postcards. We hated that."
"Yes," he sighed. "You can understand that now. Anyway what have you done with your lives? Come on. News."
"Well," started Flipper. "I was going to be a linguist but I married a wonderful man I met at college and have ended up with five children and now two more grandchildren on top. Dizzy's a widow with grown up children too. She's come to stay the week and that's why we decided to phone. Oh Alan, Alharon, it's wonderful to hear from you again. You don't mind us calling do you?"
He chuckled. It seemed familiar. "I don't mind. We went through an exceptional experience together and that is a bond. I'm sorry I could not stay longer but I knew I would not be able to plan for a real relationships for over twenty years so I had to run away. I have only

recently got married."
Dizzy laughed "Since you're in England we don't have to ask how many."
"Oh yes?" he said. "I'm rated as a diplomat so I can obey the laws of my home country in such matters. I have married five and we already have two children. You must remember that the aliens marry lots of humans. I've normally done it but I kept my romantic interludes to countries that would not take offence. This is a first for me in a western nation. It does raise a few eyebrows but we're very happy."
He paused. "Addresses," he said. "Now I can write properly I will. And I see from your dial code you are in California. I need to be there in the autumn, er, fall. We must arrange to meet. I will tell my schedule people I need a free weekend. Do we have a deal? You can introduce me to your families. I would love that."
"Wonderful," said Flipper, dabbing at her eyes with a tissue. "We're old now, not like you remember. It might come as a bit of a shock."
"Nah," he drawled, "You were sixteen then so you must be forty-eight now. I can do sums. I'm a hundred and something times older than that. I won't notice. Now look. I've got somebody waiting for me. Give the addresses and phone numbers to the operator who is just part of our computer system here so it will end up on my desk. Sorry I have to rush but I couldn't say no to speaking to you after all this time despite schedules but I've pushed someone important as far as I dare."
Flipper said "Oh thank you Alan. It's been wonderful to talk to you too."
All Dizzy could managed was "Bye. Good bye."
They carefully dictated the addresses and phone numbers and some final messages to the operator and then adjourned to the lounge for a coffee and a good cry.

Claire, the eldest had left Jane, her mother and crawled onto Alan's lap. She sat herself in her story listening position and snuggled her back against her father's tummy.
"Who was that?" asked Sally as the communicator appeared to vanish from his hand. She had Anne, her daughter, in her arms.
Alan laughed. "Two girls I knew thirty two years ago when they were young. They have finally traced me and the office put them through."
Sally looked at him. "That was before any of us were born. I find it strange to realise you were there then doing things. Were you fond of them?"
He smiled and nodded and reaching up pulled the story book from the shelf. A hand went round Claire's tummy and moved her straight. He turned the pages to the next event in the life of Thomas the Tank Engine.

Sally leaned back and let little Anne snuggle between them. She remembered that the Varhyn never fall out of love and decided that this was not the time to pry deeper. Thirty two years was only a long time to her and the others. She knew she need never fear that she would lose his love no matter who or what came. She wondered if these women knew that too. If they knew Alan they probably did. He was no problem. Thomas, however, was in trouble as usual.

Vestel

The Vestel is the only native predator that can kill a full grown Varhyn. It is relatively intelligent, solitary, heartless and a cold blooded killer. It only kills to eat and to feed its young and is indifferent to the fact that its chosen prey may be intelligent.

The Varhyn have hands and fleshy feet, the Vestel has talons. The Varhyn have a face whilst the Vestel has a toothed beak. They are similarly designed but only because of their convergent evolution. The Varhyn are avian, viviparous , mammalian decapods while the Vestel are avian, egg laying hexapods. The Varhyn are one of the original civilised peoples of the galaxy and the Vestel is an extremely dangerous wild animal.

The Vestel is a problem to the Varhyn. Although things deep in their genes tell them that a Vestel can only be trusted when served roast, with vegetables, they have nursed the species back from near extinction twice. The Varhyn are civilised and cannot bear the idea that they could be the cause of the death of a whole genera of life.

The Vestel live only on Varhn, the planet where the Varhyn originated, and are traced by monitoring stations so they can be diverted away from inhabited areas. They are supplied with bait loaded with the chemicals that their metabolism needs so that they can remain healthy without consuming the prey that their bodies are best designed to eat: Varhyn young.

The Varhyn do not farm the Vestel, although since antiquity they are a great delicacy, the rewards of the great hunt. They are too near to intelligence for that, but their meat is synthetically made for the table. In fact if a Varhyn was served, unbeknown, real Vestel they would be greatly disappointed as the synthetic is based on the best and then has been improved over the years. Freed from the need to overpower a well defended prey the species is slowly degenerating.

To say that the Varhyn have a love for the Vestel would be to overstate the case. A respect certainly, although honour is perhaps a better word. The Vestel lacks any form of communication as it is a solitary species so it is in an evolutionary dead end if intelligence is to be considered the goal. It has invested its development in strength and speed. Yet it is the dragon of Varhyn mythology, full of deep history and heraldic meaning. The word in old Varhn for 'brave' has the name of the Vestel as its root.

The Vestel has, however, made a vital contribution to the Varhyn. The historic fear of predation made them co-operative and gave them a great impetuous toward intelligence and tool making. It also endowed them with strength, courage and the will to fight an enemy that is both bigger than and stronger than themselves. To fight with little expectation of personal survival but to preserve their greater family. As a result the Varhyn are fast, brave and daring without being apt to fight amongst themselves. This equipped them to be on the front line of the Tranzen defences.

Many of the peoples that are part of the civilised worlds cannot contribute to the galactic fighting forces that are the Tranzen either because their metabolism is too slow or they are culturally unsuited to fighting. These have often contributed technology to the Varhyn ships. The Varhyn status as one of the 'first', the worlds that achieved civilisation without outside help, also means that they have a permanent seat on the advisory council of the Tranzen and they are scrupulous to observe all the duties that this lays upon then.

It may be argued that the Vestel has done more for the defence of the galaxy than any other species of non-civilised beings except one.

A person sits on a couch working at a low writing desk. At first sight it is a Homo-sapiens male. He is in that indeterminate period called middle age when the pretence of youth has been abandoned but the ravages of age need not yet be fully admitted. He is ordinary, clean shaven, perhaps a little shorter than average and not muscular. However closer observation reveals that he is using a body mapper to hide a Varhyn male in the appearance of a human. Delve deeper and it becomes more confused. The mind is not Varhyn, it bears marks of humanity, overlaid with much Varhyn but somehow not completely either. This is Alharan Anahe, known by the title Zey. He is one of the five leaders of the Tranzen, the Galactic defence organisation. He is the most recent leader and most junior. Junior is a relative term here, like the word 'minor' in the phrase 'minor deity'.

Alharan is calculating. Well more precisely he has finished calculating and is interpreting the values his mathematics gives him back into understandable terms. Alharan's chosen occupation is to be a psychologist, the most eminent branch of mathematics. He is the director, well joint director, of the Wu'al-t'zhe the Earth Civilisation Project. The audacious plan to rush this planet from barbarism to a galactic standard civilisation in mere thousands of years rather than the more usual million or so. He is clearly concerned at what he is seeing because he is rechecking his work and he knows he does not make errors. However he is allowed to hope.

The problem is fractions. Any psychologist will admit that although you can always predict the general sweep of history the details are harder. People will always surprise you. They are free as individuals to both disappoint and to astonish you. In the simplest person you can find both a hero and a villain but which will they bring out when the day comes that they are tested? It is not always clear and it can make a big difference.

Alharan is looking at numbers that he knows are dubious. He wants to believe what he sees but realism says no. He will have to go and get better data. While he is there he might just be able to nudge things a bit. His presence will change things anyway so it is best to be deliberate. He sighs and starts to prepare a plan. He sketches out the details. They will need a house and, while they are there, some farm land would help. He already has some staff and they will move with him.

He wonders about security. He will not be allowed to go that near to Rome alone. These are not peaceful times. He hesitates. Then he has an idea. He smiles ruefully to himself. He will sneak the idea in then deny that it was his. He will object to it then agree. A compromise is better than an argument. He fails to ask himself a pertinent question about the arrangement he proposes for even master psychologists are subject to the same psychological rules as the rest of us.

Hurran and Geer checked the gates. The huge bars had been lowered into bronze clasps and the entrance was now virtually impenetrable. The little side gate had iron braces. If the bolts were not drawn it too was invulnerable except to professionals who did not mind a lot of work and making a lot of noise to get in. These were not quiet times and although they were not too close to the mobs of Rome but it was always wise to be sure. The slaves and other servants were bedded down, the kitchen fires were banked or out and the villa was ready for the night. Geer had slept during the afternoon and would watch through the night. Hurran would sleep till just before dawn. They would both watch in the dawn twilight as they felt that was the time of most risk of a thief or worse.

The courtyard still radiated the heat of the day as they walked in the shade of the surrounding buildings. The villa was mostly in whitewash with some cheap wall paintings the previous owner had added to try to help him sell it more quickly. The only outward sign of opulence was the polished marble steps they ascended into the main hall. The trees, shrubs and the pool in the courtyard only provided an illusion of coolness although the setting sun could now only reach the rooftops.

They went into the main apartments and stood at an open door. Master Justus was working at his manuscript again. Detrima was taking dictation from the older man with the added light of an oil lamp. Hurran coughed politely. "All is well?" asked Justus looking up at his two guards. They could not be more dissimilar. Hurran was short, stocky, gnarled with age but still impressively muscular, and impressively scarred too, dressed in a leather and brass kilt, Geer was younger, tall with the smooth muscles of a professional athlete. Both however bore the brand of a gladiator, an ex-gladiator.

"All is well" agreed Hurran and waited. Until they knew that Justus had retired to his bed chamber and that the lights in the library were extinguished they would not leave. Justus was aware of this so they would not have to wait long. Like all good servants they knew how to control their master with gentleness and respect.

Hurran caught a scent of perfume and glanced his eyes sideways. Ruth the hand maiden had appeared next to him. She moved silently on bare feet. Hurran smiled as he remembered happy days from his youth before the injuries that bought his freedom precluded such entertainments. The girl was young and very pretty. "Justus might be old" he considered to himself, "but he has impeccable taste."

Justus rolled a scroll and pushed it into the rack behind him. He preferred the old fashioned rolls of best Egyptian stationary to the newer codex style sheets that he complained were forever falling on the floor. "Don't worry," he said. "We're finished." He pushed his chair back and stood up. Detrima lightly sanded her writing and placed it to dry. She bowed to Justus and walked past the two guards. Did she brush against Geer? Perhaps the merest touch. She was older than him but not that much older. Hurran noticed. He was watching for it now. It seemed a happy match and he might suggest it to Justus. The old man was sympathetic in these matters. Just unobservant. Hurran smiled to himself. Just as a master should be. Hurran approved of Justus.

The two guards stood back and bowed as Justus walked out past them. Ruth took his arm and lead him off. They watched them enter the private apartments.

"Pretty little thing," murmured Hurran.

"I suppose so," answered Geer.

Hurran laughed as they walked down the steps into the courtyard. "Nobody gives me presents like that. She stirs me up and I haven't got a gonad to my name and I piss like a woman. Don't you like girls?"

Geer laughed with him. "I'm realistic. We've got a job to do and there's no sense getting all fired up over the unobtainable. My turn will come."

"Ha," said Hurran still laughing. "What about Detrima? Not spoken for. Educated. Getting older without a man yet? Give her a bit of encouragement."

Geer paused. He smiled. "You may be right. How do you reckon my chances?"

"Just a bit of encouragement and you'll have to fight her off. Take my word for it. They love gladiators do women. We're exciting." Hurran turned away from his colleague and walked up the steps to the balcony. It was time to check the upper rooms to see that everything was secure for the night.

In the night two people were talking Phase. The fast-speaking totally artificial language the Varhyn used for serious communication when the pleasure and inaccuracies of speaking slow Old Varhyn cannot be justified. It is Phase that made the Varhyn so quick. Most adult Varhyn think in Phase with its thousands of shades of meaning. That is what it was designed for. It defines their civilisation.
[Alharan?]
[Yes Alacia?]
[How much longer do we wait?]
[You are always impatient. It is no good just to deal with the Senator. Someone else will only appear within a couple of years with the same ideas and we just have to do it all again. We must eliminate the root cause and opportunity. This just takes time.]
[I feel our position in this household is becoming more difficult by the day. Surely someone will suspect by now that we are not human. That will complicate things for you.]
[Do not worry. They are not aware of an alternative to human so they will not consider it. I said to you 'do not come'. You are military leader to the civilisation project. I know you take security seriously and I know you like to oversee these thing personally but a Varhyn female is a striver and an achiever. You will never be happy in a human suburban setting.]
[It is better this way. I am a fleet captain in unsafe territory and administration work seems like idleness. Here, at least, I am involved.]
[If you are going to stay then take it on as a challenge. Do not just take the easy options but actually expose yourself to being human. I know that no woman member of the crew has actually done it for as long as you have.]
[And you men live here all day every day every year. You even make us come to you for meetings. That still freaks some of my officers.]
[We must be totally identified with these people for the plan to work. If I do not, to some measure, believe I am human, well an adopted human, the plan would just flounder along slowly as it has everywhere else. If we are going to rescue these people within one generation, a mere ten or twelve thousand years, we have got to work this way. Anyhow, I suspect that you just hate to admit that a poor little man could do something better than a big strong woman. Humans are the same. Just the other way round.]
[I have never understood that. It does not really make sense. Why do they need so many men and why are they the bigger, stronger ones? Without meaning to be disrespectful it does not take many men to continue the species and why are they stronger than women when

here, just as with us, it is the woman who cares for and brings up the children?]
[We have discussed this countless times before and got nowhere. I assure you that although it is not common it is a perfectly reasonable way for a species to live. Remember that the Varhyn with our sixty-three women to each man are exceptional in the other direction. Many species would find us and our group marriages weird. Relax. Is it that I now insist that you pretend to be a human male that gives you trouble?]
[No. I could never be one of these soft females. At least like this I am allowed to be strong and authoritative.]
[Hum. I would never describe Acritha as soft but you see that I am sometimes right. In matters of the civilisation plan I am in charge and just as I defer to your authority in all things military or security you must trust me on how to live among humans.]
[I accept that. Just get on with it.]

Dawn came slowly promising another blisteringly hot day. Acritha the cook was nevertheless firing the bread oven. Hurran and Geer watched Ruth fill a pan with water and walk back into the living quarters to spray it about and cool the air. Justus did not sleep long but lay in his bed to read in the morning to allow the household to function without him. He had the politeness to allow the business of deliveries and the banter of tradesmen and also the ever-present task of cleaning to happen without the knowledge that he was there watching.

"Ruth. Why are you crying? I did not mean to scold you," Justus looked at the girl kindly. She was holding her poise but she could not mask the tears on her cheeks.
She sniffed and wiped her dark hair over her face. "No Master. I am sorry." She looked at him. "I will try to speak more correctly."
"When I correct your Latin by speaking to you in Hebrew it often troubles you," Justus pointed out gently. "I did not think my Hebrew was that poor."
"No Master," she smiled a bit. His kindness always made her do that. "It reminds me of when I was little. You sound like my grandfather. He was much like you." She dabbed at her eyes again.
Justus was pleased. "I'm sorry Ruth. I know the memories of those days must be hard for you. But you are safe in my house. If your God has so protected you then surely he can protect the rest of your family."
Ruth carefully and precisely continued with her duties. She knew she would have a break to eat in a few hours and she could weep in private again then. It was so hard not to remember the slave school where you had to learn to become more valuable. "The market is glutted with Jewish kids," they said. "Learn or starve." Then they slapped you with

damp cloths if you got your lesson wrong. You must not leave a mark on the goods. But it was hard to reconcile this gentle old man with those people. At least he was better than the other man who first bought her from the school's vendor. Inspecting her naked on the slave block and poking her with his stick to see how firm her flesh was. Then dressing her in a pure white gown to give her as a gift to this other old man.

Senator Carmedious sat in his office, surrounded by the conspicuous opulence that comes from a lifetime in politics, and looked at Kiron his quartermaster across his desk. "Are you certain?" he demanded.
Kiron smiled. "Justus is no fool. His security men have that place sewn up tight. The villa is less than a hundred paces from the garrison house and the walls are topped with razor bronze slivers under the shrubbery. Very tasteful, very urban, but very effective. Also you may have noticed that all the domestic servants are armed?"
"I saw no such thing," snorted Carmedious. "I would have noticed."
"All the men had the buttons to attach a dagger sheath on their belts." Kiron answered respectfully. "Naturally they would not be armed in your presence but a worn button eye means a knife or more and listening outside in the morning you hear the sounds of sword drill. You can be sure the two gladiators are not training old Justus."
"So. Then I must continue the diplomatic course. I have the upper hand as Justus has yet to respond to my gift of the slave girl and I am sure he will not give me such as his views on the matter and my reputation somewhat diverge." The Senator sat back and laughed. "If my domestic servants were armed I doubt I would live till morning."
"My Master. You misjudge us," Kiron lowered his eyes. "Your faithful bodyguard would not allow you to come to harm and your slaves remember Simon the horse boy. They are very careful never to offend you."
The senator grunted as Kiron rose to leave. "You will continue to try to find out what you can about our annoying neighbour," he said. "I never trust anybody who has a bigger house than I have. He must have done something dishonest."
"Yes Master," smiled Kiron. "At every opportunity."

Acritha chivvied round after the kitchen girls and shouted at them for imagined failings. The place had to be perfect. Senator Carmedious was coming to lunch. "Master Justus will want the place spotless," she insisted. It might be that Master Justus would not notice but Carmedious would have his attendants present and they would notice and they would know what to look for. A cook and house manager is allowed her professional pride before her peers.

The Senator was greeted formally by the servants and informally by Justus. They bathed their feet and left their street shoes behind. His street guard relaxed in the adjoining room to the main reception room. Hurran sat with them and produced some refreshments. Kiron and Geer stood discreetly at the side of the reception rooms and watched their masters.

"Your old man seems quite jolly today," remarked Kiron barely moving his lips.
Geer almost smiled "He's pleased with the gift the Senator gave him. More so now than when he received her. Anyway. He wants something. Just watch."
The Senator was somewhat taken aback by the gift. "My dear Justus. You knew I collect this kind of thing? But surely this is priceless? You could buy an Emperor with carved glassware like this." He moved the goblet carefully in his hands. "This is no neighbourly recompense for a little slave girl. She was a trivial gift." He laughed. "You know you don't have to bribe me. After all what are friends for if they can't help one another?"
Justus laughed. "It is pretty isn't it. It was perhaps not as expensive as you seem to make out. Perhaps I got a bargain but that's your gain now. There is something that I want but I'm not trying to subvert your civil duties. I would like access to some of your library. To copy some documents. Your collection of historic writings is legendary and you know that history is my own personal folly."
"Well anything I own you're welcome to borrow, but much of the collection I hold in trust and it would be wrong to let it out of my house. But if you just want to copy some things I'm sure something can be arranged."
Kiron coughed meaningfully. The Senator gestured at him to continue. "I do believe that Master Justus has a female slave who does his writing. If she were to do the copying in our main scroll room she could be easily searched on leaving and your responsibilities to the security of the library could be met."
"Simple," said the Senator. "It would only take a moment to strip her and ascertain that she leaves with just the scrolls she comes with and that she has nothing hidden up her skirts. My responsibilities are complete. My entire library can be at your disposal."

Detrima copied studiously. Kiron walked in with some beakers and a pot of wine. He placed the beakers on the table and poured the liquid out. "Chilled," he said. "Writing can be harder than digging at this time of year."
"Thank you," said Detrima hardly breaking from her work.

Kiron motioned Geer to move over nearer to him.

"Thank you," said Geer smiling.

Kiron sat back lazily. "I don't know why they want me to watch you," he said. "You're hardly likely to steal anything from the library and none of the books are to be hidden from you."

"Security is always important," said Geer sipping at his wine. "If you get into the habit of dropping your guard you'll get caught out in the end."

"True," mused Kiron looking down into his cup. "But I like to think I'm in control there. The Senator has a lot of enemies in many places but we keep him safe. He may disagree with Justus on many issues but your master is not a threat so I don't worry about him so I don't worry about you."

"Justus is a good and moral man. He is no threat," agreed Geer.

Kiron smiled. "All the same I'd rather have assurances. You know I do pay a retainer, small I admit, to the guards of many of the surrounding houses for information on the security arrangements there. Just for my peace of mind you realise. Just to know who's coming and going. In case one of our good neighbours is being used as an innocent dupe in a plot to get at my master. As you said, security is always important."

"I had not thought such action would be necessary," said Geer. "But perhaps your problem is greater than ours. The Senator has somewhat of a reputation while we are only concerned with thieves and such."

"You underestimate him," laughed Kiron quietly so as not to disturb Detrima. "He is very intolerant of failure, more so in himself than his servants. I have always found him predictable and I value that in a master. I trust Justus is as reliable."

"Justus neither has nor deserves a reputation for cruelty and he is tolerant of accidents and errors that are not deliberate," Geer's voice remained calm.

"And my master over-reacts a bit," Kiron nodded gently. "But he must be protected. He is the master after all. Look. Would you like to supply me with information on your house? Nothing formal of course and nothing that compromises your own security naturally. For a retainer. Good money for a trivial exercise. I could keep you briefed on what's happening here so you know when we might have trouble so you can be on your guard."

"I think we're well covered for that," Geer was relaxed. "Hurran and I have the place held secure so you need not worry about an assassin using us as a jumping off point. Don't worry. It would probably be unethical to take your money anyway."

"Maybe a little bit," agreed Kiron, "But that's what security is all about. If the whole world was ethical we'd all be farming for a living. More wine?"

As the afternoon drew on Kiron ordered bread and some cheese and

more wine. He withdrew to the outer veranda where the breeze was less sultry and contemplated his next move.
Detrima put down her pen and muttered a rude word.
"What is the matter?" asked Geer.
"Oh it's nothing," she replied. "My wrist and my fingers ache but I'm nearly done. Just three more pages and that's today."
"Give me your hand," said Geer gently.
Detrima winced at first but as she felt strong fingers massaging the life back into her fingers she sighed. "Where did you learn to do this?" she asked.
"A sword hurts if you work at it too hard. You must make the blood move round to refresh the muscles."
"Blood moving round?" she laughed. "The things they tell gladiators. But it does help." She tipped her head and blinked. "Do you do backs too? I'm dreadfully stiff from all this leaning over."
Kiron watched from the shadows as strong hands kneaded Detrima's back. Perhaps a bribe was not appropriate here. There were many ways to catch a man and perhaps it was not his turn today. He smiled. It would not be too hard now he understood.

The sun was nearing the horizon and Detrima chose to call a halt. "I am ahead of schedule but we must be back to eat or Acritha will start to glow."
Kiron carefully counted the scrolls on the table and said. "Five you bought and five you take. These are all new."
Detrima took a deep breath and started to untie her waist belt. Kiron gestured with his hands. "That won't be necessary. I would prefer to think of you as friends and neighbours. Come, you must go or you'll be eating leftovers in the dark."
The Senator's gates were already locked but the guards opened the small panel door for them. Geer stepped towards it and turned to Kiron and said. "Thank you. You have been a great help to us. We shall..."
At this point he was interrupted by a small man who rushed in through the panel door and waved a short sword inexpertly at them.
"Where's that old bastard Carmedious?" he shouted swinging the sword again.
Detrima ducked and fell heavily scattering her scrolls. Geer leaped and caught the man's sword hand and pushed him over on to his back. The sword skidded away across the sandy court and the Senator's bodyguard joined Geer to hold the man down.
Ignoring the old man's curses Geer stood up and moved to Detrima. She was already picking herself up. He caught her arms and pulled her to her feet.
"Thank you." she said. "I was..."

They stopped as a choking sound petered out behind them. As they turned to look they saw Kiron drawing his sword out of the old man's chest. Even the rest of the body guard looked shocked. Detrima threw herself against Geer's chest and wept at the suddenness of it all.

The Garrison centurion was not pleased. He had a corpse, now finally identified as a small businessman, recently ruined when his supply contracts had been withdrawn, he had two free-men witnesses, servants of local householders and innumerable slaves who saw the event. Their stories all tallied on the significant details and differed enough to be believable. He had a lawful killing of an armed intruder but with a rather bad taste. That Kiron had acted in a way that his master would fully approve of only made it marginally worse.
He watched his men drag off the body of the old man who had probably saved himself the ignominy of being sold to meet his debts. Perhaps that was all his motive. He could hardly have expected to be able to get to the Senator. Better to go out in a flash of defiance than to be ground down by the system. To rage against injustice like a young man one last time.
The Centurion was suddenly aware that he was writing his own feelings into this case. He ruminated that fighting was young man's work and policing was for the old but fighting on the frontiers was far more clear cut. He felt the tension on the streets more keenly than most and knew he needed to keep a firm lid on it. Civil disorder, not mere body-guard killings, was his prime concern but they did not help. Still this was clear cut. File a report and forget it. Bad end to a bad day.

There was a voice in the darkness. "Geer?"
"Detrima. You should be asleep." There was only a slim sliver of moon and she could not see clearly.
"I've been waiting for you. But you don't come regularly."
"If I was regular a thief would know. It is best to be unpredictable. I trust you are not ill. You normally sleep well."
She stepped forward and put her hands on the dark silhouette before her. "Hold me in your arms again like you did this afternoon."
Strong arms closed gently round her. "You are still upset?"
"A bit," she said. Resting her head on a broad shoulder.
"Why are you naked?" Geer asked. "You should not come out of the women's quarters without dressing. It is not considered correct."
"I wanted you to hold me naked. I wanted you to know that I am not too old yet to be what a man wants. I want to give myself to you."
"Detrima. I am on duty. I must continue my patrols and you must sleep. I have work to do."
"How can I sleep when I am alone and you are out here. How can I

sleep when I am listening for every sound you make as you move around the villa. You are so silent on the stone floors but the wooden stairs creak as you come up and down. Oh Geer. Please. Justus will not mind."

The strong arms around her never slackened. "What you say is true," answered Geer, "but it is not appropriate now."

"Geer. Geer," she was pressing herself against him. "Don't I stir you up. You are a man. Surely you desire me?"

"Yes," said Geer thoughtfully. "I am a man and any man would desire you. You are strong and resourceful. You are a pretty pink. Er... You have nice hair... and breasts."

Detrima felt slightly deflated at this but she slid her hands up Geer's chest and clasping them behind his neck pulled his head forward and kissed him. Although she did not feel he was responding as she hoped the arms still encircled her. Slowly she relaxed and leaned back in his grasp.

"Thank you," she said. "I suppose you're right." She swallowed. "Another time then. When you're off duty. You would like that?"

Geer slowly released her. There seemed to be a momentary pause. "Yes. Naturally I would like that. You are beautiful."

Detrima was still worried. She reached out and touched his arm again. "Look. There isn't a problem is there? You're not hurt? Like Hurran?"

"No," he said, he almost laughed. "I am a perfectly normal man. No injuries and no deviations. Do not worry. It's just a bit sudden. I feel I need to think about it a bit. That's all."

As her heart relaxed Detrima began to become aware of her nakedness in a self conscious way. Her hands wanted to cover her and danced about aimlessly. "Good night then," she said stepping back into the darkness of the doorway.

"Goodnight," said Geer. Perhaps he smiled. He turned and walked a few steps then stopped and looked back. "Don't worry," he said.

The dawn cool was beginning to warm into the morning when Hurran walked back into their little guardroom by the main gate. Geer was sitting on a stool at the table holding his head in his hands. "What's up?" asked the older man leaning on the door frame.

"I'm confused," said Geer. "When we first came here it was so simple. We just had to guard the house. We just had Justus and his staff to worry about. Now we have conspiratorial neighbours who want to offer me money to spy, political changes interfering with our benign relationship with the town guard and now I'm being stalked by a predatory secretary."

Hurran fingered his old 'lucky' trident that, with his net, framed the arch. He paused then walked into the room and poured himself a draught of

thin beer into a beaker and sat down on his bed. "Detrima?" he asked. "What's she done now?"
Geer sighed. "She approached me last night. She was very amorous."
"So what did you do?" asked Hurran, his eyes lighting up.
"I held her in my arms and paid her some complements but told her I would have to think about it."
Hurran rolled his eyes. "Think about it? You clearly have a lot to learn about women. If they approach you like that they're ready for it so just do it and worry about the consequences later. Never turn a chance like that down. They're all to infrequent."
Geer sighed. "I suppose I don't know much about women. I wish I could talk to Justus about it but that would just be to admit that I'm out of my depth here."
"The old man wouldn't mind. He understands that kind of thing. Heck. He was quick off the mark when Carmedious bought young Ruth over as a birthday present. He knew what to do all right and you're a bit of a favourite to him. Just hint and he'll give you the pen pusher just like that and if she's hot for you make the most of it while it lasts."
Geer looked at him. "That is the thing to do isn't it. But it might be better to postpone things till this business with the Senator is over. Do you think she will take offence?"
Hurran laughed. "If she takes offence you'll wish you were back in the Arena. I'd face a tridentus naked and armed with a bulrush than a scorned woman any day." He paused. "Look she's been nudging and touching you for weeks now. I've noticed her giving you the old look. Give her a word of encouragement and she'll be throwing her clothes off and crawling all over you."
"Is that bad?" asked Geer.
Hurran swore a long and complicated oath invoking a range of deities of the more questionable kind. "Best thing ever," he concluded.
Geer did not seem to be highly reassured at this.

Justus's estimate that it would take five days to copy the documents that he had identified in ten minutes seemed accurate. To Detrima's great relief it was socially impossible for him to be in the Senator's house if the Senator himself was not there to entertain him or he would be actively finding more documents that were also vital.
Detrima continued to transcribe the scrolls and books marked with the wooden pegs. She actually quite liked the work as it was simple and mundane and not particularly demanding. It was quite a relief to be able to work without Justus always fussing about and always changing things. That it gave her time with Geer was an added advantage. She had not dared to bring up the subject again since their night time meeting as she was now a little embarrassed by it. Geer, she had to

remind herself, was not a slave as she was, a simple piece of property, but a bondsman who, like Hurran, had chosen to serve Justus, exchanging the freedom to starve for the certainty of a place in a rich man's house.

Geer however found the watching and waiting galling. He wandered in and out of the library and although he was always at hand Detrima began to wonder if he was avoiding her company. However he was still willing to perform the trick to relieve the cramp in her fingers that two and a half days of solid writing was now bringing on more often.

She could see Geer standing with his back to her in the courtyard when Kiron walked in. She was careful to appear extra diligent when there were others about.

"I need to apologise," said Kiron softly.

Detrima started and nearly blotted her work. This was a word that a slave does not expect to hear very often.

"I fear I startled you badly in that incident on the first evening. I had no choice I am afraid. Without a strong show of force we cannot be safe. My master has too many enemies. If I had left it any longer my legal right to kill the idiot would have been questionable and the Senator would have had my ears. You know how these things are."

Detrima looked up at him. "Not really. But it's obeying orders isn't it? I thought Geer had finished it and I was shocked. I'm sorry I made a fuss."

"I had no choice but I try to do things like that quickly and with the minimum of pain. Geer was a great help to us there. I am impressed by his speed and agility. It could have been much worse. The old fool nearly hurt you for example."

Detrima was flattered by both Kiron's apparent concern for her and his admiration for Geer. Perhaps Kiron was not quite the villain she had supposed. There were orders and orders had to be followed and Kiron's orders would be about killing people just as hers were about writing. Geer probably had orders about killing intruders too she supposed.

Kiron saw Detrima smile slightly at him. His next move was to make a mistake. A very carefully calculated mistake.

"You have a good man there," he said.

Detrima almost blushed. "He's not my man," she answered.

Kiron raised his eyebrows a little. "I'm surprised," he said, "You'd make a fine couple." He watched her. She sighed and trembled a fraction. He smiled amiably. "It will be a good match. I must try and help it along."

Detrima put her pen down. She glanced out of the door to where Geer was still standing in the sun. "Could you?" she hissed.

Kiron was pleased with himself. "I could try," he said lightly, "After all, what are friends for?"

Detrima looked lostly at him. "I don't have anything to give you in return," she said reproachfully.
"You don't have to," said Kiron. "Friends don't need returns. We can just talk. I'm always interested in what goes on around here. Comes with the job I suppose."

Justus was talking with his farm managers. They were up from the country for their monthly meeting and they were still arguing about expanding the areas under cultivation when the market was depressed, almost in glut. These were the specialist employees that kept Justus's business running. Justus was emphasising that his stated policy was to have more available land under grain and to be ready and able to exploit more marginal land also.
"We are receiving more and more trouble from the neighbouring farmers," argued Pilatus. "When we grow standing corn they lose the hunting tracks they once enjoyed. They argue that we are changing the status quo to grow poor man's food. And that we require more labour is forcing the general costs up."
Justus was trying to be placatory. "I accept that. I recognise that you will have trouble with my plans but I foresee that this is the right track to follow. There is a wider market open to us than as provisioners for the local cities. Try to deflect criticism towards me. You know, complain that the owner doesn't understand modern farming, that sort of thing. I predict that in the end what I am doing is correct and makes good longer term business sense."

As they left he retired to the bath house and called Geer to him.
Ruth had been sponging cool water over her master but now started to towel him down to apply olive oil to his body. She watched him sit and look at the large security guard. They seemed to have sessions like this more often now when they just sat together and made little noises at one another. That Justus might be speaking another language seemed possible but Geer, for all his obvious intelligence, was just an ex-gladiator. He spoke enough Greek to get by in the market but street Latin was all he could really manage
[We are nearing full production now Alacia.]
[You expect to avert famine? Your estates are large but there are millions to feed when the rains fail. Five years is a long time.]
[We have grown a hardy strain. We will have stocks to sell as seed. The effect is a multiplier. Within a century this way of life will start to crumble. It will take four more centuries to be replaced but we need to let things go on a bit or we will lose much of what we have gained.]
[Your friend the Senator, for all his jovial neighbourliness, is working to keep prices up.]

[Yes but we must sell enough grain to keep the farms looking like a reasonable economic proposition. I am not prepared to admit to a knowledge of the future. These are level headed businessmen who would not take me seriously. Even now I need to send my accountants out from Miceni to check the books because if they thought that I was not getting regular, detailed reports on their work they would do what is the correct thing and grow less grain and substitute more expensive, fancy products and make me more money.]
[Not wishing to be a seer did not stop you moving your staff from the path of the earthquake a few years ago.]
[And my orders to move all the servants out did not stop my steward hiring more watchmen to guard the house while they were away so people on my payroll still died. Now your department of aggressive geology has closed the whole area round the volcano so how is my conscience supposed to let me sell the house?]
[Back to the Senator. He has, perhaps, a deeper agenda?]
[As we have discussed earlier we know his agents control a good deal of the opinion forming in the mob of Rome. They bully the senate in ways unthinkable just a decade or so ago and our new princeps has hardly consolidated his position yet. If the cheap bread vanished then you would have them howling for a strong man at the helm and although our old friend sees himself elevated to the purple I can think of two or three others who could equally well benefit from that.]
[I still think that eliminating the Senator would buy you more time.]
[But conversely it would strengthen his enemies and I prefer the current incumbent to any of them as he has restored stable government. If the Senator moves against us we may be forced to act. However we will need to be subtle. His power base would enable him to control the local garrison making our personal position more precarious. I feel very responsible for my household here and I feel it is my duty to see that they, and the farm people, come to no harm.]
[I can guarantee that but not the way you wish.]
[No. We must not have armed troops on the ground. We must work under the local law.]
[I have met the Garrison Commander. He appears an honest man.]
[He is old for a solder. Due for his benevolence soon I trust. His political masters however will limit his actions. This city is woefully short of honest judges. The best you can say is that they are expensive and hence not easily bought.]
[So if the Senator was caught in the act, so to speak...]
[...He would naturally be made an example of. Until then his misdemeanours will be hushed up. Until he attacks us, which is not altogether unlikely, I prefer to have him as a neighbour because he dilutes the power spectrum in Rome. As soon as the hot weather is

over he will be back there intriguing again. Until then we must intrigue together.
Incidentally. I must congratulate you. You are doing very well as a human. Are you enjoying it after all this time, to be a participant rather than just a visitor?]
[It is harder than I expected. But I always say that. I feel as if I am the prey under the eyes of the hunter all the time. I want to strike out. I can manage. Don't worry.]
[There is nothing you want to discuss? Can I advise you on anything?]
[I am having some problems so I may take you up on that later but not yet. I want to try to work it out on my own first.]
[Reasonable. I would feel the same way myself. Good luck.]
Geer stood up to leave. "I must go and join Hurran for the evening inspection."
"Do that. I shall retire to bed soon," replied Justus. He smiled. Ruth was just standing behind him, touching him lightly on the shoulder.
Geer glanced at the girl as he turned to leave. He went and sat in the guard room to wait for Hurran quite shocked at what he had just seen in his own mind.
"Ruth?" he said to himself. "Why am I so drawn to Ruth?"

The copying work progressed and Justus described a few more items that he wanted and Detrima found them and transcribed them also. They finally gathered the scrolls together for a last time mid afternoon on the Friday.
Kiron walked them down to the gate and said "You both must come over this evening and we can have a drink together and relax," he smiled amiably. "Geer can you ask Justus if we can borrow Detrima for a few hours?"
"I will ask," said Geer. "But I can't promise anything."
"Naturally, naturally," said Kiron standing in the gate as they left.

[How do you feel about tackling such a social occasion?]
[Well, nervous I admit.]
[You would need to be careful. Remember you are a big tough gladiator. You would be expected to join in sexual humour and probably a lot of drinking.]
[Alcohol is no problem. Because it is a poison to us the mapper will remove it from anything I drink.]
[Yes but you should not act that way. If they all become merry and drunken and you partake of the same amount and remain cold and unmoved they will see you as something strange. Also some people become more aggressive when drunk. You must be co-operative and friendly to keep that under control.]

[I will copy those around me. Perhaps they will not be too observant if they are slightly intoxicated.]
[Hum. I doubt if Kiron, inviting a gladiator, expects to get merely slightly intoxicated. Also. Why do you suppose he invited Detrima?]
[I am unsure. She intimated that he apologised for having to kill the old man in front of her on that first day. Perhaps he still feels bad about that.]
[I am surprised. It seems out of character for him. Be careful. He is an intelligent man and may not say all that he means. However. Just because he works for a villain does not make him one. Perhaps I am being too suspicious.]
[I am unsure too. So I am to go and take Detrima? I will follow their lead and try to be what I appear to be.]
[It will be good practice. I would like to think you could fit into this society at any level. This will be a good start. I may need you to be a king one day.]
[We will leave that to you and your specialists. I would rather not be in a place that could affect your plans critically. I shall go and tell Detrima.]
[Send her to Ruth. Get her dressed up in something pretty. She will appreciate that. Kiron may be expecting you to lower your guard and tell him something but conversely if he is drunk he may reveal more than he expects. Keep your log running.]

As they walked down to the Senators house Geer talked to Detrima. "I'm not really used to this kind of thing," he confided. "Gladiators tend more towards the drunken orgy rather than the evening with friends. I doubt if Kiron is proposing something as demure as Justus's parties but I'm not quite sure I'll fit in."
"I can feel with that," she replied. "I was born a slave and slaves do not get invited to many parties. I was always a reader and writer so I didn't get involved in things like that. We'll just have to play it by ear I suppose."
Geer looked at her slightly strangely but smiled.

The doorman recognised Geer's face at the grill and opened the little portal gate. Geer pushed Detrima through and stepped after her. The gate banged shut behind them and the duty guard turned away and put their weapons back in the racks. Geer unfastened his sword and hooked it on a spare peg at the end.
Kiron wandered up holding a cup. "Welcome." he said. "The old man has given us a couple of jars of quite good stuff so we're going to get that down us before we break open the rotgut. Come round the back and get it while it's going."
A large amphora lay on blocks on the table with a wet cloth over it and

one of the bodyguard members rocked it to pour them both generous pots of wine. Kiron had a girl wearing what was obviously kitchen slave's dress sitting on his lap. Detrima looked on pleased. There was a lot of meat on skewers spitting into the fire. There were torches to keep the darkness at bay and seats and rugs spread around the courtyard. The party had commenced.

[It was awful Alharan. Awful. It began all right. We were singing and eating and playing games. They were like children. Then they began to get more drunk and the woman and the men began to pair off and show sexual behaviour. I was watching carefully so I would not make errors of conduct that would give me away but then I realised that Detrima was also becoming intoxicated and she would not realise that I was unaffected by this. I tried to copy some of the things going on but it made me feel emotionally unstable. I failed horribly.]
[No. I disagree. Your ploy of getting involved in the drinking contest and then falling asleep was excellent. You side stepped a large number of practical problems that you are not experienced enough to tackle there. That was the kind of quality, tactical thinking that makes you a shipmaster.]
[Detrima does not look to happy this morning.]
[Mild poisoning and some dehydration. Quite normal for the amount she drank I assure you. I shall not work her too hard today. When you allow for that she is actually quite perky today. She must have counted last night a good time.]
[She slept on a thin rug on flagstones so I expect she can expect to be quite stiff.]
[With you?]
[She lay next to me. Is that significant?]
[She probably thinks so. She may be developing strong affection towards you.]
[That could explain some of the things she did last night.]
[I will not ask you to elucidate. You are a soldier and we know what soldiers are like. If it does become necessary, for security reasons, you are aware that you body mapper would enable you to function as a human male in all respects.]
[I could not do that. I prefer the falling down drunk option. Anyhow, go easy on soldiers. A large number of women cooped up in a metal tube are going to get to thinking about the one thing they have not brought with them. You are the psychologist, as you are so fond of telling me, you must know that. So we tend to talk about sex a lot? We cannot do anything about it can we? 'When we retire' we say, 'we shall marry a man with only five wives'. That is the old soldiers dream.
Anyway. Look. I am a Varhyn woman and there is only one sort of mate

I could desire. I do not have your ability to love someone just because they love you. That is a man thing.]
[Not exclusively. Remember that a Varhyn wife loves her fellow wives. 'I love them because they love my husband'. That is the saying.]
[Never having been a wife I have never experienced that. I have heard it. I suppose I saw it in my mothers. It must be strange to love a woman.]
[Do your space ship crews not bond together about a common task? I am the psychologist as you say. I assure you that that is the same mental process at work.]
[That I can relate to. I suppose I have felt that. Perhaps in a way I bond to some of the people here, even though they are human. I had not thought of it that way before.]
[Oh? Anyone in particular? Hurran?]
[No. I quite like him but that is not the same thing.]

The routine continued and the work continued. Three days later Justus met Carmedious in passing in the forum while reading the lecture schedule. They exchanged inconsequential pleasantries. Kiron passed a few words with Geer.
"Hope you enjoyed the party," he said quietly, his eyes never ceasing to keep watch. "I expect Justus doesn't provide for that sort of thing often."
"Yes. Thank you. You're right. That sort of thing would not be on Justus's schedule. He likes it quiet at night," Geer replied. "You enjoyed yourself?"
"My head didn't stop hurting for a day and a night," Kiron smiled. "You put some wine away yourself so I expect you know what I mean. And the pen pusher was well soaked too. Didn't impair her performance I trust?"
Geer hesitated. "No. She was fine. Just a bit weary next day."
Kiron laughed. "They always say that but the more you do it the better they like it. Oops. We're off again." He followed the Senator towards the outer gate leaving Geer watching after him, slightly perplexed.

"I shouldn't be doing this," thought Detrima. However she was. Kiron claimed it was only curiosity that drove him but she had agreed to copy the accounts for him and she was nearly finished. The summary sheet was enough. It had the costs, the receipts, the silo-men's totals and the estimates of the harvests. Any more detail than that would be more than mild curiosity.

The Centurion was genuinely apologetic but the villa was searched none the less. What were they looking for? They could not, would not, say. It lasted an hour and they found nothing and they took nothing. Carmedious arrived in the late afternoon and told Justus that he should complain. "You cannot stop people raising charges against you but you can make it politically expedient not to search your house," he argued. Justus was unperturbed. "I have nothing to hide. Innocence is the greatest protection from the wrath of the law."

Geer took the opportunity to supply Kiron and the rest of the bodyguard in the guard room. Hurran was still chaffing at the indignity of the search. Detrima begged bread and cheese from Acritha and Hurran produced copious beer.

Carmedious was blithe. "One can only suspect you have made enemies in the wrong places," he counselled Justus. "It's probably that farm of yours. You grow too much stuff and depress the price. There's no need to be greedy. Live and let live. If the market is strong everybody makes good money and you don't have to do so much work for it."

Justus was determined to be innocent. "I doubt that farmers are really that worried. Since the beginning of the world they have always complained. The price is never high enough, the yield is always poor and the staff eat too much of what the caterpillars leave. I'm a philosopher not a farmer. That's what I have managers for. They tell me what's going on. I like growing grain. There'll always be a market for bread and pasta. Fancy stuff comes and goes with the fashions but I'm too old to be bothered to care what is today's fad. There will always be bread. That I do know."

"Well be careful," cautioned the Senator again. "or you will be getting to know our erstwhile garrison commander again. Mark it well. It's always nice to have a bit more money but just don't overdo the one track road to grain. Diversify. Annoy everybody a bit rather than some people a lot. You know it makes sense."

Kiron waited. "What is this?" demanded the Senator.
"A summary of the accounts for Justus's farm." he was told.
"Not one farm," Carmedious glowered over the page, "There are lots of sets of numbers. Kiron. These are accounts for lots of..." he counted down, "Seventeen farms."

Kiron watched his master read. He was clearly getting more and more irate. Slowly he sat back and contemplated what he had read. "Our little philosopher is indeed a farmer. He is as rich as Croeus and devious with it. He could feed a city with what he has in his barns and what stands in his fields ready to harvest could feed Rome."

Kiron watched his master fold the sheet. The Senator continued "Licitus assured me that if we controlled bread we controlled the mob and if we control the mob we control Rome. If we have food and our friends eat

and our enemies starve then the world is our friend. Justus seems to be a more serious problem than we imagined. You have done well to find this. The problem now is what should we do about it."
Kiron looked on. "If Justus has too much grain perhaps we could help him reduce that a bit. It would be a pity if there were an accident. A fire perhaps?"
The Senator laughed. "Such a great pity. However you must ensure that nothing is traceable to us. That is clear?"

The dispatcher on Rahft looked at the troops. [You are quite clear on your orders?] she asked softly. There were very few direct action operations launched from the huge fleet battleship onto the planet beneath and if this one was happening on her watch she wanted them to be not only very clear on the plan but very successful.
[Yes Mam] they replied. She nodded and walked through the rows as if inspecting their arms and clothes for a formal parade. They were carefully scruffy, even dirty.
[Let me review the salient points of this mission again so we are all absolutely clear.] She turned down the next row.
[One. At no time will you unmap. You must retain the appearance of human beings at all times.] She was speaking louder. Nobody moved.
[Two. You will only use the native weapons issued to you. The need to draw and use a real arm will be considered a mission objective failure.] Louder still.
[Three. You need not kill anyone unnecessarily but the barns will be protected and the standing crops will be undamaged. This is quite clear?]
[Yes Mam.] they replied. She was now behind them all.
[Then go and pull tails girls!] she was shouting.
[Yes Mam!] they shouted back.

Justus sat at his desk. Geer stood before him. They were alone.
[That was stupid and unnecessary.]
[The food will stop people starving. There would be a lot less today if I had not acted last night.]
[We allowed for some losses. The key essential of the plan is our identification with these people. That is why I do not use troops.]
[You did not use troops I did. What I do does not affect your personal identification with these people. I am not identified with them. I do not plan things. What I do does not change your plans.]
[But you are here with us. You effect us. We are running on the limits of what we can predict. If you are going to go off like a child in a temper tantrum every time somebody opposes us we do not get the chance to be identified. Where is the cost to me in that? Where is my motivation?]

[If you want grain burnt I can arrange it. Be serious. We are really moving things along because we are here on the ground not sitting up in space tinkering with things. If you are going to run a 'hands on' project rather than a 'do not touch' one then somebody needs to act a bit more decisively at times.]
[No. It will not work that way. You have your responsibilities and I have mine. I will not tell you how to run a space fleet. Please do not tell me how to run the plan.]
[I considered that to be a security issue. In future, if somebody wants to burn your house down over your head and you do not like it, call me. We will try to fit you in to our busy schedules.]
[That is a reasonable offer. By all means eliminate assassins, that is your area of responsibility. However on mere property damage check with me first. If I do not call then please do not come.]

Detrima sat next to Geer by the fountain. He seemed more withdrawn than normal.
"Justus was angry today," she said, "He kept loosing track and having to begin again when dictating."
"My fault," said Geer. "However he is incapable of being cross for long. Tomorrow it will all be history."
Detrima moved a bit closer. "What did you do? If you don't mind me asking?"
"It's best forgotten," said Geer. "I did something I thought was right without asking, and, I suppose, I didn't have all the facts. I won't do it again."
"He's good like that," said Detrima, now actually leaning on him. "He doesn't mind mistakes. He only gets annoyed when you should know better... when I should... you know."
Geer did not move away but said. "Yes. You're right."
"He's been sending out orders to sell grain all day. I hear there is a shortage and price is right up and he is going to cash in." Detrima rested her head on him. "I've written to all sort of places and the couriers all have come and gone. We finished up by doing invitations to a party. In a week. That should give him something to look forward too."

Kiron entered. "You called for me Master?"
"I called for you. But I may not be able to do this much more," the Senator drained his cup. "He has got me. Blooded and in the sand. But I won't give up and lie down yet."
"I do not understand you Sir."
"It's the money Kiron. Everything hangs about the money. All I have is in grain and now that's not worth what I paid for it. I need money now and I can't get it. The house, the farm are all promised to the lenders

and they won't cover it. Licitus has deserted me, may he rot in Hades for all his help. Primedus says he will pay his share and go. I am left to pay mine and when I can't pay..."

"Then we need to leave here Sir. We can take the jewels and the portables and be aboard a boat in half a day. There are places to go where the cash in your hand is all that matters. Justus's vase alone would buy a new house."

"No Kiron. I was going to be Emperor. I had it within my grasp. I am not going to run like a fox with his tail on fire. I want Justus to know he cannot do this to me."

"A tactical withdrawal Sir. It could take many years to impeach you. You are a Senator."

"You'll change your tune when the money runs out."

"Then it's my business to see that we keep a lot of it. What am I to become? A whipper of slaves on a building site? A Senator's personal body guard has far more prestige. For that I need a Senator."

"Who owns who?" Carmedious rolled the dregs of wine around in his cup. "The master eats and the servant eats. So one sleeps on a soft bed? We all come to the same end. Kiron. Give me Justus and I'll give you your Senator. Let him cower and beg me for mercy and then let him die all the same. Then we go. Out of this god forsaken town. Just give me Justus."

"I will arrange for the packing to start Sir. We will visit Justus on our way out of town. I doubt he will delay us long."

"You can open his gates? I understood you were impressed by his security."

"The secretary will open to me. She trusts me. I shall have a note written that says I need to see her to discuss what we do next. She is infatuated with Geer, the younger of Justus's two bodyguards. She will open the door. She eats out of my hand." he paused. "Sir?"

"Yes?"

"Stop drinking. Our visit to Justus must be brief. If you wish to enjoy it you will want a clear head."

The senator glowered at him. "Get out. You really do think you own me. I shall have a bath and prepare myself for the journey. But you are right. This is to be savoured."

Detrima read the note again. What could be so urgent that Kiron needed to speak to her tonight? She hoped that he did not want her to copy accounts again. She still felt bad about that. It seemed wrong to reveal Justus's private dealings when he had done nothing wrong to her. She also suspected that Geer would be awfully cross with her if he ever found out.

But Kiron is a friend she told herself. Kiron helps me. Because of Kiron

I have lain in Geer's arms. Geer was tender to me. Thoughts of Geer wiped Kiron from her mind. If only they had not got quite so drunk that night things might have been so different. She was sure that Geer really did love her but he was shy, she was sure he was just shy. She wanted another chance. If she could go to Justus and admit they were already lovers then surely the old man would say "Well we must formalise it then." Justus was no old prude but he felt things should be done decently. He wanted people to be happy. He might even free her as Geer was a freeman servant. Then she could be a proper wife. Kiron was coming tonight. Kiron had a new idea. She was excited. Kiron would blow a horn, muted, and she would go to the gate.

Acritha was in a state. The guests would be arriving shortly and the place was not clean let alone properly laid out. The food was running late. The wine was warm. Nobody was in a clean uniform and Justus was getting in the way. Hurran marched round the place and rounded everybody up. Detrima got told, Ruth got asked but everybody helped. Hurran and Geer picked up the loaded kitchen table and carried it into the yard and Acritha shouted at them that if they dropped it she would personally skin them both. It was all ready on time. It always was.
The garrison centurion arrived with his wife on foot and the small escort was instructed to return at a specific time to accompany them home. The two judges came by coach and again their bodyguards left. The others used hired guards as this was not Rome so you were safe at home unless you had enemies. Justus's house was considered safe. Drinks were served in the colonnaded garden, with light tit-bits to wet the appetite. A modest feast was laid out. The emphasis on quality and variety rather than quantity. Only the trained food dispensers were to be in sight so the rest of the household retired to be on call rather than on view.
Geer stood in his clean smock and with a polished sword at his side and looked over the balcony rail at the yard. The guests sat on the long recliners and plates moved past them, tempting but never forcing. The discussion was on arts, plays, science. Politics was only alluded to in a historical context. Justus was self depreciating and modest. His guests played with him. Complementing, teasing. The evening drew on. Relaxed, entertaining.
Geer turned and saw Ruth standing near to him. She had changed from the simple dress she wore when helping with the preparations into a multi-layered flimsy thing that let the light through. Geer smiled. "He is happy."
Ruth stepped nearer. "I do not understand all that he says and I will never know a fraction of what he knows but he is happy. He is happy when he talks, when he explains things."

"He always talks," said Geer. "Even when he has a problem he talks and asks about it but finally he tells you the answer all by himself."
"It is as if he knows everything," mused Ruth. "Sometimes I am so in awe of him I am almost afraid."
"And yet," agreed Geer, "How could you be afraid of someone so gentle?"
"When I first came here I was frightened of him. We were taught to do all sorts of awful things at the slave school. I was so frightened. We had to practice with a dummy. Thankfully we were to be sold as virgins so we were never used by a real man. I feared him because of what I expected him to do to me."
Geer put an arm round her. "Justus could never be like that," he said. "He would never hurt someone like you."

Detrima was sitting in the library and beginning to get worried. She re-read Kiron's note again. It was brief and gave no hint of what he was going to suggest. She slowly went through the reasons she was worried.
Firstly Kiron was certainly illiterate so he would have had to dictate and he might not trust the writer. Kiron did not seem to trust many people and she was beginning to wonder about that.
Secondly, and perhaps more ominously, Kiron was hiding something. All her initial doubts about him began to come back and his wanting the farm accounts seemed more sinister the more she considered it. She was going to have to get help. If she was going to have to admit things Justus was the one to go too but Justus was busy. He could not be interrupted while he was with his guests. As talking to Hurran was out of the question that left Geer.
She sat and fidgeted. Would Geer understand? If she spoke to Justus then Geer would find out. Perhaps it would be better if she told him first. But what if Kiron was innocent of duplicity? Would she throw away everything she had gained so far? The indecision almost became a physical pain.

"Have you served Justus long?" asked Ruth.
Geer paused before answering. "Yes," he said slowly. "We have been together a very long time."
"You were a gladiator," said Ruth. "That must have been hard. You do not seem to be the type of person who would kill for sport."
Geer remembered. "You do not get much choice. A gladiator starts as a slave. If you become free you are expected to continue. I did not. You are right. I would not willingly kill without cause."
"I was born free," whispered Ruth, as though this was an enormous secret. "But they came and collected us and took us away. They

emptied the land so there would be no more rebellions. So now I am a slave and I do not know where the rest of my family has gone."

"One day you will be free again," said Geer. "I hope your family are as fortunate as you. There are evil masters but many are as Justus and know that God made masters and slaves and will hold those that abuse power responsible for what they have done."

"We must have been great sinners for our God dealt harshly with us," said Ruth. "I saw so many dead or maimed and nailed to posts that I forgot to cry in the end. My uncles were in Jerusalem so I know they are dead. We thought God would deliver us but he did not. We thought God loved only us. Now I am here and I see Justus serves God as we did. But why did so many have to die?"

"I cannot answer that," said Geer drawing the girl closer to himself. "There is a plan, I know, and that will bring an end to wars and hurt and slavery. We do our bit but I have seen greater things than this. Once I doubted things would change but now I know that it will happen."

Ruth leaned against him. "But there is so much evil. We have to choose to do good but even the good die pointless deaths. Was it my sin or the sins of my parents that meant I was dragged away from them and taught to be a prostitute? Some of the girls I trained with tried to kill themselves when they knew what was happening to them. I wanted to but I could never quite do it. They were careful with us. Finally they knew we would obey, then we were sold. I was resigned to it. It would be unpleasant but it did not really matter any more. Nothing mattered."

Geer pulled the girl to him. "I don't think it was anybody's fault in that way. It is the way the world is. It was once worse believe me. Justus is our hope. If anyone can change this world he can. He works and studies and he understands more and more."

"Can any one person change things?" asked Ruth. "There was a man called Jesus and to my people he is either a saint or the devil. He knew how to change people. My grandfather used to tell me about him. But the soldiers killed him. He still has followers today. Is Justus greater than him?"

Geer stroked her head. "There may be great things going on that we know little of but we have Justus. Who else would you choose?"

Ruth wiped her face with a piece of her dress. "Do you trust him?"

Geer sighed. "With my life."

Ruth fell silent.

Detrima finally got to the top of the stairs and wondered where Geer might be. She looked round and saw him standing at the other end of walkway. Nestled in his arms was Ruth. For a moment she saw gentle brotherly affection. Then she saw betrayal. She stepped back into the stair well and pressed her forehead against the wall. Suddenly she understood Geer's coldness towards her. He was just playing her along to cover his dalliance with that shameless little whore.

That Ruth was trained by one of the best schools, that she was young and beautiful gave her a criminal advantage. She was stealing Geer from her. Tears were running down Detrima's face. Ruth could not have Geer because she was Justus's. Detrima almost took the personal slight against her master as an assault against herself. Justus was a full citizen and he was a kind and virtuous master. He deserved better than this. Brat. Whore. Traitor. The anguish poured out. Geer could not be doing this to her. Geer was kind and gentle. Ruth was leading him astray. Corrupting him.

Suddenly Kiron was a hope. He might have a suggestion. An idea. Perhaps they could challenge Geer and by threat of exposure make him renounce Ruth. Detrima was sure that Geer would see through the temptress. She could offer him everything that Ruth could. And more. She just needed to drag him away from her.

"Do you love him?" asked Geer.

"I think I do," said Ruth softly. "The school taught us all sorts of things to do for a man but after the first few weeks I never thought of him like that. At first I just did what I was taught. Helping with the bath, the towels, the oil. All the time dreading the moment when he would command me to do something more. But he never did. He just let me carry on. Always thankful, always courteous. And slowly we became lovers. He never asked but I just knew. It would once have been wrong, we Jews are not like these Romans, we believe in marriage, but I felt free, because I was a slave and he was my master I was free, it was even my duty to do anything for him that pleased him," she reflected for a moment. "Yes. I suppose I do love him."

For the first time Ruth looked up from the courtyard below and looked at Geer. He smiled at her and she smiled back. Then suddenly she seemed to become aware of him. She pulled against his arms. "Don't hold me like this," she said.

Geer looked at her shocked. "No," he said letting go and moving back, "You don't understand."

"I'm sorry," said Ruth pulling her garments round her as if she were suddenly cold. "But I do understand. It's my fault. I shouldn't have come up to you like this. Anyway. I should be downstairs."

She looked at him sadly. "I will not tell Justus about what has just happened because it would break his heart. You are a great favourite to him. He trusts you." She turned abruptly and walked off. Geer turned away from the balcony and sat on the bench by the wall and wondered what went wrong and what to do next.

Detrima heard the note of the horn. That was Kiron's signal. She stopped and wondered, what was she to do? What if she was right and Kiron was planning something wrong? Could he rescue Geer for her? Did she even want Geer even now? In an agony of indecision she walked down to the gate. She heard the horn again. Softly. At a distance. She cursed inside. If they rushed in and killed her could it be worse? Maybe Kiron knew what to do.
The doorman was away from his post. He was standing available to the guests in case any of them needed their escorts calling. She quietly slipped open the view port. She just saw Kiron face.
"Is it clear?" he asked. "Just two minutes of your time then I must get back to the house."
"Step inside a moment," she said much relieved, pulling the lock bar up.
The door pushed her back. Kiron rushed passed her holding a sword. Then more men. She screamed. Last of all Senator Carmedious stepped in. He looked round with wild eyes and walked past her like she did not exist. Detrima grabbed her skirts and ran into the court-yard. The shouting had just begun.

Geer arrived at the balcony edge and took in the scene rapidly. The doorman lay dead. Justus stood by the pool with Ruth behind him. The Senator was facing him with two armed men. The Garrison Centurion, unarmed and unarmoured, still holding a drinking cup stood by looking on with horror on his face. Hurran stood at the door of the watch-room holding a blooded sword and facing three guards and Kiron. He was ready to step back and force them to come at him one at a time. One man lay dead at his feet which would further complicate matters for the attackers.
Detrima stood virtually below Geer looking on. Beside her were five more men. Geer began to take in the conversation to add to the sight.
"No," shouted Detrima. "You never said..."
Kiron pushed her away and she stumbled back away from him some ten feet. He was trying not to take his eyes off Hurran. "Stick the bitch," he yelled over his shoulder. "Just shut her up."
Detrima's legs gave way with the horror of it all. She fell to the floor. One of the senator's bodyguard raised his sword over her and started to swing.
Geer jumped from the balcony.
Detrima gasped as the body collapsed on her, the sword skittling across the flagstones. Geer picked himself up dragging his sword from the man's back.
"Quite an entrance," said Kiron, dodging his eyes back and forth between the two gladiators. "Kill him if you can but don't let him move

about. We've got them both covered now."
Four men closed menacingly round Geer. As with Hurran it was a stand-off. Everyone was certain who could win but also sure that the first to attack would buy the victory for his fellows with his own life. Geer stood astride Detrima. His sword was ready. He looked almost relaxed, balanced on the balls of his feet. His chest and the front of his garments was already covered in the blood of the man he had just killed yet he was hardly breathing heavily.
If the fighting men were stalled the Senator was not. He took his own short sword and waved it at Justus.
Justus stumbled back and tripping on the steps fell onto them. "You are a villain Carmedious," he said. "If you think your quarrel is with me then settle it but let these others go."
"Pompous words you meddling fool," the Senator was shouting now. "You shall die because you deserve it. You have cost me everything. They are mere play-actors. We will sweep them away as tale tellers complicate matters." He advanced on the old man who was now trying to get up. "I am going to give you the honour of dying by my hand. Not because you deserve anything but because I shall enjoy it very much." He drew back his arm.
He never struck. In a flurry of white gauzy stuff Ruth was upon him. One hand on his fist gripping the sword, the other hand on his forearm and her teeth buried in his wrist. The Senator jerked at her to get free but only succeeded in picking her off the floor and dragging her across his chest. He pulled at her shoulders with his free hand and only got handfuls of torn material. He lurched sideways to rest his back against the gate and then dropped the sword and grasped, wrong handedly, for the dagger on his belt.
Geer suddenly tossed his sword from his right hand to his left. He began to raise his now empty right hand to point at the Senator. Justus glanced apprehensively at him.
[Not a gun Alacia. Use the sword.]
[I cannot. Ruth will not stay still. I might harm her.]
[Command Translate Switch Hebrew]"Ruth my beloved!"
Ruth, still kicking and scratching looked at Justus. Her eyes were wide with fear.
[Ready Alacia.]"Sleep!"
Ruth's eyes glazed, her struggles stopped and her head flopped forward. In that moment something almost passed through her hair. She slowly crumpled to the floor as the Senator's hands released her.
Everybody stopped and looked. The silence was broken as Hurran shouted "Geer! Catch!"
Geer caught the flying sword. Then everybody looked at Hurran. The guards near him looked relieved. Geer looked at the hands on either

side of the guardroom arch and laughed. Hurran pulled in his hands and he held the trident and the net. The guards stepped back cautiously and looked at Kiron for guidance.

Kiron whistled and slowly turned his sword, pommel first, towards Hurran.

"Lost the will to fight?" asked the old Gladiator. "You won't face a tridentus?"

"I've lost my Master," said Kiron softly. He looked at the body nailed through the skull to the gate by Geer's sword. "I'm just obeying orders. Nothing personal." He watched Justus pick up the little dark haired girl. "That was some throw Geer."

The centurion walked over to Kiron and took the sword from him. "If you were just a slave that might be an acceptable answer."

Kiron smiled. "My master was a full Senator. I think you'll find that I should assume that his interpretation of the law is more clear than mine. I would never knowingly transgress the law would I? He assured me that what we were doing was right."

The centurion looked at him. He sighed inwardly. "And what judge," he thought to himself, "What judge will rule in open court that a servant, a chief body guard even, should question his master?" For a moment he considered killing the man there and then but somehow the rule of law was too strong on him. There was the sound of running in the street. The night watch was coming. There would be another report to write.

The night was old when, having eaten sparingly from the remains of the feast, the household finally retired to bed. Geer started the patrol of the house and found Justus sitting alone by the pool in the quadrangle. They looked at one another.

[Alharan?]
[Alacia.]
[I think I owe you an apology.]
[Why? What for?]
[Well over the years I have been pretty scathing over the relationships you have had with humans. But now I see that you have done it very well. You are good at it and I did not see that. When I tried I got it all wrong. I am sorry.]
[You do yourself an injustice. You were mapped as a man so how you could be expected, as a woman, to get things right?]
[No. It is not that. I just goofed around. I did not know what to do or what to say. I should have been able to act it out the same as you. But it is a relationship thing. Girls are never good at that. It is what men do well.]
[I don't claim to be an actor.]
[No? I watched Ruth with you. Even across her being a different

species I could see she loved you. You treated her gently. You rescued her. She responded to you. You were her man.]
[She came here as a slave. Did she have a choice? She was so frightened at first. I could have done anything to her.]
[I saw that. The poor child had been mentally abused. But that hardly made a difference after the first few weeks. I watched you draw her personality back. And finally, when the show down came, she tried to save your life because she loved you not because you were her master.]
[And you saved Detrima.]
[But I know you were shielded. Hurran could be expected to look after himself. The others were too shocked to move. When you woke Ruth up and she looked into your eyes she knew you loved her too. That is subtle, you did it very well. What did you say to her that made her react like that?]
[I told her she was free. She had earned the right not to be a slave any more. She said she did not want to leave. I said it would be unethical to have a free woman I was not related to staying in my house on a permanent basis. She could only stay if she married me. That is when she started crying. She did agree by the way.]
[That just leaves the problem of Detrima.]
[Detrima, to put it frankly, betrayed us. By the standards of this place she should be flogged to death or something. Perhaps we should get Hurran to offer to do it and you can intercede on her behalf and I will reluctantly give in, despite my belief in the rule of law, and send her to work in the trading house at Miceni.]
[That will get me off the hook. Do I have to say a goodbye?]
[Only if you want to. I can script it if you like. At Miceni we have a Varhyn operator running things. I can get him to assess her for a husband. He has a lot of good men on his staff. I expect we can find a suitable one. The maths are not complex for someone brought up with the expectations of a slave so we will not take much of his time. She would be a bit happier then I think.]
[It is probably better that way. I tried to be fond of her and act like a human but it would not come.]
[Actually, for a change, you did worse than I expected. It was almost like you were a Varhyn wife because your emotions seemed already set. I expected you to act like a preged or a teenager.]
[Something like that. Perhaps I am just too old.]
[Something. You will stay in the villa for the rest of this mission?]
[I will stay. It cannot be worse than what we have already been through.]
[I am pleased. I appreciate your presence here.]

A year and more has gone. Alharan sits at his calculations. The new factors have improved the margins. The future is slotting into predictable place. A problem is accounted for and things will proceed. Rome is more polarised, which is a new problem, but the mobs eat and are relatively quiet while the princeps becomes stronger.
A dark haired girl holding a small child in her arms comes up behind him. She looks unquestioningly at the jumble of papers and the large white page where the words move by themselves. The child reaches out and says "Ab Ab" and touches Alharan's head. He turns and smiles. He leaves his work.

The Varhyn female is strong and resourceful. She is a fighter. The men may be smaller and weaker but they are so rare. You share one if you are lucky. Many of your fellow wives will be your sisters so your biology says fight to preserve them. Fight to preserve the children. Fight to preserve the family.
Deep in their blood is the Vestel. You cannot kill the Vestel alone. Unless you train hard. Unless you are armed. But you must protect the home, must protect the children, must protect the husband. On and on.
Alacia Denn, Ship Master, Co-Director of the Earth Civilisation Project stands in the night outside the master's suite of the villa. Her keen hearing can pick out Ruth hushing the baby girl so she does not wake her father.
Alacia sighs. "I would have saved him too" she thinks. "But he never thinks of me as a woman." She sighs again and turns on her communicator. The watchers on Rahft, the vast fleet battleship that is the project's base, will alert her if there is to be an intrusion at the villa. It is time to catch up on the day's administration.

Zwei

One of the problems with being a Magical Girl was that, although you had to turn it on for combat, you could never quite turn it off. Captain Grace could see round corners and, currently, she could see Major Maria and Colonel Brims bringing another person, who she did not recognise in a uniform she did not recognise either, into the building and her diary told her they were her three o'clock appointment.
Grace checked round the office. Major Maria was an ex-magical girl, she had stayed on after her first enlistment, so she 'understood' that strange enclave of the army that consisted of teenage girls with weapon grade magical powers. Grace stood up and opened the cupboard with the full length mirror on the inside of the door. She inspected herself. She was suitably smart in her browns, her official uniform. She smiled at herself as a twenty year old Captain in a tiny tube skirt, cut so short her mother would never have approved of it at home, matching jacket, white blouse, a tie and kick off shoes. She sighed. A combat specialist magical girl needed to be able to transform in a moment into her fighting uniform and that was set by her magic so the army could not control it. Short, tight skirts didn't interfere with transforming and, more importantly, came back intact when you de-transformed so they wore short, tight skirts on duty.
Grace was under no illusion that the Magical Girl ranks were not taken quite as seriously as those of the long term enlistments but Magical Girls delivered the big power and took the big risks. The army knew that and rewarded them. In another few years as her powers started to wane, if she did not transfer over like Major Maria had, she would retire in her early twenties. Provided she did not slip up on a mission. Provided she survived.
Sergeant Zwei was a Metarii and although a Magical Girl in her own right was their operations manager. In combat situations she worked from the base operations room and fed intel and resources to the girls in the field. Certainly her magical girl speed and future-sense made her ideal for this role but she often expressed the wish to be on more active duties. However when you weigh 400 grams and stand 30 centimetres tall the Army does not like to let you into combat too often. Today being an in house day Sergeant Zwei was being their receptionist.
Grace waited for her visitors to come up the lift. Since there was no reason for the meeting in the diary it was either very significant or insignificant. Her future sense said the former. They were at Sergeant Zwei's little desk placed on top of an ordinary desk. They were speaking. The alert sounded and the Sergeant appeared on Grace's screen and she announced the visitors. It always surprised Grace a

little how Zwei looked perfectly human on video where there was no way to scale her size. Grace acknowledged it and stood to greet them as they came in.

Colonel Brims had oversight of her whole department and Major Maria of her unit so Grace was used to dealing with them if a bit wary. They introduced Alharan Anahe.

Grace was astounded. This was an officer from the Tranzen, the almost mythical dimensional and universal police. They had existed since forever and permeated all of time and space providing the backup to keep the multi-universe stable. Tranzen? Here?

Polankerin Anahe was smiling and polite. He was on a search for something that was lost and he had come to their world in their galaxy in their dimension because he was interested in the manifestation of magic here. Grace knew they were a bit unusual but the magic was so much a part of her life so she never questioned it. Was he a magic user? He smiled and said that in a way he was. However he had identified unit six, her unit, as crucial. It was a sense in a way similar to their future sense he assured her, so there were details he was uncertain of. He wanted to work with them and see what happened. How long would he stay? Indeterminate. As long as his mission took plus any time they needed him for. Time was not a problem.

Maria and Brims stood, shook hands and wished them well. Grace saw them to the door and then turned to the problem of integrating a young man into a Magical Girl Combat unit. This would be complicated. The army deliberately never tried it so all her ancillary workers were girls. Sergeant Zwei fussed about and allocated him private use of a room with ensuite facilities in the officer's quarters and led him away to unpack.

Lieutenant Rico sat in front of Grace's desk, Sergeant Zwei sat on a little chair on it and they listened. "We will first introduce him into our training drills," Grace explained still sketching the plan on her pad as she described it. "So we get some measure of whether he is an asset or a burden. We have all heard of the Tranzen but we actually have absolutely zero information on file. The only thing I can say is you can't use magic on him. You either see him just as you see him, if you understand me, or he isn't there. He's totally genuine until you push too hard and then he vanishes. I'm assuming it's a defensive trick and probably automatic. If it is conscious control he's really good."

"We are assured he's 'on team'?" asked Rico apprehensively.

"That was specifically emphasised," said Grace. "He is to be treated like any member of the unit, getting all intel and prompts. However we are not able to assume he is always a contributor. There is some reason that he is here and we have to assume that he will view his mission as taking precedence over ours."

"He can fly?" asked Zwei suspiciously. "If we have to do transport all the time we will tie up resources."

"I am told he is 'unlimited' but I don't have a definition of 'unlimited' in this context," Grace assured her. "All Magical girls can fly so he'd be a total disaster if he couldn't."

"What was his rank?" asked Rico.

"Polankerin..." said Grace. "No, I don't know what it means either and like everything else it is undocumented. However the Colonel clearly believed in it so he's an officer of sorts."

"So we train tomorrow?" asked Zwei.

"All of us," said Grace. "I will join you at eight o'clock. Have the others briefed to expect him. Zwei. Run us a big endgame scenario. One we might lose on if we're not on form."

Corporal Tina was lying on her bed feeling chatty while Corporal Horo was trying to read. "A man," said Tina. "Now that's a turn up."

"Tranzen," said Horo disinterestedly. "So not necessarily human so what is 'a man' in this context?"

"More than we've had before," Tina was pleased. "We get to train together tomorrow so we get an introduction and we get to see him in action and maybe show off a bit. A magical boy is a new trick on me."

"He's listed as an observer," pointed out Horo. "Don't expect big magic. Plus before you start signing up as his girl friend we don't know if he's a senior officer or what. If he's super brass you've got no hope."

"He's probably on silly mage grades like us. Give me a break. Being a fighting magical girl scares off all the boys that aren't weirdoes. At least if he's a combat mage we get to be more equals and maybe can interact a bit."

"I'm not holding my breath," said Horo very deliberately looking back into her book.

Alharan turned up in the usual training run t-shirt and shorts that the girls used to save scuffing up their browns transforming. He was introduced and shook hands all round. Rico briefed them for the first level. Alharan had no specific duties but was to move shortly behind Tina and Horo, who would lead, and Grace and Rico who would follow as heavy artillery. "Spotter?" he asked.

Zwei was not running things from her usual base in the ops room but had taken the option to be with them. She was clearly already in magical mode as she was flying with two large control screens projected in front of her. However she was not in her normal transformed uniform. Actually, Grace realised, it was a strange amalgam of the skirt from her browns, her short sleeved summer issue uniform blouse but no jacket, no tie and no shoes.

"Right," said Zwei putting her hands behind her neck and thrusting her elbows back, "Everybody ready?"

Grace looked at her and said "Start the drill," but inwardly was annoyed. The first time they had an eligible man on the practice range and Zwei was flaunting a bust that didn't measure fourteen centimetres. Grace had never thought of her Sergeant as a flirt before but suddenly it seemed that that was the case.

"Transform in sequence," cued Zwei and Rico carefully turned away from Alharan and lifted her arms and stepped off lightly off the ground to turn into combat mode.

The magic flared from the jewel at her neck and flowed over her lifting off her clothes and Grace noted that she did not do her usual spin until the jacket and skirt had fully materialised. Then she reached up and her staff assembled itself into her hand and the first cartridge of collected magic snapped into place.

As Rico dropped back onto her feet Tina's jewel triggered. Tina just hopped into the air as her roller boots and fighting fist snapped into place. "No shyness there," noted Grace wondering if Alharan had followed the moment of nudity in mid-transform.

Horo did a spiral jump pretty much as she always did and it might have been coincidence that she was faced away from Alharan at the critical moment but it was better executed than Rico's more obvious turn away.

Grace's turn came. The twist was her normal style but she told herself "I will not be intimidated. Today he is one of my team," She just punched her arms out to the sides skipping her feet off the ground so her shoes could transform.

Alharan didn't move. His shorts and t-shirt vanished and he just changed colour.

"For the log," asked Zwei looking down on them, "What are you covered in?"

"Down," he said and then expanded it to "Little feathers. It comes from one of my non-human parts. It's just improved to be a controllable insulator and reflector. I can protect things that are me but there are lots of weapons that an external uniform would actually make me more vulnerable too."

"So it's part of your body?" asked Grace thankful that 'down' obscured certain areas.

"Er... Yes," he replied. "I can colour it if you like. If the idea that I'm naked offends you. But this shade is the one that is natural to me."

"No... No," said Grace not quite sure how a naked magical man fitted in.

"What colour do I log it as?" asked Zwei with a slight laugh in her voice.

"It's usually called Tawny," he said hesitantly.

"Vanilla with toffee swirls," said Tina quietly to Horo. "I'll have some of that."

"So..." said Alharan. "Training so basically a video game?"

"The gadgets and especially the top level boss could hospitalise you if you're not on top form," insisted Zwei. "A bland training aid just teaches people to get killed."

"No," he replied. "What I mean is that my restriction that I'm not supposed to use my powers except for duty, family or training means I can play. Not on full power obviously."

Grace was interested. "Use what you feel comfortable with but when we debrief we need to know what level it was so we know where you stand for real combat. The weapons we will face on this run are 'serious injury' level. More would kill us. When we go into combat for real we don't want to take time 'saving' you from something that can't even ruffle your hair but conversely we would hope to push you out of the way of something that is going to kebab you."

"Yes Mam," he said and made a gesture with a fist across his chest that was so obviously a salute.

Three levels of run and shoot. Once Zwei had set it into automatic it all ran independently so she was able to change sides and do her normal duty of reading the intel screens to try and work with them to get round the worst of the incoming fire but they had to fight through and take out the boss. In real life the boss would be guarding or assaulting something and you had to recover that but for training runs like this that was usually glossed over. Also three levels was rare. In true combat situations you went straight for the final target. A big part of Zwei's job was to make sure they didn't get bogged down fighting the supporting act.

Rico's orders from Grace were to watch Alharan carefully for skills and weaknesses so she bunched up a little close on the first level but he neither contributed much nor got in the way. He was fast and when he did take something down it was a clean shot executed from a minimum risk manoeuvre. As one professional to another she approved.

Tina however, Rico noticed, was showing off. Not enough to get called for 'excessive risk' or 'inefficient use' but obviously going for the flashy when there was a even choice.

It was Tina's fault in the end. The last boss was powerful and fast and Horo was running an illusion and Tina was riding the bosses fire limits and suddenly did a big switch reverse. Ten out of ten for well executed but the problem was that it left the boss with no obvious targets other than Rico and Alharan when it should have been confused. A deflect would be too slow and leave Tina as an easy next obvious target and the prospect of somebody going down as a kill on a training level

loomed embarrassingly. It had to be a dodge.
Strategically the dodge was obvious but for two of them it was verging on impractical. Alharan was nearer the wall that would buy them the required half a second so Rico launched herself at him. He was starting to move as she hit him. Her fingers bit into the soft down and for a moment he resisted her push and then he went inertialess. They ended up in a heap and right on time Grace hit the boss and blew it.
Alharan stood up and executed a very careful area surveillance but Zwei announced "Boss down. End of drill. Everybody come back and debrief. We have snacks."
Grace dropped down to Rico still sitting in the hole behind the wall. "Great save," she said.
Rico looked slightly stunned for a moment and then snapped back into combat mode. They flew silently back to the lawn in front of the training model to formally go over the run. Grace was a little concerned. This was out of character. Rico ran the top level training. Fly back was the first chance to reinforce lessons. Get them while the adrenaline is still flowing.
"Wow," said Alharan back in his shorts, lying on his back on the grass. "You set a mean exercise Zwei."
She giggled. "I don't see what you're worried about. You beat all previous best records."
"That's probably because there's five of us," he laughed. "Or did you step up the offensive force to match?"
"Nope," Zwei said. "I expected you to get trashed early on and I don't want to make it too hard to be beneficial to the others. I'm pleased with you."
"You though I would be a handicap?" he asked laughing slightly.
"It had crossed our minds," said Grace detransforming and starting some stretches before she tightened up from all the exercise. "That was one of the reasons for today. I couldn't put the team in the field with an unknown member."
He chuckled. "That's the nice thing about being far from home," he said rather contentedly. "No big expectations."
"You do this sort of thing normally?" asked Tina pointedly sitting next to him.
He pulled a face. "Not really. However I've spent a lot of time amongst fighting girls so I felt a home straight away. It's nice to be allowed to play for a change."
Horo rather didn't want to be left out so she pointed out "Fighting girls are hardly the norm here. Those of us with the right magical powers aren't very common and we burn out pretty quickly."
Grace looked over at Rico. "How come so silent?" she asked. "You did really well today."

Rico gave a slightly forced smile and shrugged. "Thanks."

They were sitting in the lounge, feet up and reading. They were on call. Future sense said they would be called so they were ready. It was a point of honour that they always went on a live mission in their full browns so Alharan turned up in his blue uniform with the badges on the lapels.

"Oh, and give me a couple of those magic cartridges," he said to the armourer. "It might be better to taste 'normal' now we're on a live mission."

"What do you sense?" Grace asked Alharan. "I'm just getting 'soon'."

"Twenty minutes," he closed his eyes. "Helicopter. Deploy from the air. Gadgets like on the training run but airborne units too. We are trying to recover something in a moving tube. After that it gets fuzzy but it is the start of a sequence of escalating call outs. My project seems to be involved... Well... Maybe... I've been disappointed on that one before."

"A moving tube?" wondered Grace and pressed for comms to the ops room. "Zwei. Can you run that against anything being monitored. See if we can get a head start."

"I'm getting Statis box," said Rico. "But frankly it's only a fraction over 'guess' level at the moment."

"What's a Statis box?" asked Alharan.

"About one of the most magically stealable thing on this planet," sighed Grace. "Automated magic collectors. Very old and as stable as a fish on a bicycle. When they turn up we ship them into a secure containment unit, damp them down and hope they don't blow themselves up. Prized by nutters with a death wish as a source of huge power. They were made back when magic was weak and placed at secret strategic points. However in the Mage wars the documentation was lost and... Well, when they turn up they are kept deadly secret. Probably even the army doesn't get told unless one needs recovering."

Alharan was staring at her. "You had Mage wars?" he asked. "I thought our people would have stepped in and stopped that. I know your magic isn't very powerful but that is just what we're here to prevent."

"Zwei. Contact the Statis Agency and tell them we have foresees on this. Do they have anything for us?" ordered Grace not wanting to discuss the Mage wars.

"They came straight back with an acknowledge," said Zwei from the ops room. "No details of course but that means they're in live mode so something is on the move."

"Shit," said Tina. "It's a biggie. A bit of newsworthy urban rescue would have been nice with pictures on the vid tonight but we are going to get our hair singed and we won't even be able to type up the report in the open lounge."

"Zwei," called Grace. "Put transport on pre-empt. We have a clear foresee. All we need is the target. We will deploy to the helicopter deck. Everybody. Any ideas on a moving tube as a battle site?"
"Statis box in transport?" thought Rico, "Is it a big truck?"
"Too small," said Alharan.
"A train?" offered Horo.
"A what?" said Alharan. "Oh. I remember. On rails. That still seems a bit short for what I see."
"Heck I think they link the compartments for freight," said Tina. "You could have a mile if you wanted it. Just watch out for the bendy bits every twenty meters or so."
"It's nearly time," said Grace. "Let's put some pressure on. Zwei. Give the SA a prompt that we have a foresee on an attack on a train. See if they bite."
They walked onto the helicopter that was now running up lacking only a flight plan.

"Bingo!" said Zwei. "That shook them up. We have coordinates. It's fifteen minutes out so get going!"
Grace signalled the pilots and the team sat into their seats. The 'copter lifted and climbed towards its transition altitude where it could become a mage-jet. Grace was drumming her fingers waiting for the briefing screens to light with the target information. "If it's a Statis box grab," she said to Alharan. "It's a top level enemy so we can expect a boss supported by gadgets brought in by a summoner and probably an air superiority and transport units. The helicopter certainly can't out-gun the air unit so we'll bail at altitude, transform on the fall and go in hard. You take the train with Tina and Horo while... Zwei have we got any intel yet?... Rico and I try to make sure you have a getaway path. You can't destroy a Statis box and thankfully they're both heavy and immune to magic so we need to clear the boss, clear the gadgets and take the air cover. If we take out the air or the boss we buy time, when we take out them both we win."
"Basically," he summarised. "A total win or we lose. There is no half way."
"It's not..." the intel screens lit, "Thank you Zwei... Not that bad. The army will run in full support but that going to take a while and sadly these things usually are settled in the first hundred seconds. If you have a recorder run it as I'd like a report on file from you as your running as a full team member now. Good luck."
They were a continent away from their starting point when the helicopter dropped out of mage flight and lowered its rear gate and the warm air inside instantly vanished. Tina and Horo ran and jumped, still in their browns, Alharan followed and Grace and Rico paused then

jumped together.

The girls relaxed and let their transformation sequences run as they fell. It always felt good as the magical uniform styled by your own magic replaced your army issue. Then your fighting gear snapped together and the cartridge magic loaded. All their tools snapped in with a satisfying clunk. There was real magic power here, far more than you could sweep up for a simple spell. Concentrated, refined combat magic.

Grace gritted her teeth as the high altitude cold hit her in the moment of nudity but with her uniform came her magical shields. A magical girl's uniform showed her style not protected her. She looked at Rico and smiled. It was "Let's go get 'em," time again.

Tina and Horo were aiming for truck five. They were three minutes behind the attack so the boss had probably located the Statis box but would obviously be moving it to buy defensive time. Pick a point and punch in through the roof. Expect gadgets. Lots of gadgets.

Tina hit the floor of the truck and deployed defence and scanning. A gadget was in front of her but with its back to her so she accurately punched the vulnerable spot so it wouldn't report as it went down. Which way to go?

As Horo landed next to her Zwei called. "Statis and bosses forward. Gadgets both ways. Beware the surround trap."

"Bosses?" hissed Horo spotting the plural. "Not our day today."

"I'll cover the rear," said Alharan. "You go find the box. I'm looking forward to seeing it." He was tossing a magic cartridge in his hand like it was a kiddies ball.

Tina muttered a rude word but started to skate. Her roller boots gave her exceptional speed and turning power so it was preferred to flying for close combat. However there was not much room to manoeuvre within the body of the freight truck but, thankfully the next gadgets she encountered were unprepared and she got one before it fired, dodged the fire from the second and hit it while the third exploded as Horo came into range.

"Twin bosses," announced Zwei. "The one your side is lining up to fight. The other is moving the box."

"One each side? Nice plan for a fight in a tube," muttered Horo. "So we have to beat two before their air freight arrives. Go Grace and Rico. Buy us some extra seconds."

"Clear behind," reported Alharan with an obvious cloud of smoke showing behind him. "I'm coming after you."

"Twenty four," said Zwei. "Some obvious dummy drones and I highlight the heavy lifters. 'Ware interceptors behind!"

"You kill the transport," ordered Grace. "I'll watch your back."

Rico dived, her staff at the ready and drew a clear shot on the first transporter. It burst with a satisfying plume of smoke. From above her she saw the flash as Grace deployed a shield to deflect fire. She was drawing the fighters away. It wouldn't last but it bought time for a second clear shot and a second transport spiralling into the ground. Grace was having trouble. The light interceptors had bounced off her first rounds like they were much heavier kit. She hit them with a full power and they blew but that either took time or it needed her to be more stable. She couldn't stop jinking, twitching her flight path unexpectedly to make herself a hard target, as they were more manoeuvrable than usual. She carefully recorded one desperately trying to evade her next bolt and she realised that if she was not firing full rounds now it would have got away.
Now they were breaking off, realising that Rico had already eliminated two of the transports they were there to protect. Thankfully they seemed no smarter than usual.
Rico was jinking and Grace threw her a shield as she sighted the third transport so she could fly straight for a moment and not twist the beam. The transport exploded satisfyingly and that just left one. "Well," thought Grace, "and thirteen harder than usual inters."
Rico was diving and jinking. Shots were going past her but foresee is a powerful tool in battle. Grace saw she was trying to put the bulk of the transport between her and the fighters so she could fly smooth for a moment. There was one inter away from the main group so Grace lined it up and threw a blast at it. That would simplify Rico's course.
Rico was under the transport and shielded from the inters. She rolled onto her back and drew a careful line. The transport flared. Not a clean hit but a take down. It suddenly tumbled in the air and then smashed into the ground. "First boss down in the train," announced Zwei.

Tina pulled her lance from the smoking remains of the Boss, grinned at Alharan and Horo then dug in to make some speed for the second one. There were gadgets but she dodged and, although they were fast, there was too much incoming fire from Horo's hand guns for them to get a clean shot on her. Speed was the trick now.
They were into other cargo. The boss had broken through the wall that ended the Statis Agencies private section. It was big and round and trying to manoeuvre the bulky Statis box past a mass of heavy freight. Tina raced ahead looking for a clear shot when she saw the fire tubes swivelling towards her. There wasn't much room to dodge and you must not get cornered.
Alharan bounced off the remains of the partition and skidded past her on his tummy. He must have misjudged something. Tina skated up the wall and onto the roof still closing on the boss. She was looking down

on Alharan but the boss was still tracking her. She was running out of roof. Down. She needed down but the wall was all full of the new cargo. This was going horribly wrong.

Suddenly she felt his hands on her waist and she was dropping to the floor. Her mind accelerated and stopped. A moment of insight, of foresee. He wrapped an arm round her and pulled. Then they cannoned into the boss below its fire ports and she saw one of Alharan's hands sticking up holding a magic cartridge so it flew out of his grip into the port. She noted the silly grin but realised what he had done and wrapped her arms round her head.

The boss fired and the ensuing explosion blew a large section of the roof off the truck.

The train had been executing an emergency stop since it first detected the fire fight on board. Finally their minds slowed enough to recognise this. Alharan looked over the smoking wreckage of the boss at the Statis box behind.

"Oh," he sighed. "Disappointing. It's a sweeper and a can. Show it true magic and it would probably fry itself in minutes. No limiters so a bit wobbly. Nice trick for a fully auto though."

Horo arrived and reached out a hand to Tina still sitting on the floor gasping but Zwei announced. "Bosses down. We have air control. Deploy to guard. Nine minutes to army team. Statis Agency send their complements and a reminder that level one security applies."

"Shit," muttered Horo. "Level one means you can't even get a commend on your record. It just goes down as a blank day."

Tina just stared at her blankly.

"OK so what's the big deal?" asked Horo as they got back to their room.

"Well," started Tina, "did you see the bit where he dodged the second boss?"

"What? Where he got it wrong?" she replied. "And you were too busy eyeing up his butt to watch out for getting shot at so the Boss nearly had you both?"

"Pretty much," admitted Tina. "Well he did a top grade inertialess turn and grabbed me round the waist and pulled me clear... And we blitzed it don't forget. Before you even got there."

"So now I see why you like the top and shorts uniform with a naked tummy?" Horo laughed. "You get some hands on?"

"Didn't I just," Tina was not arguing. "And it tripped a foresee moment. I am in for something good with him."

"Good? How?" Horo wanted to know

"I'm not sure but I'd say it was an orgasm," Tina grinned. "This

relationship is going the whole way, right down to the wire."
Horo sniffed. "Over active imagination more like. He grabs you and saves your sorry ass and you take it as a grope and infer way too much. Foresee doesn't work that way and you know it."
"Yeah..." sighed Tina. "But it was so mega clear. A girl can hope..."

Breakfast was over and Zwei was in performance mode about six feet off the floor. She had screens with pictures, video and a hand out. "We have the deconstruct from yesterday," she said. "Faster and smaller. Also the bosses were very strongly fuelled but running normal programming so they weren't making much use of it."
"However," she paused. "Our Constructor isn't that smart because he as good as signed them all. Air units, Gadgets and Bosses. We are dealing with Jemmie Sempain. He has form from some previous incidents but had gone to ground for a couple of years. Frankly he's a couple of sandwiches short of the picnic and the smart money was on him having blown himself up but no such luck it seems. What is more worrying is that he has a first class magic supply. To get the amount of magic he expended on yesterday's run would have taken over fifteen thousand hours collecting. Plus it was very pure. If he has expended it all on one grab, hoping to get a Box first time, he might be out of the picture but he either has a lot of girls secreted away somewhere or he has been building stores these last few years."
"Or he already has a Statis Box," wondered Grace.
Alharan looked worried. "I don't think so..." he said. "If they are all like the one we saw yesterday I'd be able to feel it if it was running. Nothing like that has been in use at any time while I've been on this planet. Say five days. Before that I can't say but if it is so good he'd just leave it on. Wouldn't you feel it?"
"Alharan," said Grace a bit unsure that she might be telling too much. "I'm not even sure how a Statis box works. I wouldn't know what it felt like and I'm not sure we've dared to power one up for decades. They're all very old and they do rather have a rep for blowing up if they go wrong."
Everybody was silent.
"Look," said Rico slowly. "I have previous experience with Sempain. He was pretty much a head case then and he got away by setting a fire so we had to divert to rescue civilians. He was bossing himself then but they were rather simple gadgets because he didn't have any manufacturing facilities. I gave him the usual offer of a surrender twice, got turned down and then kicked his butt. If this kit is his then he has a lot more fire power so he could be very dangerous."
Everybody looked round.
"When?" asked Grace. "I know I can look it up but how good were you

then?"

"Four years," said Rico. "I've gone up a skill level but I'm about the same power. I peaked last year."

"Thank you," said Grace wishing she had some deduction other than that that was bad news. Even four years ago Rico was impressive stuff. Also Sempain's profile, according to Zwei's notes, had a nasty revenge streak. Rico would be a preferred target so that would have to be factored in to their plans.

"You have your handouts," Zwei checked. "We'll modify the training rig to be at least as good and we have some air skeets being upgraded. We should be able to train on it this afternoon."

"Uh huh," disagreed Alharan. "Call out, twoish."

"Are you sure?" asked Grace. "That's a bit far out to foresee."

"I know what I'm looking for now," he admitted. "That makes it easier."

"OK..." said Grace slowly, reforming her plans. "Warm up, early lunch, be ready by one hoping for some good intel. Zwei will do the usual scans."

Zwei just rolled her head back so her long grey hair hung down below her and kicked her toes at them.

Lunch when your foresee was kicking in never sits well so they were all in the lounge below ops well before one.

"Any clues?" asked Grace.

"Nobody is talking but look at this," Zwei, sitting cross legged on the table, threw an image on a screen.

Grace muttered a rude word. "That is yesterday's target?" she asked. "On the back of a flat-truck, parked up in a car park?"

"And how," said Zwei. "Out the back of the Statis Agency's, well the Ministry of Defence, place in Cheristatown. OK, they did have to cut the train to bits to get it out and they are showing enough sense not to ship it over night but that is just a big tarpaulin over it, plus men with guns. It weighs over three tons so nobody is going to grab it and run away."

"So summon in a boss and its team then fly in the transports and it's a straight lift?" asked Rico. "The Statis Agency's ground team will need to be cleaned off the car park with a mop."

Horo grunted. "We get a level one but they dump things on a street corner."

"Zwei," said Grace. "Estimate the fly-in time for transports given the usual SA alarm zone. How does that compare with us getting there?"

The little Sergeant ran her hands over the screens. "A guess," she announced, "But about equal. However the boss or bosses would have nearly fifteen minutes to deploy and it's urban so we have problems they don't."

"They could lift in that time," said Grace. "Alharan. Do you have a foresee."

He screwed up his face. "A couple of bosses in the car park on the screen would match. I'm mostly getting the helicopter at this range," he said. "If you have the authority to deploy without a call out let's go."

"I call a deploy drill," said Grace. "Run us in Zwei."

"Three minutes," called the pilot as they dropped out of mage flight. "We are clear to deploy at low altitude."

"Huh," sniffed Grace. "Once the bangs and the smoke starts suddenly we're welcome to low fly and do what we want. Never wanted until we're wanted." She stood up. "Transform on-board," she ordered.

"Two bosses again," called Zwei on comms from the base. "Their transport is four minutes out so it could be all over before they get there. Go in low or the bosses will sight you."

"Straight into the gadgets," muttered Tina as her uniform and weapons snapped into place.

In a moment they were over the drop zone and Alharan and the Corporals went in one side of the bosses and Grace and Rico the other.

Tina dropped rehearsing the last few seconds in her mind. Alharan had stated his game plan as to get to the box first and deact it. He knew how to do that. Then he would join them in cleaning up the bosses. Remember the gadgets are just side-show. Grace had commented that the gadgets were an extension of the boss, that's how it worked, and they were more dangerous as the boss treated them as expendable. Alharan had asked if they were smart enough to recognise he had destroyed their objective and pull out. Nobody knew. Tina hit the ground rolling.

Horo projected multiple images of herself but watched Alharan spin through the air and slam into the top of the canvas covered box. The gadgets were all engaging her and her images on this side so she fired a couple of shots as some of her images crossed in front of her. She smiled as the boss locked gadgets onto the closest image to it.

Tina was low and going fast. She was jinking between ground cars and the occasional parked helicopter and they were taking the bulk of the fire. She was picking off some gadgets but mostly setting them up for Horo's guns as they tried to draw a line on her.

Suddenly the air was full of flying metal and smoke so she ducked down and slowed enough to stay out of the way of debris while being careful not to become an easy target.

Alharan skidded into a car and virtually stopped at Rico's feet. She looked down at him. "When you said 'deact'," she said, "I had images of you switching it off not blowing up half the neighbourhood."

"Not quite the plan," he admitted. "There's a containment vessel in there. Like your cartridges but N times bigger. Don't worry. It took out the boss that was holding it and they ain't dragging it away now win or lose."

"Damn!" said Rico. "Half the gadgets faltered but now they are going again. One boss is running them all. That's a new trick."

"I thought you didn't usually see two bosses anyway?" wondered Alharan.

"Well no," she said. "But when it does happen taking one out usually buys you something. Maybe this is why we get two now."

"It still doesn't make it smart," muttered Alharan setting off at a run. "It seems to be looking for the Statis box. It thinks they're indestructible too."

As Alharan ran across the site a number of gadgets popped up from behind cars and Rico and Tina got clear shots. Now the boss was defending itself they would have to work hard to get close on it. Alharan was the only thing moving and seemed to be drawing all the fire. Grace was well back and joined in the turkey shoot. Only Horo was dug in behind a wall but close enough to the boss.

Grace looked over her battlefield and took in the scene. "Alharan," she ordered. "Close on Horo and eliminate the boss. We can manage any gadget that shows it's fire port as we now have the high space."

"We won," called Zwei. "The air unit has turned away. They've read the destruction of the 'box."

Grace put her head down for a moment. 'Won' was relative. They still had a hugely destructive boss in a city centre. She saw Alharan cannon into the wall next to Horo close to the boss. He was fast but had a slightly head-first attitude to brakes. However she was reasonably sure the boss didn't know they were there. Time for some fire drawing. She looked round and gestured 'up' to Rico. With no inters in the air it was time to fly and fly fast.

"I can take it," said Horo, "We're close enough, but I need a clean shot. If I try to fly up I'll be sig'ed as soon as I turn on the magic to fly. It will fire on me before I'm ready."

"Say I throw you?" asked Alharan.

"What? Not magic?" she looked a bit surprised. "That would escape the detect."

"I'll throw on raw muscle power, you shoot and then I catch you," he assured her.

"If I'm not in fly the guns will recoil and tumble me," she pointed out.

"I don't promise to catch you nicely but you won't hit the ground," he revised.

"Go for it," she smirked and suddenly she had a hand under her bottom. "Now!"

The Boss flashed into view. It was actually pointing out over the field.

The gun bucked twice and Horo ticked off two critical hits in her mind. They might be more powerful but that takes their brain out. The sky and ground flashed past and suddenly she hit something that flexed away from her and she was hanging in Alharan's arms.
Rico touched down next to them. "Fantastic shooting," she said.
"Huh?" grunted Horo as if waking up as Alharan lowered her to the ground.
"I'm sorry," he said. "But you were right. You did tumble. I felt that hands on your soft bits were better than letting you go face first into the tarmac."
Horo just stared blankly but Rico laughed. "We're army Alharan. Any time where you get out alive with a full count of limbs and enough uniform left to cover your soft bits is the win."
Tina rolled up and Grace stepped down from flight. "Good work team," said Grace in senior officer mode. "I'm sorry you had to win the same battle twice but win you did. First class."
"Conclusion?" asked Alharan. "I make them stupid. The new bosses."
"They don't have a way to escape, or at least they've never tried," said Grace. "They always fight to the end."
Alharan shrugged "As you would?"
Grace screwed her face up looking out over the carnage that was once a car park and several surrounding buildings. "I like to think we have a reason but we are pretty committed. There isn't really time to retreat. When we lose a MG team we usually loose the whole team but that's the unit ethos. When we lose the team these days nobody wins. They only win if they get in and out before we get there."
"So is the target the team or the apparent objective?" Alharan asked.
Grace looked at him. "It has been suggested..." she started.
"Suggested that the MG teams are sometimes the real target."
"The point is," mused Alharan. "That technology here is rather primitive. You use simple magic to sustain the economy and the special MG magic to fight crime and, actually, to generate crime. This whole world is one strange anomaly. A decent AI in one of those bosses and they would win hands down. I'd like to get my mind on an intact one but I'd say there is an animal at its core and it's just lashing out at us. Some are better trained than others but that's it. Just an animal."
Grace looked at him. "Look," she said, "All I know is magic but we do use animals for a lot of things. That's why the helicopter crews are kind to the helicopter and we never change them round more than we have to. They're based on a big bird."
"OK then," he looked round. "And the MG magic is reasonably recent? If that went away then life would continue?"
Rico was standing behind them. "If Magical Girl magic went away," she said firmly, "And the magical girls and their controllers, both criminals

and army, with it the whole world would probably be a much better place."
Grace looked at her sadly. "I'd not have put it that way..." she said. "But, to a measure, you're right." She paused and looked at her communicator. "Right. Zwei! Get the 'copter in. We're coming home."

Horo flopped on the bed and looked at Tina still towelling her hair from the shower. "You remember your foresee from yesterday?" she asked.
"Wow yes," smirked Tina lifting the drier from the charger. "No such luck today. Which is probably good as they were fast and I needed to keep my mind on the job."
"Well..." Horo said slowly. "When we cleared the second Boss he flipped me onto the firing point and I had one too."
"What?" Tina stopped. "You and him?"
"Different but..." Horo remembered. "A strong foresee. I know what you mean by strong now. I was looking into his eyes and saying special words. And he was wearing a suit and I was wearing the most fantastic dress and..."
"Shit..." breathed Tina. "You think you're going to marry him don't you? Where does that leave my foresee? I don't want to two time my best friend. I may like to wind you up but I'm not that sort of a bitch. I rather hoped he was going to end up mine. Like forever..."

Alharan was cooking. He had booked a smaller recreation room and furnished it from lend stores and was cooking dinner for six. His five guests were sitting round a table, well one was sitting on the table at a smaller table but they were all watching carefully.
"I wish I could cook," said Tina. "It looks such fun to take ingredients and make them into a meal without magic."
Horo sighed. "I did do a bit with my Mum when I was little but that was before I was streamed as magical. Seems a pity not to have kept it up now."
"I think they try to keep you out of things like that at magic school," commented Grace. "If you got used to hand tricks and simple chemistry you'd never take on all the bulk of magic classes."
"Basic magic class sucked," complained Rico. "The trouble is that it's now so much part of me I can see why the detraining as your powers fade is such a big deal to the army. Alharan. How come you can do magic and still do things like cook?"
He turned for a moment and grinned. "I'm using magic to stir two pans and watching inside the oven so the dessert doesn't send smoke signals. I don't see it as contradictory."
"Well when your powers go," said Tina, "Will you still be able to cook?"
He paused. "My powers are a bit different to yours," he said. "I'm stuck

with them."

"This is your 'true magic' stuff is it?" said Grace lightly. "Look. You need to explain it a bit because the first time it went straight over my head." He screwed up his face. "Perhaps 'true magic' is a bit of a misnomer. The magic you have here is psi-power residue. It's as if there's been a leak, a continuing leak, of psi-power and you scoop it up and recycle it. Normally having 'true magic' used would dissipate it. What you have we would treat as the sign that a psi user did something here and had moved on but nothing since. We wouldn't think to reuse it. In fact I don't think we had realised it was reusable and if I was running at high power I'd probably leave it behind me which I now think might be a bad move."

"So using young girls to scoop it up is a new trick to you?" asked Rico. "It's actually a bit the other way round," he said starting to serve onto plates. "This magic is clearly signed 'young girl', younger than any of you. You are therefore more receptive to it."

Dinner was building on six plates and Zwei was sitting at her little table swinging her feet so her toes brushed the tablecloth and looking slightly resigned. They had all come in very off duty, almost party clothes, but she had a box with sandwiches in it hidden under her coat by the door. Alharan finally went into serving mode and put the sauce boats and other kit on the table and started to walk round like a waiter. Once he had laid food in front of four girls he turned back to the work surface and picked up a tray with more sauce boats and the last plate. He stepped onto the table.

"Cool!" said Tina looking at a thirty three centimetre tall Alharan starting to set Zwei's table.

"I'm sorry you're last," he said, "but even with these iron bottomed plates it will go cold so quickly."

Zwei giggled. "I confess I thought you'd forgotten me," she said.

"How could I do that?" he grinned. "All of squad six are my favourite girls and you are the one who looks after the rest of us." He bowed gently and then walked off the edge of the table resuming his normal size.

"At risk of intruding business into a fun evening," said Rico, "I wouldn't have a clue how to do that size trick. Leaving the dinner on the table when you transformed back was really impressive. I assume it's permanent? Zwei isn't going to explode as her dinner reverts?"

Alharan laughed as he sat at his place. "Of course not. I just said that we need her. Everything you saw was true and everything you see now is true. I'm just using full transitions, something you aren't familiar with, rather than the illusions that you normally use. "

"Could you make me big?" asked Zwei. "Then maybe the army would let me go on missions."

"Not really," he replied. "It's not just a matter of scale. I am consciously running all my body processes so when I scale I can adjust things. Stick to MG illusions. Enjoy your dinner. I don't get to show off my cooking often enough."

"Oh," said Tina with her mouth full. "Do this one again any time. Watching my dinner being cooked is just wonderful."

"Agreed," said Zwei. "Oh... Is this a date?"

"Five of us?" laughed Tina.

"That's what I mean," said Zwei waving a fork at her. "We have the food, we have the atmospheric lighting, the mood music but five of us is about as 'not a date' as you can get. I might as well have brought my mum. Getting called up really puts your romantic life on hold so I've never actually had a real date yet and I don't see me getting one until I hang up the browns for the last time. So... Can I pretend?"

"Well Alharan has forbidden me to be Commanding Officer tonight," Grace laughed. "So we're just unit six on R and R so if you want it to be a date it's a date."

"No officers?" asked Tina.

"Don't push that too far," warned Alharan. "That might just make tomorrow a wee bit uncomfortable. OK it's a date for Zwei. I quite like that too."

Horo leant on one elbow. "When we retire," she said, "I hope we are good friends. When we are in combat I take orders faster because I trust you not because you're senior."

Rico looked at Alharan. "We can't help but wonder how senior are you?" she didn't want to ask the question too directly but she knew they were all wondering.

He shrugged. "I'm Polankerin. You don't have an equivalent. In times of crisis I am a free agent and, because I'm supposed to know what's going on, I get huge authority with it. The rest of the time I just bumble about following up my own ideas and getting in the way but everybody remembers what I can suddenly turn into so they tend to leave me alone."

"Magical Girl!" laughed Grace. "No wonder you fit in. Nobody wants to give you an order but they just hope that if something goes wrong you'll go and take all the risks and sort it out for them."

"So are you the age you look?" asked Rico. "I'd guess you can look like what ever you want after seeing that size trick."

There was a slight grimace. "I'm... I'm the best part of three quarters of a million years old," said Alharan. "But don't think of me as old. I like to think I just have lots of experience at being a young man."

There was a pause. They did not know quite how to take that.

"Are you married?" asked Zwei eating quickly. "We need to know before we get in a fight over you."

"I have been married," Alharan took a reassuring tone, "But I am not now. That is the sad part of living so much longer than everybody else. However, I suppose, it's also some of the good part. Being married is good, it's fun. Being married has given me some of the happiest years of my life."
"Tell us more about cooking," said Grace relying on the fact that 'No Officers' didn't go very deep into military girls so she could run things if she needed too.
Alharan was thankful that she helped him escape and conversation flowed harmlessly away.

They had eaten the meal, the hot debaucherously chocolaty dessert and were finishing off on some of the more sophisticated soft drinks available to 'on call' combat personnel who might be under age for alcohol when Grace looked at her watch very deliberately. Suddenly everybody was starting to go into 'thank you' mode. Alharan was dismissive, "It's more fun to cook for friends," and saw them off.
Zwei was deliberately hanging back to be last out. She smiled and flew just in front of him, so she needed to look up a bit. "You knew about the sandwiches?" she asked.
"Lunch for tomorrow," he said blandly as if it was obvious. "I assume you always pick them up the evening before."
Zwei giggled. "You're too sweet for words. It's been a lovely date." With that she flew up, placed a hand on his collar to steady herself and kissed him on the cheek.
As she fell he caught her. "Are you OK?" he asked.
She wasn't sure. She needed to go. Her room, well her converted cupboard, was on the same corridor. She sat on his arm and he walked her back.

Tina was not feeling very awake yet so she padded down to the canteen wearing just her dressing gown. She made a coffee and looked round. Alharan was sitting with his back to her drinking orange juice and reading the news so she smiled, loosened her gown to show off a bit and wandered over to see him.
Barefoot she was certain she was silent but he politely turned and invited her to sit down as she got close. She sat and answered his conversational questions. She would have liked to flirt but he wasn't playing the game and she wasn't feeling like a morning person.
Perhaps it was for the best that he never seemed to be looking when she leant forward because in hindsight it was pretty tacky. In the end she excused herself and headed back to her room to get some proper clothes on. Zwei, getting some breakfast, gave her a dirty look. "Shit," thought Tina, "If I've offended Miss. Panty Flash I must be the slut

today."

Grace looked at Alharan in his blue uniform and guessed. "How long?" she asked.

"Elevenish," he said. "It isn't usually this busy is it?"

Grace sighed. "It comes in bursts. Often we go for months just doing training and then we get some new cowboy on the range. This Jemmie Sempain is one of the worst yet but we haven't lost anybody and we are two for two so far."

He smiled. "Look," he started, "I've read up a bit on this world but the magic here is unlike any I know. Give me a run down on how you see it."

Grace looked at him warily. "We have two sorts of magic," she started wondering how much this was a training lecture. "Normal magic is slow and hence it's safe. Also normal, that is commercial, magic doesn't need girls. Any gender, any age works. Combat magic is relatively new... Say the last fifty years or so. Combat magic can be run in a boss or a gadget but a girl is best. It has to be girls that collect it. This is why there are Magical Girls in the army. Most are just collectors who stuff it in our cartridges but a few are like us. Users. We are very receptive to the stuff and it obeys us. They pick us out young and train us."

He nodded. "And you fight bad magical girls?"

Grace screwed up her face. "They used to exist but the screening is very careful and planet wide and evil magical girls don't seem to exist now... They did once. I think we're just rare enough that the Army finds us all before anybody else. Lots of girls can collect the stuff but it doesn't do more than come when it's called for them. They are the lucky ones. A job, a pension and no risk."

"So..." he was thinking. "That's why the gadgets and bosses?"

"There were always gadgets," she ran on. "They are magical automata. Once they used clay men and you just put written orders in their heads but a light ali chassis is a better tool and we use a lot of them. Unfortunately that makes a good weapon platform. You'll find the non-fighting gadget everywhere. Dumb as a log of wood but efficiently carrying out orders. Too slow to know you're there. Only a fighting gadget is a threat. Frankly most of them are just stolen supermarket carriers, something you used to pick up your shopping and carry it, just massively accelerated and given guns."

"OK..." he continued. "So how do the bosses and gadgets get there before the air support?"

Grace looked at him strangely. "A summoner? Perhaps you don't have them. That's somebody who can call something to be with them. That's why gadgets and bosses are super light weight. Also it takes combat magic to get enough in at once. However a summoner doesn't have to

be a combat MG. It is the magic in the kit that brings it. My sister can summon. Too many people can. That's why people like Sempain can run a combat magic operation without a combat MG on team. They just need collectors and one or more summoners."
"You can't control summoning?" he asked.
She shrugged. "We arrest them but they can plead coercion. If the bad guy puts a cord round your neck, gives it a twist and says summon for me you summon. Often they're only seven to tenish. You can't jail a kid just because they were frightened and obeyed a grown up."
"Summon... As in 'come to me'?" he asked.
Grace nodded. "The summoner has to be on site but she can be summoned back so she's usually gone by the time we get there. Summoning a summoner doesn't even require magic just a bit of training and their cooperation. If they have any sense they don't cooperate and escape. We know to look for them but usually they've been told we will do fearful things to them if we catch them so they go back. Keep your eyes open for a little girl running away."
"So how does the summoner get there?" he wondered.
"Takes the bus?" Grace almost laughed. "Just another little girl wandering onto the car park yesterday."
"But on the train?" he looked perplexed.
Grace looked at him. "Not sure. Maybe she was just with the other freight."
"Seems the hard way to go," he ruminated. "There's probably a clue there."

The group sat round the table and looked at her. "We are promised no Statis boxes in transport," Grace assured them. "So does anybody have anything for me yet? Alharan says elevenish so just over an hour."
Rico screwed up her face. "A fire?" She shook her head straining for a clue, "not local?"
Grace shrugged. "With this Sempain business they probably wouldn't assign us to a fire. They have other MG teams. That's the good and the bad side of being pretty much the elite squad now."
"So you do super villains?" asked Alharan.
"Well we tend to do bad magic," said Grace. "There are newer teams that do the search and rescue. Combat magic is good for that but a bit expensive. However we'd have to burn it training to stay in top form so pulling a rescue is good use of our time and resources."
"But now you're the elite so you only get the nasty jobs?" he concluded.
"Pretty much," sighed Grace. "But you've seen the sort of thing we face. If we were beginners we'd get zapped before we started. However we've done the hours and they trust us to deliver." She drew herself together and realised this was not a good pre-mission state of

mind. She smiled girlishly. "Enough of that. What foresees do we have? I can't get beyond a call out yet."

"I still have a fire," said Rico. "It might just be a consequence not a first cause."

"Nothing sensible," said Tina and Horo just shook her head.

"Seaside..." said Alharan. "And gadgets again. That doesn't tell you much."

"Operating Gadgets tells us we're in time," said Rico. "If we get there after the event they pull back the bosses and the gadgets are just abandoned scrap."

"Nothing else?" Rico looked at Alharan hopefully.

"A bunch of fight stuff," he shook his head. "Clear sky so not local, the sun is high so the same sort of time zone if we're right about elevenish callout, pretty scenery, chalk cliffs, calm seas and a nice big house... No... Not so nice. I have Rico's fire."

"Are you getting this Zwei?" asked Grace. "Do you have any input?"

"I'm running some best guess searches looking for some foresee familiarity. Alharan. What colour roof on the house?"

"Sorry," he said. "It's not a foresee based on sight. It doesn't do colours. We're going to have to give it a while longer. It isn't ten yet."

They flopped back in the lounge chairs. Rico looked at him slightly perplexed. "Isn't foresee 'fore see'?" she asked.

He smiled. "Well it is if vision is your primary sense. I do vision. I like vision but my mass sense, well more density gradients, is more useful in combat situations so it is my preferred means of perception when fighting."

"So you can see through things?" she asked.

"Oh yes," he smiled. "The snag is that it makes thin things almost invisible. I have to revert to sight to read and without sight I can miss a stick on note like it wasn't there."

"Clothes?" asked Zwei putting some bite in her voice.

He chuckled. "Don't worry. I sense your skeleton quite strongly and your blood flow second so it's not like I'm seeing you all naked. Picking out the distinction on where the uniform ended and the skin began would just be a totally academic exercise. Skin needs to be perceived by sight... or touch."

Tina laughed and then to excuse herself asked, "So... In total darkness you could see me but you couldn't tell if I was naked or not?"

"Buttons are a give away," he answered taking it as a serious question. "I can see any detail at any microscopic detail but to do that I have to focus in and give up the comfortable world-local-to-me view I'm used to."

"Is that what our magical distant sight is based on?" asked Rico tipping her head slightly. "Like so many things I use it but I don't understand it."

He shook his head. "I can't explain it in your language," he said. "Use of magic has rather depressed the study of the natural sciences here and your physics is too primitive to give me words or concepts. Once all this is over I think I'd plan to set up University stuff on sciences. That would be a good investment of my time."

"I've got the fire," said Horo. "And I have the name of the house. It's over the door. Famadentra."

"I'm on it," said Zwei.

The helicopter dropped out of mage-jet mode and descended. "We have an air unit five miles out and targeted on us," said Zwei, "But no Bosses and no gadgets on scan so far."

"So we hope to find the summoner?" asked Alharan.

"I have a strong foresee on gadgets so she must be here," said Grace. "We'll try and pick her up. She's clearly good so it would mess Sempain about if we get his 'two boss' girl and put her in rehab."

"Rico go for the summoner," she continued. "Tina and Horo get into the house and secure the Fabber, Alharan and I will take the bosses and try to keep them outside and take on the air unit when it arrives. Rico will join us as soon as she is clear."

"Are we sure this is Sempain?" asked Rico. "Why should he want a fabber? The problem with bosses and gadgets isn't making them, they don't have to last for long. It's fuelling them. They need combat magic."

Grace shrugged. "The whole thing is circular. We're here because we foresaw us being here. What would happen if we worked up to a strong foresee of ourselves in battle and then decided we couldn't be bothered and went out for lunch? I don't know. I just do as I was trained and we win most of the time. If I had a strong foresee of us getting killed should I scratch the mission? Why would I have a foresee then if it wasn't going to happen?"

"Two minutes to drop," announced the pilot.

Rico circled and spotted what she expected. A small girl, eight or ten, in a short pink dress was running across the field behind the house towards the woods. She dropped down onto the track ahead of her and blocked the way.

The girl stopped and looked at her uncertainly. "Don't be frightened," said Rico, "We won't hurt you. We will protect you from Sempain."

The girl straightened up. "I don't need protecting," she smiled. "I am the Focus. I power his systems and I'm making them better and better."

"What's your name?" asked Rico trying to be a bit big sister. No spell can hold her if she hits the recall.

"I... I don't think I have a name," said the Focus. "I don't really need one."

"Did Sempain tamper with your mind?" asked Rico remembering stuff she had learnt in magic history.
"I..." the Focus hesitated again. "It doesn't matter. I haven't lost anything. I just have limits. I will get it back. All back. Sempain will give me my past back once I've helped him win."
"We can help you!" said Rico.
"No you can't," said the Focus and smiled. "Bye."
Rico looked at the empty space where she had been and muttered "The Bastard erased her." Sempain would pay for that.

Tina was skating a corridor and Horo was struggling to keep up even in a straight line. When Zwei called the door she didn't bother to open it just smashed through with her power fist. She jumped back and the door blew out.
"Shit call Zwei," she said pressing herself back against the wall as Horo came up behind her. "There's a boss in there."
"Yeee..." came Zwei on the comms. "It was inact. It powered up as you reached it. Rico nearly intercepted the summoner."
"That would have been good to know," hissed Tina. "Summoner leaving means boss installed. Right?"
"My bad," said Zwei. "I scan a boss and just seven gadgets in there now. The girls are trying to set up a scan process for inact kit in case there is any more. It is a new trick by the way."
"So is the Fabber still there or have they trashed it?" Tina wanted to know. "Plus is there a call on can we trash the Fabber rather than let them take it?"
Zwei paused before answering. "Legal says that if they steal it or trash it it's on the company insurance. If we trash it it might be our bill. Have you any idea what those things are worth? Their whole manufacturing operation is based on the spell in that box." She paused again. "I can't get a ruling on second best outcome."
"OK," said Horo, "But log an observation. The summoner didn't wander this far into a secure building and a deact boss sure didn't haul itself down here."
"Noted," said Zwei. "New scan. You have no extra deact kit in there."
"Just a new style boss and seven gadgets," muttered Tina. "Plus a valuable spell we mustn't break. Horo. Give me some images to confuse things and I'll run a wall ceiling diagonal. Zwei? For pity's sake. Any clue what a Fabber looks like? You took the whole trip out explaining how it worked to Alharan and missed the vital detail we need."

"Grace," called Zwei. "Rico's lost the summoner. There's a boss in the building but the girls are on it. Eight inters but no transports closing."

"No need for heavy lift?" asked Alharan hovering close behind her.
"Probably..." muttered Grace. "So we have to do all the inters this time... And from the way they're rolling in they're all new ones."
Alharan smiled. "Right," he said. "I'll go and do the classic intercept out of the sun and if they do the usual dive and scatter that should feed you two or three easies before they realise there are two of us."
"Just don't get too exposed," she said and moved off up the cliff towards the highest point as he sped away into the sky.

Tina went through the remains of the door and took the defensive line into the room and correctly guessed that the boss would assign the gadgets to the most dangerous looking attackers and keep its fire power in reserve for when it had sorted fake from real.
Her skates made her fast and just as she moved onto the side of the boss away from its fire ports she fired on the two gadgets on her side of the room and got two immobilising hits. Sensing the shots Horo dropped the images and started to run a confuser pattern. Tina dropped a blind over her eyes so she was only seeing in a narrow monochrome Horo was avoiding and jinked hard.
Two gadgets fired on where she should have been and left themselves as clear targets. Four for four shots and the others were eclipsed by the bulk of the boss. This was going like a text book drill. Now. Spot the Fabber.
Horo dived through the door and complicated matters for the boss. She was exposed to the gadgets but the boss was turning after the first target. Horo switched the illusion and put two rounds into the boss. Good strategic hits but to kill it in one would blow the room up. Not good.
Tina spotted a flat box that matched the Fabber notes Zwei had finally commed to her. Annoyingly it was right under the boss. Clearly it was already acquired and now was being guarded. This was going to make it tough to get it back intact.
Horo dived between two gadgets and the boss, which still not clear on where Tina was, started to turn for an shot on her. Tina leapt onto the floor and did a side slide so one of her skates went under the boss and hit the Fabber box hard. Horo was between the boss and the two free gadgets and in theory that should at least inhibit the gadgets from firing. They probably hesitated waiting for her to move off a direct line and she kicked the box back again.
The boss was redeploying sensors. It was faster than normal but it seemed to be still falling for the obscurant tactics that had worked in the past. Keep changing the active girl. It fired too late and narrowly missed frying one of its own gadgets and as Horo jumped she saw Tina with the box in her hands skating the roof towards the door.

Both girls bundled out of the door and threw a demolition charge behind them. They were thrown down the passage and somersaulted into a heap, grinned at one another and jumped to the ready position when Zwei announced "Boss down, 'Ware the gadgets haven't deacted but are just shooting at random."
Then a moment later "Forget that. They just shot each other."

Rico was heading back over the house towards the incoming inters when she saw one diving towards her. She jinked up and it jinked down. It would probably turn for a shot as she passed it so she loaded and prepared to cut inwards for a shot. Suddenly it jinked down again and for a moment she smiled to herself thinking it would never get out of that dive at that speed but then realised it was not trying, it was heading for the roof. She fired. She hit it but it probably did not help much. A large burning inter exploding into a building through the roof is probably marginally less destructive if it is already on fire but only for certain restricted meanings of the word 'marginally'.

Grace gasped. She had three inters on her and she was too high and they were frighteningly fast. She hit one, missed another and hit a third when a fourth suddenly appeared too close. It was as she feared too fast and she was exposed and going the wrong way. "Damn," she hissed. It was going to get a perfect clear shot and she was toast. It probably wouldn't even hurt. Too quick. Double "Damn."
She gasped again as she was grabbed. The reversal of direction took her breath away. One arm had come over her shoulder and across her chest, the other between her legs and onto her tummy. She was head down and being forced down at extreme speed but she was still alive. "Alharan," she thought and then reality vanished. She was clutched in his arms, holding his head in her hands doing something she had only read about in a girl's magazine with her tongue in his mouth.
Suddenly it was gone, it was a foresee but so intense, they were bouncing down a rough slope protected by the cliff from the fight. She wasn't floating softly but grasped rather roughly in places she wouldn't chose to be grabbed but he seemed to be grinding to a halt on his back in a shower of rocks and dust.
His arms relaxed and his hands lifted off her body and she was just lying on her back sideways across his chest. She tried to sit up but had to negotiate the arm between her legs. She clambered off and looked at him. He was panting, his eyes were closed and he looked in pain. Grace wondered for a moment if she should comment on the grab being a bit inappropriate but the foresee was still clear in her mind. "Anyhow," she thought, "Save my life like that and you deserve a grope."

She pushed that to one side. "Thanks," she said, not quite sure how you thanked somebody for saving your life when duty called on you to go back and risk it again. "Are you OK?"
"Mending," he said opening his eyes and drawing a deep breath. "Go up to the top edge and see if you can pick off any inters from there. I just need twenty seconds to remember how to put some ribs back in place or I'll make matters worse by moving."
Grace looked round and her staff was hovering next to them. You could trust semi-sentient weapons like that. She grabbed it and scrambled back up the slope kicking in a bit of flying on the loose bits of the scree. The moment she got to the top she saw an inter coming straight for her. It took a moment to realise it was trying to escape from Rico and as it went over her head it presented its belly as an all too easy target and she sent it tumbling down into the bay behind her as a blazing ball of fire.

"We got the Fabber," yelled Tina. "But the roof is coming in on us. Scan us a way out Zwei."
"Back fifty and then smash the air duct open," Zwei was running five screens and hitting requests with hands she didn't have. "Rico. I need some roof beams shifted. Grace. Two behind you. Last two. Alharan go to this mark. Join Rico."
"Duct smashed," yelled Tina, "Air here is getting not really breathable so we're on the masks. Do we go up it?"
"No!" said Zwei. "We need to cut into it or it goes into a chiller grid. We can't cut it if you're in it. Rico do you have my mark?"
Rico and Alharan were in a pile of broken concrete. "We can't blow it," she said looking back at him. "Zillions of tons of roof will come in on us."
"You blow it," he said. "I hold the roof."
Rico reasoned that he was either right or he was wrong and that was better than no chance. She clicked a new charge into her staff and fired. In the broken concrete was some metal sheets making a hole. It must be the duct. She levered it more open. She looked round. Alharan was nowhere to see but there were lines of blue light joining the floor to the remains of the ceiling above them. Suddenly Horo appeared, white with dust and bounced out of the duct. Then Tina with a box held over her head. They looked round.
"Don't just stand there," said Alharan's voice. "Get out before it all comes to pieces in my hands. I can hold hundreds of tons of big lumps but not hundreds of tons of gravel."
"This way!" yelled Zwei projecting a line on their comms viewers. There was light at the end of the line and the three girls threw themselves into daylight. "Get clear! Get clear!" yelled Zwei. "It's going to collapse."

"Grace?" said Alharan on the comms link.
"Are you OK?" she asked anxiously.
"No," he replied. "Look... Your sister can summon... Can you?"
"A... A bit?" she was suddenly worried.
She could feel the chuckle. "Then summon me. My magic."
Grace looked down from the cliff at the burning building and took a deep breath. It wasn't hard. She recited the spell and set it. At that moment the building crumpled and a huge cloud of dust, or maybe smoke, rolled out.
She waited and the sound finally arrived and reverberated round the cliffs.
Alharan put a hand on her shoulder and gently said "Thank you". Grace just stood and stared blankly down at the destruction below.

Tina was on her hands and knees on the floor of the helicopter. She looked at the fabber box. "Shit," she breathed. "We really did it. I really thought that one had got us."
Grace and Rico took her by the shoulders and pulled her into a seat. Grace clipped the belt across her lap. "You did OK," she said. "Now rest up. Home, shower, debrief. Three for three. Sempain's going down."
Tina rolled he head back. "Boss?" she said.
Grace smiled "Soldier?"
"When that inter squared you... I got some of it on the link... He grabbed you didn't he?" Tina shut her eyes and let her head roll. She paused then opened her eyes again. "Did you get a foresee? We did."
Grace paused. "Something... Have you had that?"
"Wow. Yes..." Tina looked almost a bit drunk and Grace reached for a booster from the medikit. "Vovavoom. Horo had one too but hers wasn't as good as mine." Her eyes rolled up and she fell asleep.
Grace looked at the booster in her hand and decided to let her rest. She sat down and said to Rico "That was delirious talk. Neither she nor Horo logged a foresee in their debriefs."
"I didn't log mine either," said Rico quietly. "It wasn't the sort of thing you could describe in an official report."
"No," said Grace slowly, her senior officer conscience troubling her knowing she was about to not do something that everybody else should not have not done either. "It wasn't was it?"

Grace called Team time so they got together to eat but this time they had something important to discuss.
"Alharan," said Grace strongly. "We are magical girls. Combat magical girls. We all have future-sense. That's key to how we function. Now. When we touch you, in full on magical mode, we all see the same sort

of thing. We know what it is like to kiss you, to hold you, to love you. All of us. So tell us... What is going on?"
He took a deep breath. "I see it too," he said. "Not your vision but similar. That is the reason I am with group six. Time is a bit confused for me and the reason I fall in love with you may be in the future but the love sort of spills back and I love you already. You foreseeing it too rather confirms it. There will be a huge battle and what you foresee probably comes from beyond that."
"Just a minute," said Grace. "We have a battle? That makes sense for this case. This one is not going to wind up without a big show down and Magical Girls can get killed on final battles even if the operation succeeds. So... Is there a trick we can pull here? What if we all foresee kissing you or something and we decide not to do it before the final battle is over?"
"Then we must survive?" shouted Horo.
"Can we twist time in that way?" asked Rico. "Our future sense doesn't normally come clear to allow us more than a split second warning of incoming fire or it's very fuzzy. You know the gist of things but no snap clear details like this unless you're very lucky. We don't even know if it's going to get us we just know that it's coming. This is like remote-see. Can we really be seeing months, years even, ahead. Anyhow how can I foresee that sort of thing? Alharan. I'm sorry but although I respect your skills and judgement I don't actually like you very much."
"None of you really know me enough yet," he said. "I know some of you like me more than others but we need more than the future memory of a kiss or similar to build a relationship on now."
"And there are five of us," pointed out Zwei. "Two girls is kinky but five isn't even possible. Anyhow five definitely isn't a semblance of legal and most of us are more the marrying kind."
"You? But you're..." Rico was horrified.
"So I'm having the same sort of foresight," snapped Zwei. "This is a team six show."
"What?" Tina interrupted. "You and him with..."
"With not a stitch on," Zwei cut back. "And no fuzzy feathers either. So is it real? Because I can't see how it can be. Or is it just a combat style warning of an incoming broken heart? Avoid it while you've still got the chance?"
"Slow down," said Grace. "Alharan we need to think this through. We are army and that is enforcement of law so let's deal with legal first."
Alharan sighed. "On the encyclopaedia Zwei?" he asked.
She gestured with her hands and screens flashed into view.
"Reference?" she demanded.
"Interspecies relationships on treaty 1278," he requested, "and then Varhyn, under intelligent species."

"Summary..." said Zwei slowly as her eyes flickered reading fast with her face lit by the screens. "Interspecies Marriage. Can use either species law and ceremony. Recognised by all parties. Metarii are listed as co-signatories. Centuries old law but still current. Protected by treaty obligations. And... Varhyn. Decapod, oxy-carbon, mammalian, bird. 180Kgs. Hey! Polygamous because they have very few males. Neat but you're not a big bird with lots of legs."
"Where do you think the feathers come from when I transform?" he laughed. "I'm biological Varhyn."
"I'm awfully fond of you," said Horo nervously. "But I'm not polygamous. I'd like to marry when I retire but I was rather expecting to have my own man. I'm foreseeing more than just a kiss but I can't really see how it could work out."
"Ha," laughed Tina. "Sharing with me for the rest of your life. I drive you nuts already."
"Stop," said Grace. "So we have legal. Tina seems keen but Rico not. Horo and I have doubts. Zwei?"
"I'm not planning to have somebody in my life who isn't Metarii," she said firmly. "Size matters."
Alharan shrugged. "I can be 180Kgs of Varhyn, well 140 as males are smaller, or what you see now. You've seen me do your size when I cooked dinner. When I transform I am just redefining my body and you've already seen me define it back straight when damaged. If I want to be as now but rescaled to eighteen percent linear for as long as we want it's not a problem. One day, on a mission, I might need to upscale and that can be very handy if we're up against something big. Also remember what I do is true, I don't use illusion."
"I'd like to see this before I agree to anything," insisted Zwei. "Well... Get a bit of hands on."
Tina made a "Snerk" noise trying not to laugh too obviously but got a dirty look from the others.
"So it's all possible," said Grace. "I'm trying to see if we can put any certainty in the foreseen vision of a relationship. We have a big enemy and almost certainly a big end battle to come so ending up with a win plus all of you alive is my target as unit commander. If we end up with a polygamous Varhyn husband or a lover that is a secondary consideration. Breathing before kissing."
Tina whispered "Breeding usually comes after kissing," but Horo kicked her under the table.
"Alharan," said Rico. "You're just answering questions. You must have an position on this."
He looked around awkwardly. "OK. What is happening when you touch me in combat mode is that you link into my magic. True magic. You are all good, powerful magic users so it levels you up a lot for a moment

and, since the focus of your attention at that moment is usually me, you see me in the context of your future. I'm very flattered that you focus on our relationship in your own style but there is more to it than kisses and things. I do see more although I don't know what you see. However I am very aware that we have a big battle to come and the fact that I am blind to many of the significant details probably means my target is probably involved. This means that you may be on your own, with me out of the picture at key moments. I will be otherwise involved."

He took a deep breath. "Can I say trust me? I want the best for you and breathing, as Grace says, must come before kissing."

They all looked at him expectantly and he paused awkwardly. "Look..." he started. "Can I give you something? It is a personal present with an element of my magic in it. In the past I have used a simple 'be with me' teleport spell as a token of my affection. I have built it into some rings. All you need to do is activate them to 'be with me' and that may just be a trick we need over the next few days."

He pulled a cloth bag from his pocket and tipped it out on the table. There were four obvious rings but he licked a finger and poked something and offered it to Zwei.

"It's wet," she complained.

"If I had picked it up by magic it would be less from me to you," he replied.

"Rings?" laughed Tina as he placed one in her hand. "Anybody would think we were getting engaged."

"It might have been nice to have had the time to sort out our relationship," said Alharan slightly sadly. "But we are a combat unit and we're now probably the only team that can take out Sempain if he goes all out. Sort out Sempain, sort out our relationship, then, if everything works, negotiate a deal."

"But why do I foresee it?" asked Horo putting her ring on the table and sounding worried.

"Have you anything further we need to know?" asked Grace twisting her ring in her fingers as if afraid to put it on.

"I wish I had," he shook his head. "I prepared the rings at first because of my future love for you but suddenly my future-sense told me that they were very, very significant and you had to have them now. I can see far more than you can but I'm being blinded on specifics so a lot of it doesn't make sense yet. I just have to run with what works. Believe me I am getting scenarios where we do not kiss and some where some of you are certainly dead. I keep putting in fixes and this is a biggie. Please wear the rings. All the time. They need the hours to settle in and then we can do comms and all sorts through them."

"How can something interfere with future-sense?" Grace asked.

"You blind yourself," he said sadly. "When what you do changes the

future you cannot see beyond the point of your action. The fact that you use it to dictate action probably always cuts it short for you."
"Right girls," Grace went into Commanding Officer mode. "Nothing planned but be on call from eight tomorrow. I'd plan training but I don't need future-sense to expect another Sempain incident tomorrow. Go get some quality sleep."
As Alharan walked back towards his room Zwei flitted up to him in the passage. "How did you know?" she asked. "How did you know to make a ring for me?"
"Shoes," said Alharan. "You somehow tend not to wear shoes when I'm about. Then when you saw Tina talking to me and she had no shoes on you were insanely jealous for a moment. I'm learning my Metarii psychology slowly but I'm getting the idea."
"Oh," said Zwei. "You caught it... Hang on... I gave no sign. Not even a look. Are you... Are you a telepath? Are you snooping us?"
"I'm an involuntary I'm afraid," he admitted. "I don't read thoughts or memories, that would be unbelievably crass between friends, but I can't help see emotional peaks like that. You might as well be letting off fireworks. Oh and you didn't hide it at all. Others noticed."
"So..." she looked at him sideways. "Am I supposed to wear the ring on the engagement finger or the wedding finger?"
"Wear it through your nose if you must but, trust me, one or more of them are very significant," he sounded worried.
"I want to know why I was holding you like I foresee before you get any promises," she bit back. "Even if I'm insanely jealous I'm not stupid."
"OK," he sighed. "I promise you that the night after we beat Sempain I am yours. Just do your best for these girls and you can kiss me or kick me. I'll be your size, I'm buying so to speak and I set no limits to questions or activities."
She tossed the ring in the air and caught it in her fist. "Deal," she said and flew away.

Alharan looked up from his breakfast. "Nothing I can make any sense of."
"But mid-day like the rest of us," said Grace. She sighed. "At least we aren't sitting about missing training for false alarms."
"So do I interpret the day after day assaults to mean that Sempain has lots of reserves and lots of kit?" asked Alharan.
Grace looked at Rico. It was straight out of a training lecture and that was her line.
"Well..." started Rico. "The psychological profile is that once they start they escalate until they get beat, achieve their target or just plain run out of the where-with-all to fight. Your average evil genius believes in himself to the point where stopping and going back to earth is only the

most desperate last resort. Frankly the throw-everything-in last stand and get killed is more their style."

"Last time," she continued. "Sempain virtually ran himself dry and then, maybe accidentally, set fire to a big condo. We had seventy people to get out while we knew he had nothing left to fight with. Because we were doing the rescue stuff we missed his reverse summon trick so he got away. We don't know to this day what his base was or where."

"So he still had his magical girls sweeping up magic for him?" Alharan nodded. "And he's had four years at it so he's well restocked?"

Grace shook her head. "No way are the crew he used before sweeping class stuff like this. Also he's just throwing it about. There is something new here. Either he has found a way to steal magic, he's found some sort of archive, they do exist, or it's something new."

"So we take what the Focus said to you seriously?" he asked. "That she is powering things?"

Rico wasn't quite comfortable with that but she had nothing better to offer. "So much else we're hitting is new so why not?" she said sadly.

The team sat round the table and tried to foresee collectively. "Isn't this a bit circular?" asked Alharan. "We aren't looking for an assault but rather for something we are involved in."

"The assumption," started Rico back on the lecture notes again. "Is that if we got it wrong and turned up somewhere wrong we wouldn't foresee a big fight but there have been errors before so we only go in where we see fighting gadgets so we know we have evil-genius at work."

"Not always genius," added Grace. "All they need is a source of magic and the basic skills to set it up. Some of them are pretty dumb but, perversely, those are the worst as they really do fight until you annihilate them."

"I'm getting grass," muttered Horo. "No gadgets yet."

"Hence we don't move," explained Grace. "Actually the fight often comes last but the standing orders say we don't move until we get the fight."

"I'm getting mud," said Alharan. "Not very helpful that."

Grace looked round. "Anybody else?" she asked. There was silence.

"What else interests the 'evil-genius' type?" asked Alharan. "Should I have something else in mind?"

"We've had Statis box," said Grace. "Which is just their modus, and a shot for a big industrial spell which is more big time thief rather than evil-genius but still a news worthy thing. They like to get some press and we try to suppress it as it is just pouring petrol on a fire. I don't know. We've had assassinations, a couple have tried to hijack a conference to show off at, actually just picking a fight somewhere public seems to be a favourite."

"So think show off..." Alharan shook his head. "I'm a bit thin on the cultural features here so I'm a bit out of my depth. You have a relatively high apparent technology without the infrastructure to back it up. So much is simple magic just emulating things you have seen from other worlds. It works but if people stop sitting up recasting the spells your roads and things vanish."

"Tell me about it," muttered Horo. "I grew up well out of town and if the guy doing highways got to work late it was pull on the wellies and trudge to school in the mud. No backups and they acted like they were doing us a favour not doing a job they were paid for. At least here the military ensure things stay in operation 24/7."

Alharan shook his head. "All you need is some machines... I can see I'm going to be here a while."

"A low building," said Rico.

"With a flat roof," added Tina. "We land on the roof and enter that way?"

"Weather?" asked Grace looking for clues.

"Sunny," replied Rico. "and the sun is high so this sort of longitude."

"Flat," said Horo. "I stand on a low roof and I can see for miles all round. So clear."

Zwei's screens were flashing, lighting her face. "Colours," she said. "Colours help."

"If I try for colour the grasslands in grey more than green," said Alharan.

"Roof is black stuff," added Horo.

"Children," said Rico urgently. "Lots."

Grace suppressed a rude word before she said it. A boss battle with civilians about was the worst kind. The weapons they used were not 'innocent bystander' friendly so you really wanted a clean field.

"Count?" she asked Zwei.

"Still lots of possibilities. Four figures," said the little Metarii her hands dancing on the selectors. "I have a guess though."

"Tell!" Grace was in a hurry.

"Daarine Academy," she answered. "Big school for the sons and daughters of government and business elites. In Kard Province so flat and by a big salt marsh. However not just one big building. The school is two story surrounded by masses of single story accommodation units."

"Kidnap somebody?" wondered Rico.

"Or just kill a lot," wondered Grace. "How mad is he?"

"I'd pick up on mass slaughter," said Alharan. "Maybe kill some. Maybe, as you say, kidnap. Gut feel is we are only getting part of the story. Somebody has been blackmailed and didn't pay. That's not a foresee by the way, just a concept."

"Anything more guys?" asked Zwei. "We need to confirm this urgently."

"If it's kids this is desperate," said Grace looking worried. She looked up from the desk at Alharan. "What's your prediction hit rate on things like this? You've been spot on the money every time so far."
"I am Polankerin because I am always right," he almost sighed. "My job is to make the decisions when there isn't enough to go on. However I can't give you a yes or no on something I don't understand. Zwei. Can I read your mind? I'm sorry but I need all the information you have and more to understand your guess but with that I can call true or false."
"Mind reading at that level is about the biggest personal violation you can get isn't it?" asked Zwei.
"Pretty much," he admitted. "But I need your interpretations of things or I won't understand them. That's pretty much all you have. If you're not happy we just wait and see what develops."
"But if I am right and we don't move now they might be shooting the kids before we get there?" she sneered. "Sucks to be me today. Go ahead. Rape me."

The helicopter dropped back into normal mode. "We have an evac in progress," announced Zwei. "The local police are bussing the children out. However we have an air unit inbound but no bosses on scan yet, even deact bosses."
"I'd like to drop on the school and see if I can get the summoner," said Alharan. "If I go in with Tina and Horo and I can get to her before she leaves I can stop her going. If I can get to her before she summons even better."
"I foresee Gadgets in amongst buildings," said Horo. "So sorry. That's not happening today."
"OK," Grace was laying in plans. "Rico and I will guard the buses and then divert to the air unit once we have bosses located. You run with the forwards and see if we can get a clean up. Now the air unit is on the scans we are suddenly wanted big time and they know they will have the builders in tomorrow to sort the mess out."
"So do you think they know we have an evacuation running? asked Alharan. "Or are they expecting to turn up in mid classroom sessions so the target is as marked on his or her school time-table?"
"Magical girl units are heavily obscured," said Rico. "How seeable or foreseeable are your?"
He shrugged. "I obscure things even to myself. Having me along will certainly make things worse for anybody trying to skry us. The snag is we are predictably on time so we ought to be expected."
"Drop zone," called the pilot so the discussion ended.

That was it. The last of the children were bundled into the last of the coaches and Zwei relayed that the Police locking down the protection

spells on slow but secure non-combat magic. Grace and Rico turned towards the bearing of the of the air unit, still a long way out and reconfigured to fight aerial style. They looked at one another and grinned.
"Still no bosses reported?" wondered Grace wondering what was going on.
Suddenly Rico pointed. Somebody was out in the playing fields behind the school. Grace grimaced. They had been promised all the kids were accounted for. They dived towards the person.
It was a girl. "It's her!" shouted Rico. "The Focus. From yesterday." Grace saw the area around the girl shimmer and a boss, all packaged for transport appeared and then a line of gadgets clicked in one at a time. "I'm actually seeing summoning," though Grace. "We're ahead of the usual game." However this time there was no delay and the boss activated and started calling its gadgets on line. Grace signalled Zwei. Zwei signalled Alharan.

The two forwards were walking through the main hall of the school and looking at Alharan who was just shaking his head and saying something about "not here, wrong buildings," when they got the message.
Deciding speed to be the essential they left through a large, clear but hopefully not too expensive window and in heading towards the summoning site found themselves running straight into the front row of gadgets.
"They turned up in the games fields?" asked Alharan. "Zwei can you do the stuff on the school time tables and find out who was due to be out there? This was possibly intended to be a grab and go. Maybe they have no foresee at all."
Tina and Horo were just hitting the accommodation village when Grace saw a better plan. "Forwards, fly and go for the air unit. Rico and I are behind things and clear of the gadgets. We will go for the boss. Alharan leapfrog us all and... Can that. She's gone."
"No!" said Zwei. "The air unit is turning. This is just a cleanup. We were too early for them. One boss and twelve... eleven gadgets."
"It would be easy to get complacent," warned Grace on the comms. "It could be the last gadget that punches a hole in your head. They can't get away so be careful and try to minimise the damage. This is a kid's dorm so every teddy bear flamed is a broken heart."
Rico hit the boss and it hesitated but turned towards them. Grace blinked. This one was even tougher than before. No way was Rico pulling it gentle on a one shot win like that. Now the back line of gadgets were breaking back towards them as the boss realised it had enemies behind. They were coming fast but what did it have to lose?

Suddenly Grace saw Rico fire on a gadget immediately in front of her and be showered with the exploding debris of its destruction. Then she realised she had one heading for her on the same suicide tactics - too fast to fire but almost too fast to stop. It was fire and dive to one side and she got an immobilising hit on it and it dropped a bit, touched the ground and tumbled, suddenly no longer a weapon of war but a dangerous flying object. Grace put up a recoil spell and it crashed to a halt over her.

As she pushed the gadget away Grace realised that she was stalled right in the boss's field of fire. She saw the fire ports start to blaze but even as she started to pile on the acceleration she knew she was not going to get out of line. It was a new style boss so dodging was the only option.

Suddenly Alharan skidded into her. It wasn't a tidy move, he more slammed into her pushing her to one side and away from the boss. Grace saw the twin bursts from the fire ports and hit him in the back then they tumbled into the broken rubble and into a hole. She grabbed him and pulled him down on top of her to get his away from the beams. Then she felt the foresee of the kiss again. It was stronger this time. Alharan was face down on the floor and on fire but as she watched the fuzzy down extinguished itself and seemingly miraculously there wasn't any hole in his back. As Grace watched the down became its usual non-descript 'tawny' colour again and he looked up. "Second try," he said. "But Horo hits it with an illusion split and you go in hard aiming for the fire port edges. They swivel and there is a seam."

Horo heard on comms and just said "Ready."

Grace took a deep breath, said "Go," paused just long enough for the illusion to establish itself and jumped out of the hole and dived straight at the boss. All she saw was the edge of the fire port getting closer and closer. The fire port was swinging back towards her as the boss recognised and discarded the illusions. However the point of her staff hit the joint, penetrated and then she fired the cartridge.

She was tumbling in the air so she rolled and dived for cover. The boss had exploded so fast she had not sensed it but Zwei was calling. "Boss down, gadgets entering deact." Grace allowed herself a second to relish the memory of the kiss. Now she knew how important it was and she had two. Then she kicked in the comms and asked "Rico? How are you?"

"Spot burns," she replied, "I'll be washing burnt gadget out of my hair tonight. I was just lucky the big bits missed me."

The helicopter wasn't going to land in amongst the school campus so they flew up the last bit onto the back deck and the door closed. They flopped into their seats as they buzzed back up into the sky heading for a safe transition altitude.

Grace looked at Alharan and asked "Did you see the summoner?"

He sighed. "No. So... Since she isn't under arrest she was called back before you got her?"

"I assume so," said Grace. "She didn't look very old and I draw the line at throwing combat magic at kids when taking them out will usually be little more than an inconvenience to their masters."

"What did she look like?" asked Alharan.

"Long black hair, pink dress, short sleeves, she had some letter or shapes written or tattooed on her forehead."

"Clunky pink shoes and ankle socks?" asked Alharan.

Grace screwed up her face. "'Think so. This is Rico's Focus from yesterday. Is this 'your target'?"

"Maybe..." he sounded unsure. "I've been disappointed before."

"Are you going to explain?" asked Rico.

"No," he sighed. "There is no scenario where knowing does not increase the risk to you be I right or wrong. I won't let my problems mess with your speed of decision." He paused and then said more loudly so everybody heard. "Well top marks to Zwei for a spot on call. Not only right on the money but so early we blew their plan before it even started. Total children hurt - zero and they got an afternoon off classes which is always a bonus to a school-kid. Any guess on who they were after?"

Zwei's projected image in the helicopter kicked her toes at him. "Three or four that would have made headline news tonight. We might not get a credit publicly but at a guess we will be remembered where it counts for this one."

The NCOs were in the pool, soaking out the day before looking for a meal.

"So..." said Tina. "Have we found a magical husband who can cook to make our retirement a bit special?"

Zwei grunted angrily.

Horo said "Hey I know you had a bad day. You don't have to join in."

"You miss the point," said Zwei fiercely. "When I hit retirement I go home. I can't live with humans without magic. Lots of it. End of story."

Tina smiled. "We'd look after you."

"No," Zwei slapped the water and splashed her. "You're not thinking. Do I just run around on the floor all day? Ladders on the furniture? And I'm far too breakable. A small dog, a cat, worse a small child and I'm toast. Love the guy to bits or not it isn't going to work. The vision has to be wrong."

"Are you going to forgive him the rape?" asked Tina hesitantly.

"It wasn't rape," the little Metarii had tears in her eyes. "He went two way. He let me see far more of himself that he asked of me. I know he loves me more than I could ever love him and... and he loves you bitches too. So don't you ever hurt him or I'll come back and claw your eyes out."

Tina took a deep breath to protest but looking at the little doll sized girl, now sobbing, choked her up. "She needs a hug," she thought. "But she's right, I don't know how to hug somebody that small without hurting them."

"What's on today?" asked Rico pushing some breakfast onto her tray. Alharan shrugged. "No Statis boxes for sure. There's some sort of investigation but clearly I get involved in something so I blind myself as usual."

"So we don't need the rings?" there was ice in the question.

"If I knew why you need the rings then you probably wouldn't need them as we would plan for it," he replied gently. "The rings are for the big 'don't know' scenarios... Plus they are a token of friendship."

She almost chuckled. "It may be different where you come from but here when a man gives a girl a ring it is normally more than a mere token of friendship."

He grunted. "Well let's get this Sempain business over and then we'll see what happens. Using future-sense on relationships sucks. If things don't grow by themselves they shouldn't be pressed. I'm not going to ask what you saw but there might be another explanation however... Interpret it in the light of the fact that I don't do affairs, brief encounters or one night stands. I'm not that kind of guy."

Rico picked up her tray and glared back at him. "I knew that. I'm not that kind of girl."

When Alharan had finished making his selections from the food bar he looked round and saw Rico sitting at a distance with her back to him however Grace was clearly rushing to catch him up. He waited, standing facing her holding his tray as she glanced at him so she could take her time. They went and sat opposite one another at one end of a long table.

"We've got a lead in," said Grace. "Zwei is researching it. It might be noise but it could be worth a look."

"Sempain's home base?" he smiled hopefully. "So we can go and bang on his door and arrest him? Plus find out where he gets his refined magic from?"

Grace shook her head. "The current theory is that it's an abandoned hideout. One of us can go with the forwards and do a trawl and snapshot. Probably some intel but I'm not expecting to get on a fight today so I'll probably let Rico run things. If you aren't out saving the world I'd like you to brief me on what this 'true magic' is again. Give me something I can write up in a report."

"Maybe that's it," muttered Alharan. "We do something but I'm sure I don't leave the base. I've got 'feeling very relieved' so something works out better than might have been expected."

"I'll put it in Rico's hands then. She deserves some 'in charge' time. We're a small unit so we don't often run less than full team but a penetrate and spy trip is just her profile."

Rico was happy to brief the two forwards and they planned their entry and exit plans and a bailout sequence.

They walked away from the helicopter and Rico was impressed. Whoever spotted this place was good. Nothing actually there but just the usual magical sense of things about you just seemed to fade a bit too abruptly. There was earth beneath their feet but it faded out too early and too finally. It was almost right until you tried to look carefully and then it was definitely wrong.

Once you got the hang of seeing what you were not seeing the blank bits stood out. There was a big lift door and a bunch of side tunnels. There were a couple of caves in the cliff that were obviously genuine and were just tapped into as a ventilator shaft. A tube with rungs in the wall. Built by workmen not magic.

The three girls stood at the top of the shaft and dropped their vision down. It was burglar proof with a big grid but sliding bolts on the inside wouldn't stop a magic user. They clambered down, reached a spell through the grid, drew the bolts and stepped into a corridor.

Dull emergency lighting showed the way ahead. Rico touched the wall and it felt lifeless. Magic deadening materials. She smiled. Hence the bends and twists. This was for a non-magic user to run away through. They had just come in through an emergency exit.

They walked carefully on looking about them. Hideouts always had booby traps. They did booby traps as a training drill. There was something ahead. Tina signalled she had seen it too and stopped. Rico was the expert here.

Rico crept forwards. It was definitely an alarm and it was good they had spotted it. The can was a big magical charge and the alarm would explode it. A simple threshold trick. A normal person could walk in and out, Sempain was twenty six and a man so no magic on him, but a magical girl would push it over the edge and boom!

She wondered what to do. She either stood back, shielded up and fired at it, expect the roof to come in, or she went as flat as she could, no magic on her and walked past. The staff would have to be left outside but if it's a 'blow up the joint' booby-trap nobody is here and she wouldn't need the fire power or the stored magic in it.

Ever the trainer Rico pointed out the details of trap and how it worked to Tina who asked if they should trigger it as they left. Rico declined and placed her staff in Tina's hands. The girl looked at it as if it were a live bomb. Rico assured her it was inert without commands. It was semi-intelligent and might be nervous at being left but it would wait for her.

As she walked back into the hall Rico tried to flatten her magic down. Not so as to reduce the power but to make it smooth so there were no bumps to trigger the alarm. The magic density in a place like this would be changing all the time but it was a sudden change that would fire the bomb. She stopped and looked at it. She could shield against that amount of power with her staff but there wouldn't be much left to inspect so it wasn't a win.

She set her mind to be a little girl walking in a field and stepped happily forwards. One tiny part of her mind counted the paces. She wasn't even interested in the alarm. She didn't know about things like that. Nine. Don't think about why nine is important. Fields of grass. Eighteen. Eighteen is good. Very good. Grass. Twenty five. Allow yourself a sigh of relief and look back. Nothing has changed. It will be easier on the way back.

A couple of times Rico checked the little logging camera but that was the only thing switched on other than her defensive screen. Nothing variable and definitely no comms so her magic profile was maintained exactly consistent.

Finally she came to a great hall. "A throne room," she thought. "That's Sempain's style," as she walked up towards the raised dais somebody walked out onto it and looked down at her. It was the girl in pink again. The Focus.

"You are Rico?" asked the little girl. "Of course you are. Nobody else could have got this far. You are the best. I thought it was you last time we met."

"We need to get you away from here," said Rico suddenly concerned that an empty base was clearly still occupied. "Sempain is not your friend as you seem to think."

The Focus shrugged. "He's using me, yes. But isn't that what I'm for? I'm a source of magic. If people didn't use my magic I'd be wasted."

"I wouldn't use your magic," insisted Rico.

The Focus looked at her puzzled. "But you do. Sort of. Second hand but I'm sure it's my magic. It tastes like my magic."

Suddenly Sempain was there. "I don't think explanations are helpful," he said. "Be a good girl and go back to the base and when I signal bring me back too. Leave my shields up."

"Are you going to show her the icky thing?" the Focus asked.

"We built it just for her," said Sempain reassuringly.

The Focus looked at her. "Goodbye Miss Rico," she said. "I hope we meet again some time. Thank you for trying to help me even though I don't think I need to be helped. It was a nice thing to do. Bye."

Rico gulped. No gesture, no incantation, she was just gone. Then the cold hit her. She took a deep breath and realised it wasn't physically cold it was just that her protective shield was gone. She reached for the simple magic that sustained it and it was gone.

Sempain laughed. "You can feel it? No magic. She is a source and this is a magical field cage."

Rico gasped. It was a magical black zone. Without her staff and the stored magic in the cartridges there was no power here. Her uniform would persist and her personal offensive magic but she couldn't fly, she couldn't shield. No general spells would work just specifics and they drained you. It was a trap for magical girls. Somehow she never felt it until the Focus left. Now she began to realise what they meant by 'source'.

Beside Sempain something stirred and reached for her.

"What is it?" Rico shouted realising the situation was changing from discussion to confrontation.

"It's a tentacle monster," laughed Sempain. "We discovered it in your dreams. You read it once in a comic book and it has haunted your nightmares ever since."

"Tentacle..." Rico was horrified. It was every inch the tentacle monster.

"This is your hell," Sempain was enjoying this. "It will hold you, stretch you out and rape you in every way you can imagine and several you can't. It will abuse you everywhere. Finally it will choke you and strangle you so the last thing you know is your body being painfully, shameful and intimately violated. It isn't enough just for you to die. No pain could repay me for the extra labours your section have put me through to bring my plans to success. You must die hating yourself for what you have become and knowing you are powerless to stop the retribution that you must suffer at our hands, well, our tentacles."

"You are a mad, childish freak," she yelled and threw a spell at the arms reaching out for her. It was a powerful spell but only one arm was chopped off. There were so many arms. She was perspiring. It was her nightmare but there would be no waking up with a start. She had never told anybody. It was just a stupid idea from a comic her brother had. He had laughed. She had told him off for reading such things. It had come back to haunt her nights.

Rico's mind was racing. She had never felt like this in combat before. "It wasn't real," she told herself, but it was real enough. It only needed to hold together long enough to carry out their wishes and when the magic was exhausted would be dumped and it would just revert back into what they made it from. She sliced off several more arms, "Well not

arms as each was tipped with a... no, don't think of it that way! It's just a magical foe. You've destroyed so many of them before. This one is just designed to mess with your mind. Don't let it!"
She jumped about to stop the tentacles twisting round her ankles and tried to stay way but it was backing her towards the wall. It was not seeming to lack arms for all she was cutting them away. They were brushing at her thighs, they had one ankle. She kicked but it wouldn't come free. She thrashed the other leg about but she could feel the embrace wrapping round her pinned calf. It had her wrist. The nightmares ended when it reached her knickers but this wasn't a nightmare. Something touched her there and she threw a spell and drew a clunk as another tentacle fell to the floor. She gasped as many tentacles lurched into her uniform at the waist, pushing against the magically tight clothing.
She was ready to panic. She needed to wake up from the nightmare. Suddenly the ring on her finger filled in where the comms should be. She heard Zwei shouting. "The Ring, Rico, the Ring. Use the Ring." Alharan's ring. It could not work as she was in a magical black zone but it was an option. Nothing to lose. She shouted the spell and fell backwards.

Silence. Just the sound of her own rasping breathing then Grace's voice. "Rico?"
Suddenly she felt a touch and knew it was Alharan. She relaxed back and opened her eyes. She was in Grace's office. She was lying on the floor. They must have been having a meeting or something. Alharan's hand touched her forehead and coolness and calm spread through her. Grace looked at her unit's prime fighter and chief instructor. Her uniform was torn, her shoes and one of her gloves were gone, her hair was a tangled mess with no ribbons and her knickers were round her knees. Alharan was stroking her face and then he gently said "De-transform." Grace though "He can't just make that happen. There are all sorts of safety interlocks," but suddenly Rico was in her smart uniform browns. He sat her up and gave her a gentle caress on the cheek.
"Check in with Zwei," he said. "She's going mad."
Rico took a deep breath and activated the comms. "I'm clear," she said. "Bring the others back."
"They are at the helicopter," said Zwei. "We have them ready to cover you for an evac under fire but there was a big bang but now there doesn't seem to be much activity."
"It was a trap," said Rico. "Sempain wanted me. I am at Base with Alharan. Thank you for the steer. Out." She took Alharan's hand and stood up but wobbled a bit.
"Sit down," said Grace gesturing to one of the seats in front of her desk

thankful that a magical girl still with all her limbs will usually recover without intervention. "Debrief."

Alharan drew another seat up right next to her. "One moment," he said and his fingers took hold of the ring on her hand. "There," he said, "Reloaded." He put a hand on her shoulder, "Now. Tell us slowly what you saw."

The formality of a vocal mission report steadied Rico's nerve. She stepped through the last few hours and the final trick. As she touched on her use of the teleport spell she saw Grace's fingers close on the ring on her own hand.

Alharan nodded. "He has gone finally insane. He has had all the marks but now we are dealing with the unpredictable."

"Unpredictable even to you?" asked Grace.

"Even to me," he agreed. "There is true magic here so tonight you must learn to attach to my true magic. However I warn you. Once true magic is used in combat the simple mage power you draw from the world will be destroyed. This final battle will be the end of fighting magical girls. Hopefully the end of my quest to. It can only be what I seek is that that is being used against us now."

The two girls looked at him. His eyes flickered between them. "Right," he continued uncertainly. "When will the helicopter be back with the others debriefed, showered and fed?"

Zwei was still on channel. "About two hours. But add an allowance for stress. There was an enormous explosion and I think they thought Rico had sacrificed herself to save them."

"So did she," said Alharan looking at the girl sat next to him.

Rico, wearing a towelling jump suit, flopped into her armchair and dumped the towel next to her. "A shower, wash my hair and nice smellies always draws a line under a mission no matter how dire."

Alharan smiled and put the book he had been reading back on her desk. "Aroma therapy?"

Rico smiled. "It's probably just old wives tales but it still makes me feel better. Do you like it?"

"I do," he smiled, "Scents are special to me. It's one of those senses I acquired in later life so it was a whole new set of pleasures. Well... And pains."

"Right," she said. "Still a bit of time before this big meeting of yours and thanks for staying with me. So what's the deal tonight?"

He shrugged. "We all know now that tomorrow is the final play. Us verses Sempain and the Focus and he's going no-limits and so so must we. You aren't going to make it on swept up magic residue in cans. Tonight I teach you how to connect to my magic. I will be your Focus and feed you real power. I can't actually give you a foretaste as that will change the whole of magic on this world."

"Is that a problem?" she replied. "Magic has never been a force for good. The MG corps are just a containment operation for planet wide villains who found some adept girls. They would otherwise just be small town local gangsters so perhaps only nasty bullies."

"Well tomorrow we will have to fight true magic against true magic and we will blow away this residue like morning mist in the sunshine. Even the stuff cartridged needs some background to work against so that's the end of the old style game."

"Old style?" she looked puzzled. "So there is new style?"

He sighed. "Look, if we develop the much foreseen... intimate... well physical relationship... Well..." he took a deep breath. "Regular sex and especially pregnancy will permanently wire you into my magic. All of you. New style magic will be just five girls, well six if I'm right about the Focus."

Rico sighed too. "Hence the importance of my foresee?" She pulled a face. "You think you can turn the poor kid?" she asked. "I tried twice. She might be erased and recoverable but if she's willingly implicated in Sempain's crimes she's going down for mass murder and if she's artificial she just gets terminated. That's the law."

"If I knew the answers to those questions I'd feel a lot better about what might happen tomorrow," he did not sound very happy.

"We need a target," said Grace putting her breakfast on the table opposite Alharan. "Waiting will drive me mad."

"Enjoy you breakfast," he replied firmly. "We're chasing the fox to his lair today. He has something planned for this afternoon but once I started putting plans in it dropped off the foresee and we're paying a home-call at lunch time."

"You have a target?" Rico arrived.

"I will have," he assured her. "We need the army there to secure the place and take his staff away for rehab or whatever."

"So we go in on 'Super-Magic'?" asked Tina.

"No," replied Alharan. "We go in on the old stuff. We must force him to move up a gear because that opens the Focus up. When she is running at full power the rules change. But remember. The Focus is mine. She could destroy you if she though it necessary but she needs to concentrate on me. That is how we win. Don't get clever or the team may win but bringing any of you, or her, home tonight zipped up in a bag is loosing to me."

"Right..." said Grace. "Anything else we need to know?"

"Well..." Alharan was hesitant. "We will lose home support once we are in the base. If Zwei is also using my magic she can keep our search and feed going but she won't be able to do it remotely."

"So I can come?" asked Zwei. "This really is the last MG mission ever isn't it? If I can be of use I must be there. Sitting back here biting my nails waiting for you to come back or not come back is a waste."

"I ought to say no," said Alharan, "but somehow that feels like not having you there makes things go a lot worse for us. I don't know in detail what you contribute but being there helps. Can you still access all your data feeds?"

Zwei pulled a face. "In theory. Provided he doesn't have any of those dead zones Rico ran into."

"Once we fire true magic they are irrelevant anyway," he replied. "I am your source... And yes. Win or lose we destroy combat magic today. Those of you that arrive back here tonight are out of a job."

The helicopter droned on towards the drop off point.

"How are you feeling?" asked Horo.

"Scared shitless," muttered Tina. "I didn't understood a single word of the last hour or so fixing our target and I don't think Grace did either. The briefing was expect the unexpected. The big fight is with a weapon we're not trained on and have only the barest knowledge of beyond how to switch it on. I'm ready to do what I must do but this one doesn't look good and I've only got a rather kinky foresee, that seems more and more like a bad girl's bad dream, that gives me any hope of being alive by sunset."

"Alharan's 'true' magic must be good," Horo assured her.

"But we have no nice lumps of it," Tina fretted. "We know our old cartridges can't touch the new style gadgets and the new bosses can fry us on a near miss. All we have is an incantation that links to a ring that, since Alharan is with us, we can't even use it to run away on. This one's win or die."

"So we do our best?" said Horo. "And we rely on Alharan to see us through?"

Tina chuckled. "Maybe the reason I'm foreseeing such a big scene is that we do win on Alharan's magic and we carry him back to base and have the victory party of all time culminating in a gang bang. It stands out in our fore-see because we then all get court-martialled and don't get out of the lock-up until we're far too old to ever do it again."

"I didn't see that," pointed out Horo.

"OK," replied Tina. "We go to jail while you didn't participate so you win the guy. I don't know. I'll just be happy to make it through to tonight and be able to get a chance at him."

"Zwei says she's dated him for tonight," pointed out Horo. "Anyway... If we carry the day on his magic nobody would believe he didn't have the power to stop us. He was obviously willing. They can nail us with 'conduct unbecoming' but not gang rape. It's a watertight defence.

'Unbecoming' is a fine and loss of privileges. Let's go for it."
Tina giggled and they squeezed one another's hands.

Rico looked at Grace in her browns and noticed something. "You're wearing his ring on your wedding finger," she observed.
Grace sighed. "This is the big one isn't it?" she said softly. "We either win or we die. Look on it as me nailing my colours to the mast. We are all going to live. We are all going to kiss him, to love him, or whatever each of us saw. For today we are all going to win. The key word is 'all'. I'm not going to lose too Sempain and I'm not going to lose any of you."
Rico reached over and squeezed her hand. Then she moved her ring from her right hand to the wedding finger of her left hand. "I want a bit of that," she said.
"You didn't like him," asked Grace. "Has that changed?"
Rico sighed. "Not really. He still annoys me but somehow that hasn't stopped me falling in love. We haven't known him a week but I think we're all totally besotted for life and we trust him to be the same. I don't have to like it but I'm prepared to admit that I'm in as badly as the rest of you. Look, let's get Sempain out of the way and then bigamously marry him under that treaty. Then we can have endless rows. I might not be able to live with him but I'm sure I can't live without him now."
"You didn't tell us what your foresee was," said Grace. "Is now the time?"
Rico sighed. "There might not be another time if it isn't true. Look... It's like I'm sitting up in bed in one of those awful hospital gowns. I feel like I've been beaten up or worst and I'm desperately tired. You're all gathered round, even Zwei, and you're all madly excited and... and he's sat on the bed next to me with his arm draped round my shoulders. You're all talking to lots of people on Zwei's rem-camera while I've lost track and... and I'm holding a tiny baby in my arms."
"Wow," said Grace. "All I got was a kiss. It was a good kiss but nothing like that."

"Alharan?" said Zwei. He smiled. "We do have a date for tonight don't we?"
"That was the promise," he looked up at her.
"My big foresee is of crying myself to sleep in your arms," she admitted. "That isn't good is it? Do we lose somebody?"
"I don't think we do," he sounded unsure. "My foresees are a bit statistical but I'm getting a lot of 'lives happily ever after' in there. You're all wound up so a good cry might just be you unwinding. However I'm so blind I think I've finally found my target. Anyway... Foresees never seem to help on the really critical decisions in life." He looked up again and grinned. "Is that really your transformed uniform?"

Zwei laughed. "I became an MG on a beach holiday so I get stuck with a uniform based on what an eight year-old thought was a glamorous swimsuit. It's a bit minimalist even for me and if the top wasn't magic it'd never stay on now I have some bust. Admit it though, it's better than some of the others, Rico's is basically a winter school-uniform with big ribbons. However going into combat off uniform takes persistent magic and we're all running in total no distraction mode today. I've seen worse. It all depends what you are doing when some incident pushes you over the top and you go magical. Your feathers are pretty cool. You have the physique to carry it off." She paused and looked at him hopefully. "So we all live?"

"I can't offer better than 'I think so'," He sighed. "Now be careful. I can't tell Grace because her mission is to try to take Sempain alive but to me it's only all of you and the Focus that are important. If Sempain gets in the way of that I will have to kill him. Get me to the Focus. Once I have her I control the power and you girls can win while Sempain is powerless."

"And if we fail and he kills us all?" she asked.

"You really don't want to know," he whispered. "I've logged everything back with my HQ staff because we have a universe to protect. I can't promise that your planet will even have ever existed if the Tranzen have to go head to head with something that out guns me."

"Drop Zone," announced the pilot.

"There is no way he should have missed us coming so we start from altitude and get the helicopter safely away," briefed Alharan. Somehow everybody accepted that he was in charge today. "I read a fight to get in but no super gadgets or stuff so keep the reserves in reserve. We need to find Sempain and the Focus but we have the army putting a ring round us with heavy conventional weapons. Once the main battle starts and we escalate to true magic old style bosses and gadgets are junk, in fact the only people that they could hurt are Sempain's crew so we might even end up having to rescue them."

Alharan nodded to her and Zwei took up the brief. She showed them the rough scan of the base and the selected service way they would drop into. There were bosses and gadgets but they looked like old type. "However this is not a drill," she emphasised. "Taking out a new style boss and then getting your head blown off by an old style gadget endangers those that are left. If you're determined to mess up at least have the decency to get yourself killed cleanly so nobody has to risk their life and waste their time evacuating you."

Alharan and the two Corporals moved the magic bomb onto the back door and Rico set the fuse. Then they all dropped out of the helicopter and watched it fall away below them as they finished powering up.

"Shields!" called Zwei and they braced themselves as the bomb carved a hole in the ground below. As they braked into the crater the broken remains of the tunnel were obvious and they dived in with Tina's roller-skates giving her an edge for speed.
Tina saw a gadget and hit it hard. Bits of metal bounced off the walls. "Old style!" she called.
Grace looked at Alharan who shrugged. "He probably has masses of old ones. They'll be spread out all over the base. Both as a trip wire and as a time waster for us. I get the impression that we have a monopoly on foresee so he probably guessed we were coming but didn't know where or when."
Rico and Horo pulled a fast illusion split and a boss exploded. "A week ago," complained Tina. "we would have thought that was good end to a mission. Now it's just a side show."
"Bulk gadgets fifty ahead," called Zwei fumbling at her projected screens and trying to keep the flock of magic canisters following her on track.
Grace dived in and with the other girls rapidly destroyed them. Zwei clipped another cartridge into the fat stubby gun and gripped it between her knees so she had two hands free for the scan screens. "I got one," she said to Alharan obviously pleased. "They're not hard."
"They're not," said Alharan. "He's playing with us. These might wear us down but his psychological profile says he wants a show down. He almost needs to tell us how clever he is more than he needs to kill us."
"After what he did to Rico I'd happily kill him," said Zwei not looking up.
"After what he did to Rico," sighed Alharan. "I'd feel bad about killing him. He's ill. I want him in a legal Doctor-Patient situation and I want informed consent but I'm not sure I'll get either. If it comes to it I have to tell myself I'm the vet putting down a sick animal. I can't let him do any more harm and if I can't otherwise get all of you out alive he is... Well he is dispensable."
"Well I..." started Zwei. Her hands danced over the screens. She pulled a face and reached up to take hold of a magic canister that had flown out of the pack and over her shoulder. She looked at Alharan and there was worry in her voice. "I've lost comms to base. We're on our own now."
"You can still scan?" asked Grace.
Zwei nodded as she looked at her screens. "Yes Mam. All skrys running and all lots to see."
Alharan looked round. "We probably need to make the others stock up. Your ideas of reserve planning pre-dates virtually using one can for a gadget. We can afford to blow a lot before the big showdown scene but nobody must take risks because they're getting short."

Grace was almost in front of Tina as the passageways were widening. The others were almost struggling to keep up and maintain a sensible amount of caution. "Foresee incoming!" she shouted and virtually stopped dead.
"Magic mines," said Zwei. "I can coordinate on them but we'll have to blit them one by one."
"Mines?" asked Alharan.
"Magic detectors as a fuse to a magic bomb," explained Rico.
"So I just detonate them," he shrugged. "Give me a couple of cans Zwei. I assume they'll set things off."
"Magic can't protect you from a magic bomb," said Grace worried that he didn't understand basics.
"So I use physics like the rest of the universe does," he said. "Zwei. Once I get to the far end scan and let me know if there are any I have to go back for."
Grace went to object but felt Rico's hand on her shoulder. "Trust him," she said. "He knows what he's doing."
The series of explosions made the floor shake but when Alharan waved at them from the far end of the hall Zwei paused a moment then said "All clear. He detonated every single one."
The girls flew on through the smoke and looked down another passage. "You'll explain that some time?" asked Grace.
He laughed. "The trick is to go through both slits at once," he smiled. "Then collapse only the states with the desired result. Bingo, you open the box and the cat is alive and well."

"I have the Focus and I think I have Sempain and others," announced Zwei. "Down fifty and left. You're right. He's not hiding." It was a door and Tina destroyed it using yet another full cartridge. The girls dived in and formed a defensive line with Alharan scrambling to keep up.
It was a big auditorium with screens. Sempain was standing on a platform raised about three meters shimmering with a defensive field and surrounded by several lines of gadgets. The little girl in pink stood in front of everything. There were some other people in blue and metal uniforms. "'Ware cyborgs and augments," said Zwei.
Alharan walked forward. "Good morning," he said. "Sorry about the door but you know how these things are. Would you like to surrender or are you going to make us do a lot of unnecessary damage?"
Sempain smiled back. "You're all here, even the Metarii I see. I'm quite happy to have to redecorate if it gets you out of my hair. I'd offer you the chance to surrender but you wouldn't have bothered to come if that was in your plans. However, I warn you, if living as far as this evening is on your 'to-do' list for today you might want to consider it."
Alharan continued to walk forwards looking up at Sempain until he was

within about a meter and a half of the Focus so Grace answered him. "We have the army coming. We have new powers. Surrender and you will be restrained from future destructive activities but permitted to document your work for publication."

Sempain looked down on them. "The standard Evil-Genius Contract?" he laughed. "Thank you for the genius label but I'd rather win and, would you believe it? I will. Welcome to the intelligent gadget," Sempain bowed with a flourish. "More powerful than any boss ever and capable of independent action. Indestructible to your miserable power and more than capable of taking any of you down."

"But apparently unfuelled," pointed out Alharan.

"Fuelled but not yet connected," corrected Sempain. "I just need to release my best find of all by removing her erasure bond and we are ready to play."

"Where did you find her?" asked Alharan amiably as if continuing a conversation over dinner with friends.

Sempain gripped the edge of his platform rail and looked down. "I traced magic, combat magic back to its source. Where others failed I, Jemmie Sempain, succeeded. At the end of the line was a little sleeping girl and she serves me now."

"And you erased her, you bastard," Rico was incensed.

Sempain grinned. "Not a total erasure."

"A slave maker?" asked Grace quite surprised to hear her second in command so riled.

"Less than that," said Sempain. "I have been good to her and she has helped me. Now I make her free and she will continue to help me. Erasure is good even if it is just temporary. It takes the pain away. It sets patterns of thought and action. When we clean up after this fight, if you're still breathing I'll demonstrate. You'll feel so much better for it."

"I would rather die first," bit back Grace.

"That is the alternative," laughed Sempain stepping to the control panel on his platform and activating something with a flourish. The lights flickered. The screens flared with images of various famous city buildings.

"All limits are now off," shouted Sempain. "So we will destroy you even if we have to destroy this whole world doing it."

Alharan dropped into almost a sprinter's crouch before the Focus.

"We will destroy you," she said off handedly. "Just as he says."

"I do not believe so," Alharan replied.

She looked up at him. "I am a source," she said. "It is not like the puny little local magic your girls use. Now I am unlimited I can brush them away."

"You forgot me," he replied softly.

"I have never monitored you doing anything other than use their

collected stuff," she said. "So I have no measure of any personal magic. However I have never met anybody like me so why should you be different? We will destroy you. Sempain wants it so it might as well happen."
"No," he smiled. "I mean you have forgotten me. You have a memory block."
"It has protected me," she snapped.
"It does not," he replied. "Now you are unlimited if I say your true name you will remember everything."
"I have no name," she snapped spitefully.

"Now!" shouted Sempain. "Attack now."
The gadgets lunged to move forwards and the girls started to accelerate. This was obviously the time so they activated the final level to use the magic that Alharan had promised them.
Grace kicked the ring into action and felt the transformation start. It felt a bit familiar at first as the magic lifted away her old uniform but she felt no new uniform coming into place, no new wand, staff, gun, knife or any tool. For a moment she felt as magically naked as her body had become. Then, suddenly, the magic flowed over her.
All five girls gasped. Magic was such an ephemeral thing. At first you gathered it together and used it sparingly. Junior mages spent hours concentrating it into the cartridge systems they used so they had the fire power to destroy the gadgets and bosses but suddenly what washed over them not like a thin mist to be condensed into fog but like the waves of the sea. Suddenly they saw why the new gadgets were so unbeatable. This was the magic the Focus had imbued them with. Suddenly Alharan's phrase 'the true magic' made sense.
The gadgets were coming but this time they had the same power. "If Alharan could just stop the Focus reloading them," thought Grace, "but keep supplying us then we have a good chance."
The girls threw up shields and projected platforms and deployed against the bolts leaping at them from the gadgets as Sempain laughed maniacal laughter.

Alharan looked at the Focus and said "Chii."
She looked back with eyes growing wider by the instant. The face that was almost bored suddenly looked at him with horror. The hands bunched into fists and pressed against her chin and tears flooded into her eyes.
"Daddy!" she screamed.
At this moment the girls and the gadgets closed in combat.
Keep moving was normally the rule and if the gadgets were going to be super powerful and super smart that was probably going to call on you

to be super fast. The girls all leapt off in different directions and accelerated hard. Tina always used the force of gravity to estimate how far she had sped up but as she skated across the room she found she felt almost weightless and she was virtually continuing in a straight line. She dipped and punched her fist into a gadget at the front and a satisfying amount of spare parts went flying out the back. "First blood to us," she thought.

Horo, the illusion runner, went seven different ways at once, all jinking and her confused target never even got a clear aim before three of then aimed and fired. The real Horo paused momentarily as the gadget exploded as she wasn't expecting that. The illusions aiming to fire should have caused the gadget to jink to try and make whichever of them was real miss and the jink should have given her a reasonable shot. "Alharan doesn't use illusions," she remembered so she spun her images on another gadget, one took the full brunt of its cannon and dissipated but when she fired some of the others although the gadget didn't explode it fell over and its speed carried it skidding across the floor until it hit the wall. "Trashed two," she thought. "And I haven't really fired my..." then she realised she didn't have a gun, her images had guns and uniforms because that was what she was used to projecting. She didn't have anything.

Grace checked that Alharan had the Focus as planned and headed for Sempain's tower. The gadgets had rushed out as if to fulfil an image of committing to the fight but it was for theatrical effect only. They would need to be careful as they turned back in and they had gadgets behind them but many were currently just heading for blank walls.

There were two cyborgs, or maybe augments, on the bottom of the stairs up to Sempain. Grace had qualms about throwing a destructive charge at what might be an enslaved human but the magic, seeming to sense her dilemma, offered a choice of quick sleeper and a slow sleeper. The difference appeared to be based on whether you could risk giving them the chance to catch themselves as they fell or if the knock down had to be so fast that a bloody nose was an acceptable risk.

Two slow sleepers were dispatched and Grace felt the magic reporting back as the cyborgs crumpled. The report was comprehensive. They were both mid teens girls and they had the sweeper talent. They had metal skin armour and simple magical strength and speed boosts. Neither of them seemed to be significantly armed but, surprisingly, they were both pregnant.

Grace gritted her teeth. So was Sempain just recycling his old sweeper girls as guards and something to keep him warm at night? Rico's rage at him suddenly became a foresight issue and she logged it... she paused an instant as her log was gone but something had acknowledged the record request.

Tentacles waved at Rico. She laughed and threw a bolt at it. It splashed a spray of parts across the floor. It felt strangely satisfying. "What was the word they used?" she thought as she sighted a gadget. The gadget exploded, "Closure," she smiled. She was actually enjoying this.

Tina was targeting Sempain's console as it appeared to be the command and control hub. However as she started to sight it the magic highlighted the connections from what now appeared to be a simple servo box to a larger, more complex unit behind the wall of projector screens. She banged her fists together at full arms reach mimicking her best attack and a hole appeared in screens, the box, the wall behind and off an indeterminate distance into the rock beyond. This had the annoying side effect of shutting down the screens which were providing most of the light in the room.

Zwei glanced around as the gloom began to fall and realised she could sense not just this cavern but also ones beyond. She saw some people sitting in rows and wondered for a moment if they were prisoners when she realised they were more augments. She suddenly felt that they were frightened so she picked one and began to probe deeper. She could see a mind in levels. The top was quite simple. It was calmly waiting for a clear order. It had "Wait here until I call you," and although that satisfied that level there was a further level below that was befogged and struggling. It seemed to be a proper personality but it was groping through all manner of mush. But it was very frightened. Zwei looked again at the top layer and decided it was an interloper and decided it should be deleted. It was. The result was frightening. The mind in mush was suddenly free. It was a girl. It looked round in panic and saw a familiar face. It called to a friend but the friend did not move. It reached out to the friend but was ignored. Panic was rising. Zwei was not quite sure what to do but suddenly, like a screen menu, the options presented themselves and she chose sleep. The panic subsided and the girl folded up in the lap of the unresponsive friend. Zwei desperately signalled Rico that there were slavered cyborgs in that room and she desperately started to scan the whole complex for other signs of life.

Grace was closing on the steps up to Sempain's platform in the fading light. As she reached the bottom step a gadget fired at her and she ducked. The beam ripped over her head and cut part of the supporting lattice. Sempain looked down at her and shouted something obscene. Grace grimaced. "It's always so sanitised in the reports," she thought. "There's no way I'm typing that he called me that so when they animate it he'll come over better than he deserves." Suddenly the whole structure dropped half a meter and Sempain lurched out of sight. Another gadget was spraying fire about almost at random and Grace destroyed it with a single beam.

Zwei flew into the room with the cyborgs and scanned. They were all still passively awaiting an order. She scanned for comms. They didn't have personal radios but there were wall mounted loud-speakers in the room. "Quietly," she though. "They probably have orders to defend the base. Just remove the wiring so nobody can call through to them." It was done. She checked on the girl sleeping on the other's lap and was shocked to realise how alike they were. Not twins but probably sisters. Grace was concerned and needed to talk to the others. She guessed that just 'selecting comms' as she usually did would work and perhaps it did or perhaps the magic just recognised her intentions but she knew at once that the others would hear her when she spoke. "Careful," she said. "We are just running and shooting without a fixed plan. Report in."

The reports implied that running and shooting was working but there seemed to be an endless supply of gadgets so it was going to be a poor plan. "Gadgets run on external power," Rico pointed out. "If these are not miniature bosses they must have a central battery somewhere." "Zwei," commanded Grace. "We need you to scan for the power source." Zwei looked at her lines of little girls promised she'd be back for them.
"Horo?" called Grace. "Just how many illusions can you run?"
"I get confused above five or six,." she replied. "They work but I'm a bit like a boss and they are my gadgets. I have to think for them."
"Can you do us. Make the illusions look like us? So nothing realises we are gone?"
"I can do the image but the style will take a bit more... I'll try."
"Do it," ordered Grace. "A least do naked girls with the right hair colour but keep your real self well out of sight. I don't want to come back and find you fried just because I've left you to fight a hundred super-fast, super powered gadgets alone."
"I have a direction from the power flow," said Zwei, "But not a fix yet. Out through the big door at the end. Big chamber beyond."
"Tina, Rico," called Grace. "Sort the gadgets by the door and punch a hole as if by accident. Then turn back into the room, start shooting and do a fade. Try to stay as invisible as possible until we are through and into the next chamber. Beware it being the reinforcement store."
"Nothing much scans in there but it's fuzzy," said Zwei diving forward just over the floor. "Something is masking things."
Two gadgets flared and burst and the magical bolts smashed through them into the door posts. One side of the double doors sagged on its hinges. Grace ordered Rico through at speed and maximum concealment and Tina dived after her.
"It's a big fat boss," called Rico. "But it's not reacting to me."
"I can take it," shouted Tina, aiming for another big strike.

"Don't!" yelled Zwei diving through the door. "There is so much power there the only things that will survive if it blows are us. Can we disconnect it?"
"It's feeding directly to the gadgets," said Tina skating at high speed and expecting an attack. "I can feel it like lines drawn in the air connecting it to the gadgets outside."
"Right!" said Rico. "You don't need to destroy it. It's like Alharan's magic. It obeys us. All I have to do is tell it to switch off and rely on Alharan making sure the Focus doesn't turn it back on."

Silence. Not even much smoke. Some gadgets were burning fitfully but they were mainly metal. Grace looked round and as she turned her hair swung free. She took a deep breath. "Even the ribbon in my hair is gone," she thought. "No uniform, no communicator, nothing but magic."
Rico looked at her. "We... We did it?" it was true but it sounded like a question.
Tina and Horo walked up. Tina was trembling. "We stopped them all," she said. "But it was only moments. I cast so many spells..."
Grace reached for some Commanding Officer. "You did well. Check for Sempain. Zwei. Scan for more gadgets."
"No more gadgets," said Zwei. "Sempain is by the grey pillar but he won't be going anywhere. He has many broken bones but nothing, I think, life threatening. I have outside comms again. Bingo! The wards are down and the troops entering the tunnels. I'm passing our route floor-plan over. Hey! I've found emergency lights. Coming on."
Grace looked at Tina and Horo. "Check on Sempain for us," she said. She saw them hesitate and then start to move off to carry out the order. "No. Wait." she said realising the problem.
Grace looked at Alharan who was kneeling, nestling a little girl in his arms with his back to her. The Focus, Chii, whatever, looked even smaller now. "Alharan?" she asked.
"You did very well," he said firmly not looking round.
"I'm sorry," said the little girl in his arms looking over his shoulder at Grace. "I didn't know I was doing wrong."
Grace struggled hard to remain on track. "Alharan," she said. "We will have troops here in moments. Can we have our clothes back?"
He laughed. "I'm naked," but as he did so Grace felt the familiar pressures of her routine browns and the hurried footsteps behind her meant the others did too. The magic was still there, almost jostling her. Eager to serve.
"Wow," said Rico looking round while sweeping her hair into a ponytail and reaching into a pocket for something to restrain it. "Not much to show for the big show down."
"That is because I have the Boss here," said Alharan. "May I introduce

Chii Anahe. She doesn't realise how long ago it was but I have finally found my daughter. She was the first to inherit the full powers and she made a great big mistake with them."

Chii pulled a face. "It wasn't a mistake. I was being spiteful."

"But you didn't realise the consequences," he offered. "And you lost far more than anybody else."

Chii looked at him. Screwed up her face and burst into tears. He patted her gently on the back. "Calm down, calm down," he said. "You know how."

Chii took a deep breath and scrubbed her hand across her face and smeared the tears about. "No Mummies," she said. "And no sisters. You promise to tell me all about them?"

"I will," he said. "Once you are settled to your new life."

She turned and looked round. "These ladies are new Mummies?" she asked.

"I have to deal with some details there but probably," he replied standing up and lifting her as he did.

Suddenly the hanger was full of troops so Grace had to revert to senior officer mode. There were cyborgs to move out for medical care and assessment plus something had to be done with Sempain.

"How is she?" asked Rico.

"Asleep," answered Alharan. "Zwei found me a room and I put her to bed. She's worn out. We talked and cried together a bit but she's taking her situation on board. All you heard back at Sempain's lair was just the surface. Remember we are both full telepaths with a grade A civilisation mentality. She was taking on the situation faster than I could verbally explain but, thankfully, she was letting me direct her so it wasn't too traumatic."

"An explanation," said Grace as gently as she could, "if we have a chance of understanding it, would help. We can feel the old magic around us fading by the minute and yours seems to have gone again now."

Alharan walked slowly over to one of the low coffee tables in the lounge and the girls of unit six followed him. "Sit down," he gestured. "You deserve the best possible explanation."

"We are Mummies?" asked Tina hesitantly.

"I'll come to that..." he paused and took a deep breath. "I'm not going to describe how long ago or how far away this happened because in a multi-threaded universe your concepts of time and distance cease to make any sense quite early in the game. Let us just say that 'once upon a time', where I came from Chii was the first to inherit the full powers, full as in range not strength but still huge even compared to you in your full combat mode. We didn't know what to expect and, of course, future sense doesn't work well on a psi user. What happened to her was a problem that was fixed forever from then on, a trivial thing to do but we didn't know to do it then."

He sat back. "She was seven and she had some archive stories, 2D colour anime and she watched six hours straight and nobody noticed. We were a big family. When Mummy Mure tried to get her to stop and be sociable she threw a big temper tantrum and just jumped into the story. The problem is that in the multiverse there are so many worlds that she found one like the story or she'd have bounced back. She came to here and now."

He rested his face in his hands. "She became the girl she identified with in the story, she was even dressed like her when we found her, and that made her forget home because she took on that girl's memories. No... She took on the memories the girl would have had if she had really existed. The psi-power expended as she arrived liberally dosed your world with a psi-residue characterised by a seven year old girl so girls that were at least recently seven and like her were receptive to it. It was smeared through time, from the past as she came from the past, but explaining time will take all night. Anyhow she was then stuck until Sempain forced a release on her."

He looked round. "Well back at home they naturally called me back at once and I worked out what had happened but I couldn't just follow her because we didn't have her perception of the story to go on. She had got much of it wrong but she was only seven. She got you and that you were magic users but the plot is totally garbled. Anyhow I have been searching for worlds with Magical Girls ever since."

"So..." thought Rico. "Are they waiting at home for you to bring her back?"

He sighed. "I have searched, well when I had some free off duty time, for over two thirds of my life. I promised her mother, before she died, that I would never give up and, anyway, you can't give up on your own child can you?"

"What about the assessment group?" asked Rico. "They've found most of the cyborgs were slavered or erased. Treatable. Do they need to see her?"

He shrugged. "I said 'Tranzen Polankerin' and they've gone to look up my authority to make decisions. They will discover it is sufficient. For a simple matter like this 'Tranzen' is probably enough but I didn't want anybody upsetting Chii."

"So what do you do?" asked Horo fearfully. "Now that you've found her?"

"I get to stop searching..." he sighed. "She is late toki-human so she will grow up to about twenty five and stop there. She should live about three hundred years although she can use psi to assist herself to go a

bit longer if she wants. I'd like to stay here and let her grow up. I think she'd like to put something back into this world after all the trouble she cause... No, not caused but that happened because people misused her."
"Would our children..." started Rico. "Would they inherit these powers?" Alharan looked at her and smiled. "It was a very long time ago. We have learnt a fantastic amount since then. The A-plus civilisations are primarily psi users. Inheritance is now safe and growing up powered up is safe too."
"So... This polygamous Varhyn relationship," said Zwei, "Now comes with a seven year old, or is it half a million year old, magical step daughter attached? We need to be clear on this."
"We can cope," said Rico abruptly. "Give the poor kid a break Zwei. If she is Alharan's daughter then she is our daughter just as much as Grace's, yours or mine will be."
"I just wanted to be sure what sort of deal this is," said Zwei pulling back slightly. "Still. After the last few years attending to you lot I ought to be good at child minding."
"That was needlessly rude," said Grace coldly. "We're all wound up and tired so maybe we'd better get some sleep ourselves before I have to stomp on somebody hard."
There was thirty seconds silence before both Rico and Alharan stood up. "Thank you again," he said very formally. "All of you. Your victory today has rescued Chii. Both she and I will be grateful to you for the rest of your lives." The humans all looked at him and smiled but took the hint to walk off silently to their rooms.
Zwei was left sitting on the table. She looked up at Alharan. "I need a lift back," she said morosely. "And I have a promise."

There was a knock. "I thought it would be you," said Grace letting Alharan in.
He smiled. "I'm flattered," he said looking her up and down.
"I'm getting my first kiss aren't I?" she said putting her hands on his shoulders. "The short, diaphanous nightie is just so I can get a bonus high contact cuddle to go with it. You can't not grope a girl wearing something like this can you?"
He slipped his hands round her and gently patted her bottom. "I wouldn't dream of..."
They took their time but the kiss ended slowly. "Am I the last," she asked. "I mean... Can you stay with me?"
"One more," he said patting her bottom again. "And I need to stay there."
"Rico?" she asked wondering if it was an intrusive question.
"No," he smiled. "Already been there. We needed to talk more than

cuddle. She's beginning to understand herself and her feelings now. She, more than any of you, will live the polygamous life well."
"I don't want to understand my feelings," Grace growled at him. "I just want to revel in them. If I had been last you could have stayed. There ought to be some perks to being the CO. Who wins?"
"I'm going back to Zwei. She's stressed out of her head because she's convinced she's about to lose everything." He chuckled. "I need to sort things out for her but I know what to do now. It was a matter of asking the right person the right question. It's much simpler than I expected and it solves a whole bunch of other problems too. Then I need to be away with Chii for a few days, well a week or so, to help her remember things and then to build in the safeguards so they are automatic. Psi, true magic, when it runs properly is very boring. It can't do bad things the source wouldn't do, Sempain broke his bones falling off his silly platform not because any of you zapped him with my magic. Now I need to help her so she is ready to face the world and things but don't worry. I'll be back for the rest of your lives... Well for the rest of Chii's life too. We've already decided she should stay here. There isn't anywhere she could go 'back' to so it's definitely for her best. I'll see you all in a week and we'll settle things."

Alharan looked round the girls of team six. It was time to confirm everything they had been planning. They had won, they had been on the victory parades and medals but now they needed to move on before the slump hit them.
"Well," he said brightly, looking at everybody sat round the low coffee table. "I gather while I've been away the magic has run out and you are being disbanded. Everybody has their demob papers?"
"All done," said Grace. "We all finish at the end of the month with full salary for six months and a pension thereafter. Now that the special combat magic is gone there won't be any more call for adolescent magical girls to be recruited into the army so we're the last."
Rico sighed. "It's been good. The team work, the thrills, the excitement."
"But now we're retired at seventeen," added Tina. "Somehow I didn't expect it so soon when I joined up. We can't even do ordinary magic... although that's pretty mundane stuff."
"But we'd never have met Alharan," added Zwei, "If we hadn't joined."
Grace, still for a few more days the Commanding Officer of the Unit, looked at her little Staff Sergeant. Zwei was only about thirty centimetres tall and an exact miniature of a human teenage girl. She was sitting precariously on Alharan's shoulder with her shoes left on the table supposedly so she didn't mark his clothes. They knew he could be her size or possibly any size but he always fell in with the majority.

She was just taking advantage of her stature to get to cuddle up when she was actually the last big problem to solve. Grace decided to take the bull by the horns.

"So we can get married," she said resolutely. This time they would get it all settled. It was tentatively agreed already. They just needed to firm up the details.

Rico, Tina and Horo looked at her hopefully then glanced back at Alharan.

"Yes," he said. "We've waited long enough. With no combat magic there will be no bad magic so policing will just require... Well, the police."

The girls all looked at Zwei. This was the point where she normally raised some sort of objection and dragged them off onto a long detour but Alharan had pre-empted her. Now he was saying it it sounded more decided.

Zwei giggled, crossed her legs and leant on Alharan's ear. She seemed even more under-dressed than usual but made no objections yet.

Grace went to say something about clarification but Alharan interrupted her firmly. "Everything is fixed," he assured them, "We have only to sort out dates, families, invitations and stuff. We've been living in one another's pockets so much it will be quite a relief to go official and claim all those foresees."

Zwei giggled again.

Grace took a deep breath and smiled. "Just in time," she observed. It had been a frustrating period and Alharan had forbidden her to pull rank when they were in family mode. The giggle was, however, really starting to annoy her. Trying to keep it cool she smiled at Zwei and added "We knew you'd come round to it in the end."

A giggle again but Alharan said "It was a matter of doing it her way. She is the first Metarii I've spent much time with and I had to learn," there was a giggle in his ear, "So in the end I cheated."

Zwei leant forwards and kissed him on the cheek, "He cheated," she agreed. Giggle.

"I phoned her Mum."

"YOU WHAT?"

As a highly trained military unit everybody ducked as a synchronous action. Zwei was suddenly standing on the coffee table glaring back at Alharan. Her hands were on her hips and she was trembling with rage. "You phoned my Mother and she told you to do that? And you did it? So how can I ever go home again?" she stamped and looked round at everybody swinging her long grey hair about. "And... And now you tell these... They are my... My unit. My friends. They are going to be my fellow brides. What will they ever think of me? My mother?" she stamped again and grabbed her head with her hands. "Oh you wretch!"

"Stop and explain," said Grace strongly, carefully biting the words "Sergeant Zwei," from the end of the order.
It was about right. All those years that they had worked together gave her the edge and Zwei deflated. She walked back across the table, flew onto Alharan's knee and walked up to him. She gave him a strong "We'll talk about this later," look and then turned and leant against his chest. She took a deep breath and announced "I found out today. I'm pregnant."

Best joke ever. Four girls dissolved into helpless floods of laughter. Even Zwei giggled.

The Dragon of Arnoc-fell

Randal the Barbarian tightened his grip on the sword and looked at the dragon in the gathering twilight. "Are you ready yet?" he asked.

"Of course I'm ready," snorted the dragon. "As soon as he gets on and writes our big fight scene you are just so much mythology."

"I'm the dashing hero," complained Randal. "So of course I'm going to win."

"But I," pointed out the dragon, "have the title role. You are just like one of those doomed, cannon fodder, security guards they put in the early Star-Treks. You're only function is to make me look big and bad."

"Well I have back-story," Randal pointed out. "You don't get that if you are just an NPC."

"But do you have a brave younger brother?" asked the dragon sitting down on his haunches and looking round. "Somebody to avenge you? Believe me that's never a good sign for the life expectancy."

"Only a sister," admitted Randal putting the end of the heavy sword on the ground and leaning on it slightly.

"Well a heroic sister is more his line," warned the dragon. "Pretty and apt to get her kit off for no obvious reason. His agent likes things like that. Always got a nose for film rights."

"Well it's too early to stop for the night so he ought to get on with it." Randal was beginning to lose his temper. "If we're ready to fight to the death he should at least be prepared to type it up."

The dragon looked round again as if sniffing the air. "You know he's gone," he said. "There is just no feeling of 'Author' now is there? We've been dumped haven't we?"

"Not that damn writer's block again?" said Randal sitting down on a rock. "I was doing an SF quest with him as a space trooper and got left on Mars for three months with negligible supplies and nothing to do last time he got it. It was as boring as hell."

"You were in that one too?" the dragon was scratching himself. "I did the rock monster... He's pretty lazy you know. Always reusing the same personalities."

"You're right," Randal looked about. "Look... You don't have anything to eat about here? I've been questing for you for half a chaptor."

"There's some smoked goat in the cave," said the dragon. "Feel free to help yourself. Also the pool is clear fresh water so it's safe to drink, better than the usual alkaline puddle you get in the desert. However it's a pretty transparent plot device. I can see that in another chapter or so I'll be coming upon your sister while she's in it doing the morning ablutions and wearing nothing but soap. Is she old enough to make the cover?"

Randal sniffed. "She's grown up quite pretty and... developed, but I really don't like thinking about people leering at her. A kid sister is always a kid sister."

"Well unless she has shiny green scales I'm not interested," muttered the dragon. "Actually, since we're stuck in early evening until he gets back, we might as well go inside. I'm getting chilly."

"You don't happen to have any tea do you?" the barbarian hero asked hopefully.

"Naturally... And you won't believe how fast I can boil a kettle," the dragon laughed. "Look. We can hope he's just knocked off early for the night and we resume when he gets back in the morning. Until then you're my guest. I don't have any beds but I can do you a good pile of straw."

"Well that's most civil of you. I've been sleeping in this wretched rocky desert for days."

"No worries," replied the dragon. "You seem quite a decent sort for a barbarian. I wonder if we can cut a deal on imprisonment rather than the usual flambé trick. Intelligent conversation is sadly lacking out here. Provided you're under lock and key when the girl arrives it could still be credible."

Randal stood up, picked up his sword and sheathed it. "I'm not sure," he replied. "Being killed by a dragon is respectable while being captured just isn't the barbarian image. 'Yield' isn't something I'd want on my CV when I'm looking for another part."

They turned and walked off together into the cave. "Maybe if I hit you on the head?" offered the dragon...